PENGUIN BOOKS

Cobraville

Carsten Stroud is the author of *Black Moon*. He lives in
Thunder Beach with his wife, photographer Linda Mair.

D1341310

For Linda . . .

'The enemies of reason have a certain blind look . . .'
– *The Duellists*

Cobraville is dedicated to
all the men – the living
and the dead –
who were serving on
the USS *LIBERTY*
On the Eighth Day of June 1967

And to Marysue Rucci,
who edited *Cobraville*
with consummate grace and style

Washington, D.C.

The navy-blue envelope lay on the polished oak table in the center of a pool of warm yellow light, the embossed crest of the National Security Agency in its center gleaming like a fifty-dollar gold piece. During his tenure as a senator attached to the Intelligence Oversight Committee, Drew Langan had been handed several navy-blue envelopes exactly like this one, and he had learned through bitter experience that what was contained inside them was often dangerous to know. Gunther Krugman was sitting on the other side of the low round wooden table, watching Drew through half-closed gray eyes in which a pale light glittered. They were in the Library Bar of the St Regis Hotel. It was Krugman's usual base of operations; where you looked for him if you needed him, where he waited until you did. The richly detailed, wood-paneled room was nearly empty on this rainy Monday evening. It was the last full week of the August recess, and those few government staffers still in town were safely back in Georgetown or Cherrydale or Adams Morgan.

Drew Langan's Secret Service escort was parked at a table a few steps away; Dale Rickett and Orlando Buriss, two sleek young hard-cases with gelled hair wearing Hugo

Boss suits and Armani glasses, as alike as a pair of artillery shells. They were both tactically deployed; one man facing the service door behind the long wooden bar, the other watching the entrance to the lobby of the hotel. Black coffee steamed untouched in white porcelain cups on the table top between them. He knew very little about them, and he intended to keep it that way. Cigar smoke was curling and rising through the yellow haze and Krugman was watching it with an air of Zen-like calm, as if he had a universe of time to burn. Drew sat back in the chair and studied Krugman's blunt, irregular face, the skin cracked and seamed, the pale eyes slightly hooded, the jawline clear cut and lean, his bloodless lips thin and tight, as if their only purpose was to seal his mouth; the result of a lifetime spent keeping other people's secrets.

Krugman returned Drew's look with the unblinking self-possession of a tombstone. An artery pulsed slowly on the left side of his throat where the perfect white linen of his shirt collar cut deep into his leathery hide. His tie was a silken ladder of Egyptian hieroglyphs in bright copper against a deep ocher field. Hieroglyphs, thought Drew, one of the first ciphers. A nice touch. A Django Reinhardt number was floating faintly through the cigar-scented air; Cole Porter's 'Night and Day.' A distant echoing murmur was coming from the lobby, the milling stamp-and-shuffle of guests, the crystalline ping-ping of the bellman's signal and, whenever someone opened the French doors that led to the street, the hissing rattle of rain drumming on car roofs and pooling in the gutters.

'Who sent this?' asked Drew, feeling that he had lost something by speaking first, the scotch working on him now, a smoky burn in his throat and belly. He was tired and he needed to sleep. He'd felt this way for longer than he could remember. Krugman put the cigar down onto the crystal ashtray in front of him, his long fingers moving precisely. He had no fingertips at all, just ten blunt fleshy conclusions at the ends of his fingers. Krugman had never told him how he lost his fingertips, but then Drew had never asked him directly. Krugman's military service had been as an intelligence officer in the Marine Corps during World War II. He had served in the South Pacific, in the same unit as Drew's father, Henry Langan. Once, a long while back, Drew had asked his father what had happened to Krugman's fingertips. The old man's demeanor – usually quite genial – had immediately altered: he said nothing and a cold and distant expression hardened his face. Drew never raised the subject again. Krugman's tone was one of polite regret.

'Obviously this is from the National Security Agency. The specific sender wishes to remain anonymous.'

'Why? I can figure out who sent it by what's in it.'

'You can infer what pleases you.'

'So he wants . . . what? Deniability?'

'There is no such thing. And I didn't say it was a "he" at all.'

'Fine. Tell me what you think is the reason for this contact.'

Krugman gave the question his glacial consideration.

'Well . . . actually I think it's a warning.'

'A warning? A warning to me?'

'Not necessarily you.'

'Then someone connected to me? Someone on the committee?'

'Possibly.'

'Do you know this?'

'I suspect it. That's why I agreed to deliver it.'

3

'Why to me? Helen McDowell is the chair. If I have the protocols right, she has to approve every rated release, doesn't she?'

Krugman closed his eyes and inclined his head gravely. Drew took this for agreement and restated the question.

'So why is this coming to me?'

'Let us say that a decision was made to deliver this directly to you. I assume that the same communication will find its way to her desk in a timely way. I infer but cannot define a specific reason.'

'You understand that by accepting this document I may be committing a breach of the Oversight Committee protocols?'

'I take full responsibility for that. You will be indemnified.'

'Even from Helen McDowell?'

'Particularly from her. She has vulnerabilities.'

'McDowell? What sort of vulnerabilities?'

'I'm not at liberty to say. But I assure you they are sufficient to keep her at bay, even in a protocol breach.'

'You're a cryptic old bastard, aren't you?'

'I prefer to think of myself as discreet.'

Drew picked up the envelope, weighed it in his left hand.

'What's the rating?'

'VRK ... Umbra,' said Krugman. His voice was a breathy whisper in a throat burred by heavy smoking. Drew shook his head and forced a counterfeit smile.

'Spare me, Gunther. Please. Almost everything is Very Restricted Knowledge now. And everything that isn't Gamma or Zarf is Umbra. If it isn't a Goddamn press release, they code it VRK. We're not on good terms with the intelligence sectors and you know why. You read the

4

findings from the Select Committee. Everybody did. It was all about shifting the blame to another agency. Even the nontactical geeks at NIMA and the National Reconnaissance office, for Christ's sake.'

'Hindsight is a deceptively pleasing opiate.'

'Hindsight! You could see the threat building. You said so yourself. It was exponential. This all started with the embassy bombing in Beirut back in eighty-three. They send in Captain Crunch and he ID's Elias Nimr – and what does the CIA do with that nasty bit of Lebanese crap? They let him walk and fire Keith Hall for treating him badly and a year later the same group – funded by Nimr – kidnaps Bill Buckley, Hall's station chief. They torture him to death and send us the video. And what do we do about *that*? Not a damn thing. Except Clinton issues a directive forbidding the CIA to associate with unsavory sources, which effectively killed any chance they ever had of tracing real terrorists. And all through the nineties the CIA lets the DEA suck up all their operational resources so they can be pissed away on The Never-Ending War On Drugs while a bunch of Saudi killers take flying lessons in the heartland. And in the end – after September eleventh – they all lied like wild dogs, burned their own people, the field people, the operational troops. The analysts blamed the operational people, and the agency brass blamed anybody but the men in their shaving mirrors. They tried to save themselves by torching the only real talent they had in this game. And what happened to the senior officials at the FBI and the CIA, the mutts who let this atrocity happen on their watch? The hapless drones at the top, who should have been frog-marched out of the building by a platoon of security guards?'

'That's a bit harsh, Drew. Some very strong private condemnations have come out of the Executive Branch. Quite a few senior people saw their careers wither in the chill that followed.'

'Chill? Hardly that. Most of the people who appeared at our hearings have either been promoted or retired with honors.'

'My point exactly. Promoted out of operational areas or retired. That's how it's done. We don't put them up against a wall.'

'Maybe we should. And now somebody at the NSA wants to back-channel this thing to me? I've been here before and I always get screwed one way or another. I'm being worked for somebody's endgame and I'm getting tired of it. Tell me why I should care about one more eyes-only packet of disinformation from the NSA?'

'You are free to regard this in any way you choose. I have no brief for or against it. In this matter, I am merely the courier. However, in my view, it may have some intriguing implications.'

'What exactly is it?'

'It's an intercept from the Kunia listening post in Hawaii. They rated it a CRITIC Flash at three-eleven this afternoon.'

'What was the originating language?'

'Tagalog. Not a native speaker. A senior Reader translated it.'

'They gave it to a senior Reader. Why the urgency?'

Krugman shrugged, reached for his cigar, drew on it. The ring of red fire in the tip glowed and spread up the shaft of the cigar. Krugman's face was briefly obscured by the smoke, then slowly rematerialized through it like a drowned man rising in a lake. He said nothing, merely shrugged his shoulders and smiled. In his heart Drew wanted Krugman's package to mean nothing. He wanted to go home and crack a bottle of Gamay and let that sanctimonious old gasbag Larry King irritate the hell out of him until he fell asleep on the sofa.

'Look, Gunther, if it's rated CRITIC the President already has it. He gets them within ten minutes. Then they show up on the National Sigint File website. If it's relevant to our brief I'll get it when the security adviser hands it to the oversight committee.'

'I think that would be a bold decision. In this case, time is a critical factor. Something in this has implications for someone on your side of the debate.'

In Krugman's vocabulary, 'bold' meant 'stupid and risky.' And 'the debate,' as Krugman put it, probably meant the antagonism that had arisen between the Congress and the Executive Branch over what people on Drew's side of the House saw as the deepening world-wide morass that had started out as a War on Terror. Aside from the ongoing complications that had resulted from the destruction of Hussein's regime in Iraq, there were combat troops in Afghanistan and other American military elements engaged in over seventy 'advisory missions' all around the world. Even the chronically commitment-phobic UN had managed to get itself buried up to its wheel wells in a nasty little peacekeeping mission in the southern Philippines – for once body bags were coming home in places farther away than Terre Haute and Laramie – and the Hill was trying to get the current Administration to define an endgame, a point where the States could get out of the ugly – and so far worse than thankless – task of saving Western Civilization, without any substantial success. The idea that American soldiers were out in the global swamp trying to reshape a hell-bound world into a Republican pipe dream of good order was a constant goad to him.

'I take it you've read this already.'

'I have. I never deliver a packet I haven't read; people who do that kind of thing sometimes end up being blamed for what's inside.'

'And . . . ?'

'And this is hardly the place. Drew, as a long-time friend of your family, and for your father's sake at least, who is one of my oldest friends, my earnest and heartfelt recommendation is that you take this envelope with you and read it at home. With your Beringer Gamay. Then do whatever seems required. It may be that nothing is required. It has been my experience that many of life's truly vexatious problems go away of their own accord, without any action ever being taken against them. We can but hope.'

A brief revelation of his long white teeth, his canines prominent. He pushed the envelope closer, picked up his antique rosewood cane with the solid gold horse-head, and got to his feet, breathing heavily, favoring his left hip.

'You'll forgive me if I slip away. I'm being stalked by Britney Vogel. The *Post* thinks I'm still green enough to let myself be profiled in their weekend section. Now, are you in touch with Cole at all?'

Drew suppressed his startled reaction to this un-expected mention of his son Coleman – their relationship, already strained by Cole's midterm departure from Harvard to enlist in the US Army, and further complicated by his equally sudden resignation from the army after a long combat tour in Iraq – was now almost nonexistent, an estrangement of which Krugman, an old family friend, was perfectly aware. After a prolonged pause during which Krugman regarded him with detached amusement, Drew shrugged.

'Cole and I don't talk. Haven't for over two years. I think he's in Thailand on a walking tour. At least that's what his mother tells me.'

'Thailand, is it?' said Krugman, nodding absently as if this confirmed something he already knew. 'Well, if you do hear from him, give him my very best, will you?'

Drew said that in the highly unlikely event that Cole ever called him, he'd convey Krugman's regards, and rose with Krugman, taking the envelope from the table top and holding it under the light. It felt solid and heavy – NSA packets were usually lined with inert metals as a security measure – and seemed to contain a plastic disc. Krugman extended his hand and Drew shook it. Krugman's skin was hot and dry, his palm leathery, his grip hard. He held Drew's hand in that tight grip for a moment longer as he leaned forward and slipped a silver cigar tube into the breast pocket of Drew's suit jacket. Krugman then spoke very softly, his breath scented with cigar smoke and scotch, his whisper barely audible.

'Read the report, Drew. Look at the CD. Enjoy the cigar. I think you should have it tonight. I really do. I'll say goodnight now. And if we don't see each other for a while, I want you to know that I have always been proud to have been associated with your family ... I'll take my leave now and I wish you good luck.'

He smiled then, perhaps at Drew's visible surprise at such an intimate expression of friendship from a man so famous for his wintry heart. Krugman offered him a half-ironic faintly Prussian head-bob and a smile that seemed strangely off, almost regretful. Then he turned unsteadily and cane-walked away toward the lobby, the slender rosewood shaft flexing under his weight. Drew watched him go – Krugman's ambiguous smile floating in his mind – and promptly felt the heightened attention of Rickett and Buriss, like heat on the back of his neck. Krugman's last words felt like a farewell to Drew, and he wondered if the ancient Cold Warrior might be sicker than he let on. Rickett and Buriss were staring at him, taut and at the ready. 'Okay,' he said, as the men got to their feet. 'Take me home.'

The Philippines

WG&A Superferry Seven
Inbound to Iligan City, northern Mindanao
From Manila, Luzon, the Philippines
Tuesday, August 19, 1:00 p.m. local time

At roughly the same moment that his father – half a world away – was walking out to the Secret Service car in the St Regis parking lot, Drew Langan's son Cole was leaning on the railing of a passenger ferry inbound to the island of Mindanao, surging in over a pale jade-colored sea, and staring at the long lean sharklike hull of a French naval frigate riding at anchor in the Iligan City harbor, a cast-iron naval knuckle-duster, plated with ceramic armor, packing heavy guns. A huge white sphere dominated the foredeck; the ship's air-search radar dome. He recognized her as the frigate *Suffren,* detached from France's Mediterranean fleet and posted to Mindanao two months ago to shore up what was still being doggedly referred to back on the East River as a successful UN peacekeeping mission. What was actually happening here was obvious to anyone with a functioning cortex: Iligan City was the yawning iron gate of yet another United Nations feel-good rat-fuck fiasco, a doomed-from-the-get-go Cub Scout Jamboree that was slowly but inexorably sinking into the blood-drenched malarial swamps of Southeast Asia.

The *Suffren* was surrounded by a fleet of smaller gray vessels, supply ships and tenders in the main, but Cole could also see a medium-sized white passenger liner with a huge red cross on the hull parked at one of the big wharfs. A Super Frelon chopper was lashed down on her fantail pad. She was *La Magdalene,* a French hospital ship stationed here to do what she could for the legionnaires and the German armor stationed thirty-five miles upriver inside the DMZ, patrolling the Iligan Line around Lake Lanao. The poor bastards.

He braced himself against the pitch and roll of the huge ferry, sweat trickling maddeningly down his spine while he fought for a breath of steaming air inside a crowd of mangy-looking Eurotrash backpackers and aggressively sullen Filipino teenagers. The sky above him was dull, brassy, streaked with clouds the color of a fresh bruise. Far away in the hazy stratosphere he saw twinned glittering sparks. Probably a couple of Mirage fighters flying close air support and reconnaissance for the grunts and mud puppies deployed up-country. The flattened disc of the sun shone through the damp heat haze like a gold coin glimmering at the bottom of a stagnant pond. Working his way through the dense crowd until he reached the railing, he lifted his binoculars to take a closer look at the town itself.

In the sudden leap through the long lenses, Iligan City looked every bit as butt-ugly as he expected it to be; trailing out like a drunkard's litany of blue ruin – erratic, haphazard, and eventually quite pointless – for several miles along the mangrove-matted coast, a ramshackle collection of low concrete-block and scrap-wood buildings teetering drunkenly along the narrow roads that ran behind the wharves. To his right he saw a huge pile of run-down slums and shantytowns built on rickety stilts set out in the churning surf. The waterfront looked as if it had been hastily clapped together by a shore-party of Spanish missionaries five hundred years ago and promptly abandoned to decompose in this sweltering heat ever since.

They were almost at the three large wharves now, and Cole could see the officials lining up at the chain-link gates where they would dock, compact little mahogany-faced men in pressed tan uniforms, backed up by a double rank of very large very bulky legionnaires in jungle-green fatigues and full battle dress, with their FNC's on lock-and-load and their nerves obviously twanging like banjo wire. Cole drifted backward into the crowd until the ferry butted massively into the dock bumpers and then let the rush of disembarking passengers carry him along toward the exit gate.

He had a reasonably convincing Canadian passport in his backpack, along with laminated press credentials from a Toronto-based newspaper, both of these under the name of Jordan Kemp. The rest of his gear had been scrubbed and relabeled and sanitized. The clothes in his duffel and the contents of his shaving kit had all been bought at retail stores in Windsor, Ontario, along with his Sony digital camera, his cell phone, all but one of the components inside his laptop computer, and all the accessories. He had the receipts to prove it.

In spite of his usual precautions he felt his belly muscles tighten as he reached the end of the ramp and stepped out onto the wharf. Although he had been in the field many times, and in regions even more dangerous, this moment of arrival always affected him the same way. When he came out from under the shade of the covered ferry deck the heat of the day rolled over him like a blast of steam. A squat bowlegged bullet-headed Filipino policeman with a sloping forehead, a gap-toothed overbite, and the face of a disappointed grouper watched him with dull but palpable hostility as he reached the end of the gangway and came up to the entry gate.

'Passport!'

This in a yipping falsetto bark that would have shamed a corgi. Cole, whose tolerance for the insolence of office had always been low, barely suppressed a snarl as he handed the cop his passport.

'Purpose of visit?'

'Journalist. I'm writing a travel article about –'

The man rudely waved him into silence while he flipped through the various immigration stamps on the back pages. Although the passport was plausible, every one of the stamps was a forgery. He looked up from it and studied Cole closely, seeing a very muscular young man almost six feet tall in a tan military-looking shirt, faded blue jeans and denim-blue hand-tooled cowboy boots, his bony blunt face sun-creased and tanned almost black, with long curly brown hair and light gray eyes and a small silver ring with a Celtic cross set in the lobe of his right ear.

'So. You say you are writer?'

Clearly the cop had his doubts. Most of the 'writers' and 'reporters' who hung around Luzon and Mindanao were sodden third-rate stringers for small-time news outlets or oily little pederasts cruising the bar circuit through Southeast Asia. Sometimes both. The rest were sanctimonious neo-hippies and backpacking eco-anarchists looking for their next brick of hashish and a fresh beach to foul until the local bulls moved them on. The crowd all around him was full of these types even though this was a war zone. Well, most of Southeast Asia was a war zone and had been for two thousand years.

'Yes. I'm a travel writer.'

'You have been to Egypt, Mr Kemp. Also Qatar. Why?'

'Like I said, I do travel articles for –'

'This is a United Nations zone, Mr Kemp. A peace-keeping zone. You cannot go up-country. You must stay in Iligan. There are big troubles up in the hills. Terrorists. People disappear. People are dying. No civilians. No journalists. No travel writers. You follow?'

'But I have –'

'Not possible to go. You have a laptop computer?'

'In my bag.'

'Show it.'

Cole dug the machine out of his duffel bag and set it down on the little table in front of the cop he was beginning to think of as Frog Jowls. Watching the man handle the black machine, Cole could feel the pit-bull attention coming in off the legionnaires a few feet away.

'Open it. Turn it on.'

Cole did as he was told. The machine cycled up and showed Frog Jowls a desktop screen with a Canadian flag on it. Cole disliked the Canadian flag almost as much as he disliked Canadians. Frog Jowls picked the machine up and shook it hard.

What? thought Cole. If you shake it, it will rattle in that unique way that bombs inside laptops always rattle?

Frog Jowls put the laptop down, snapped the lid shut.

'Cell phone.'

Cole produced it. Frog Jowls turned it around in his tobacco-stained fingers, flipped it open and hit the ON button. It beeped at him and he held it up to his ear. Maybe he could hear the ocean in it.

'You have a hotel?'

'I'm at the Milan. Two eighteen Truong Tan Buu Street.'

'How long you stay?'

'A week. No longer.'

'You want good girls, you go to Ang Kusina Folk House. Clean girls there. Or boys. Badda-bing-bing all night long. No problem.'

Cole smiled and nodded as if an interlude with a scrofulous thirteen-year-old Filipina whore was right at the top of his to-do list. Frog Jowls showed him a set of mildewed brown fangs. It took Cole a moment to realize that this nasty rictus meant that Frog Jowls was smiling at him. A chin-thrust toward the gates and a pimp's conniving leer as he handed the phone back.

'Okay, boboy. Ang Kusina Folk House. Too much fun.'

Cole got his passport back and walked slowly through the double rank of the legionnaires. They looked young but fairly professional, all of them fit and well-equipped, including body armor and well-oiled Berettas in strap-on thigh holsters. Their FNC's looked clean and well maintained. None of them was wearing the light blue beret of the United Nations, but they did have blue armbands on with the letters UN in white. The men stared hard at Cole as he passed, each man locking eyes with him and holding the look steady as he went by; they seemed edgy, tense, overheated, and severely homesick. Nobody was smiling at him so he didn't smile back either.

He crossed the two-lane bridge over the muddy river onto Truong Tan Buu Street and saw the Milan Hotel a few blocks away, a five-story concrete pile covered in peeling white stucco in the middle of the market district. By the time he reached it his shirt was dripping and his jeans were damp with sweat from his thighs to his cowboy boots. The interior of the hotel was a relief from the heat and the glare. The Milan was a four-star palace by Mindanao standards, which meant the bellboys didn't have leprosy and the lobby wasn't visibly seething with cockroaches. It was very dim and very chill, lit here and there with ancient art-deco wall sconces and a few garage-sale lamps left over from the fifties.

After the riot of the streets outside the stillness was profound, the only sound the brassy rhythmic piping of some tribal music coming from the speakers in the walls and the sweeping rush of the ceiling fans. The place smelled of clove-scented Filipino cigarettes, stale beer, human sweat, and fifty years of lemon polish. There was a long bamboo bar at the far side of the low-ceilinged lobby, tended by a withered bloodless Filipino hermaphrodite with the face of a grinning skull and a port-wine stain across most of his – or her – forehead. Pike Zeigler and Loman Strackbein were sitting at the bar, three stools apart, with their backs to the lobby. Chris Burdette, their close-quarters-combat specialist, was sprawled in a peacock chair by the elevator doors, apparently asleep.

Pike Zeigler was the team's weapons man, an ex-Army top kick whose combat experience ran all the way back to the Vietnam War. He was the unit's oldest member and he looked it, a massive slope-shouldered bull of a man with a battered haggard face deeply marked by everything he had ever done in the line of duty. Loman Strackbein, as always a little apart, was their electronic specialist, the only black man in the whole place – looking like a senior button-man straight from the Vatican, lean and hard-looking, wearing an open-necked black shirt over a crisp white tee and trim black slacks, drinking what looked to be a mojito in a tall cylindrical glass. Neither man gave Cole more than a flicker of recognition as his reflection passed in the mirror behind the long bar.

Chris Burdette was the unit's only ex-marine, a champion professional surfer who had paid for his English history degree at UCLA with his winnings; twice-divorced, with a twelve-year-old daughter at Quantico he was lucky to see at Christmas and two vengeful wives – Chris was fidelity-challenged – who managed to suck up most of his civil service salary. This forced him to live in very spartan BOQ rooms at Camp Peary when he wasn't out in the field and living a little better on their deployment per diem. Burdette's military operational specialty was close-quarters combat – silent killing, up close and personal.

Cole studied him as he walked across the lobby toward the reception desk; his shoulder-length blond hair tied back in a blue bandanna, his leathery cheeks shining with sweat, his long lean body loose-limbed in ragged jeans and a pair of worn leather sandals that looked like they were stolen from Christ himself when he came down off the cross. Although Burdette was only in his late thirties, his sun-dried hide was full of fissures and seams, and the skin on his face was stretched drum-head tight over the craggy bones underneath. He had that corrupted look of desiccated languor you see in people wealthy and insane enough to indulge a daily heroin habit. His eyes were closed but Cole knew it was unlikely that he was asleep. A pair of Ray-Bans was tucked into the top of a surfer T-shirt with a Banzai Pipeline graphic, his muscular forearms folded across his flat belly.

The rest of the men in the lobby were uniformed soldiers having an off-duty drink: German armor by their markings, well-muscled, with short-cropped hair cut high enough on the skull to look like mohawks. They were talking fast in a grating Silesian bray. The oldest – white blond with the chiseled bones and the sulky good looks of a perfume model – couldn't have been more than twenty. He was power-chugging a heavy glass stein of some mud-brown beer with a layer of creamy foam on the top while the rest of his unit chanted a line of rhythmic doggerel and watched his throat muscles working.

Over against the far wall a powerfully built older man with a bumpy bald skull and small mean eyes was watching the men as they drank, a look of acid contempt on his broad, slightly Slavic face. He was also in faded German battle fatigues, light armored reconnaissance like the kids at the bar, by his markings a staff sergeant and by his ribbons a combat lifer. He had the stone killer look down cold, an effect supported by a livid burn scar that covered most of the right side of his face like a congealed flow of black lava.

Cole was aware that Pike Zeigler was now obliquely tracking him in the mirror as he walked across the wooden floor, his tanned face shadowed, his deep-set eyes hidden in the glow of the downlight over the bar. Pike had both of his long-fingered oddly delicate hands around a bottle of Stella Artois that looked as if it had just come out of a freezer. He allowed a brief connection with Cole in the cracked and stained mirror that told Cole he had already scanned the perimeter and there was no one from the opposition in the area. Then his eyes glazed over as he looked past Cole and off into the middle distance.

Strackbein wasn't looking at anything but the glass in

front of him and seemed to be cut off from the rest of the men at the bar by a self-willed zone of disconnection. Loman Strackbein was the most self-contained and private member of whatever the hell it was they were, and Cole knew very little about his life other than that he was a gay Republican and didn't give a stainless-steel damn what you thought about that. Cole liked him for that, but he liked him more for his skill with anything electronic, which was magical.

Cole returned that glancing visual hook-up with Pike Zeigler and then broke it off as he reached the desk, where a well-thought-out girl with crow-black hair and an off-the-shoulder sundress made out of what looked like green smoke from an LZ canister was watching him cross the room with an off-center smile. Her nametag had the letters INGRID deeply engraved into the polished brass plate that rested lightly – in Cole's view even happily – upon her left breast.

'Good afternoon. Welcome to the Milan.'

She had a difficult accent to place, a mixture of Australian and Swedish. Her scent was smoky and spiced with sweat. There were tiny beads of perspiration along her upper lip that glittered in the light of the desk lamp. Cole gave her the twisted off-center leer that he mistakenly believed was a happy smile bright with boyish charm.

'I'm Jordan Kemp. I have a reservation.'

Ingrid's smile widened as she riffled through a seashell-covered box at the side of the desk, her long sun-browned fingers supple as she flipped through the index cards and extracted a sheet of blue paper, which she pushed across the desk for him to sign.

'You're in room 511, Mister Kemp. On the top floor. Oh yes, there's a message for you.'

She handed Cole a slip of lime-green paper, a three-word handwritten message. Cole recognized Ramiro Vasquez's handwriting.

The Blue Bird

Cole slipped it into his shirt pocket, smiled back at Ingrid and her lovely left breast and her fortunate brass nameplate, signed the register, picked up his gear, and headed for the elevators. He crossed in front of Chris Burdette, who moved his feet out of the way without opening his eyes or in any way acknowledging Cole's passage.

The elevator doors closed with an asthmatic wheeze and the machine lurched heavenward in a grinding screech of rusted cable. His corner room on the fifth floor had a view of the ocean and the hotel's frontage along Truong Tan Buu Street. The clamor from the street below was slightly muted by the dirty glass of the windows and the clanking chug of the medieval air-conditioner dripping a ribbon of black water down the interior wall. The room was large, painted a sickly lavender, and nearly bare, with a creaking wooden floor, an iron-framed double bed with a swaybacked mattress covered with stained yellowed sheets, and a worn-out flock coverlet in a daisy pattern. The pillow looked like a dead badger and felt like a sack of rocks. There was a small cooking counter made of plywood, a charred hot plate with a frayed cord, and a sink made of rust and encrusted toothpaste-spit with a tap that produced, in a low clanking growl, a viscous red discharge that might have been water. There was also a big wooden ceiling fan that wobbled on its hub and made a sound that reminded Cole of that scene in *Apocalypse Now* where Martin Sheen wakes up to the sound of a chopper going over the roof of his rat-bag hotel in Saigon. He walked to the window and pulled the blinds apart and looked down into the churning crowds swarming up and down Truong Tan Buu Street. Tinny native music was coming from a rooftop across the way. The air smelled of seaweed and grease and was tinted pale blue with diesel fumes. His sudden grin was wide and wolfish. He felt intensely and vividly alive. And they were safely in.

Solitaire

While Cole Langan was standing at the greasy window of the Milan Hotel and looking down into Truong Tan Buu Street, his father was leaning into the soft black leather seat in the back of the Secret Service car watching snakes of rain coiling down the tinted glass. The streetlamps flickered, their lights haloed with mist, and beyond them the ruffled gray-steel surface of the Potomac was churning with scintillating glimmers. Drew flicked on the halogen reading lamp and opened the blue envelope, tipping the contents out onto the seat beside him; one page of computer printout and a CD in a slipcase with the NSA label. He held the printout up to the light:

CRITIC FLASH VERY RESTRICTED KNOWLEDGE

NSA KUNIA INTERCEPT NUM 15/340/0097:

1425 HOURS EDT INTERCEPTED MODE: MICROWAVE SUB

FREQUENCY PACKETS WITH FREQUENCY MODULA-
TION WAVE ENCRYPTION; EXTRACTED FROM ILIGAN
CITY POWER AUTHORITY DIGITAL RETRANSMISSION
FROM MARIA CHRISTINA FALLS GENERATING
STATION: LATITUDE 7.5832 LONGITUDE 124.2944
LANGUAGE TAGALOG: SPEAKER ONE

PROBABILITY HIGH HAMIDULLAH BARRAKHA
VOICE ANALYSIS INDICATES SPEAKER TWO TAGALOG
SPEAKER / BARRAKHA OPERATIONAL CODE NAME
MISTER GABRIEL NATIONALITY YEMENI (see SIGINT
bio ref number AXR-881089) / SPEAKER TWO NATION-
ALITY POSSIBLE FILIPINO / SIGNAL QUALITY — VERY
POOR — RELAY TRANSMITTER FAILING /

LOCATION OF SPEAKER TWO NOT ESTABLISHED

TRIANGULATION FAILURE DUE TO INTERCEPT
SENSOR MALFUNCTION. LOCATION OF SPEAKER ONE
— BARRAKHA ESTIMATED HAMBURG GERMANY —
(HUMINT / NIMA NOT CONFIRMED) AUDIO CD TRAN-
SCRIPT ENCLOSED

SPEAKER ONE — HAMIDULLAH BARRAKHA:

YOU ARE WELL INSHALLAH?

SP TWO — UNKNOWN:

I AM. YOU ARE NOT YET (inaudible) IN THE HOTEL?

BARRAKHA:

NO. IS EVERYTHING (inaudible) DONE, EVERYTHING
PREPARED?

SP TWO:

ALMOST EVERYTHING — WE NEED A DELIVERY
PERSON

BARRAKHA:

I UNDERSTOOD THAT YOU HAD ONE — A CHOSEN
ONE.

SP TWO:

HE DECLINED — HIS WIFE HAD (inaudible)
OBJECTIONS, HIS CHILDREN — HE SAID HE COULD NOT
LEAVE HIS FAMILY.

BARRAKHA:

STIFFEN HIM, THEN. YOU KNOW HOW TO DO THAT.

SP TWO:

IN THE END HE MUST BE (inaudible).

BARRAKHA:

IF HE DOES NOT WANT TO LEAVE HIS FAMILY TELL HIM TO TAKE THEM WITH HIM. THAT SHOULD EASE HIM.

SP TWO:

I WILL TELL HIM. HIS WIFE IS JUST NOW A BRIDE. HE IS STRONGLY ATTACHED TO HER AND WISHES NOT TO —

BARRAKHA:

IF THEY HAVE CHILDREN ALREADY HIS BRIDE IS A WHORE. SEE THAT THIS IS DONE AT ONCE. EVERY-THING DEPENDS ON WHITE MEAT. I WILL BE (inaud-ible) WITH THE FERENGHI PERSONALLY WHEN THE TIME IS RIGHT.

SP TWO:

IT WILL BE DONE. EVERYTHING IS IN PLACE HERE. HAVE YOUR ARRANGEMENTS BEEN AS YOU WISH?

• BARRAKHA:

WE ARE TO MEET SOON. I EXPECT THE SATISFACT-ORY CONCLUSION OF OUR NEGOTIATIONS.

SP TWO:

GOD WILLING.

BARRAKHA:

AS YOU SAY.

SIGNAL ENDS

Drew read the transcript twice as the car turned off the Whitehurst Freeway and rolled north into the George-town district. It meant very little to him, although he had seen the name of this Hamidullah Barrakha – generally known in the terrorist underworld as Mr Gabriel – on a list of suspected Al Qaeda operatives currently on the CIA's hit list. The conversation, on the face of it, suggested that something suitably cataclysmic was in the works for northern Mindanao. 'White meat' was the Al Qaeda code for any Western victim. 'The Ferenghi' was an odd phrase, but one he recognized; it was a corruption of the ancient Arabic word *franji*, for anyone foreign. It actually meant 'Frank,' as in a Frankish knight or crusader. It was an odd use of that word. And 'The Hotel' was their secret phrase for the Philippines. Well, something ugly was always brewing in Mindanao, the definitive Third World snakepit.

The tribal conflict between the Islamic Fundamentalist hill people in central Mindanao and the Christian population that lived spread out along the Zamboangan peninsula had been festering for years. After an escalating series of Moro Liberation Front and Abu Sayaf terrorist bombings in the Sulu Islands and the coastal cities during the previous summer, the Philippines government had asked – begged would be closer to the mark – the United Nations to send in a peacekeeping force, preferably an American one. Since the institution of the International Criminal Court at The Hague in 2002, the United States had a standing policy of not allowing American troops to fall under any UN-controlled military authority. So the UN peacekeeping force was currently composed of German and French troops, two nations still viewed with suspicion by the executive branch after their opposition to the war in Iraq. The UN had assigned them to sit on the dividing line between the peninsula and the highlands in an attempt to keep some kind of order there – so far, perhaps not surprisingly, with very mixed results.

Iligan City, the northern end of the UN-imposed DMZ called the Iligan Line, which cut the peninsula off from mainland Mindanao, was a squalid industrial port town on the north coast of the island. The port town's industrial base was electricity, generated by a hydroelectric station at Maria Christina Falls that tapped the runoff from Lake Lanao, 35 miles away in the central highlands. Since Lake Lanao was deep in Islamic-controlled territory, there was a lot of nasty conflict in that jungle-choked region. A month ago, five German soldiers on a peacekeeping patrol had been ambushed near the town of Cobraville, a Samal village buried in dense jungle a few miles down-river from Lake Lanao. Their bodies were found a week later, naked, strung up with cords laced through their ankles like durians in a fruit tree. They had apparently been tortured for hours by people with a flair for sadistic innovation, then – as shown in the VHS tape found stuffed into the partially disemboweled belly of one teenaged soldier – rather ineptly castrated and partially beheaded while still more or less alive. In the video a pack of machete-wielding, khat-chewing Moro teenagers could be seen dragging the naked and bloody corpses around a clearing while they chanted Islamic hate mantras in broken English. The report itself was depressingly similar to many other CRITIC-rated Sigint intercepts that he'd received since he had become a member of the Senate Select Committee on Intelligence.

Six years ago, when he had first been appointed to the Select Committee as the junior Democratic senator from Pennsylvania, every security report he got had sent a sleazy frisson right through him; he felt that he was a vital part of the secret world, a trusted professional insider, hard-wired into the high-voltage power-cable that snaked through the capital like the Potomac itself. That was then.

Five years and one September eleventh later, most of these communiqués now struck Drew as operationally useless and frequently out of date; little more than busy work thrown down from the NSC to distract the Congress from what was really going on. But Krugman had made it clear that there was something in it that he needed to pay attention to. Krugman was an old family friend and a grizzled veteran of the secret game since the time of Allen Dulles; his direct advice was rarely given and never safe to disregard.

When they finally pulled up in front of his rented townhouse on Dumbarton he folded the document, slipped it back into the envelope along with the CD, and waited in the vehicle while Rickett did his usual walk-about in and around the house and Buriss surveyed the empty tree-shaded avenue. The rain had softened into a drifting mist and a warm dense fog had rolled in off the Potomac. After a few minutes, Buriss touched his ear mike and said something cryptic into his sleeve, leaned down, and opened the rear door, his unmarked young face uplit by the yellow light from the car interior. Damp air as warm as steam rolled into the air-conditioned interior.

'The house is secure, Senator. All systems are nominal. Our duty watch ends at midnight.'

'I thought you were staying on until I left D.C.?'

'They put Canmore into a psychiatric facility last Friday. He's no longer a threat.'

Dwayne David Canmore was a disgruntled former employee in one of Drew's father's steel plants. He had made several death threats, and the Secret Service had been assigned to guard Drew until his case was settled. Last week he'd been sent to a facility in Allenwood.

'I know. But Luna Olvidado told me you guys were staying on until I left town.'

'We thought so too. We've just been reassigned. But I can stay if you want. I'll call my wife.'

'No. You're right. The Secret Service has better things to do than leave their personnel parked outside the house of a totally obscure junior senator all night long.'

Buriss smiled, shook his head.

'How about a drive to the airport in the morning? Just so you can have somebody to wave good-bye to?'

Drew gave Buriss a closer look; a slight smile was playing across his features. It was pretty common knowledge that since the collapse – no, the implosion – of his marriage, Drew Langan was the Hill's most famous solitary celibate. He grinned back at Buriss.

'Yeah . . . that would be nice. Who's up?'

'Luna Olvidado, for one. Not sure who else.'

Drew kept his face the way he wanted it to look, but the issue of Luna Olvidado – the only female member of Drew's Secret Service protection unit – was a highly sensitive one. Lately she had been making cameo appearances in his dreams. Short but memorable cameos. He was trying not to have these dreams, but he wasn't getting a lot of cooperation from himself. Buriss gave Drew back the same forcibly blank expression.

'Okay, if she doesn't mind? If it's no trouble?'

'I think she'd be happy to. Sweet dreams, Senator.'

Drew smiled at the man.

'I'll do my best. Go home, have a beer. Or three.'

Both men watched him as he walked up the stone steps to the front door of his Federal-style townhouse and keyed the lock. He pushed open the door, the entry alarm shrilling in his ear. He entered his code and the tone cut off suddenly. The silence that always lived in the upper reaches of this ancient seventeenth-century stone house seemed to flood down the central staircase and spread out into the main-floor rooms. He walked down the oak-planked central hall – the ancient floor creaked and groaned under his weight – to the old kitchen, set his briefcase down on the marble countertop, draped his suit jacket over one of the bar stools at the side of the center island, pulled open the fridge, and stood there in the yellow spill of light, staring blankly at what little there was on the racks.

Finally he extracted a folded paper packet of sliced beef and some rye bread and laid this out on the bar top. He was halfway through the process, running on auto with his mind turning over the levels of meaning in Krugman's package, before he realized he was, out of an old late-night habit, making three sandwiches: one for himself, one for his wife, who was probably never coming home again, and one for a son who was almost a total stranger.

Years ago, he and Coleman, known as Cole, had exchanged very hard words over Cole's decision to leave Harvard and join the US Army. Drew's fundamental conviction – a hard-nosed isolationism – was derived from a reflexive distrust of American military adventures designed to make the world a better place for people who weren't American. This sentiment was born during the Vietnam era and indelibly confirmed by the disastrous American mission to Mogadishu. Cole had not agreed with him. And he said so. Often.

His shattered relationship with Cole had not been repaired when Cole suddenly resigned from the Third Infantry Division right after the Iraq War. Cole had made captain and had performed so well in armored combat –

that his superiors had told him he could fast-track his way to his own brigade if he wanted it. And then he just ... quit. Walked away.

Cole's resignation of his commission came as a shock to everyone, but particularly to Drew, who had no idea why his son had left the military. Cole had made it clear that he didn't want to talk about it. At least not to Drew. Calls made were never returned, e-mails went unanswered. Even letters were ignored.

Now Drew was grimly resigned to a solitary life, but he took comfort from the fact that, for whatever reason, Cole was safely out of harm's way. He was quietly delighted when Krugman had told him that Cole was currently based in New York, working for a trade mission connected to the IMF, a bureaucratic but honorable line of work that Drew could happily live with, although it was a bit out of character for a man as fond of adrenaline as Cole.

Whatever Cole was doing for the IMF, it seemed to require a great deal of travel, especially in the last two years. Cole said very little about his work to his mother and nothing at all to his father. What he did say to mutual friends seemed carefully calibrated to bore the living jeepers out of his listeners. His son had taken Drew's separation from his mother pretty hard and Drew had so far been unable to repair the plate tectonics that had disintegrated his family. He stared down at the sandwiches with a familiar but still piercing sense of loss, then shoved them away.

There was a bottle of Gamay in the pantry. He pulled the cork, selected a gold-rimmed crystal flute from the rack above the bar, and went into his den, where he flicked on the green glass lamp over his desk – pointedly ignoring the flashing LED on his answering machine – and opened up his laptop. While the machine cycled through the start-up program, he put on a Harry James CD and sipped at the Gamay with an effort of concentration, savoring the taste, deliberately holding his mind in suspension. He knew where it wanted to go, and there was no point at all in letting it go there. The machine beeped twice. He clicked on the SEARCHLIGHT modem button and brought up the Intelink portal, with the NSA crest floating in deep-blue space above a red-lettered warning:

ANYONE USING THIS SYSTEM
EXPRESSLY CONSENTS TO MONITORING

He typed in his passwords – twice – and sat back while the system verified his access. In a moment, he had reached the Intelink home page. The screen was running hyperlinks to various classified intelligence information streams as well as the home pages of more than ninety subagencies within the American intelligence community. He clicked on NATIONAL SIGINT FILE, waited for additional asymmetric encryption software to load, typed in his UMBRA clearance-level password, and opened up the home page. He keyed the SEARCH function and typed in 'Hamidullah Barrakha,' followed by the reference file number, AXR-881089, then hit the ENTER key.

In a moment he had a grainy color shot of a cranky-faced Middle Eastern male with narrow black eyes glazed over with chronic hatred, like a migraine of the spirit, a mono-brow like a furry black centipede, an under-achieving beard that failed to conceal a receding and sharply pointed chin. Barrakha was sporting a checkered Palestinian kaffiyeh and wearing a dirty white djellaba, holding a rusted AK over his head. His mouth was open –

he looked like the kind of person whose mouth was always open – his meaty lips twisted in a feral snarl that reeked of vaudeville, showing a jaw full of teeth that were a standing reproach to Middle Eastern dentistry. To Drew's weary eyes, he looked like a dyspeptic ferret with Tourette's.

The biography was predictable but Drew read it carefully, looking for something to justify Krugman's interest:

BARRAKHA, Hamidullah:
Born Adan, Yemen, 1958. Operational Cover Name Mr Gabriel. Father Yemeni Ambassador to United Nations. Attended Al Khalid University, Riyadh, and took a graduate course in postcolonial divinity studies at the Sorbonne, studied in Saudi Arabia and London School of Economics. Joined Taliban during Soviet occupation. Trained at Al Qaeda camps in Tunis, Libya, Iran, Syria. Active in Berlin-based terror cells. Suspected financial assistant September 11th attacks. Escaped Afghanistan during Operation Anaconda. Next seen in Karachi. Humint suggests Barrakha will soon relocate to Indonesia to organize Islamist resistance cells in Bali, the Sulus, and the Philippines. Health issues: chronic asthma. Otherwise healthy. Suspected pedophile but no record of substantiated proof anywhere and allegations merely anecdotal. No substance-abuse deficiencies. Considered emotionally stable and intelligent; adapts well to strategic and tactical changes. Upper-echelon Al Qaeda officer. FBI Most Wanted Number Six. CIA Expedient Demise Authorization granted by Presidential Finding November 2001. (See KUNIA Intercept this date) (See extended extract CIA Terrorist Overview on this page)

There was nothing here that struck him as remarkable, other than the very existence of a course called 'postcolonial divinity studies'. Certainly nothing with an obvious hook for him or for his people. Barrakha's story was right in line with the biographies of most of the terrorists he had been reading about for years: second sons or trust-fund leeches, cunning but with a weakness for grudge-holding and revenge fantasies and the mean streak required to indulge them, who had then hooked up with a charismatic prof at a Parisian university or a gotch-eyed mullah in some parched Syrian backwater, where they promptly swallowed the whole noxious tincture of global jihad at one go and headed back out into the world with red-rimmed eyes to make the West pay dearly for whatever the hell it had done or hadn't done or was about to do.

This crude interpretation of the terrorist crisis was in no way the view – at least the publicly expressed view – of any of his fellow Democrats on the Hill; hell, it was probably only his view in late-at-night hour-of-the-wolf sessions just like this one. Come daylight, he'd strap on the shining armor and go back out there like a brave little Democrat to fight whatever the hell the Good Fight was supposed to be these days. Anyway, he was no further ahead in his inquiry and it was running late. He wasn't even supposed to be in Washington right now; August was the month for sucking up to your constituents back in the home state, and he was booked on a flight for Harrisburg tomorrow afternoon. Even in the summer recess he had more critical things to do than go on dancing in the dark with one of Gunther Krugman's elusive chimeras. He'd give this an hour, then pack it in.

He hit SAVE AS on the Barrakha file and downloaded

it into his hard drive, cleared the site, and picked up the CD that Krugman had included with the transcript. He slipped it out of the case and inserted it into his CD drive.

While he waited for it to cycle up, he stared at the blinking red light on his answering machine. It was intriguing to consider, in this wired, interconnected world, that real power lay in the ability to stay out of touch, to be totally unreachable until you chose to reconnect. He leaned over and scrolled through the Caller ID list. He recognized the phone number of the *Washington Post* city desk – probably Britney Vogel's direct line. Vogel was the *Post*'s junior Senate reporter, a chipper little vixen made of solid titanium with blue eyes as pale as glacier water under a helmet of glossy blond hair and the tender sensibilities of a pickax. She'd hacked herself a special niche under Drew Langan's ribcage when she had spiked a particularly nasty rumor related to the disintegration of his marriage.

The fact that the rumor had been completely accurate had earned her a degree of special access to him, and she had been working that access like a piston at the wellhead ever since, surfing on the crest of the recent wave of sparkly young snakeheads fresh out of Columbia and now working the Capitol beat.

'Senator Langan, this is Britney Vogel. I'm sorry to be calling you at this hour but I was hoping you could persuade Mr Krugman to answer one of my calls? I know he'd want to hear from me but for some reason I'm not getting through? If you could just let him know I'm trying to reach him that would be wonderful!'

'You can count on me,' said Drew, as he hit DELETE and went on to the next caller, a Denver number. The only connection he had in Denver was Helen Claiborne McDowell, the senior Democratic senator for Colorado and the Chairman of his Intelligence Oversight Committee. He hit PLAY and listened to McDowell's rasping whisky tenor: 'Drew, this is Helen – if you get this message early enough I'm here in Denver for another hour and then I'm on my way up the Front Range for some hunting. I'm gonna give you my private cell –' Here she barked out a string of numbers, forcing Drew to scramble just to scrawl them down on a note pad – 'and where the hell are you, anyway? I know you're home because I already woke up your daddy and the cranky old fart told me you were still in Georgetown. I need to talk to Gunther Krugman pretty damn quick. Can't find the son of a bitch anywhere. He's a friend of yours. You get your ass in gear and tell him to give me a call!'

Drew shook his head and poised his finger over the DELETE button. Then, in consideration of his lousy clerical skills, he decided to hit SAVE MESSAGE instead. If he got her damn cell number wrong at least he'd have a record of the call to retrieve the right one. Drew had found that it didn't pay to irritate McDowell, a once-beautiful woman whose years in power had turned her into a raddled old banshee.

Helen Claiborne McDowell was a living paradigm of the ancient proverb that 'any politician who retires from civic service with more money than he had when he went into it is a scoundrel.' She had consolidated her metastasizing D.C. power-base by shamelessly working her political connections to secure federally funded foreign-aid construction contracts for Colorado companies all over the western hemisphere. Starting out from a very rich Denver family, she had managed to reach truly obscene levels of wealth during her forty-nine years in public life. She owned a sprawling hunting lodge high up in the Front

Range with a hundred-mile view that included Denver and most of eastern Colorado all the way to the Great Plains, and her house in Georgetown was a white marble Palladian mansion that took up an entire block of Calvert Street. Her real-estate holdings in Baltimore and her recent sale of a family estate in Palm Beach had placed her in the highest echelons of wealthy Washingtonians, which made her one of the most powerful people inside the Beltway. At seventy-one, she was the last of her long greedy line and, unless she miraculously gave birth to something arguably human before she died, this Croesus-like hoard would fall into the hands of some obscure flatlander relative, a bleak prospect that – based on her recent fits of near-hysterical bitchery during committee meetings – was driving the venal old bat totally nuts. He had no intention of calling her at this hour, no matter what the hell her problem was. Maybe it was connected to Krugman's package, but it could just as likely be some petty procedural bullshit.

He made a mental note to call her in the morning – maybe she'd be out of a cell-phone area by then and he could just leave a message – and went on to the next caller, a D.C. number with a PRIVATE CALLER tag. The number looked familiar. It took him a moment to recognize it; it was the NSA – Levi Sloane's personal line. Sloane was Assistant Deputy Director of Operations for the NSA, and a call from him was not at all safe to ignore. He hit PLAY and heard Sloane's brusque Arkansas twang – 'Drew – Levi here – need to have a talk with our buddy Krugman. He still with you? Heard you two were all snuggled up at the Regis tonight. Not answering any of his phones, the miserable old bugger. No panic. If you don't get in too late you might give me a call, okay?

If not let's talk first thing in the morning. Have a good one.'

Drew played the message twice and then shut the machine off. Three calls and they each had something to do with Gunther Krugman. Whatever Krugman was up to, he was a popular man this evening. Everybody wanted to reach him and they didn't mind calling Drew up at whatever the hell hour and dragooning him into the sweep, as if he had suddenly become the central clearinghouse for all things Krugman. He was reaching for the handset to give Levi Sloane a callback when there was a flicker of motion in his peripheral vision and he looked back at his computer screen. He'd been expecting the CD player to kick in and give him the audio version of Krugman's transcript. Instead he was looking at the entry screen of what looked to be an ordinary copy of a Microsoft Streets and Trips CD. Had Krugman made a mistake? Or the person who sent him? Not Krugman, at any rate. So what did this mean?

He ejected the CD and studied it under the light, looking for some kind of etched writing on the plastic surface. Nothing. He tore open the slipcase and looked at the interior, then he picked up the large blue envelope and studied the interior of that. There was nothing, nothing at all. And no slip of paper hidden inside it. But there was *something* here, something Krugman meant for him to decipher. Drew tried to recall Krugman's whispered final comment, the last thing he had said before he left the bar: Read the report. Look at the CD.

Look at the CD. Not listen. But the print transcript identified the enclosed CD as an audio CD. Had Krugman replaced it with this one? There was no reason to believe that. It was just as likely that whoever had sent Krugman had enclosed the CD for his – or her – own reasons. If so, what were they? The CD was a locator aid. The only location data on the print transcript was latitude 7.5832 and longitude 124.2944. He put the CD back in, let it cycle up, found the SEARCH tab and typed in those coordinates.

The CD processed the data and, in less than a second, showed him a basic map of the Iligan City area in northern Mindanao. Okay. Maria Christina Falls was right where the coordinates said it would be. What was he intended to infer from that? Nothing that came immediately to mind. Had Krugman said anything else? His final words played out in Drew's mind again.

'Read the report, Drew. Look at the CD. Enjoy the cigar. I think you should have it tonight. I really do. I'll say goodnight now. And if we don't see each other for a while, I want you to know that I have always been proud to have been associated with your family. Your father is a man I have always admired. I'll take my leave now and I wish you good luck.'

Thanks. Good luck to you too, you cryptic old bastard. In all the years of their association, Drew had never heard him use the phrase 'good luck.' Gunther Krugman was a creature of solid calculation.

Numbers, then? A locator disk needed numbers. Were they any other numbers on the transcript? Only three other sets of numbers: Barrakha's file number, AXR-881089; the intercept file number, 15/340/0097; and the time marker, 1425 hours Eastern Daylight Time. He went back to the CD, found the Location Sensor tool, and clicked onto a map of the world.

AXR 881089.

That could be latitude 88.1089 or longitude 88.1089.

A few minutes of painstaking mouse work later he had

established several things to his own satisfaction; first, a north latitude of 88.1089 put him on a globe-spanning circle around the North Pole that started in the middle of the Arctic Ocean about five hundred miles north of Greenland, or an equally large circle that started somewhere in Antarctica and never left it. He considered just calling Krugman's home number and asking him what the hell this was supposed to mean. If anything.

One more try, then the hell with it. What's next? The intercept file numbers, 15/340/0097? A few minutes' work and he was certain that there was no secret map grid reference in them, nor were there any in the time marker either.

Jesus, I hate puzzles.

Now what, Gunther? Any more clues?

Yes. There was one.

Drew went back to his coat jacket and pulled the cigar case from the pocket, twisted the top, broke the seal, and slid the long brown cigar out of the tube. A Monte Cristo, fresh and soft and sharply scented. No plastic wrapping, though. There was nothing else inside the tube. He held the cigar up to the light and studied the paper ring wrapped around the shaft. The Monte Cristo logo. He carefully opened the ring and peeled it off the cigar. Numbers were written on the inside of the ring in light pencil, tiny but legible. 39.06675–76.80991. It was like Krugman to put his message inside a cigar ring; unlike the younger generation of cigar smokers, who liked to leave the brand ring on their cigars to impress their friends, men of Krugman's generation had always peeled off the ring before lighting the cigar. And the numbers? Latitude and longitude. Had to be.

So where did they get him? After a few seconds of

processing, they got him to Beltsville, Maryland, a small town about 14 miles north of Washington, D.C. To be more precise, the numbers indicated a point right at the intersection of two country roads a little over three miles east of the Powder Mill exit off Interstate 295. Springfield Road and Good Luck Road. According to the map, there was nothing there but meadows and farms and industrial malls. Jolly. Now what?

Did any of this connect with Sloane's sudden interest in reaching Krugman? Drew had a feeling it did. The fact that Krugman expected to him do something with this information was implicit in the trouble that Gunther Krugman had taken to conceal these coordinates. It occurred to him that the simplest way to deal with this puzzle was to pick up the phone right now and ask Krugman what the hell it all meant. He looked at the clock in the task bar – a little after one-thirty – and picked up the phone.

He dialed Krugman's unlisted home number. It rang busy for about thirty seconds and then the line went dead. That was odd but not unlike Krugman, who had a habit of dropping out of contact whenever he pleased. Judging by all the calls he was getting from people who were also looking for him, it had pleased Krugman to drop off the grid this evening. He thought about calling Levi Sloane, but some vague concern about Krugman made him put the phone down and think about it. If Krugman had gotten involved in something that had gained the attention of people like Levi Sloane and Helen McDowell, then he wanted to hear what it was from Krugman himself before he called these people back. Maybe there was something about this Beltsville location on the SIGINT database. He could type in the coordinates and see what popped up. He logged back on to the home page and saw the NSA crest with that red-lettered warning:

ANYONE USING THIS SYSTEM
EXPRESSLY CONSENTS TO MONITORING

Drew looked at that warning for a long time, his finger hovering over the ENTER key. Then he logged off, cleared all his temporary Internet files, and shut the damn thing down. Then he pulled the laptop out of the docking bay and shoved it into his briefcase. Wherever he went, this computer was going with him. And whatever he was going to do about this – and he knew in his heart that he was definitely going to have to do something – Krugman's clear intent was that Drew do it quietly. And alone.

Iligan City

Room 511, The Milan Hotel
218 Truong Tan Buu Street
Tuesday, August 19, 3:00 p.m. local time

It took Cole Langan almost forty minutes to sweep the room for taps and monitors. It was clean. He attached a number of tiny low-frequency emitters on the windowpanes to block any laser mikes directed against the glass and had just sat down at the laptop when there was a soft triple knock on the door.

'Who is it?'

'Al Gore,' said Pike Zeigler. 'I need a job.'

'Try the Ang Kusina. They're looking for clean boys.'

'I did. They sent me here. Open the damned door.'

'It's open.'

Pike Zeigler came into the room carrying a large plaster image of the Buddha, followed by Chris Burdette and Loman Strackbein. Pike set it down on the fold-out bamboo table that was holding Cole's laptop. Cole looked at him with one eyebrow raised and the Buddha looked back serenely while Chris Burdette went to the fridge and pulled out some chilled Singha beers. Loman Strackbein gave Cole one of his sardonic grins and picked out a chair that didn't look too virulently infectious. Burdette popped a few of the Singhas and handed them around, then he hitched himself up onto a window ledge and looked down into Truong Tan Buu Street.

'Saigon,' he said. 'Shit. I'm still only in Saigon.'

Pike looked over at him. 'You were never in Saigon. I was in Saigon.'

Burdette gave him a grin. 'I keep forgetting how incredibly old you are. I mean, you got more wrinkles than a seersucker suit. Tell us, Pike, what was Jesus Christ really like? Was he a knock-around sort of guy?'

Pike, whose sense of humor, if it had ever existed at all, was now buried under more than thirty years of open and covert combat, ignored Burdette and took a long pull of his beer as he sat down on the far side of the table. Pike had been in the US Army since 1967, when he had walked away from a juvenile detention facility in Butte, Montana, and volunteered for combat duty in Vietnam. He was a career lifer and a gifted combat leader, retiring from the Seventh Cavalry three years ago with the rank of Command Sergeant Major. But he had been one of those soldiers for whom peacetime military service was one bar-fight-cluster-fuck-motor-pool-fire-AWOL-court-martial-punishment-parade after another, in his case often for drinking and violence. He retired with full honors, but his one-year hitch as a communications security director for a Verizon R and D branch in Syracuse had ended badly – for the usual reasons – and it was basically reup or eat his gun for Pike Zeigler. The Army had wanted nothing of him, but Pike was prime grade A military beef, seasoned and marbled and perfectly aged. At the time, the CIA Special Collections was in the process of building up a new paramilitary arm to counterbalance the rise of the Special Forces and Delta units the Army was fielding, and they needed men like Pike Zeigler to form the training cadre. And he was a brilliant success at that. He was fifty-four years old now and looked as if most of those years were spent at hard labor under a mean-tempered yard bull. He had heavy plates of thick muscle that were always working under his chest and sliding across his shoulders when he moved. His neck looked as if it should have a good strong rope around it. He had great hands, long-fingered and very strong; he could play the piano well enough to make a decent living at it in any stateside bar, a career path that many men who had encountered Pike Zeigler in his professional capacity had reason to wish he had taken. Cole looked at the veins in Pike's cheeks and the tight line of his mouth. His skin was yellow. He smelled of limes. He was obviously still drinking, but right now he seemed sober enough. Not that Pike was a mean drinker at all – he was a quiet man, a patient and polite listener – but he was easily angered by barroom louts and had a tendency to fold, spindle, and mutilate them if adequately provoked. He had this general air of impending doom. Not necessarily his. If you were in a room with Pike Zeigler the room always seemed too small, like being in a box stall with a high-strung draft horse who didn't really approve of you.

'Why the Buddha?' asked Strackbein.

Pike lifted an eyebrow at him and then studied the statue.

'I got the replacement transmitter inside it. It's safe. Nobody fucks with the image of a Buddha in this part of the world. And his name isn't Buddha; it's Earl. He just looks like the Buddha.'

Burdette took the statue from the table and hefted it.

'Twenty pounds easy. How far did you travel with this?'

'He was waiting for me in Hawaii. I flew out of Kunia

with him under my arm. It was easy. The flight thingy gave him a Mai Tai.'

Burdette handed the Buddha to Strackbein, who turned him around in a shaft of slatted yellow light streaming in from the window.

'I take it they sealed the relay before they cast this?'

'They're geeks, Loman,' said Pike. 'Not morons.'

'They didn't X-ray this at the airport security?'

Pike sent Strackbein a weary knowing smile and popped the lid off his Singha. He drained half the bottle, his powerful neck working. He set the bottle down again and looked at Cole across the table as if he were trying to remember his name.

'You look all wrong.'

Pike's Montana accent was strong and his voice rumbled in his chest like big rocks rolling around.

'I look all wrong? How do I look all wrong?'

'It's not even that stupid earring,' said Pike. 'It's your hair.'

'At least I have some.'

Pike rubbed a hand across his scalp. Cole could hear the furry zipping of Pike's close-cropped bristles from across the table.

'I tried. It grows out in patches. I look like I got the mange.'

'Maybe you do,' said Burdette.

'What kind of writer were you going for?' said Pike.

'What? With the long hair?'

'The whole thing,' said Pike, making an inclusive gesture and looking around the room, finally settling his attention back on Cole with a kind of inaudible snap like locking a magazine into a grip.

'Caring. Concerned. A compassionate Canadian writer.'

'A bleeder,' said Pike, rocking back in his chair.

'Bleeder' was Pike Zeigler's word for anyone who was even remotely left-wing. In his world you were a bleeder if you had never had a chicken-fried steak, and his definition expanded in concentric circles from that point. His opinion of the United Nations was hard to convey in words longer than one syllable, and you only asked him for his views on the French and the Germans if you wanted to see all the veins in his neck and forehead pop out. Cole did a slightly fey preen-and-smirk.

'I'm not a bleeder, Pike. Like all of us insanely brave yet humble newshounds, I follow wherever the truth may lead in my sacred mission of letting everybody back home know how badly you dumb-fuck soldiers are buggering things up for the poor and the downtrodden. I'm really here for the children. The dear little ones.'

'So you're like a combat proctologist?' said Pike.

'What's a combat proctologist?'

'A war correspondent. When the shooting stops they crawl out from behind a rock and sodomize the wounded.'

'Not *all* the wounded,' said Cole. 'Only our guys.'

'What are you reading?'

Cole turned the laptop around and pushed it across the table. Pike and Burdette leaned forward and squinted at it, then Pike pulled out a pair of reading glasses.

'Don't say a thing about my glasses.'

'What glasses?' said Burdette.

'What is this? Looks like a Critic Flash.'

'It is,' said Cole. 'I just decrypted it. It's an intercept out of Kunia.'

Pike leaned in and read the screen and Burdette read it over Pike's massive shoulder.

Pike leaned back and frowned at the screen.

'We have any idea who Speaker Two is?'

'Who he is?' said Cole. 'Likely some Filipino. Where he is? No idea.'

'Who the hell is "the Ferenghi"?'

'Us, I guess. The good guys. The white meat.'

'Can we check that out on the SIGINT database?'

'Not from here. The firewall would never let us in.'

Pike was still focused on the word.

'Ferenghi. I tell you, it sounds like somebody in their organization. Like it's a code name for a specific person.'

Strackbein came across and looked down at the screen. Then he put a hand on Pike's shoulder and patted it.

'Don't go all crypto on us now, Pike. We don't need another puzzle wonk in this unit.'

Pike kept at it, which was like him.

'Think about it, Cole. This intercept was stripped out of a microwave transmission from the power plant at Maria Christina Falls. Which means somebody on the staff there has the technical skills to embed a frequency-modulated signal in a microwave carrier broadcast. Around here, that would be a very short list of guys.'

'I love it when you talk like that,' said Burdette. Pike ignored him again. Over the years ignoring Chris Burdette had become one of Pike's core skill groups. He could now ignore Burdette almost at will.

'Or somebody on the outside who has access,' said Cole.

'Is anybody on our side looking at the staff?'

'Highly likely.'

Pike's face was getting redder.

'But not us?'

'No. Not us.'

'Man, look at all those "inaudibles,"' said Strackbein. 'It sounds like the intercept signal's getting worse.'

Cole nodded.

'The relay is failing. That's why we're here, remember? By the way, Pike, they're not likely to have any white meat in Abu Sayaf. "Ferenghi" would be a reference to a westerner of some type. Jihad is strictly for the rag-heads. No infidels allowed.'

'Maybe. Maybe not,' said Pike. 'One thing you can count on. They're going to pull something right here in Iligan.'

Strackbein walked away and sat down in his chair.

'Your death grip on the stunningly obvious remains as firm as ever, Pike. Your point here?'

Pike looked around at each of them. His blood was up.

'And we're going to do . . . what? Let it happen?'

'Not our job,' said Cole. 'That's what SOUTHCOM is for. And the DIA. And the Filipino cops. We're just the maintenance crew. But let's not linger around Iligan City any longer than we have to. Where is Vasquez?'

Burdette frowned at the question.

'Ramiro's at the Jiddy Lodge with Jesus Rizal, who some lunatic back at the farm decided to make our liaison guy. He's checked in under the name of Ramón Goliad. They're passing themselves off as a couple of chicken-hawks on a short-eyes junket, which I think was an inspired choice. I haven't heard from Dean Krause yet.'

'Krause was delayed in Bangkok,' Pike put in. 'He'll be in this evening. He'll be at the Iligan Star under the name of Cannon.'

'We're using Vasquez on this one?' asked Pike. The question caused an uncomfortable silence in the room. It wasn't that the unit believed in bad luck, but the last two missions that Ramiro Vasquez had been involved in – an extraction in Paraguay and an insertion mission in Waziristan – had gone very badly. The Paraguayan mission had run right into a rebel patrol and had been forced to fight its way out of the jungle. The Blackhawk lifting them off the mountain had taken over a hundred hits from small-arms fire before running clear, the crew chief hanging dead in his harness half out the bay door, still clutching the butt of the minigun.

The Waziristan mission – bad intel had dropped them into a hot LZ – had resulted in the deaths of three of their members, good men whose stars on the Wall of Silence at Langley were now all that was left of them. Vasquez had been the only man to get out of Waziristan alive. And the year before the Paraguayan mission, on June 17, 1997, Vasquez's wife, Katie, and their two children, six-year-old Rafael and nine-year-old Pilar, had been struck by a hit-and-run driver while walking home from their school in Charlottesville. Katie and Rafael were dead at the scene, and Pilar was still in a deep coma in a Richmond hospital years later, technically alive but with little hope of recovery. The driver had never been caught, although Vasquez had spent all six weeks of his bereavement leave looking for the white Windstar van that had done the damage. No suspect had ever been found, no charges ever laid. They liked and admired Vasquez, but they all thought that such sustained bad luck was very likely contagious; Cole finally answered.

'Ramiro's one of us, Pike. We all trained with him at the Farm and at Camp Peary.'

'It's not that I don't trust him,' said Pike. 'It's his nerves I worry about. Who assigned him?'

'Sloane did,' said Cole, 'and that's good enough for me.'

'Sloane personally?' asked Pike.

'Yeah.'

'Putting a guy in the field after a string of severe emotional hits runs strictly counter to operational rules. During the last six years we've had eight guys shifted into analytical or supervisory roles, taken out of the field, after having missions go a lot less sour than either of Ramiro's last two missions. My question remains. Why is Sloane putting Ramiro Vasquez into the field again? It's just plain nuts.'

Cole shook his head.

'Pike, the field is all Vasquez has left. Take that away from him and what does he have in his life? A daughter in a coma and a house full of grief waiting for him back in Charlottesville. Vasquez needs to have some success in the field and this is his chance. I've seen his psych review and Sloane thinks he's up to it. So do I.'

Pike wasn't convinced. 'Three of our section's last nine missions were organized and run by Levi Sloane. All three of those missions ended in a cluster-fuck of record proportions. Including Vasquez and his unit in Waziristan. Maybe Vasquez isn't the problem here.'

'Who is? Sloane? You're saying Sloane's . . . what?'

Pike hesitated, then shook his head like a buffalo.

'I'm not saying Sloane's anything. Maybe he's just losing his touch. Maybe *he* needs to be reassigned, instead of Vasquez. I mean, ask yourself, if we're not supposed to *do* anything about this thing the rag-heads are planning for Iligan, why did Sloane let us see the fucking thing? It just shakes up our concentration. What was his point?'

'That's another issue. We saw it because it relates to the terrain we're operating in. Look, Pike, Vasquez is in. Deal with it.'

'Well ... okay then. To that I got nothing to say. On your head. And Sloane's. What the hell. Maybe Vasquez can put up with that Filipino prick. Better him than me.'

'I take it you don't like Jesus Rizal?' said Strackbein

'I think he's a flake,' said Pike. 'Where'd we find him?'

The question was directed at Cole. Strackbein answered it. 'Sloane got the referral from Crypto City. Rizal's one of their links here. He's got family all over the Philippines.'

'Sloane again,' said Pike, his voice a low growl.

Nevertheless, Burdette was suitably impressed.

'Crypto City uses him? What languages does he have?'

Strackbein seemed to have Rizal memorized.

'The basic tribal stuff in Lanao del Norte. Bukidnon, Diyandi, Maranao. Tasug. Tagalog. Cebuano, which is what most of the Iliganos around here speak. Samal. Some Spanish. His family name is big in the Philippines. His ancestor was José Rizal.'

'The guerrilla?' said Burdette.

Strackbein nodded. 'The freedom fighter is how he likes to put it.'

'I don't trust any of these local people,' said Pike. 'Rizal's a touchy little prick, too. Always ready to pick a fight.'

'Show me the Filipino who isn't,' said Cole.

'This guy gonna go all the way to the relay site with us?'

'No. Not if I can help it.'

'What does he think we're here to do?'

'He's been told we need a linguist to help us gather basic intel about the rebels up around Lake Lanao. That's all he will ever know. Loman, you figured out how to get us up-country yet?'

'I've got a jeepney cached on the outskirts,' said

Strackbein. 'Rizal thinks we can ride it up into the hills a little north of the falls. We rendezvous at the jeepney, put on some jungle gear, and then into the bush. It's a big ugly hump to Camp Casey. There's a weapons cache on the site, been there since we pulled out in ninety-two.'

'Man,' said Cole. 'That is a mean trip. Thirty miles. Uphill.'

Burdette gave him his trademark jarhead grin.

'In case you haven't noticed, sir, it's been my experience that most of your actual combat takes place out of doors. I've also found that some pretty strenuous exercise is usually involved. Officers are sometimes asked to take part. It has been reported – I admit I've never seen this myself – that occasionally they even fire their own weapons.'

'Really?' said Cole. 'The things you tell me.'

'Combat is an all-weather sport, sir.'

'Stop calling me sir. We're not in the Army anymore. We're not supposed to be getting into any combat. This is strictly a service call. Hear me on this, all of you. We go for a ramble up-country, we fix this little problem for those wonderful folks across the Potomac, and then we get the hell out of Dodge.'

'If you ask me –' said Pike

'I don't remember that I did.'

'If you ask me,' he said, with more force, 'I don't get this entire mission. Okay, we have a surveillance relay going off-line. It's not the only relay in Southeast Asia. I've never heard of dropping a repair unit into a UN-controlled peacekeeping zone. If we get caught, I mean caught alive and tagged as American intelligence, all those schmucks at the UN who already hate us will go totally bats and we could end up wearing baggy pajamas and leg-irons in a prisoner's box at the International Criminal Court. Tell me why I'm wrong?'

'We do what we're told,' said Cole. 'Levi Sloane told us to do this. We *need* this relay working. It's the only one we've got that's deep into Al Qaeda territory up around Lake Lanao. America needs to know what those little greaseballs are up to. And you don't know that none of our teams has ever been dropped into a United Nations zone before, do you?'

'That's another point – why this extended hump up-country? Why not HALO us in or do a Blackhawk insertion?'

'I presume you saw that deuce of Mirages go over?' said Burdette.

'Presume? You're using the word "presume"?' said Strackbein.

'Every chance I get, Loman. It's fun to say. They're flying regular reconnaissance and cover out of a base in Luzon. Plus the Krauts have some of their one zero five choppers up around Lake Lanao. They'll have infrared and heat sensors. And twenty-millimeter cannons. That's a lot of serious air. You think we can just slide on into their zone without tripping a wire? Pike's got a point. Why didn't we just insert or do a HALO drop? Or better yet, let some of our local agents do the repair?'

Cole shook his head.

'And I presume – you're right, Chris, it is fun to say – I presume you saw the radar dome on the Suffren out there in the harbor. They'd see a Blackhawk coming from a hundred miles away, even if they came in at ten feet off the deck. Same with a HALO drop. And there's no way the NSA is going to hand the kind of technology we've got inside Earl over to a slap-happy band of our local freelancers. Even if they did manage to get up-country without setting fire to their grass skirts, they'd probably plug the thing in backwards and get their noses blown off. We do it or nobody does it. Collections said anything else was too risky.'

Pike snorted. 'Too risky for Levi Sloane and his merry band of rear-echelon-motherfuckers, you mean.'

'It's political, Pike. They don't want to risk freaking out the French and the Germans in the middle of another UN operation.'

'Fuck the Frogs and bugger the Krauts.'

'If you have the stamina I'll hold your coat. Look, Pike, you don't like this. I don't like it either but that's the assignment. The jungle canopy up there is thicker than a bath mat at the Waldorf. I'm told Jesus Rizal knows the terrain. He thinks we can get by the UN patrols if we follow the river beds and stay off the trails. Most of the UN troops are cooping up inside their perimeters and doing very little in the way of foot patrols. And if the monsoon sets in they won't be running a lot of chopper missions either. The whole mission is a down-and-dirty in-and-out. Elapsed time maybe seventy-two hours.'

'What kind of ordnance are we gonna find up at Casey?' asked Burdette.

Pike had the list. 'Sloane said the Army cached some M-Sixties, a bunch of M-Sixteens, forty-fives, maybe some bloop guns.'

Burdette wasn't happy to hear this.

'We're gonna deploy with a pig? Christ, Pike. That shit's Vietnam gear. That sucker weighs over twenty pounds. I haven't even fired a Sixty since Lejeune.'

Pike managed to look hurt and offended at the same time.

'It's *not* a pig. The Sixty is a righteous piece. And it's not the same weapon that we used in Eye Corps. The ones up at Casey are total rebuilds like you jarheads are using right now. And I got a soft spot for anything that can put out five hundred rounds a minute. Stop whining. I'll hump the Sixty. Now what about the rag-head? I get the idea he's coming into Mindanao. We gonna go see this –'

'Let's not say his name, hah?'

Pike gave the men another sweep and settled back on Cole's face, opened his eyes wide, radiating purity and innocence. It was like watching a Komodo dragon do a Barney impression.

'Whose name? Barrakha's name? I can't say Hamidullah Barrakha's name. Why the fuck not? Half the wogs in this 'ville are doing his laundry.'

'That's what I mean. And don't call them wogs.'

Pike stayed with it, zeroing in on Cole. 'Is he on our wish list or not?'

Cole shook his head and tried to look regretful.

'This is a United Nations zone. The Krauts lost five troopers last month, and anyone they see in the bush even looks like a soldier they'll light him up like Joan of Arc. We are not to be seen. We will not engage even if fired upon. If we get into a contact we cut and run.'

'And if they're shooting at us?'

'We are not to engage any peacekeepers, Pike. Under any circumstances. Nor are we to be taken prisoner.'

'No firefights and not to be taken prisoner?'

'I think that's what I'm saying here.'

Burdette had heard enough. He cut in.

'That leaves dead. Is dead our fall-back option here?

Because I got to tell you, Cole, being dead doesn't work for me.'

Cole leaned back and drank some Singha and smiled at Burdette. 'I'd rather not go the dead route either. I'm morally opposed to being dead. We just can't afford to tangle with these UN weenies.'

Pike was clearly displeased and not at all ready to leave this alone. 'Then what the fuck are the weapons for?'

'Lions and tigers and bears,' said Burdette.

Pike stayed on it, his blood rising in his face.

'That doesn't leave us a lot of tactical options.'

'The basic idea is not to get seen at all. By anybody.'

'And if we do, be sure to avoid headlines and die politely?'

'This is a repair job, Pike. We tippy-toe in and twinkle on out like pixies. That's mission policy here. You all okay with that?'

There was a long strained silence.

Cole held Pike's hostile look until Pike's eyes shifted.

Cole pushed the issue.

'Pike?'

'Don't ride me, Cole. I'm not in the mood.'

'Are you good with that?'

'No. I'm not good with that.'

'You'll work on it? Right?'

'I'll do my fucking best.'

'Are we all good with that?'

They all nodded. Eventually. Except Pike.

There was a short tense silence. Traffic noise from Truong Tan Buu Street drifted up through the hazy afternoon and filtered in through the shutters. Cole's lap-top hummed quietly. In the distance they could hear the sighing hiss of sea rollers breaking on the flats.

'I have a question,' said Burdette. 'Pike's humping the Sixty?'

'He volunteered.'

'So who humps the Buddha?'

'I'll hump the Buddha,' said Cole.

'You'll hump the Buddha?'

'Is there an echo?'

'Can we watch?'

Georgetown

2699 Dumbarton Street N.W.
Georgetown, Washington, D.C.
Wednesday, August 20, 3:00 a.m. D.C. time

Drew snapped abruptly out of a deep dreamless sleep, aware only of the fact that his body was now listening to the surrounding dark with such a concentrated intensity that he could hear his own blood pulsing in his throat. The house seemed to be silent, but it was a silence so profound, so strangely *dense,* that it felt like a dull pressure on his eardrums. Lying there in his king-size bed, alone in an empty house, Drew felt his skin contracting across his chest and belly in uneven tingling waves. On his back, staring upward into the velvety blackness, hearing only the sound of his own blood singing in his arteries and the soft tidal hushing of air moving in and out of his lungs, Drew realized that this absolute silence was the reason he was awake. It was all wrong. There was no muted bass hum from the central air-conditioning. The noise of the refrigerator downstairs – usually registering as a soft electric murmur that drifted up the staircase – was also absent. As his eyes adjusted to the darkness he could dimly make out the blades of the ceiling fan overhead, turning gently, the blades slowing ... slowing ... He turned his head to look at the red numbers of his bedside clock and saw only a blacker rectangle in the darkness. Okay. There you go. The power was out.

Judging by the still-turning fan blades, it had cut out no longer than a minute ago. That was what had wakened him, the sudden cessation of the ordinary rhythms of the sleeping house, the unnatural silence. He lay there in the bed within this urgent silence, beginning to wonder why the answer to the puzzle was failing to calm his nerves. It came to him then that there was one more *absence* left to explain; in a power failure the household alarm system went to a stand-by battery pack. That activated the built-in cellular phone that carried the alarm's signal to the monitoring station. Whenever the system went to stand-by, there was a continual warning beep, faint, muted, but audible throughout the house. Yet there was no beep; only this pounding silence. Drew pulled the covers off and slipped softly out of the bed.

He stood in the middle of the room for a time, listening for any kind of motion. Nothing. Then he padded barefoot over to the window and looked out through the leaded glass panes. Down the tree-shaded block a soft mist was drifting in a luminous cloud around a pale yellow streetlamp. A house across the way still had its porch light glowing. So whatever had happened to the power, it wasn't a major failure. He craned his neck to see if there were any other lights on and saw the pale glow of a streetlight down at the corner. Above the black silhouette of the rooftops the suffused glow of the Capitol was reflected on the underside of a low bank of clouds.

He was still standing at the window, idly wondering what kind of power failure affected only one side of the street, when he heard a soft groaning creak that stopped quite suddenly. It had come from downstairs. He knew the sound. The battered old oak planks in the front hallway. They groaned whenever you stepped on them.

He turned to face the black rectangle of the open bed-room door, his breathing shallow and his heart beginning to race. Was someone in the house? He strained to hear another creak and heard only the thumping of his own heart. A number of separate thoughts tumbled through his mind, the first being that the pistol all senators were allowed to carry in D.C. – in his case a stainless-steel Taurus – was only a step away, wrapped in a blue polka-dot handkerchief in the second drawer of his mahogany armoire. The second thought was that this pistol was unfortunately unloaded. Like all right-thinking, gun-hating urban liberals he had made sure to store the magazine separately: it was in a drawer in a Chippendale cabinet in the downstairs hall. The third thought was that he had just recently put a trigger-lock on the pistol, the key to which was on his key chain, and his key chain was lying at the bottom of a large sterling silver vase, which was also downstairs, on a table just inside the front door. It was safely stowed away there right next to his cell phone and the small emergency pager the Secret Service had told him that he must always keep on a chain around his neck. It had chafed his skin badly, and after a few weeks he had taken to leaving it in the silver vase with his car keys. The cant phrase 'a defensive gun in the home always presents the greatest risk to its owner' rang with a special hollowness in his mind. This was apparently only true if you followed all the recommended rules for safe storage. If you actually needed a gun for self-defense, you had basically screwed yourself, although in a wonderfully law-abiding and socially responsible sort of way.

Another slow tentative creak, this time closer to the bottom of the staircase. This was not the ordinary working of a very old house, cooling in the evening, ticking softly to itself as its old bones shifted. The sound stopped, again quite suddenly, and then more silence. He stepped quickly to the bedside phone and snatched it up. The line – as he knew it would be – was dead.

Two more soft groaning sounds from the bottom of the stairs. He looked around the room for something – anything – that he could use as a weapon, finally pulling open the drawer of his armoire and taking out the useless semi-auto, holding it so his fingers concealed the trigger-lock. He crossed the room, his bare feet silent in the deep Persian carpet, and reached the open bedroom door, where he stopped, listening. The darkness in the hallway was complete. The sense that someone was waiting in that darkened stairwell – looking upward at the entrance to the upper hall with one foot on the bottom stair – became painfully intense. He resisted the urge to call out a warning – 'I'm armed; I've called the police' – for reasons he could not have explained. Some instinct was telling him that whoever was down there – *if* anyone was down there at all – was not going to simply run away; too much trouble had been taken. Then he heard a clear deliberate step as someone put weight on that bottom stair. Drew waited until the next step began – he had climbed these same stairs for so many years that he knew each step's unique groan by heart – in time it came and as it did he stepped lightly across the hall and into the bathroom on the far side, half-closing the door as he did so.

Someone was now climbing the stairs, slowly, with perfect patience, moving as silently as this ancient house would allow. Drew pulled back into the darkness of the bathroom, reversed the pistol so that he could hold it by the barrel, and waited. After a timeless interval, he became aware that a blacker shadow had filled up the space in the hallway outside his bedroom door. He held his breath and watched as this blacker shape – a man, small, slender – stopped in the hall. Drew caught a slight change in the intruder's upper body as he turned his head, and now Drew could feel the man staring into the darkness of the bathroom. The figure seemed to radiate a terrible concentrated intensity, a palpable menace. Time passed, the shape shifted again, and the figure seemed to glide away into Drew's bedroom. Drew waited for almost thirty seconds, listening as the man moved farther into the bedroom, his feet whispering across the carpet. Then silence, and Drew could picture the man standing there at the side of Drew's bed, staring down into the tangle of blankets and sheets, listening for the sound of a sleeping man. A sudden motion – the sound of something slicing through fabric – Drew stepped out of the bathroom and in one quick motion reached into the open doorway, found the handle as the black shape by the bed turned and came at him – Drew slammed the bedroom door shut and twisted the exterior lock – taking his hand off it just as the man on the far side of the solid-oak door struck it with incredible force, rattling the hinges. Another huge blow – the man was kicking the door – the frame around the door cracked slightly under the blow – Drew raced down the long staircase, slipping and sliding on the polished wood – fumbled at the cabinet drawer and found the loaded magazine, which he rammed into the open grip – just as he reached the front door he heard another deep shuddering blow and the sound of wood splintering – he thought about simply running out the front door but an image of being chased down like a deer in the deserted street by an unknown killer stopped him – and this was *his* house,

Goddammit — at the top of the stairs the bedroom door shook under another powerful blow — he rattled through the jumble of keys in the silver vase — another kick and the sound of splitting wood from the upper hall — Drew found his car keys at the bottom of the vase — a sharp crack as the door-frame snapped, followed by the sound of the bedroom door being ripped open — rapid footsteps as the man ran along the hall and started down the stairs — Drew jammed the key in the trigger lock — the dark shape was halfway down the stairs — the lock popped open — Drew racked the slide and let it go, the sharp metallic snap filling the hallway as a figure ran at him from out of the darkness — Drew braced himself and fired the weapon into the middle of that blackness and saw in the bright blue flaring of the muzzle flash — the weapon kicking in his hands and the sound huge in the narrow hallway — a small man in black clothing — white wet face and pale blue eyes very wide and something thin and glittering in his hand — Drew put two rounds into his chest and belly from less than three feet away — the man tumbled backward onto the narrow runner, sliding as he hit it, coming to rest in a heap of splaying limbs just under the hallway cabinet. Darkness rolled back in, and the afterimage of the muzzle flashes and the man's wide blue eyes full of murder pulsed rhythmically in his retinas. His ears were ringing and his head seemed to be stuffed with cotton. After a while he realized he wasn't breathing, and he sagged against the wall, pulling air into himself in short sharp gasps. Time passed. Across the street a door slammed. Then he reached into the silver vase, found the security buzzer on its neck chain, lifted it out, and pressed the red button over and over again.

*

Buriss and Rickett were the first to show up, and they stayed right by him, radiating ownership, while the local PD took his house apart. A container-sized black detective named Brutus Packett, wearing a shiny charcoal silk suit, had interrogated Drew for what seemed like a year while the little red-haired man in the black clothing had stiffened slowly in Drew's front hallway.

Drew, in a kind of dream state, watched the flash of cameras and listened to the soft muttering tones of the various officials who came, observed, directed, contradicted those directions, argued quietly in the kitchen, whispered in Drew's ear, and finally went away. Buriss made several pots of coffee, which the cops drank gratefully. After a long time, Packett came up to Drew carrying a sheet of computer paper and a color printout of a mug shot.

'You know this guy? Ever seen him?'

Drew studied the picture. In it a slight middle-aged man with bright carrot-red hair in a widow's peak, a broad white forehead, wide, Chinese eyes very pale blue, and a triangular face that narrowed to a strong pointed jaw stared back at the camera with a calm, self-contained, confident look in which something cold and detached glittered. Drew looked at the picture for a while and then shook his head. The big black cop looked down at Drew with a kindly expression.

'We got a tentative ID on this guy. The Feds think he's a guy named Dietrich Voss. Turns out he used to work with ADT – get this – designing domestic alarm monitoring systems. ADT says he might have hacked into their system a couple of hours ago and taken your alarm off-line. They're doing a firewall check right now. Whatever he did, it worked. He used bolt-cutters on your electric meter. It looks like he came in that fan window above your side door.'

Drew shook his head. 'Are you telling me this was just a simple break-and-enter?'

Packett looked at Drew for a while. 'He fits the general description of a guy the Feds have been looking for, pulled a string of high-end burglaries in the area over the last three years. Made off with jewels, bearer bonds – total losses to this unknown guy over the last year alone something around a million dollars. Left prints, but since Voss was never on any fingerprint file they didn't do us much good. We're running a set right now, see if the prints match. Always the same method – hacking into the alarm system and taking it off-line. Only two face-to-face contacts with residents, and in each case no unnecessary violence. Both victims described the same guy we have here. Caught him on a camera once too, and the Feds e-mailed us the shot. Not a good angle, but again, looks like the same guy. Too early to say for certain, but I figure a real professional thief like this one only comes along every few years. Now he's dead. And it looks good on him. You have any reason to think it was anything else?'

Buriss and Rickett had stiffened at the tone. Packett studied them the way a cop would assess a couple of Dobermans.

'No,' said Drew, wondering how far the term co-incidence could be stretched, finally deciding to keep it simple. 'I do have a question. Has he ever killed anyone?'

'If he's the same guy, no. Never. It's unlikely he was going to kill you. Most guys stay with a winning system.'

'Why was he in my bedroom with a knife?'

'That's a good question. It's not his style. Maybe he heard you moving around and decided to come up and check it out. In two other jobs – if he's our guy, I mean – he did confront the owners when he realized they were awake. But he just tied them up. One old lady, he even brought her a glass of water.'

Drew let that pass.

'Am I going to be charged?'

Packett paused, shook his head.

'No. You have a permit for the gun. A permit to carry. Both bullet wounds were in the front of his body. He had a weapon in his hand. He'd broken into your house at three in the morning. It was a righteous shooting. It's up to the DA, but I'm sure there'll be no charges. We're still allowed to use lethal force to defend ourselves in this country. Those of us with gun permits, anyway.'

'No press either,' said Rickett.

It wasn't a question.

'The neighbors are all up,' said Packett. 'They'll call somebody. But I promise they'll get nothing from any of my guys. What do you want us to say about this? Officially?'

Buriss and Rickett exchanged looks. Something silent but significant passed in that look.

'We're the senator's security detail –'

'Then where were you?'

'It wasn't a full-time detail.'

'Why not?'

'Last month the senator got a series of crank calls. Death threats. We chased the guy down. A guy named Dwayne David Canmore. He had lost his job at a steel plant owned by the senator's father. Psych case. We decided that we'd give the senator some stepped-up security until the court case came up. Last Friday the judge ordered a psychiatric assessment and sent Canmore to a mental health facility in Allenwood. So we got pulled off and reassigned.'

'Yeah, I remember seeing that name on one of the department's watch-for sheets. So you guys got pulled off exactly when?'

'At midnight.'

Packett smiled at them.

'Seems a little hinky that the senator would get B and E'd three hours after his Secret Service detail is pulled off.'

'Hinky in what way, detective? Hinky like maybe somebody in our unit shot his mouth off?'

'Like I said. Seems a bit weird. No offense.'

'If your guy was such a pro, he could probably case a street and see there's no cover on a target,' said Buriss, stung and angry. 'When we cover the senator we don't do it from a mile away. We're right out front of his house. So when we pull off it's pretty obvious. And don't start with he was tailing us, because nobody ever gets away with that shit on our watch. If you're looking for somebody to blame for this crap maybe you should start with these FBI major-crimes guys who apparently couldn't find this asshole even with a photo and two solid descriptions from his victims.'

'Fuck you too,' said Packett, smiling.

'Duly noted,' said Rickett. 'We were talking about what you can say to the press. How about this: There was an intruder and he was subdued by the senator's detail?'

'We're not saying that the senator blew the guy's doors off?'

'No. We're not.'

Packett shrugged. 'What are we saying?'

'He was subdued.'

'Subdued? No kidding. The senator here subdued the living shit out of him.'

'That's not going to be in any agency's record.'

'Says who?'

'National interest. A seven zero nine form. We'll have Justice send you the paperwork. That covers you and your department.'

'Ah. The old Night and Fog stunt? I must be in Georgetown.'

'You are. So are we. Make it happen and we'll owe you.'

'A lot of Feds owe the Washington PD.'

'I didn't say the Feds. I said we'd owe you.'

'You two?'

'Yeah. Us two.'

'This personal?'

'Yes,' said Rickett. 'It's personal.'

Packett looked at their hard faces for a time.

'Okay. I can get next to that. Personal I understand.'

Maria Christina Falls

Lanao del Norte Power Authority
Maria Christina Falls Generating Station
Tuesday, August 19, 3:00 p.m. local time

Even inside his soundproofed office the booming thunder of the falls rocketing down the inlet courses and the iron-throated bellowing of the six huge turbines was a deep bass-tone vibration that thrummed through his limbs and seemed to liquefy his brain. When the phone on his desk rang, the tinny buzzing arced through his mind like a thin blue spark. He looked up at the glass wall that showed him the turbine floor. Three of his engineers were huddled around the brass and steel crown of the Number Five turbine; it had been spiking and the rpm's were a bit wobbly. They were standing around the hub spindle and staring down at it as if that alone could do something to change it. Maranao, he thought, as he reached for the handset, were like children playing with spinning tops. They were untrainable fools.

'Generation.'

'We have a problem at the inlet manifold.'

The earthquake rumble of the turbine floor seemed to recede into the distance. Mr Gabriel. Mr Gabriel was calling. Gideon stared at the cluttered surface of his desk for a moment with his own heartbeat sounding in his ears.

He pulled in a breath and answered in as steady a voice as he could manage.

'Fine. Yes. Okay. Which manifold?'

'Number Six.'

'Number Six. Fine. Good. I'll come down to look at it.'

'I'll be waiting.'

He put the receiver down, leaned back in the chair and rubbed his eyes. When he pulled his hands away they felt oily and damp. He wiped his face with his sleeve and pushed himself away from the desk. Taking a deep and shaky breath, he got up and walked out of the office into the aural wall of roaring turbines. He turned to his right, crossing the huge turbine floor, the deep rhythmic vibration in the concrete floor humming up through his bones. A glass wall fifty feet wide and twelve feet tall showed him the hurtling whitewater cataract of the falls, the slick granite rocks of the spillway cut. A shaft of sunlight spearing through the spray and the silvery mist that floated in the gorge glittered in blue and red and violet.

He reached the heavy steel door that led to the staircase, pulled it open, and went down three flights, his heavy boots making the steel risers ring like iron bells. At Level Three Gideon used his security card to open a door marked ENGINEERING / NO ADMITTANCE and pushed his way through it into a tiny concrete-walled cubicle packed with pressure monitors and fuse panels. There was a padlocked steel box resting on a wooden shelf at the rear of the cubicle, painted red, with the words MANUALS stenciled in white on the shiny surface. The key for the padlock was on a chain around his neck. He fished it out with hands that shook very little considering the adrenaline that was pumping through him. Under a sheaf of papers and spec sheets he had hidden a dedicated single-line Nokia cell phone. He picked it up, turned it on, and pressed SEND six times, then hit the OFF button and held it as he watched the minute hand on his Timex Indiglo sweep around the face. Precisely six minutes later the phone rang.

'Hello. Gideon here.'

'Kemp. Jordan Kemp.'

The voice on the other end of the line was heavily accented. It was difficult to understand his English.

'Please say again.'

'Kemp. K-E-M-P. The first name Jordan. I'll give you the passport number now. G-H-9-1-8-9-5-3-3-F-R. You have it?'

'I do.'

'Repeat it, Gideon.'

He repeated the information slowly.

'Good. Canadian. A white man. A journalist. With a newspaper in Toronto called the *Morning Star*. Thirty-one years old. Born in Hull, Quebec, on July seventh, nineteen seventy-two. He is staying at the Milan. Room five eleven. He is six feet tall, with long brown hair. Gray eyes. He looks very strong, hard, something like a soldier. He has a silver ring through the lobe of his right ear. You might see him at the Ang Kusina. Or the Blue Bird. How long will you need?'

'Canadian?'

'Yes.'

'It is night in Canada now. Maybe several hours.'

'No. That's too late. Get us this one now. Get it quickly. You must have it before eight o'clock tonight. You will be in your apartment by eight tonight. You will be at home. You understand?'

'Okay. I will –'

The phone was dead. Gideon looked at his watch, thinking about the job. It was a quarter after two in the afternoon. Thirteen hours of time difference. Almost four in the morning – yesterday morning, since North America was east of the international date line – in eastern Canada. He put the phone away, locked the box and set it back on the shelf. All the way up the stairwell, as the roar of the turbines grew stronger, he worked to calm himself.

By the time he reached the turbine floor and crossed it to his office he was feeling much better and the sharp pain in his chest had diminished slightly. He would code and transmit the request from his office and then perhaps this evening he would go to the Milan and then to the Ang Kusina. If this Kemp was not there he would be at one of the other clubs, the Arc en Ciel or Annie's Bar and Grill, or maybe the Blue Bird. He would be looking for girls. The Westerners were always looking for little girls when they came to Mindanao. They were dung pigs, not even fit for slaughter. When he got back to his apartment he would have the answer to Mr Gabriel's question.

He could do this. He had done it before. A single beer he would have with dinner, or maybe some wine, but only to help him think. No more than that. He would be back in his flat by eight. Or soon after. He was capable of this thing. It was very important work and he was an important part of that work and he felt he could do it properly if he was slow and careful and he did not make any mistakes.

The Blue Bird

Cole could feel the music coming out of the Blue Bird from a block away. At fifty feet west of the doors it sounded like a runaway bulldozer taking out a Crate and Barrel. He snaked his way through the crowds of tourists and soldiers milling around the entrance and pulled the big bamboo doors open. At the back of the huge smoke-filled club a quintet of young Filipinos in Goth gear were using vintage Fender Stratocasters and an amp the size of a minivan to pummel the living daylights out of a Bruce Springsteen song that might have been 'Thunder Road.' The crowd was talking so loud over the music that the general effect was a wall of noise like a force-field you had to break through to get into the place.

The Blue Bird was a huge low-topped dive with a big arched roof shaped like a corrugated-iron Quonset hut. The interior smelled of spilled beer, cigarette smoke, sweat, and – from somewhere in the rear behind the house band – the pungent stench of a totally maxed-out latrine. The walls were lined with bamboo stalks and the ceiling was covered with fake palm fronds and hung with a thousand paper lanterns that glimmered in the smoky haze like red and blue fireflies. There was a huge

74

U-shaped bar in the middle of the large wooden-planked floor; the bar seemed to be constructed entirely of dented ammunition cases stenciled in white letters: 5.56 MILITARY BALL.

The bar-top was made of huge slabs of battered rough-cut mahogany almost six inches thick, and it was surrounded by a milling riot of ferociously party-minded people – young Filipino males with trick hair; beefy German and French troopers in flowered shirts over their salt-stained fatigue pants; here and there the odd group of older white men who were eyeing the Filipina bar girls with the avid look of predatory dentists hell-bent on a life-affirming debauch. Their pockets bulging with Euros, they were being cuddled and conned by a professional-looking platoon of grinning gap-toothed bar girls who were hanging onto them like spider-women from Venus.

Cole spotted some of the tourists he'd seen on the Superferry that day – also being expertly fleeced by the bar girls – next to a small knot of skeptical-looking legionnaire officers who were holding out on a corner next to a rack of beer taps with their backs to the bar, keeping a wary eye on the crowd. Behind the chest-high bulwark of ammo crates at the bar eight young Filipinas were slinging tankards of Tsing Tao and Bull's-Eye down the line with the dogged efficiency of *maquiladoras* in a Tijuana sweatshop. As he came up to the service line, a trio of young Filipinas about the size of ten-year-old boys aimed their pointy little breasts at him and closed in with the wide white smiles of cruising sharks. They had to shout to be heard over the din. Their voices were high and cut through the noise like razor wire.

'Hello, *honeyko! Kumasta ka na!*'

They all said this in unison and came in much too close,

pressing themselves against him. The effect was a little like being gang-groped by the Lullaby League in Munchkin Land.

'You buy us ladies drinks, *malaki boboy?*' This from the head lollipop, who looked like she could fillet a carp with her canines. 'Malaki boboy' was Tagalog for 'big fat pig.' She had little matte-gray eyes like a fer-de-lance and when she talked she rocked her head from side to side on her short muscular little neck. 'Ladies drinks' would likely be soda water passed off as champagne and cost him twenty US bucks a pop. The price of an evening with these little flowers could settle the French war debt. One of the girls was sliding her bony little claw down the front of his jeans. This appealed to him about as much as having a tarantula stuffed into his pants. The fer-de-lance gave him a gravedigger's leer.

'Come on, *boboy*. You bar-fine us? We cherry girls!'

Cherry? The last day this gargoyle was cherry there were saber-tooth tigers in the Catskills. He pulled the groper's mitt out of his pants and backed them off with what he hoped was a winning smile.

'No thanks. *Buntis ho ako*, kids.'

They all laughed in the same high tinkling falsetto. He'd just told them he was pregnant. As he pushed through the trio he kept his left hand on his wallet and his right hand over his crotch.

'*Bahala na*, ass-wipe,' said Fer-de-lance as they faded into the crowd. He thought 'ass-wipe' was a bit harsh. He was still saying 'Bahala na ass-wipe?' to himself when he reached the bar, perhaps a bit too loud. A wiry Filipino teenager with a shock of black hair hanging over his blood-shot eyes stiffened in his path, said something deeply manly, and shoved him very hard in the middle of the chest, the net effect of which was to force the kid to back-pedal about a yard. The boy looked shocked, then shamed. He reddened and reached into his pants for something to help him retrieve the situation when a tanned and tattooed arm snaked out of the crowd, jerked the kid's arm around and levered it up his back all the way to the base of his neck. Cole looked past the kid, who was now bent over double and squealing with real conviction, and saw Ramiro Vasquez smiling at him over the boy's back.

He hadn't seen Vasquez since he'd visited him in Walter Reed Hospital after his disastrous mission in Waziristan. He'd been clean-shaven then, desperately thin, sunken eyes, his bony skull shining under a Marine Corps crew cut, and in Cole's unspoken opinion, tormented by untreatable and corrosive grief. The man in front of him now was a different Ramiro Vasquez entirely; his gleaming black hair was draped around his shoulders like a cape, he was tanned almost black, and he was sporting a razor-edged goatee under a handlebar mustachio with sweeping curls that ended in needlelike points. He was still holding the kid in an arm-bar and grinning at Cole through the smoke; caught in the downlight from a paper lantern overhead, he looked like a seventeenth-century Spanish duelist.

The Filipino kid started to buck. Vasquez twisted a fine-looking switchblade with an antique carved bone handle out of the kid's right hand and shoved him so hard into the crowd that he sprawled face-first on the dance floor. Vasquez snapped the blade shut and offered it to Cole with a low bow, keeping one eye on the kid, who was now being dragged to his feet and forcibly restrained by a German noncom with a shaved head and the squared-off build of an APC.

Cole was aware of him too. He recognized the grizzled old German tanker vet by the big ugly burn scar that covered the right side of his face. It was the same man he'd seen in the bar at the Milan earlier that day, watching the greenhorns chugging their Dark Horse from across the lobby. Cole turned back to Vasquez and accepted the switchblade with a smile. Vasquez offered a hand, and when he spoke it was with a reasonably convincing Spanish accent considering that Vasquez had been born and raised on Long Island. Cole slipped the switchblade into his pocket.

'You should keep that, sir, as a gift from that *cabrón,* since it was his intention that you should receive at least a part of it.'

'Thanks. I appreciate it. I'm Jordan Kemp.'

'Kemp, was it?'

'Yes. Jordan Kemp.'

'I'm Ramón Goliad. Can I buy you a drink?'

'No. But you can let me buy you one.'

'Wonderful. I have a booth at the back here.'

Cole followed Vasquez through the crowd until they reached a row of large, curtained booths lined up along the western wall. Vasquez pushed his way through a curtain made of plastic palm fronds and sat down at a round wooden table lit by a hanging lamp with a pressed tin shade. A Filipino man was sitting at the table with his chair tilted back against the bamboo wall, his eyes closed, roasting a spliff the size of a rainbow trout. He opened his eyes and blinked at them both as Cole pulled a chair out and sat down with his back to the hanging curtain. Cole hated sitting with his back to an open room, but it seemed rude to insist on the man's chair. Vasquez introduced Cole to Jesus Rizal, a compact man in his mid-forties, with a hard little frame and round, pock-marked cheeks.

His features were classic Filipino, a cross between South American Indian and Japanese. When they shook hands his palm was wet and his fingers cold. His skin was liverish and sallow, but his flat black eyes were clear and bright. He was wearing a starched guayabera shirt over black silk trousers, and from the way he was holding himself Cole figured he had a large and uncomfortable pistol shoved into the belt at the small of his back.

'We can talk here?' asked Cole, looking around the booth. The bar band had successfully reduced the Springsteen set to an unrecognizable pulp, and they were now busy lowering their zippers behind an unsuspecting medley of Sinatra classics.

Rizal held his hand up, soft pink palm out, and then touched a finger to his upper lip. They waited in silence until the waitress, a Bukidnon girl with a face full of tribal tattoos, took their drink orders and left, again, returning in seconds with a cork tray full of dewy Bohemias. As she left, a chubby man in a hula shirt and baggy linen slacks stumbled through the curtain and skidded to a stop, looking confused and embarrassed. He nodded briefly to Rizal – whose face had hardened up into a stony mask – excused himself in a flustered rush of Filipino-accented English, ran a soft, brown, long-fingered hand through his shiny blue hair, flickered his kohl-tinged eyes at Ramiro Vasquez, sent him a lingering smile, then backed out of the room leaving a sandalwood scent lingering in the air.

'Who the hell was that?' asked Cole, directing the question to Jesus Rizal. Rizal, resenting the tone, bristled up.

'Gideon Sabang. He is a friend of my cousin Diego. He

79

is harmless. What we call a *cotquean*. He merely wanted to look at Mr Goliad.'

Cole glanced at Vasquez and then favored him with an obscene smile. Vasquez, smiling as obscenely, gave him back the finger. Rizal grinned and drew heavily on his spliff while he blinked at Cole some more, his rough skin pebbled by the downlight and two yellowish sparks glinting in his eyes, his face shadowed by the overhead lamp.

'We are safe here. The Blue Bird is always good for us. This place is owned by my cousin Diego D'Aquino. Everyone does business here.'

'This Diego knows why we're here?'

Rizal looked offended. The way he did this looked practiced and theatrical. Cole was trying hard to approve of the man, but Rizal wasn't making it easy.

'No. I have told him you and Mr Goliad are business friends of mine. I am showing Mr Goliad the sights of Iligan City. Are we not to be joined by the others of your party?'

This got a blank look from both men.

'Others?' said Cole. 'What others?'

Rizal looked a little uneasy and recovered badly.

'I am sorry. Of course there are no others.'

Vasquez was watching this exchange with thinly disguised impatience. The little room was filling up with marijuana smoke from Rizal's spliff, and Cole's sense of clarity was suffering a gradual decline.

'You understand what's involved?'

Another slow blink.

'We are to go up to Lake Lanao and meet with my associate in the village of Cobraville. He is a most reliable man, a Christian missionary. With the help of his contacts you wish to obtain some useful intelligence about the Abu Sayaf people who infest the jungles around Cobraville. You are not in any way to be . . .'

'Visible,' said Vasquez, helpfully.

'Yes. You are not to be visible. I will admit that we do not understand why you cannot simply allow us to gather this information for you. You are unfortunately highly visible. The presence of two – or perhaps more? – Western men in a tribal area, this will be hard to keep secret. But I ask no questions. I will help you to be invisible.'

'This Christian missionary. What's his name?'

'Father Desaix. Constantin Desaix.'

'Does he know the country around Lake Lanao?'

'He taught an interfaith course at Marawi University. In the year before the war started. Now Marawi is closed off to all infidels. No one can reach it. Even the Germans and the French only go there in helicopters or in armored columns. The Moro and the Bukidno keep watch. People do not try to go into Marawi anymore.'

'How can a Catholic priest work in an Islamic region?'

His face became hard, almost brutal.

'These Abu Sayaf terrorists, and the Moro Liberation Front, they are killing more of our people than they are of yours. Father Desaix runs a small medical clinic in Cobraville. The villagers of Cobraville are not Moro or Maranao people. They are Samal, a tribe far older than those Maranao newcomers. They are persecuted by the Moro and hate them. Father Desaix has made a mission among them. He has been in Mindanao for over fifteen years and in Cobraville for almost eight. Every day he treats Samal and Manobo people who have suffered at the hands of the MLF or the Abu Sayaf. Like me, he does not preach his faith. But the manner in which he lives it is a credit to his order. He is much loved by the Samal of Cobraville.'

Cole felt a wave of fatigue roll over him. He had inhaled so much of Rizal's spliff smoke that the bar band was beginning to sound good to him. It was time to get out of here.

'It's a long haul up-country, Mr Rizal,' said Cole. 'We leave early in the morning. You may want to back off on the weed.'

Rizal looked at the stubby roach in his left hand as if it had just materialized there. He lifted the roach and sucked the last of it to death, the tiny red spark flaring in the shadowy light. Bits of red ash floated to the tabletop as he blew the smoke out across the table again. Most of it reached Cole's face, as it was intended to. Cole smiled thinly through the haze, nodded once.

'I'll say goodnight then, Ramón. We have a jeepney cached at the end of the Agus River Road. If you're coming, Mr Rizal, be there at dawn.'

He got to his feet and Vasquez rose with him. Rizal stood up and extended a hand.

'You should stay for a last drink. Please?'

'Maybe,' said Cole, lying through a cardboard smile.

'Wonderful! Now, if you will both excuse me for a moment, I am going to go to the latrine and have myself a most necessary piss.'

Rizal bowed and walked out through the palm-frond curtain, almost knocking over the plump Filipino male in the hula shirt and baggy linen slacks, who was fondling a young waiter and whispering something into the boy's ear that was making the boy smile like a piranha. The little man blushed as Rizal shoved past him far too roughly and disappeared into the crowd, heading for the latrines at a jog trot, holding himself like a man with a bladder that had too often been a disappointment to him.

The perfumed man bowed and gave Rizal's back a flowery apology. Cole stepped out of the booth and looked hard at the man long enough for the man to stop babbling, let go of the boy, and fall into a strained and wary silence.

'You looking for someone, sir?' asked Cole.

'I, sir? No . . . I apologize . . .'

He and the waiter both looked so completely terrified that Cole felt ashamed for locking onto them. If he had a problem with Jesus Rizal, picking on a pudgy little lounge lizard wasn't the right way to handle it. Cole stepped around him and pushed his way across the crowded dance floor. Vasquez caught up with him by the bar.

'Not impressed?'

Cole looked around him and came back to Vasquez.

'No. I'm not.'

Vasquez nodded, looked around him, checked his watch.

'How about we have a talk outside.'

They pushed their way through the crowd and out into the busy street. The twilight block party was in full tilt down here on Aguinaldo, with wandering couples and packs of drunken teens and far too many tourists jostling for sidewalk space. A trio of French legionnaires in their summer whites was sitting around an outside bar table next to the Blue Bird talking to a small crowd of young Filipinas. The rumble of trucks and the music from the Blue Bird and the buzz of the passing jeepneys and scooters made it hard to think, let alone talk. Cole walked Vasquez across the street and into a doorway that provided some cover from the noise. He leaned in close and spoke in a harsh whisper.

'That mutt's a flake, Ramiro.'

'Sloane thinks we need him.'

'We'll have to take him as far as Casey. I don't want him wandering around the market square in downtown Iligan bragging about his exciting life as a covert agent. But as soon as we get to the weapons I'm going to keep him cooped up somewhere safe until we wrap this mission up and get out of here. And he'll be coming out with us. I'm not leaving him in Mindanao to shoot his mouth off.'

Across the street, the bamboo doors opened up and the sandalwood-scented lounge lizard in the hula shirt came out of the club with his left arm draped around the shoulder of the young Filipino waiter. He had his lips very close to the boy's neck. They turned to the right and began to walk eastward along Aguinaldo, and then they flattened against the wall as a Vespa scooter swerved out of the traffic and began to snake a drunken path down the sidewalk, scattering the walkers. A kid who looked sixteen was steering it one-handed and holding a bottle of Tsing Tao in the other. He had what looked like his whole family on the scooter, a Filipina girl and two young children. The children were laughing brightly as the driver forced the machine through the crush. Vasquez turned to follow Cole's look, then came back to Cole, his face hardening up.

'You see this guy as a security issue, that's fine with me. Some terminal shit could happen to Jesus Rizal tonight.'

Cole gave that some thought, watching the Filipino kid playing sidewalk cowboy with his Vespa. The driver was grinning so widely his teeth were visible from ear to ear. His eyes were glazed and drunken and his skin was slick with running sweat. He had a huge crate of Tsing Tao beer lashed to a wire basket on the back of the scooter. His pretty young wife had her head down and she was holding her two kids in tight to her belly as she rode sidesaddle behind the driver. After a moment of thought, Cole shook his head.

'No. Won't work. They still have cops here. And he's a big man on the local campus. We need his help getting through the peacekeepers. He knows the terrain better than anyone else we could get. Whatever we do to restrain him, we'll have to leave him with enough face to keep his honor. You really going to go on a crawl with him? He's a train wreck. You'd be better to slip him a mickey and drag him back to the Jiddy Lodge by his heels.'

'You got this very convenient mickey on you?'

'What? Like a Rufinal? No.'

'Then you can relax. I do.'

Vasquez held out his hand. He had eight small red caplets in his palm. Across Aguinaldo Street the man on the Vespa had reached the sidewalk area outside the Blue Bird. One of his children – the little boy – hopped off and ran through the crowd toward the big bamboo doors. A legionnaire smacked him on his butt as he ran past and said something to his friends. They opened their mouths and hooted. The little boy reached the bamboo doors and pulled them wide. Up the block Cole could still see the little flower-shirted guy and his date. They were moving away through the crowd at a brisk walk. As he watched them they broke into a flat-out run. He heard the Vespa snarl as the driver gunned his motor and jerked forward.

Cole stared at the kid behind the handlebars. He wasn't really a kid. He was just small. He could have been anywhere from thirty to sixty. His grin wasn't really a grin.

His eyes were black and empty. His wife had a fixed and blank look, as if she were drugged, and she was squeezing the little girl so hard now that her knuckles were white against the coffee-cream tan of her skin and the little girl was starting to cry. The little crying girl had on a pure white cotton dress and was holding a fresh bouquet in her lap. She looked like a child going to her First Communion. There was something . . .

Cole started to push past Vasquez. The scooter popped and buzzed and then roared in through the open doors in a cloud of blue smoke. Cole was halfway across the street. The Vespa had gone deep inside the Blue Bird and the little boy was letting the bamboo doors swing shut. He looked right at Cole and beamed at him like a little brown-skinned angel, a big sunny smile full of innocent joy. Cole heard heavy footsteps behind him, and then Ramiro Vasquez slammed into Cole at a dead run and drove them both down into the gutter and inside the silence that followed the corrugated skin of the Blue Bird rippled – seemed to billow outward – rose up into the night sky – blossomed into a bright blue flower with a burning bloodred center.

Berlin

With a grin so strained and false that it felt as if it had
been stapled into his cheeks, Gerhardt Eisenstadt considered the sallow-skinned little man at the far end of
his dining room table and devoutly wished him gone. He
stole a covert glance out across the city and sighed. A soft
light was streaming across the tops of the linden trees
in the Tiergarten and pouring in through the glass doors
of Eisenstadt's wood-paneled dining room; a honeyed
seventeenth-century light, pale saffron and rich amber and
the particular tawny gold that you only saw in these rare
high summer afternoons in Berlin. The boom and roar of
the traffic on the Kaiserdamm floated over the parkland,
muted by the swaying trees to a distant murmur that
reminded Eisenstadt of the North Sea sweeping over the
Frisian shoals when he was a boy. Beyond the delicate
green of the linden forest the broad surface of the Spree
glimmered in the sunlight, bending its ancient way
through the spires and slate-roofed peaks of Moabit and
Charlottenburg. Hildi's balcony plantings had bloomed
in their Carrara marble vases and their blended scent lay
heavily in the long, dimly lit room, the smoke-filled air

87

stirred by a warm damp breeze off the river. Eisenstadt watched his guest toying with his coffee and covered a strained yawn born of petulant resentment with the back of his soft pink hand.

'May I offer you some more of this Sacher torte? Hildi buys it fresh each day. Such a delight. Or must you go so soon?'

His guest, a Mr Gabriel, a narrow-shouldered, yellow-skinned angular man with a sickly complexion and a receding jaw badly disguised by a threadbare goatee, his fleshy lips shiny with grease from the osso bucco, a sharp protruding beak of a nose, pushed his coffee away and bared his unnerving brown teeth at Eisenstadt, the yellow light of the sun reflected as two points of pale fire in his small, close-set, obsidian eyes. He moved inside his wrinkled sky-blue suit like a man in need of a bath and shook his head slowly. The stillness with which he regarded Eisenstadt over the clutter of their as-yet-unremoved plates and glasses – where was Hildi? – and the scattered silverware that lay among the debris – the reptilian stillness – sent a small tremor of unease rippling through his pillow-shaped body.

'You understand what commitment is involved?'

'Yes. Of course. There will be no difficulties on my end, I can assure you. We have the resources in place already, already up and running. The infrastructure, as the Yanks put it. As you are aware –'

'I wish you to consider the importance of your commitment.'

'If you mean the purely business aspect . . . ?'

The double doors of the dining room were suddenly thrown open and Hildi bustled into the room, a slender young woman – far too young for Eisenstadt – quite stunningly lovely – with large, cornflower blue eyes and a lush red mouth, her blond hair shining in the mellow light and her rich green silk dress slightly dusted with pastry flour. She covered her obvious nerves with a stream of rather brittle chatter as she bustled about the room, her pale white hands fluttering like a pair of agitated doves over the table, gathering up plates and glasses, talking in a rush of high German.

'Forgive me, Gerhardt, Mr Gabriel – it's Rudi, Gerhardt – he simply will not go for his nap –'

'Can't you see we are in the middle of a business meeting?'

Hildi sent him a hot glare, her face flushing.

'He claims it's his asthma again. Says he cannot breathe –'

Mr Gabriel sat up and stared at Hildi with the look of a predatory bird.

'Where is his puffer?' Eisenstadt asked.

'I have given him his puffer – it is always the same. You undermine me, Gerhardt, you do not mean to but you do – excuse us, Mr Gabriel, such sorry little domestics we are. A sad bore –'

Mr Gabriel's close attention became obvious to her.

'He has asthma?'

Hildi frowned at Eisenstadt and turned to Mr Gabriel.

'He *says* he has asthma – but it seems to be a convenient sort of asthma – yes it is, Gerhardt – the doctor has told you as much – you have allowed him to be a spoiled baby.'

'How old is the boy?' asked Mr Gabriel.

'Eight years this September,' said Eisenstadt, with a rush of pride. The *fact* of the boy's existence – the irrefutable proof of his own potency at the advanced age of sixty-four – had contributed greatly to his reputation among the policy men and bureaucrats who moved in his circle of government. Little Rudi, begotten with some difficulty with his third wife, Hannah – the grueling delivery had sent her into menopause, and Eisenstadt had tired of her soon after – a sickly boy and something of a whiner, was still triumphantly his, and he glowed at the top of his long golden table with paternal pride. Mr Gabriel considered his fat beaming face for a time and then turned to Hildi with a look devoid of anything but clinical interest.

'Bring him in, then,' said Mr Gabriel, in a hard flat voice that sliced across her tidying bustle and stopped it dead. Hildi straightened and stared at him, her eyes widening. Eisenstadt stiffened in his chair and began to look a little overinflated.

'I beg your pardon?'

'I'd like to meet your son,' said Mr Gabriel, his tone even, his Middle Eastern accent thickening his rudimentary German, making his speech nearly unintelligible. He reached into his coat pocket and pulled out a small blue plastic ventilator.

'I have the asthma myself,' he said, holding the little device up into a slanting shaft of fading yellow light streaming in through the windows. Hildi began to flutter again.

'He's already in his pajamas, Mr Gabriel.'

'Please. I would like to meet him. I may be able to help.'

He stared up at her from his place at the end of the low gilt table, his hooded eyes blank, a thin smile playing on his wet lips. Hildi sent Eisenstadt a beseeching look, unwilling to insult one of her husband's clients and even more unwilling to allow Gerhardt's snotty little bastard of a child to ruin what had been – up until now –

a moderately successful business dinner, an accomplishment upon which, as the former star waitress at Savigny-Platz, she prided herself greatly. Eisenstadt saw her look and appealed to an unfounded assumption of Mr Gabriel's purely theoretical fatherly instincts.

'That is very good of you, sir. Very fine. But . . .'

His voice trailed off as he watched Mr Gabriel reach into his belt and pull out a large black semi-automatic pistol with ivory grips. Mr Gabriel laid it gently on the tabletop and sat back into his chair. His lips spread and his brown teeth shone wetly. A great silence flowed into the room. Hildi found her voice – at least that part of it which lived in the higher registers.

'I won't have guns –'

'Tell the whore to bring in the child.'

Eisenstadt attempted a reproach that died somewhere between his throat and his lips. Hildi stared at Mr Gabriel's dead eyes. She nodded once and started for the open door.

'No phone calls,' he said to her slender back, which stiffened as if struck. Hildi left the room and they sat together in the forced companionship of the extraordinary, the singular. Eisenstadt became aware of his metronomic blinking and willed himself to stop.

'Why are you doing this?'

Mr Gabriel closed his eyes slowly and opened them again. Eisenstadt thought of a gimlet-eyed toad squatting in a marsh.

'I will not harm the boy. I wish merely to make a point.'

'What about Hildi?'

'The whore is safe from me.'

'Then what do you –'

A noise in the outer hall as the old boards creaked and

then a pale young child with a spiky corona of stiff yellow hair and the soft wet brown eyes of a lemur padded into the room in a set of blue pajamas covered with brown snakes and colorful ladders. He moved toward his father but kept his watchful eyes on the stranger in the chair at the far end of the long table. Hildi stood in the open door, her hands clenched across her belly and her neck muscles visible.

'Poppy,' said the boy, in a nasal whine, 'she won't let me have my puffer. I hate her!'

Eisenstadt gathered the damp warm body into his lap and stroked the boy's head. The boy squirmed under his hand and stuck a fist into the Sacher torte. Eisenstadt wrapped the child's clotted fingers in a pink linen napkin, clucking at him. Mr Gabriel rapped the table sharply with his knuckles and they all looked at him.

'You have the asthma, boy?' asked Mr Gabriel.

A moment while the boy looked up at his father, who nodded.

'Yes,' he said, finally, his willingness to moan and grizzle very close to the surface – Hildi suppressed a shiver of dislike as she watched the little brute try to assess the best way to manipulate this birdlike stranger. 'I have a puffer.'

'So do I,' said Mr Gabriel, holding it up.

'Give me,' said the boy, holding out a splay-fingered sticky hand, jutting his lower lip. Mr Gabriel smiled at the boy but kept his own puffer by his hand. When he spoke it was to Eisenstadt alone.

'Does he really have asthma?' he asked.

Eisenstadt nodded stiffly. 'Of course. It is confirmed –'

'It is not confirmed,' put in Hildi, angry with her husband for failing to protect her from whatever Mr Gabriel really was – angry with the frequently squalid nature of his business transactions – although she had found that no lasting taint attached itself to the money, a wondrous truth – and angry with his nasty spoiled brat of a child for precipitating this whole unhappy confrontation. Eisenstadt's own anger found a safer outlet in his fourth wife.

'It is *confirmed*,' he bellowed at her, the sound of his harsh voice resounding from the wooden walls. Mr Gabriel nodded slowly, still staring at the boy.

'I have lived with the asthma all my life. A life of slow asphyxiation. A very cruel affliction.'

Eisenstadt nodded in agreement, held the squirming child and spooned some Sacher torte into its mouth, wiping the cream off its cheek. The child chewed noisily and reached out for some more, opening its food-filled mouth like a baby gannet in a nest.

'Strangle him,' said Mr Gabriel, mildly, his voice carrying.

Eisenstadt tilted his head to the left.

'What?'

'Strangle the boy,' he repeated.

While Eisenstadt processed the order, Mr Gabriel raised the pistol and pointed it at Hildi's temple. The boy, entranced by the pistol and delighted by Hildi's obvious fear, began to giggle. Hildi's eyes alone moved, burning at him. Eisenstadt stared at Mr Gabriel for a long beating moment, seeing the intent in the man's bleak face. Two white circular spots had appeared on Mr Gabriel's sallow cheeks and his breathing was coming in short sharp gasps, his black eyes now shining and moist.

'But why?'

'The child's life is of no value to him. Strangle him.'

Eisenstadt stared at the man, unbelieving, his mouth slack.

'If you need stiffening,' said Mr Gabriel, 'then I'll help you. Strangle the boy or I'll shoot the whore. I may then find it necessary to shoot you as well. One does not know.'

Eisenstadt opened his mouth to speak and then snapped it shut. Hildi's look was pleading and desperate, but it wasn't clear for whom she was silently pleading. Eisenstadt stared back at Mr Gabriel while the child fussed in his lap, struggling against his grip, the familiar moaning whine beginning to build in the child's throat. Eisenstadt felt his anger beginning to rise. The boy lurched forward and plunged his hand into the Sacher torte again. Eisenstadt jerked him backward and found himself holding the boy by the neck. Under his plump fingers he could feel the child's carotid pulsing weakly, and the swelling of the boy's throat as he breathed.

Mr Gabriel watched Eisenstadt, the muzzle of the pistol centered on Hildi's temple. An oblong of reflected amber light crawled over the far wall, and Eisenstadt noted – in some chamber of his mind – that the sound of the traffic on the Kaiserdamm had softened to a whisper. The low moaning note of a river barge's horn carried through the stillness, like a lost calf bawling for home.

Eisenstadt searched himself for fury, for resolute action, for the will to fight and die in defense of his honor – his son – his wife – and found only the mild indignation of a privileged man unfairly put upon. The idea of his own extinction was unthinkable. And the money was so critical. He was badly overextended. He had drained the accounts of several clients, some of whom were now asking for their money. This arrangement with Mr Gabriel's people would save him from financial ruin, possibly from prison. It would also make him extremely rich, the kind of wealth that could not be exhausted. The idea of a test came into his harried mind. Arabs did not value life the way men of the civilized world did, but they valued strength of purpose. The man wanted to see what Eisenstadt was made of. Well, he would show him. He would only hurt the boy a little, just to show the man that Gerhardt Eisenstadt was equal to anything.

He gathered the boy into himself, stared defiantly at the grim face across the table, and slowly began to squeeze. Unused muscles in his forearms tensed and bowed. Strength flowed into his fingers and the tips began to dig into the boy's throat. Under his palms the carotid arteries beat faster and faster. The boy began to struggle, the familiar whine dying in his closing throat. Hildi's eyes burned at him with gratitude and relief. He focused on her look and drew strength from it. Strength was required. The child, sensing that this was no longer play, began to struggle; his struggle intensified, became frantic. His face reddened and he began to pluck at his father's fingers, his little nails drawing blood from the soft skin on the back of Eisenstadt's right hand. A minute passed in this silence, the only sound the child's knee thumping against the underside of the table. The whites of his eyes began to show. Mr Gabriel watched the boy struggling for his life with a calm clinical interest.

'That will do,' he said, finally.

'What?' said Eisenstadt stupidly, like a man coming out of a trance. After a hesitation, he released the boy, who slipped off his lap and onto the floor, gasping. Mr Gabriel came around to the head of the table and pulled the child to his feet. The boy began to weep. Mr Gabriel stroked his head gently, soothingly.

'Pack some of his clothes,' he said to Hildi. 'When our business is complete, I will return him.'

Eisenstadt stared at the man, who returned the look without a trace of emotion other than cold contempt.

'I will not –'

'You would have killed him. You have nothing to say.'

Georgetown

Drew Langan woke up from a punishing nightmare, and the events of the night came flooding back in an overwhelming rush, the small black-clad figure caught in the muzzle flash, his pale blue eyes widening. The smell of the gunpowder floating in the hallway. Since the house was still filled with cops and coroners and looked like it was going to stay that way for a while, Buriss and Rickett had taken Drew to the Georgetown Suites. He had gotten to sleep around dawn and, thanks to three Valium he had found in one of Diana's purses, he had slept like a dead man. He sat up in the hotel-room bed with a tightness in his neck muscles that he at first thought might be the forerunner of the fatal heart attack he was grimly certain he was about to have any day now. As he swung his legs to the side of the bed, Krugman's message came back into his consciousness. Was this connected? Was it really just a break-in? He was standing by the bed and considering the question when the night-table phone rang.

'Langan here.'

'Drew, this is Diana.'

Jesus. Not now.

'Diana. Where are you?'

97

'What time is it there?'

Her voice sounded hoarse and hurried. There was palpable tension there under the silky Back Bay lilt. Drew looked at the clock and realized with a jolt that he was still booked on a one o'clock flight to Harrisburg and his Secret Service escort was due to pick him up in less than a half-hour. He tried to sound alert and failed.

'Time? Diana, it's ten-thirty in the morning. Where are you?'

'I'm in Paris. Were you still asleep?'

'Yeah. Hold on a second. I need a coffee.'

Drew stood up and carried the cordless across to the bathroom, where he triggered the coffeemaker. Through the hotel window he could see the bright light of midmorning. The rain seemed to have stopped. He ran a hand over his face, feeling the stubble. He had a terrible headache, and Diana's voice on the other end of the line had brought back a rush of the same sense of loss he had felt last night.

'Drew, are you still there?'

'I'm here. Is everything okay? Are you all right?'

'What are you doing in a hotel?'

'How did you find me?'

'I called the house. Some guy answered and he told me where you were. Who's at the house?'

'What can I do for you, Diana?'

'It's the recess, isn't it? Why are you still in George-town? I called you in Harrisburg and got rerouted. Why are you still there?'

'I have a flight this afternoon. I had to stay to get some furniture delivered. I'm still trying to make this place work.'

'You have money for furniture? I thought we got it all.'

'I had some hidden in my socks.'

'I knew we should have checked your socks. How are you, Drew? You sound terrible. What do you mean you slept in? Are you still drinking?'

He had no intention of telling her what had happened. He tried for the light tone Diana had once found fatally attractive.

'As much as I can. As often as I can. Are you still playing Hide the Bunny with the shoe salesman?'

'No, I'm not. As if it were any of your business. And Franco wasn't a shoe salesman. He owned the company.'

'The company sold shoes. Skanky Franky owned it. Therefore he was a shoe salesman. *"Cogito ergo sum."'*

'Let's not fight. Please? And it's "quad erat demonstrandum."'

'What are you doing in Paris?'

'I'm here with Mitzi. We're doing some galleries.'

'And how is the Lovely Undead? Still avoiding mirrors?'

'She loves you too. Are you seeing anyone?'

'Hordes. I have to beat them off with sticks. And as much as I love to hear from you without a lawyer covering my back, would it be rude of me to ask you why you're calling?'

'No. I'm sorry I woke you. It's already after four here. It's about Cole, actually. Do you know where he is right now?'

'Where he is right now? How the hell would I know? I haven't spoken to him in two years.'

'You have no idea where he is?'

'He's traveling. It's what he does. The IMF is always sending him somewhere. Meetings. Whatever. We don't talk. I'm not his favorite daddy right now. You know that.'

'This has nothing to do with him. He shouldn't be taking sides. I told him that when he was here in the spring.'

'He's a kid with very strong views on marriage.'

'Easy for him to preach, Drew; he hasn't had a steady girlfriend since he left the Army. I don't even think he dates.'

'Have you talked to him lately?'

'He called me a week ago. He was getting ready for a trip. He said he was going to Thailand. Some beach called Phuket. Have you watched the news yet?'

'No. Like I said. I just woke up. Why?'

'Turn on CNN. There's been a bombing in Mindanao. It happened less than two hours ago. A nightclub called the Blue Bird. Somebody drove a motorbike into the place and then blew himself up. He killed over a hundred people.'

The Critic Flash. Hamidullah Barrakha.

'God. Not in Iligan City?'

'Iligan City? Yes, I think it was. How did –'

'You think Cole was there? Why would you think that? You said he was in Thailand. Did you call his hotel?'

'He didn't give me the name. Anyway, I got the idea he was going to be bicycling around the countryside.'

He had actually done it. Hamidullah Barrakha had promised it, and he had delivered. In Iligan City, just the way the intercept had indicated. They picked up that intercept at Kunia hours before it happened. Why the hell hadn't they stopped him? Drew tried to concentrate on Diana's call, but his mind had split right down the middle. Why had Krugman delivered that package to him? What did the Beltsville location have to do with it? Terrible as the bombing was on its own, did his possession of that intercept damage him in any way? Was he being set up? If so, by whom? And for what purpose? And why hadn't they *done* something to stop the bombing? What the hell was the NSC *for* if it couldn't stop that kind of atrocity? Diana was still talking and he cut into her frantic flow a little sharply.

'Diana, Mindanao is a thousand miles away from Thailand. Don't go hunting grief. Cole is fine.'

'You don't know that.'

'I don't know that he isn't. Have you tried his cell phone?'

She paused then. Drew could hear music in the background, and the sound of traffic coming in from an open window. He imagined what she would be wearing and how the strange light of Paris streaming in through the open window would be lying on her cheek and in her hair. He had a strong sense of her presence in the room and could almost smell her perfume and the scent of her skin. She was an extraordinarily beautiful woman in a delicate Irish way, with skin as luminous as alabaster and a full, round, very white body. He felt her absence from his bed the way a reformed drunk misses a dry martini. There was no point thinking about her this way. Fidelity was not in her, and he wasn't modern enough to handle that, and now she was gone from his life. But she was still on the line and close to panic. He could hear it in her breathing and her tone.

'Yes,' she said, finally. 'I called his cell three times. All I'm getting is his voice mail. I've also called the IMF in New York.'

'And . . . ?'

'And they said he was in Thailand.'

'Thailand? Not Mindanao?'

'Yes.'

'Then why are you so worked up about this?'

'Drew, this bombing was so terrible. You should see the video of the place. There's a huge gutted shell of a building and the police have white sheets all over the street. They say hundreds of people were injured. There were parts of bodies everywhere . . . they showed a picture of child's doll. It was all burned away. Then I realized it wasn't a doll. The place was full of UN soldiers and tourists. They're saying it was a terrorist bombing. Some Islamic front called Abu . . . Abu something. If Cole was there . . .'

'If Cole was there – which he wasn't – you'd have heard from him by now. You know that.'

'Unless something happened to him.'

'Nothing has happened to him.'

'But you knew, didn't you? You knew it was Iligan?'

'It was a guess. I didn't know. Leave it alone.'

'Good Christ. It's one of your Goddamned spook things, isn't it? Is this something you were involved in? You owe me that much!'

'I wasn't involved in – and what the hell does *that* mean, for Christ's sake? I'm a senator, not a secret agent. We're the *last* people in D.C. to know anything. Take my word for it.'

He felt himself losing traction and made a hard left.

'Look, Diana – try to stay on point, will you? If it'll make you feel any better, I'll have my office track him down. They can find out where Cole is and I'll let you know as soon as I do. Okay?'

Everyone in his office down to the last intern was happily off home for the August recess, but he didn't mention that. He would take care of this himself. She was breathing into the phone. He caught a fleeting image – a memory – of her lips on his, the smell of fresh cut grass floating in through an open window. Narragansett, or was it Wisconsin Dells?

'Will you, Drew? Will you do that? I know this is silly. He's probably fine. But you'll do it? Please? Promise me?'

'I promise.'

'Thank you. I love you for it. You have Mitzi's number?'

'Honey, I've always had Mitzi's number.'

'Don't be flippant. You'll call me?'

'I will.'

'Bye. I love you.'

Love? He opened his mouth to answer but she was gone.

Britney

Luna Olvidado was a green-eyed, purple-haired packet of high-impact government muscle, somewhere in her mid-thirties and a perfect example of those hard-eyed harpies of law enforcement they hammer out by the hundreds down in Glynco. In spite of her rawhide exterior, she had made a number of cameo appearances in his more lurid dreams, which had caused him no end of physical discomfort. During his waking hours he had managed to keep his hands to himself. Partly because it was the right thing to do and partly because he believed she was the kind of woman who would snap his head clean off and fold it into an origami swan.

Dale Rickett had once told Drew that when Luna was only a few days out of Glynco she had been traveling north on the interstate, on her way to her first Secret Service assignment in Maryland, when she ran into a multicar pileup in a fogbound section of the highway a few miles south of the Virginia state line. A few seconds before she reached the crash area, a tractor trailer had smashed into the tail-end of a train of stopped cars, setting three of them on fire. She pulled up next to a black stretch limousine that was already ablaze. Luna had wrenched open the left passenger door, the only part of the vehicle not completely enveloped in flames, and managed to drag three of the occupants out of the car, a mother and her two children, a ten-year-old boy and a three-year-old girl. She got the unconscious girl out seconds before the limousine blew up.

The mother and the boy survived, but the little girl – badly burned – had died in Luna's arms. In saving the family, Luna had sustained severe burns on her torso and her left arm. Even after several skin-grafts, the back of her left hand and her left forearm all the way to her elbow were badly scarred, In Rickett's opinion, the event had marked her physically and spiritually, and now, although she never spoke about it, she seemed frozen in the terrible moment, in a state of emotional lockdown that kept her isolated from the rest of the unit.

She and her Secret Service partner, the one who looked like an Arapahoe banker with bad taste in bow ties, had arrived to take him out to Reagan International two hours before his flight left for Harrisburg. On the way out he auto-dialed Gunther Krugman's pager and cell-phone numbers every five minutes, and he called Cole's cell phone almost as often. So far he hadn't heard from Levi Sloane, and he wasn't going to call him until he had talked to Krugman. He could tell by the set of Luna's shoulders and the slightly tilted angle of her head as she listened to him working the cell phone that her instincts were telling her that something was very wrong with Senator Langan. For the same reason he didn't want to call the IMF in front of her. He'd call them from the airport instead.

By the time Luna had wheeled them into Departures, Drew had Cole's voice-mail greeting memorized and had heard not one beep of response from any of Krugman's contact numbers. This was not like Gunther Krugman. It had him more than a little worried. He hated being worried. He also hated that Luna knew he was worried. He knew he was going to hear about it when he saw the look on her face as she pulled open his door and stepped back to let him get out.

'May I speak, sir?'

'I'd be willing to bet on it.'

She smiled him a smile that never warmed those green eyes. A kind of unseen electrical charge was coming off her in a steady wave. She handed his gear to the Arapahoe, and he backed off a few yards. Smart man. Drew wanted to back off too.

'The whole unit wants to apologize for what happened last night. Justice has already sent the seven zero nine form over to the D.C. police chief. The press has officially been told that there was an intruder and that he was subdued by your protection unit.'

'Do you think they'll believe that?'

'They may not buy the whole story, but in the absence of any kind of corroboration from the authorities they'll have to accept it.'

'They'll talk to my neighbors.'

'Almost everyone on your street is a high-level civil servant. We've already spoken to them individually. They won't be talking to the press, Senator. May I ask you a question?'

'Certainly.'

'You know it's our job to protect you and your family. But I'd like to say that I was honored to be on your detail.'

'Thank you.'

'Having said that, Senator, is there any way in which

I can be of service to you right now? Is there anything troubling you?'

Drew noticed she wasn't saying 'we.' He worked up an expression intended to convey total innocence and perfect peace of mind that wouldn't have looked out of place on a wanted poster.

'There isn't a thing, Luna. I appreciate your concern. But I'm fine. Really. I'm fine.'

She gave him a short sharp nod and took the dismissal without further comment, but the silence that followed seemed to contain an ominous ticking sound. He had to get a little huffy with her before she'd agree to let him carry his own bag into the terminal. When they finally pulled away, the Arapahoe – Drew's private name for him was Bad Bow Ties – was staring back at him with a look of endearingly wistful concern. Luna Olvidado kept her eyes firmly fixed on the road as she drove away, but he knew she was upset.

Standing under the arch and watching them drive away in their black Crown Vic it occurred to Drew – not for the last time – that the problem with being a powerful man in the government was that you had very little personal freedom, and the freedom to move alone was the thing he most desired right now. He sighed and stood there in the sunshine for a while, looking tall and trim and near-fatally spiffy with his chiseled senatorial jawline and his steel-gray eyes and his Hermès bag hanging off him like a sidesaddle on a mule. He looked every inch the United States senator, but right now he felt like a mirage.

After a moment, he pulled himself together and went into the huge echoing terminal filled with the stamp and shuffle of a thousand ordinary Americans, many of whom who could wake up in the morning to something other than a cold sweat accompanied by chest pains. He was halfway to the start of the lineup at the check-in counter and drawing his first easy breath of the day when his cell phone rang. He knew the number being displayed, but he answered it anyway. Resistance was useless.

'Langan.'

'Senator, it's Britney Vogel.'

Thank you, Jesus. More nails, Flavius, we need more nails.

'Britney, how are you?'

'Is this a bad time? I called your office and –'

'It's closed. We're in recess, remember?'

'Yes, I know. I've just heard about the incident at your home last night. Are you all right, sir?'

'What incident, Britney?'

A hesitation. Good. She was fishing.

'Well, our police reporter said that someone tried to get into your house last night and that he was arrested by your Secret Service detail. The police confirmed that, but one of the neighbors said he heard shots being fired.'

So much for the discretion of his neighbors.

'The man was high on crack or something like that. Apparently quite strong. He resisted arrest. There was a struggle. During the struggle the man got slammed onto the hood of the Secret Service car a couple of times. That's all it could be. No shots were fired.'

'This neighbor said he saw police cars and a coroner's wagon.'

'It wasn't a coroner's van. It was an unmarked ambulance. The intruder was hurt in the struggle. And the police only arrived because my alarm system had been cut and that sends out a distress signal.'

Where did this stuff come from? Lying had never come

this easily to him until he got into politics. Now it was a core skill.

'What did the person want?'

'It was just an attempted break-in, Britney. I've got to run.'

'Can you spare just another minute? We're doing a major spread on this bombing and we were hoping for a statement.'

'What kind of statement, Britney?'

'We're looking to the Oversight Committee for reactions to this tragedy, Senator. Do you feel we are losing this war on terrorism?'

'The Oversight Committee is not sitting at this time, as you know, and any statement representing our committee would have to come from Helen Claiborne McDowell herself. I suggest you call her office in Denver and see what she has to say.'

'We have, sir, and her aides say that she's up in the Rockies on an eco-tour –'

An eco-tour? The old bat was on a hunting trip at her Valhalla-sized lodge up in the Front Range. Right about now she was waiting in a parked Winnebago with a Winchester 30-30 in her lap, hoping to blow the liver and lights out of Bambi's mother. Eco-tour my –

'– and unavailable by our deadline, so I was hoping that you might be willing –'

– to slice my own throat?

'– to give us a statement?'

Drew reached down deep for his Voice of Concern.

'Well, Britney, like all Americans, we are shocked and saddened by this pointless brutality. We trust that the authorities are doing everything in their power to hunt down these terrorists –'

'So you do think this bombing was an Abu Sayaf plot?'

'I think this was a terrorist bombing. I can't say who planned it. There are several radical groups working in Mindanao and the Sulu Islands. Your guess is as good as mine.'

He gave himself a mental high-five. Nicely lied, Drew.

'May I ask where you are, sir? Right now?'

This came in a velvety tone, almost conspiratorial; his internal alarm bell started to bong softly in the back of his mind.

'I'm at the airport. Why?'

'You're leaving for Harrisburg, sir?'

'I am. The next flight.'

'That's in one hour. Do you have time to meet me?'

I'd rather gargle my own bathwater, thought Drew. And why do you know the time of the next flight to Harrisburg?

'For what purpose, Britney?'

'It's about Gunther Krugman, sir.'

Here it comes.

'What about him, Britney?'

'Well, sir, our editors have slated a profile for him for our "Inside the Machine" series this weekend. You know about that?'

'I've been following it. Is this chat off the record?'

'It is.'

Drew fished around in his suit-coat pocket for his digital mini-recorder, clicked it on, and held the mike up to the phone.

'Just say that for me again. For my little tape recorder.'

A hesitation there, but not for long.

'Certainly, Senator. This chat is off the record, sir.'

'And what time is it?'

'It's . . . fifteen minutes after twelve.'

'And the day is . . . ?'

'Tuesday. August nineteenth.'

'Okay. Off the record, from what I've heard of Gunther Krugman, he'd rather get his bell-rope snagged in his zipper than have a sit-down with you or with anyone from your paper. And if the *Post* was entertaining an equivalent fantasy that I would have anything to say about him for publication, your editors are in possession of a talent for megalomaniacal narcissism that rivals the French. Even if I knew anything about him. Which I don't. We haven't spoken for weeks.'

There's an old and golden rule in politics: never tell an unnecessary lie. Drew knew this very well. Retribution was swift.

'About the sit-down, he hadn't ruled it out by yesterday afternoon. And forgive me, sir, but you were seen having a drink with him at the St Regis last night. But that isn't why I'm calling. Please let me come out? I'm already on my way. I'll be there in ten minutes. It's too important to talk about on a cell phone.'

Damn. And where was she getting her information?

'Why is it so bloody important?'

'Ten minutes? Please?'

She was almost begging him. And she was almost here. The catch was that he had no intention of taking any flight to Harrisburg today. What he wanted to do was register on the flight, miss it, drop off the official grid, make contact with Cole so he could reassure Diana, and then have a very long and very private talk with Gunther Krugman. He intended to ask him exactly why the Kunia intercept had been sent to him just a few hours before the Iligan City bombing. And why the hell were Helen McDowell and Levi Sloane trying to find him in the middle of the night? But if he dodged Britney Vogel she'd spend the rest of the week hounding him. She was like that. He had to meet her, if only to get rid of her as soon as he could.

'Ten minutes. I'll be in the Empire Lounge. Tell the receptionist you're expected. And Britney, this had better be worth it.'

She made it in nine. He was in a private booth at the back of the first-class lounge, tucking into a plate of eggs Benedict with a crystal sidecar of champagne and orange juice, and wondering why the obvious spook in the dark-gray worsted suit and the pencil-thin tie who was sitting at a table by the door was doing such a bad job of blending in, when she materialized in front of him like a jet of swamp fire, a vision in an emerald green skirt with her jade-colored blouse semibuttoned. Her eyes were wide and brimming with a lurid delight. Drew looked up at her like a wolf in a leg-hold trap and showed her his teeth.

'Britney,' he said, rising awkwardly, the way men do who have to be gallant while trapped behind a table. She faked a wry grimace of counterfeit contrition and slipped into the booth opposite him, placing her green alligator Kate Spade bag on the table between them the way a Tombstone gunfighter would lay his Colt down on the bar top.

'I'm so grateful for this, Senator. Really.'

Just to drive her nuts, Drew pulled out a cigarette from a solid-gold Cartier case with Diana's initials on it, flipped it open, and held it out to her, raising an eyebrow like Ronald Colman did in *Lost Horizon* – a trick he'd learned from his father, an aging rake still chasing his night nurse around the family mansion overlooking Harrisburg.

Britney looked at the cigarettes as if he had offered her a trayful of pickled cat penises and scrunched her nose up in that cute little way she had that made him want to punch her every time.

'Oh, I couldn't. Anyway, you can't smoke here.'

'I'm riveted. Time's running, kid. Shoot.'

He was talking like Bogart. He always talked like Bogart when he was around newspaper reporters. He had no idea why. It was better than hitting them with the breadbasket. She leaned forward far enough to give him a helicopter tour of her underpinnings and the soft shell-pink curve of her left breast. She spoke in what she apparently regarded as a conspiratorial whisper.

'Gunther Krugman. Nobody can find him.'

Worse and worse.

'Really. Who's looking?'

'The National Security Agency, for one. At least, their security service is concerned about him.'

Drew kept his features in order and sipped at his crystal sidecar.

'And how does *The Washington Post* know what is concerning the National Security Agency on this fine summer day?'

'I was waiting for him in the lobby of the Regis this morning. I had been there since four A.M. I was hoping that if I caught him at breakfast I'd be able to persuade him to give us an interview.'

'What made you think he was coming downstairs so early?'

'I had information to that effect.'

'How nice for you.'

'Thank you. But he never did come downstairs, and I was still there when the people from NSA security showed up. I stayed out of the way and watched the action.'

'Why would the National Security Agency be interested in Gunther Krugman's location?'

'You know very well he's one of their informal couriers.'

'Really? I know this?'

'He describes himself as a security consultant, but everybody knows he's connected to the NSC and that from time to time he acts as a back-channel liaison between the NSC and the Hill.'

'Define everybody.'

She gave him a pained look, reached out and took the crystal sidecar of champagne and orange juice and held it up like a chalice.

'May I? I'm simply dying of thirst.'

Drew nodded and watched her as she pouted her full red lips and sipped delicately from the off side of his glass. Jesus, Mary, and Joseph. The child was actually flirting with him. He was aware of his genitalia retracting slightly in contemplation of this dangerous development. Fear had its practical applications. She set the glass down again and dabbed primly at her lips with his white cotton napkin, and leaned forward again. Drew kept his eyes where they were supposed to be. For a while. Then not.

'Okay, this is off the record, right?'

'That's why you're still here, Britney.'

'The last time he was seen he was taking the elevator up to his suite at the Regis about an hour after you left. He spoke to the concierge and then had a word with the bellman on the desk about a rental car for six in the morning.'

Drew made a mental note to warn everybody on the

Democratic side of the House that at least one of the bellhops at the St Regis Hotel was a paid informant for *The Washington Post*.

'Mr Krugman told the bellman that he was going for a drive up to Maryland. He also had a wake-up call for five A.M. He never answered it. At ten after five the bellman knocked on his door to bring him his breakfast. There was no answer. They waited around in the hall for another five minutes and then tried his phone. Still no answer. They were worried about him. There had been several calls for him during the night, but he had instructed the desk not to put any calls through. Mr Krugman is a very old man. They became more concerned and used the pass card to gain access to the room.'

'"Gain access"?'

'I'm sorry. I'm talking like a cop. I mean, they got into the suite. They thought he might not be well. Or worse.'

'And what did they find?'

'He wasn't in the suite. At all. Anywhere. There was no sign of anything wrong. The bed had not been slept in. It looked as if he had taken a few toiletries, his shaving kit, that sort of thing. He was gone.'

'What did the security people say?'

'They told the NSA team that no one had seen him leave. I find that curious. Do you find it curious?'

'I find many things curious. Such as, where are we going with this? Why are you here talking to me?'

'You were the last person seen with him. I was wondering if you . . . had any comments. Observations? Anything to guide me?'

'Guide you? Where would I want to guide you?'

Maybe over a cliff.

'We feel that this is an unusual development. Gunther

Krugman is a well-connected D.C. insider and now he seems to be missing. For example, was there anything in his demeanor last night that struck you as odd?'

Drew decided to play this thing out long enough for her to commit herself, and then he was going to smack her with the breadbasket anyway.

'I hear you telling me he's missing. What we *know* is that nobody knows where he is right now. So what? He works for himself. He's a free American. The fact that nobody in the hotel saw him leave does not mean that he took measures to leave without being seen. Last month, in one night, somebody stole three stretch limos from the underground parking lot at the same hotel. The cameras saw it, but nobody in security did. Cameras never sleep, but security guards dog it on the night shift all the time. The Regis isn't a fort, Britney. I'd wait a long time before I started calling this a disappearance. He'll turn up when and where he wants to.'

He could see by her reaction that he had made his point.

'Why would he leave in the first place? Even if he wasn't trying to do it without being seen?'

'Maybe he heard you were down in the lobby stalking him.'

'I wasn't stalking him. Was there anything in his manner last night that seemed odd? Was he nervous or worried about anything?'

'Listen to me, Britney. By your own report I was far from the last person to be seen talking to him.'

'I meant the last person of significance.'

'Why haven't I heard from the NSA security team, then?'

She settled back in the booth and gave him the kind of

look that a well-brought-up young vampire gives to a lovely curve of exposed throat, a mixture of profound aesthetic appreciation and naked hunger.

'Because they haven't been told you were there.'

She never spoke the obvious 'yet.' It was hanging in the air between them like a spider hanging on a thread. His hand actually did make a move for the breadbasket. He stopped it in time. Barely. He sat back in the chair and looked at her with unfeigned admiration.

'Jesus, kid, you really are a piece of work.'

'Drew . . . this isn't fair. I'm only trying to help you.'

'You ever hear of the Secret Service? Last night I had two agents with me, and wherever I go they file a report on where, when, and with whom. I see the bellhop at the Regis forgot to mention that fact to you. I can see it in your face. Remember not to tip him. Point being, if the NSA cared that I was, in your phrase, the "last person of significance" to see Gunther Krugman, then I'd be sitting here sharing my champagne cocktail with them and not with you. Watch me. Here I am looking around theatrically.'

He looked around the lounge theatrically, came back to her.

'And yet . . . here we are. Just me and you. I don't like being shaken down, Britney –'

'I wasn't –'

Drew held up a finger.

'It felt like a shakedown. I ought to know. I get shaken down more often than a box of Wheaties.'

'It was not a shakedown. I'm a reporter. I'm doing a job.'

'So was Linda Lovelace.'

She got up without a word and turned to go,

remembered her Spade bag, turned around to get it, and stood there for a long moment with her eyes shining. Drew felt suddenly and deeply ashamed.

'Britney . . . that was out of line. Really out of line.'

She pulled herself together a little, and her breathing slowed.

'Yes. It was. Even by my standards that was pretty mean.'

'And I'm deeply sorry for it. Will you sit down?'

Several emotions ran across her face. He had cracked her open a little bit. The two pale white spots on her cheek changed slowly to pink. She sat down in the booth and the air seemed to run out of her. She focused on what was left of his champagne and orange juice. He picked it up and handed it to her. After a time, she looked across the table at him with a look that was much more human.

'Maybe I *was* trying to shake you down. I'm sorry for it. If you don't think like a barracuda, then the paper will go find someone who does. You know what we call the city desk at the *Post*?'

Drew shook his head.

'The Reptile House. Newspaper people are . . . mostly they're not very good people. Maybe they start out that way, but it never lasts. At Columbia they drill it into you – all officials are corrupt. Politicians believe in nothing. Cops are evil incarnate. If somebody's poor it's somebody else's fault. Go out there and prove it to the world. Take no prisoners. We all take on this unearned wisdom . . . We never actually *do* anything in the world, never put ourselves out to be judged. In a way we live very sheltered lives. And since we never attempt anything out in the world, we never fail, and after a few years the ones who get to be stars think it's because they're just plain *smarter* than anyone else. Maybe that's what's happening to me.'

Drew, leaning back in his chair, found that he believed her. His readiness to believe her made him feel a little better about himself, since while she had been explaining the corrosive dynamics of modern journalistic practice, he'd been thinking that it sounded very much like the life he was leading in the Senate. She fell into silence, looking down, looking inward, and at that moment he felt a rush of protective affection for her. Probably doomed, but nevertheless . . .

'Britney, this thing about Krugman . . . May I give you some advice, strictly off the record? Something bad is happening here. Something connected to Krugman. I don't know what it is, but I do know that this conversation of ours is drawing some attention. There's a man in a dark gray suit sitting at the table by the door, and I know him; he's one of Levi Sloane's people. You know who Levi Sloane is, don't you?'

'Yes. He's something at the NSA.'

'He's the Assistant Deputy Director of Operations. If he thinks that a conversation between you and me is important enough to send a surveillance unit, then you need to step very carefully around this story. Very carefully.'

'Can you tell me why?'

'No.'

'Do you know why?'

'No.'

'Are you trying to find out?'

After a hesitation, Drew said, 'Yes.'

'I know this sounds self-serving –'

'You want to be the first person I call?'

'Actually, yes.'

Drew sat back and thought about it.

'Okay ... how about this? If you'll stay out of the picture and let me work out a few things that are puzzling me, then if – and I mean if – I come up with something that I think the media needs to know about, you'll be the *only* one I call. How does that sound?'

She lifted up a folded napkin and wiped away a trace of tear from her left eye, and then she smiled at him in a way that made Drew wish he'd had a daughter.

'It sounds like a Pulitzer.'

Maryland

Drew had the rented Cadillac Escalade pretty well figured out by the time he left the airport, and now that he was closing in on Beltsville he was deeply in lust with it. Maybe the Republicans were onto something. His last family vehicle was a pious little Geo that ran on a fifty-fifty mix of Evian water and sanctimony. Every time you gassed up an urban tank like this you got an autographed picture of the Sultan of Brunei. You were so high off the ground that you could look down through a car's open sunroof and see the bald spot on the back of the driver's skull. That kind of thing gave you power. The windows were tinted almost black, and by the time the bright sunlight outside forced its way in it was reduced to a pale, polite glow that lay on Drew's right shoulder like a gentle benediction. In the slightly unreal world out there beyond the windshield, the interstate flowed through the deep green Maryland countryside like a black river, and he drifted along its surface in a gleaming black microcosm of calm cool silence. He hadn't seen an official-looking car in two miles. If anyone wanted to track him – and he couldn't think of anyone other than Britney Vogel who would bother – the truck had an On Star system that broadcast the truck's GPS coordinates to a mainframe in Houston.

The idea that somebody in Houston could sit at a monitor and watch a little computerized image of a black Cadillac Escalade rolling through southern Maryland appealed to him, and he smiled into the rearview mirror as if he were looking into a camera. Maybe there really was a camera. Somebody could be watching him right now. He twiddled his fingers at the mirror. Maybe they would wave back. Maybe they were waving back at this very moment. Maybe he was going bats. He had every right.

Krugman was still out of sight for some unknown reason. He knew he had to talk to Levi Sloane at the NSA soon, but he didn't want to do that before he reached Krugman. If Sloane wanted to talk to Drew, he had his cell number. So far Sloane hadn't called, no matter what Britney Vogel was trying to imply. He had some time and he intended to use it. He punched the On Star phone button and the disembodied voice of someone who sounded exactly like the receptionist at his dentist's office only without the wintergreen-scented breath filled the interior of the truck with a single sultry word.

'Ready.'

Damn, you had to love a country like this.

Drew spoke a series of numbers that added up to the phone number of the IMF office in New York city. The voice said, 'Dialing,' and then he heard a loud dial tone coming out of the speakers as the hands-free phone kicked in.

It rang four times and then a woman answered.

'IMF New York.'

'This is Senator Drew Langan. I'm calling about one of your employees, Coleman Langan. He's my son.'

The hesitation was very brief. But it was there. It was a very wrong thing, that little hesitation. For some reason a cold, dark thought woke up deep down in his hypothalamus and looked around at a world it did not find promising. A vision of Cole's face as a pale young boy came drifting up from that same primeval reservoir and floated on the windshield before him as he thought about that woman's brief but telling hesitation. His heart seemed to be hurting very slightly and his throat felt dry and constricted. The two most terrible words surfaced.

What if . . . ?

When she finally spoke, her tone was soft and soothing, full of reassurance and warmth, the kind of laudanum-laden voice he heard every day in the House, the silky cadences of the professional liar.

'Certainly, Senator. How may I help you?'

'I need to contact him. It's an emergency.'

'I'm so sorry, Senator Langan. Your son is out of the country. He's gone to Thailand, sir. But he'll be back next week.'

Drew put some cold iron into it.

'I'm aware of that. My wife has already told me. I need a contact number for him. He must have left you with one.'

Another not-quite-silent intake of air.

'Just a moment, Senator. I'll put you through to one of our directors. Please hold.'

A director? Why call in the big guns for a simple request like his son's phone number in Thailand? Drew waited, listening with painful concentration to the electric hum of the carrier tone as it floated around the silent interior of the truck. He was coming up on the Powder Mill exit. He slowed and eased the truck into the off-ramp. The tone of the carrier line changed very slightly, and then there was an audible click. If you could say that a carrier tone had a certain ambience, then the ambience seemed to change. The effect was rather like the way the sound changes when you go from a small room to a much larger one. Some altered quality in the phone lines, probably, but he had the distinct impression that whoever was going to answer wasn't necessarily in the same building as the receptionist. For no reason he could name he pulled his tape recorder out and set it on the dash, clicked it on to RECORD. The phone line popped and clicked twice, and then a man's voice came on, a deeply rounded and well-buffed voice with a vaguely black, vaguely Central African accent.

'Senator Langan. An honor, sir. Your son has spoken of you often. My name is Olatunji. I'm the associate director here. How can I help you?'

He had to be in a very different location. There was an odd repetitive noise deep in the background of the connection that had not been audible before, the sound of a helicopter. Very faint, a long way off, but present. The man seemed oblivious to the steady thumping sound. Drew tried to be the same way.

'Mr Olatunji, is it?'

'Yes, sir. Abraham Olatunji. This is regarding your son?'

'It is. It's very important that I speak with him.'

'Certainly, Senator. Your wife has already called us. We understand your concerns. This terrible bombing in the Philippines. I have my people on the matter now. We have traced him to a hotel in Phuket called the Lotus Blossom. I have the number for you. The receptionist there has informed us that he checked in a few days ago. As far as she knows he has not checked out yet. It is a

be back in a few hours. May I take a message for him?'

Drew gave her his name and cell number. Her voice had one of those audible smiles that usually drove him nuts. She asked him if there was anything else she could do for him in a tone that made him want to fly out there this afternoon with a list of his top five.

'No . . . wait. Yes. Can you tell me what the weather is like?'

A moment of silence . . . that stretched out far too long.

'The weather, sir?'

'Yes. The weather right now. Exactly right now. Can you tell me if it's raining? Or not? The temperature, the time of day. Half moon. Full moon. Black moon. Windy. Not windy? Describe it all for me.'

'But why?'

'Maybe I just like the sound of your voice.'

A pinging little laugh like crystal cracking.

'You too funny. Bye bye.'

The line went dead. He redialed it and after a long interval the line rang busy. He asked the On Star Goddess to find him the phone number of the Lotus Blossom Inn in Phuket, Thailand. The Goddess tried ever so hard and was desolated to report that the number for the Lotus Blossom Inn was no longer in service. He thanked her. Honesty was in her. He thanked her again. The Goddess actually said, 'You're welcome.' Then the tone cut off and the silence was on him again like a feral cat. He sat there in the Escalade and stared out at Maryland, seeing none of it, his mind in the jungles of Southeast Asia and his breathing shallow. There were very few people in the world with the ability to reroute a direct-dialed call in order to make it look as if you had been put through to a real number in Thailand. Most of those people worked for a variety of national governments in solid stone buildings with elegant little brass nameplates that had nothing to do with what actually went on inside. Finally, he pulled out a piece of paper and looked at the writing on it.

Springfield Road and Good Luck Road
Powder Mill exit – Beltsville Maryland

After a period of time that seemed much longer than it was, Drew put the truck in gear and rolled off the exit and out onto Powder Mill Road. The countryside was flat and covered with thin brush forest. Within a few hundred yards it gave way to gently rolling farmland and meadows of summer rye and sweetgrass. The two-lane blacktop curved south and east through empty fields bounded by thin stands of spindle pine. Through the sunroof he saw the contrail of a jet carving a thin spidery trace across a pale blue sky. The road turned and curved again. About three hundred yards down the line he crossed the intersection of Reservoir Road and passed a sign that read:

NASA GODDARD SPACE CENTER
THREE MILES

He stayed on Powder Mill for another six hundred yards until he reached the turnoff for Springfield Road. This was a smaller road with no clear lane markings, and it led him down through more rolling meadow country with no signs of homes or farms or anything made by man other than the low wire fencing that ran along the left side of the lane. If there was anything here to justify Gunther Krugman's interest, it wasn't leaping out of the goldenrod that lined the ditches to wave a placard at him.

The sun was gliding into the west now, and he pulled the sun-roof shade closed. The air was full of drifting cottonwood fluff, and when he rolled down the window so he could light up a cigarette the sound of cicadas droning in the fields of old rye and summer wheat was high and clear. Another mile along this road and he came to a rise and a turning where a semipaved road came north out of more empty meadowland. A low wire fence that looked well maintained and businesslike ran along the offside crest of drainage ditch next to the meadow on his left. Beyond this fence was a broad, level field of standing rye. Every twenty yards or so along the fence a metal sign had been affixed to the wire with shiny metal studs.

The signs all said the same thing in big red letters:

ALABASTER FARMS
KEEP OUT KEEP OUT KEEP OUT
TRESPASSERS WILL BE PROSECUTED

That was okay with Drew. Anyone who had the moxie to name a place Alabaster anything had a right to keep people from walking around on his turf. The three KEEP OUTS did seem a bit hysterical. One would have done the job nicely. Even two was sort of like shouting it at you. Three was just plain rude. Drew decided he probably wouldn't like the guy who owned Alabaster Farms. He looked up at the faded blue sign:

GOOD LUCK ROAD

It had been punctured with a single rusted-out bullet hole, from the size of it a heavy hunting round. That seemed a bit ironic. He pulled over to the side of the road, stopped the truck in the narrow shadow of a stand of poplars, and climbed down onto the shoulder of the road. The heat of the sun was steady, and the light that lay on the countryside all around him was old the way Maryland was old. He walked a little way up the road until he was standing right in the crossroads of Springfield and Good Luck Road. He looked up at the sky through a rectangle ringed by old oaks and dusty poplars. He took in a breath, pulled his suit coat off, and draped it over his left shoulder. Other than the dental-drill whine of the cicadas, there was more silence available at the crossroads of Springfield and Good Luck than he had heard in years. A soft wind came in from wherever soft winds live and began to sigh in the dry leaves of the oaks, and the heavy tips of the rye bending in the field beside him shimmered as the wind moved out across the field. There was also the earthy smell of dust and the licorice smell of hot pavement and the tick-ticking of hot metal as the big black Escalade's engine cooled by the side of the road. Its big chrome grill seemed to be grinning at him. He didn't like it very much right now. It looked like a warthog keeping a secret.

There was nothing here for him. Gunther Krugman was missing, for reasons that would probably become clear and would have something to do with old age and decay and the onset of dementia. It was a sad, heavy feeling, like mourning the onrushing loss of a dying friend. The lies of Abraham Olatunji would have an explanation that he would eventually hear; he was a senator and he could make that happen. He would make it happen. He had a reasonable expectation that when he heard why Abraham Olatunji and Silver Bells of the Lotus Blossom Inn were lying to him about his son and where his son might be, what he heard would not make him happy.

Even now the cold little dread that had awakened down in his hypothalamus was crawling up through the layers of his mind looking for a much larger office and many more neurons to order around. Something was very wrong in his world, and now he was going to have to find out what it was. Drew pulled in a long, slightly ragged breath and finished his cigarette. The smoke blew away across the rye field and vanished into the high, clear, blue sky over the meadow. He walked back to the truck and opened the door. He was halfway into the truck, one foot still on the running board, when a sound came across the field of rye, a deep booming sound he could feel through the hot metal of the truck itself.

He stepped down off the running board and stood there in the shade of the poplars, staring out over the meadow. The soft breeze died away and the drumming sound grew clearer. The cicadas stopped their droning to listen with him. They all listened so hard to that distant pounding sound that the muscles in his neck began to hurt.

A helicopter. He reached into his pocket and pulled out the tape recorder and switched it on. There it was, under Olatunji's bass reverberations. He turned the sound up and held the speaker close to his ear. It was steady and strong and deep, like kettle drums in a narrow canyon. It had exactly the same rhythm and cadence that he was feeling now in his chest and through his shoes and in the air all around the clearing. There was a chopper at work on the far side of the field, behind the distant tree line. Was it really the same chopper he had heard in the background while he was talking to Olatunji? Of course it wasn't. But if he didn't go and look it would drive him totally bats. He turned the recorder off and slipped it into his pocket, locked the Escalade. Then he slipped down the ditch and scrambled up to the wire fence with all the bad-tempered KEEP OUT KEEP OUT KEEP OUT signs. He looked at the signs for a second, and then stepped over the bright new copper wire and started out across the meadow, passing with a hissing sound through the bending stalks of waist-high rye with the warm earth under his feet and the hard flat sun like a hot iron on the back of his neck. He had no clear idea of where he was going or what he would find on the other side of that distant tree line. This entire expedition contained not a single scintilla of sense. This was just some innocent chopper pilot spraying herbicide. It had nothing to do with Krugman or his son. He told himself that all the way across the field. By the time he reached the tree line he almost believed it.

La Magdalene

The old soldier in the gurney was dying pretty well. Cole admired him for that, and he felt it was a privilege to sit next to him here in this hard steel chair in the hallway on board the French naval hospital ship *La Magdalene* and keep him company. He was also quietly hoping that someone would come along and sew his ear back on reasonably soon. It had been a good ear, and Cole thought that going through the rest of his life without it would be unpleasant. He had the ear right there on his lap inside a Styrofoam container filled with crushed ice. He was trying not to fret too much about this severed ear of his, but it wasn't easy. The soldier doing the dying was the big square-built noncom with the lurid burn scar that covered half of the right side of his face. The leathery old trooper was lying on his back on a hospital gurney with a big red 'F' scrawled on his forehead and staring up at a cold blue light inside a wire frame set into the ceiling of the long white hallway. A tall steel pole was standing by the gurney and an IV drip of morphine was sending him to his long sleep in a way that was allowing him some time to think about his life.

Around them people were crowding into various

ORs and other people were yelling at them not to do that, and this was all mixed up with the moaning and the burning sharp scent of antiseptic and the earthy smell of fresh blood and the busy chatter of saws and pumps and the ringing clatter of surgical instruments dropping into steel trays.

The dying German was telling Cole about the fight they had all made for a little Serbian village several years ago in which many of his men had behaved very well although nine of them had been killed in the taking of it. Since he was telling Cole this story in German, Cole had no idea what the man was saying, but it seemed to be helping the man just to have Cole sitting there beside him and nodding at him from time to time. From his post at the head of the man's gurney all he could see of the man's wounds was the great white swell of the sheet that was covering what remained of his body. On the sheet, bright red stains were seeping to the surface and spreading out over the whiteness. The German's skin was growing more and more blue with each breath, and he kept his eyes fixed on Cole's face as he spoke. There was fear in those eyes behind the pain, and Cole knew that the man was afraid of dying but he was getting himself ready for it as well as he could. Cole hoped that when his own time came he could handle it as well as this trooper was handling it. Privately he had his doubts. He had seen many men die, and few of them took it very well; even the very best tended to lose it at the end. Cole did not feel that he was one of the very best, especially not right now.

There was something wrong with his balance, and the side of his head where the missing ear had been felt as if it had been burned with a blowtorch, and there seemed to be an invisible iron bar stuck right through the middle of his forehead. He tried to pay as little attention to any of this as he could for the sake of the old soldier. In one small part of his mind he thought about the ear a little. He couldn't help it. He had been stumbling around in the smoke looking for Ramiro Vasquez when he found it. It had been lying there in the middle of some debris that might have been the patio furniture where the legionnaires had been sitting when the Blue Bird exploded. All that was left of the legionnaires and all that was left of almost everyone and everything else anywhere near the Blue Bird was a tattered scattering of shapeless lumps and shining gobs and the heavier pink bones, all the same one thing now, all mixed together and on their way back into the ground. Cole was still pretty proud of himself for recognizing his own ear in the middle of all of that craziness and for doing it in spite of the truly terrible ringing in his head. The little silver ring he liked to wear in it – the one that always drove Pike Zeigler nuts – had helped him to find it in the debris. He had been sitting there in the wreckage of the Blue Bird while sirens began to wail, when he felt a hand on his shoulder and he looked up to see Ramiro Vasquez standing over him, staring down at him with a hunted despairing look. Vasquez seemed to be saying something – Cole watched his lips moving – and the words '*I'm sorry ... I'm so sorry*' seemed to form in his mind as he sat there and looked up at his friend's bloody face. Vasquez had pulled him to his feet and somehow they both made it all the way down through the teeming streets – through the crowds and the panic and the drifting pall of smoke – to the docks, where a young woman in blood-soaked medical greens was running a triage operation. They had been separated there, Vasquez being led off by a strong but gentle legionnaire while another team of stretcher bearers had taken Cole up into the ship. Vasquez had not yet reappeared, and Cole had lost all track of time, sitting in this long white hallway beside the dying German soldier, staring into nothing, holding his severed ear.

He felt that if someone came along pretty soon they might be able to save his ear, but if they didn't then he was going to have to resign himself to having only one ear, and he found this hard to accept. He liked having two ears. He had the impression that having two ears had been an advantage in whatever work it was that he did. And there was the problem of sunglasses. You needed at least two ears to keep your sunglasses on, although three was best. They had loaded him up with some drug that was helping him to stay calm about all of this, but it was still an issue with him. He did feel a bit selfish for fretting about his severed ear and not paying better attention to the German trooper.

The trooper's voice was growing softer now, descending into a whisper that rattled around in the man's throat like a stone going down a drainpipe. Cole had to lean in and turn his head so that the only ear he had left was close to the man's lips. The man pulled his bloody hand from under the sheet and held it out to Cole. Cole took it and gripped it hard. It was as cold as a severed ear. The man stopped talking abruptly and looked up at Cole for a few moments longer like a man who had just had an important insight and was now trying to put it into words. Cole felt that he should say something to help him do that and was still trying to get his head clear enough to say the right something when he realized the man was probably just dead. He wasn't sure. The line between being dead and not being dead was blurry around here. People crossed it without thinking. It might be that Ramiro Vasquez would come back and help Cole decide. Or perhaps Vasquez had died somewhere else in the ship or it was only the ghost of Ramiro Vasquez that had walked him through the town and down to the hospital ship. It was hard to be certain of anything.

He studied the stillness on the face of the German soldier. Maybe he wasn't all the way dead yet. Perhaps he was just sleeping. Cole decided to stay there and keep watching the man's face in case he woke up. He would want someone to do that for him if he were trying to wake up from being dead. Nobody wants to wake up from being dead and find himself all alone on a gurney in a long white hallway full of strangers shouting in a language he can't understand.

Iligan City

230 Fortaliza Street
Iligan City, Mindanao
Wednesday, August 20, 1:00 a.m. local time

When the Blue Bird blew up so close behind them that the force of the concussion struck them like a blow and the air grew suddenly thick with dust and debris, Gideon had found himself unbearably aroused, pitched headlong into a delirium of sexual excitement that burned through him like a pale green fire. With the city shrouded in smoke and ashes blowing in the hot wind and the incoming sirens wailing like the ghosts of all those newly dead people, Gideon had felt himself lifted up and exalted by this wonderful sexual rage. In his room, on the creaking old cot, amid a tangle of grimy sheets and dried sweat, he had quenched it again and again in the frightened young Filipino the way a blacksmith cools a bar of hot iron by plunging it into cold water. Gideon had poured all of his own fear into the boy, and when he was drained and spent he had paid the boy too much money in American dollars and shoved him out the door of his flat barefoot with his clothing bundled in his shaking hands.

Then he had gone into his kitchenette and poured six ounces of single malt into a tall dirty glass, mixed it with a can of Canada Dry ginger ale, and gulped this down in one shuddering draft, his flabby brown body pouched and naked at the sink filled with dirty dishes, his knees trembling and weak, thigh muscles jumping, his free hand braced on the greasy countertop. Then he poured himself another just as large and carried it over to the window. He threw up the sash so hard it slammed into the wooden frame, and a jagged lightning-bolt crack sliced through the thin glass. Over the low rooftops of the New Quarter he could see the column of black smoke still rising over the blackened crater where the Blue Bird had once stood. He pulled in a long shaky breath and let it out through thinned lips, his nostrils flared out and his eyes as wide as a child. His chest expanded and his heart filled with pride. He was a man of important business now. The proof of his own power was drifting out over the city.

He turned away from the window with his heart fluttering around in his chest and padded over to the desktop computer sitting on top of the dresser in his bedroom. He flicked it on and waited for the machine to wake up. Perhaps there would be no message. Perhaps the explosion had cut the phone lines. While he waited he looked over at the phone beside his rumpled and stained little cot and saw no blinking red light. Mr Gabriel had not yet called. This did not surprise him. Mr Gabriel had told him to be in his room by eight o'clock, and although he had been a little late he knew that Mr Gabriel would not care. They were celebrating a great victory against their enemies. He would call soon. Gideon would have his answer waiting. The machine beeped and Gideon opened his e-mail server. There was a letter icon flashing in the upper left corner.

'I have mail,' he said, and laughed. The laugh went skittering around the shabby room like a trapped bat and settled on the back of his neck. He downloaded the message and got a field of what appeared to be random numbers. He stripped the numbers from the e-mail and pasted them into his decryption software.

In a few seconds he got the plain text.

Kemp Jordan freelance ID supported by local research. Not possible to confirm current location. Description as provided matches description of freelance reporter unofficially connected to *Morning Star, National Post,* assorted Canadian magazines. Passport correct and confirmed as belonging to Kemp Jordan. Unmarried. No children. No family listed. Photo correct. Problem. Tried to confirm description of Kemp Jordan by searching back issues of online newspapers. Online archives unsearchable without providing return e-mail address and valid credit card. Unwilling to compromise ID. Accessed yellowpages.ca. Kemp Jordan unlisted. Accessed periodical index at Toronto Library website and found thirty-eight articles attributed to Kemp Jordan. Note. One photo attached to an article published in 1987 subject Sport Fishing in Costa Rica – shows man reported to be Kemp Jordan in fighting chair holding a fishing pole and looking into camera. Kemp Jordan in passport photo MAY NOT be Kemp Jordan in fighting chair. Repeat. MAY be different man. Note: Kemp Jordan embedded freelance reporter with C Company, First Brigade, Third Infantry Division during Iraq War. Newspaper photos of Kemp with US military not repeat not retrievable. Explanation given; data loss due to system error. Medicare Canada database confirms one Kemp Jordan underwent radiation therapy for prostate cancer July 2003 result metastasis in situ. Referral code link to Mayo Clinic in Rochester, Minnesota. Kemp Jordan underwent surgery for replacement of cancerous left hip July 15, 2003. Prognosis poor. Palliative care prescribed. Left Mayo Clinic July 21. Current location unknown.

The message ended there. Gideon stared at it and tried to find a sober place in his disordered mind to make sense of it. The room was tilting a little to the left, and he held on to the dresser top to steady it. The phone rang. The sound was large and punched through his skull like a piece of rebar. He stumbled across the room and snatched the handset up.

'You have an answer?'

Gideon tried to sound like a man who has not just rolled drunkenly out of a debauch. Mr Gabriel's voice had winter in it.

'I do.'

Gideon carried the phone across to the dresser. The cord wasn't long enough to reach it so he found himself stretched out between the phone and the dresser like a fat bird on a very thin wire. He squinted at the screen from a distance and managed to read off the e-mail report. When he finished, the silence on the other end of the phone had a thin dry hissing under it, as if the line ran straight to the coldest place on earth. Mr Gabriel finally spoke.

'Find out where he went.'

'But how? Everything is closed for the night!'

'I don't care. Don't disappoint me.'

Maryland

Drew's walk in the field of rye went pretty much as he privately expected it to, although he had no clear idea why; he was almost at the tree line when the sound of a police siren went skirling into the summer air and flushed a small explosion of crows out of the meadow just in front of him. They rose up into the blue sky with cries like iron gates creaking and flapped heavily away to the south. He sighed and turned and looked back out across the field. A dusty Maryland State Police car was parked close behind his rented Escalade. Two state troopers were standing beside the patrol car and staring back at him, a large black man and a short thickset woman, both of them wearing Kevlar vests and knife-edged DI Stetsons. The large black trooper bent over, put a hand into the open window of his patrol car, and the siren cut off sharply. Drew stood there a few yards from the tree line and gave some serious thought to ignoring them. Then the construction noise from beyond the line of trees stopped, and the silence came back like a tide returning.

He heard one of the troopers calling to him.

'Senator Langan. You'll have to come back.'

Drew suppressed a rush of cold anger. Less than two

142

hours had elapsed between the time he had cut Luna Olvidado loose and this untimely arrival of a Maryland State Police unit. Eight years in the Senate and an important post in the Intelligence Oversight Committee, and all that his power could buy him was not quite 120 minutes of personal freedom. The black cop reached into the window of his unit, and the siren whooped again. The line of trees was only a few feet away. He still couldn't see what was on the other side. The image of a US senator being hounded across a field by a pair of overweight Maryland troopers was too ridiculous to bear. He turned away again, shaded his eyes from the sunlight, and called back.

'What's the damned problem?'

'Sir,' said one of the cops, 'you're on private property. The owner has complained. Will you please come back?'

'Who complained?'

'Sir. Please come back here.'

It was pointless. He started back. The troopers stood by their unit and waited for him, saying nothing, watching him with hard blank faces. He reached them after a walk heavy with barely suppressed anger and a feeling of impotence. The heavy-set female officer met him at the shiny copper fence and held out a hand to help him step over it. He declined the hand with his face as blank and stony as hers. She backed away and waited for him by the patrol car, next to the large moon-faced black cop. He tried not to say 'what's the problem, officers?' again but ended up saying it anyway. The large black cop nodded his formidable skull in the direction of the KEEP OUT signs and spoke in a whiskey rumble that came right out of Alabama.

'We're sorry to bother you, Senator Langan, but the

143

owner made a formal complaint. We had to respond.'

'Who owns this property, Sergeant?'

'What it says, sir,' said the sergeant. 'Alabaster Farms.'

'And who the hell are they?'

'Can you let us know what the problem is, sir? We'd be glad to help. We just can't let you wander around on private property.'

Everyone wanted to help. Mainly by getting in his way. He was going to have to find out who owned Alabaster Farms by himself. Add it to the list. He strapped on the best smile he could manage.

'I'm sorry to have caused you any trouble. I was just out for a drive and I felt like a stroll. Summer doesn't last very long. The day was perfect. How did the owner know I was on his property?'

'Sensors, sir,' said the female trooper, who didn't believe a word of it. 'On the fence.'

'Okay. One other question?'

'Sure.'

'How did you know my name?'

'We ran the Cadillac, sir. The rental company had you listed.'

They all turned as a low black Crown Victoria came up the rise and rolled down toward them. Drew knew the car and tried not to swear out loud. Luna Olvidado was behind the wheel. She pulled to a stop beside the state car and rolled down her window. She was alone in the car and her face was pale and tight. She held up a folder and tinned the two state troopers.

'Olvidado, Secret Service. Is everything all right here?'

The sergeant frowned at her ID and then relaxed.

'Yes, ma'am. The senator was out for a stroll. We got a call.'

Luna gave Drew a brief glance that carried a warning and smiled up at the troopers.

'I'm assigned to Senator Langan. I'll take it from here.'

The sergeant looked over at Drew, who nodded. Then the two troopers looked at each other and exchanged the same wry grin. Whatever was actually happening here, they'd never get cut in on it. This was Beltway business, and they were just a couple of patrol grunts in a cruiser. The big sergeant shrugged and touched the flat brim of his Stetson with his right hand in a satirical salute.

'Okay then. None of our damn business, right? Let's us two fade then, Moira. Y'all have a great day, Senator. You too, ma'am.'

The troopers climbed back into their unit and rolled slowly away down Good Luck Road. Luna and Drew watched them until the car disappeared around a curve and they were alone with the bending rye and the droning chorus of cicadas. Neither of them spoke until Luna got out of the Crown Victoria and stood beside him.

'How'd you find me?' asked Drew.

She tilted her head in the direction of the Cadillac.

'That thing has a GPS transmitter. We can track GPS anywhere in the world.'

'So you were looking for me?'

'I was worried about you. I checked the passenger list. You never boarded. So I looked at the rentals computer and found you. The truck had an On Star system. I called them and they did the rest.'

'Where's the Arapahoe?'

'Who?'

'Your partner? With the bow ties?'

'Micah? We were at the end of our shift. I dropped him at the HQ. HQ had a couple of things to tell me. I listened to him tell me and then I went back out to the airport. Why are you calling Micah "the Arapahoe"?'

'I guess because he looks like one.'

'Micah's from Hawaii. He was born on Molokai.'

'I stand corrected. What *things* did HQ have to tell you?'

He watched her face while she worked out her answer. It was a fine face, and on any other summer afternoon he'd have been delighted to watch it until sundown. When she spoke it was in a changed tone.

'Well, that's my whole problem. Would you by any chance have a cigarette you could spare?'

The hard right turn rattled him. He had no idea she smoked. Drew pulled out his Cartier case, flipped it open, and held it out for her. Luna took one of his thin black Davidoffs with the showy gold-foil filter and leaned forward to let him light it up with his Zippo. She pulled back and exhaled a plume of blue smoke that flew away on the shoulder of the soft summer wind, looking up at him with her deep green eyes, her short-cut purple hair fluttering in the wind, her navy-blue skirt-suit as sharply pressed as dress blues, the crisp white shirt underneath open to show a smooth brown curve of her throat. She held the cigarette the way people who don't smoke very often hold their cigarettes. Drew waited and finally she was ready to talk.

'What HQ had to tell me concerns Gunther Krugman. My section chief told me that you had a meeting with Krugman last night at the Regis. Rickett and Buriss reported that he gave you a dark blue envelope with the NSA crest on it. And a cigar in a silver tube. Or maybe just a silver tube with something else inside. They got the idea that Krugman was worked up about something. On the way home to Georgetown you opened the envelope and read whatever was inside. They dropped you off.

Rickett and Buriss both thought there was something bugging you. Not their business. Then sometime during the night Krugman disappears. He disappears in a way that suggests a great deal of forethought. There is some speculation that he did not leave willingly. This is not a good thing. Now there's a low-level panic attack all over the security services. Some of our people have been called in to help look for him. The NSA's all worked up because he's one of their freelance couriers.'

'Why haven't the NSA talked to me directly?'

'The field team was going to go over to your house this morning and ask you what was going on. Then there was the break-in. There was a lot of activity around you. The press was calling. Sloane didn't want to send a couple of his yard bulls off to your hotel at a time like that. He's going to run a full background check on the man you killed, this Voss guy. And he thinks that if you felt this break-in had anything to do with Gunther Krugman, you'd have come in already.'

'Why didn't Sloane talk to me himself?'

'If word got out that you'd been questioned by the NSA in connection with Krugman's disappearance – and it would – the Hill would get all bent out of shape, and then the search for Krugman wouldn't be a low-key issue. If they buttonhole you in a public way, then there's no chance they can keep it under wraps. I mean, the NSA questions a senator sitting on the Oversight Committee regarding a missing courier? It'd be a front-page lead in the *Times*.'

'I was on my way to Harrisburg this afternoon. If Sloane is as worried as you say they are, why were they going to let me leave the capital without talking to me?'

'Sloane had two NSA guys waiting for you at the

airport in Harrisburg. They figured it'd be easier to have a quiet talk with you away from D.C. But you didn't get on that plane. Instead you hired a Cadillac and dropped off the grid. We'd all love to know why.'

'I get it that Krugman's disappearance would worry them. But I don't get the full-court press. What's the urgency?'

Luna glanced at him, her face full of concern and perhaps a trace of wary suspicion.

'I don't know. My guess is some mission is involved. Something complicated. Krugman had obtained a sensitive Critic file and now he's gone. Of course they're worried.'

'What kind of mission?'

She gave him a weary look.

'Like they're going to tell me. I'm just a low-life bodyguard with a pistol in her garter. They wouldn't give me a heads-up if the French navy was blockading the Chesapeake. Anyway, my point is they wanted to back-channel a talk with you. Quietly.'

Drew pulled on his Davidoff and looked out across the field of rye. The chopper noise had stopped a while ago. He felt the instinctive unease that comes from being carefully observed through long lenses. Luna pursed her lips and exhaled a feathery white plume of smoke, but her eyes stayed on his. Clouds whirred across the sky in perfect silence and the wind stirred the heads of buttercups and Queen Anne's lace that lined the meadow. He felt like a man standing on an empty platform in the middle of the night waiting for a train. Any train.

'Let me guess. This back-channel contact would be you.'

'Yes. It would.'

'Why you?'

'I asked my section chief for the job.'

'Ambition?'

'No. Not ambition. It was personal.'

'So what do they want you to ask me?'

'First of all, Britney Vogel called you on your cell at twelve-fifteen today. You agreed to meet her at the airport, and that meeting took place a few minutes later.'

'My cell is being tapped?'

'No. Hers. During the meeting an observer reported that you and Ms Vogel had some sort of disagreement.'

'I saw the guy. Tell him nobody wears pencil-thin ties anymore. Am I under routine surveillance now?'

'No. She is.'

Drew let that slide; Britney Vogel was a royal pain in the ass, but in a vigorous democracy being a royal pain in the ass is a constitutionally protected right.

'What are they after?'

'They want to know if you told her anything at all about Gunther Krugman. About his disappearance.'

'I didn't know he was gone until she told me. And no. She said she was trying to get him to agree to an interview for the paper. I said he'd rather get his bell-rope snagged in his zipper. Then we exchanged some hard words and I told her she was spelling her name wrong. Then I felt like a first-rate heel and told her to sit down and have some lunch. By the time she left I sort of halfway liked her.'

'Which half?'

'What?'

'Never mind. Sloane says you logged onto the SIGINT database last night and downloaded a biography of a man named Hamidullah Barrakha. When you hit that file on SIGINT it pinged –'

'Pinged?'

'Like in a sonar return. It pinged back to website security and they relayed it to Operations. Sloane apparently has that file and he promptly blew an artery and wanted to know why you were querying the name Barrakha.'

'Man. Spooks. They *sent* me the damned file.'

Even as he said this, the truth of it rushed in on him. His belly did a slow barrel roll and went into a plunging dive.

'The NSA didn't send me that at all, did they?'

'From the level of hysteria, I think it's safe to assume that whatever you got from Krugman, it wasn't authorized by Levi Sloane or anyone else at the NSA.'

'Gunther would never do that. Never.'

'He just did. Accept that. What did Krugman give you?'

'A Critic Flash. It was VRK. Krugman hinted – strongly – that something about it related to me. Or to the committee.'

'What exactly is a Critic Flash?'

'Critic is a security rating. VRK means Very Restricted Knowledge. It's a very high-level security access. A Critic Flash is an intelligence bulletin – either SIGINT or HUMINT – that has just been collected by one of our assets. SIGINT is intelligence derived from some kind of monitoring operation. Satellite, faxes, e-mail, or cell phone, wireless, or landline transmissions. The NSA has hundreds of listening posts around the world. There isn't a data transmission they can't intercept. Not one. They've even got a sub – they named it the *Jimmy Carter,* which shows that the Navy still has a sense of humor – doing intercept operations on fiber-optic phone cables laid down on the floor of the Atlantic. It all ends up at Crypto City for decryption and analysis. On the other hand, HUMINT is information from a human asset in a position to collect it. You could say the CIA tries to develop HUMINT sources while the NSA specializes in SIGINT.'

'Thanks for the lecture. Remind me not to ask you the meaning of life. While it's still daylight, what was in this flash?'

'I can't tell you, Luna.'

'Sorry. Of course you can't. Nobody can tell me anything. I probably don't want to know. But I think I can assume that it had something to do with Hamidullah Barrakha because that's the thing they're so upset about. That's the link. What's the normal distribution protocol for something like a Critic Flash?'

Luna was getting very close to operational details that Drew had spent years concealing from any outsider. But Luna was a Secret Service agent and not exactly an outsider. Still, he chose his words with care and she watched him do it with a wry smile.

'Usually a Critic Flash goes to the National Security Adviser first and then, if it's important enough, she relays it to the President. After about an hour, if there's nothing in it that affects an ongoing operation, it gets posted on the National SIGINT File website.'

'The same day?'

'Usually.'

'So if it wasn't posted . . . ?'

'Then one of two things. Either it wasn't really a Critic Flash, or it was a Critic Flash that wasn't posted on SIGINT. Which means it was blocked because it affected national security.'

'Or posting it would affect a covert operation?'

'Possibly. There are other reasons I can think of. But risking the security of a covert operation is the most likely.'

'Who makes the decision to block the posting?'

'The Director of Operations for the CIA. The National Security Council. The National Security Adviser. The President.'

'But all of these people would still have access to the information? They just wouldn't post it on the SIGINT database?'

'Yes. Of course.'

'So there's a hierarchy? Various levels of distribution lists?'

'All kinds.'

'And you? You're on what level?'

'Lot of dangerous questions here, Luna. Who's asking them, you or Levi Sloane?'

'Both of us.'

'Sloane already knows this stuff. He invented most of it.'

'Okay. I'm asking. What level are you on?'

'Exactly why are you asking?'

She considered him in silence for almost thirty seconds.

'Good question. A very damned good question. To tell you the truth, I guess I'm worried.'

'Worried? About who? Whom?'

'You. I'm worried you're involved in something you don't quite get. I suppose I'm trying to help you. I really have no idea why.'

'I do. You're crazy about me and want to bear my children.'

Luna blinked at him for almost a minute.

'Was that a pass? Because if it was, maybe you should

understand something about me. This is strictly business. That's all. You've never made a move on me before, and this is sure as hell no place to start. The fact that you never made a move on me is one of the reasons I feel like sticking my neck out a little for you.'

'Okay. Sorry. Won't happen again.'

Luna held her hard look for a while and then smiled.

'Anyway, I don't like men.'

'You? No way. Hell, you're not even wearing Birkenstocks.'

'I don't like women either.'

'That sort of narrows your dating field, doesn't it?'

'I like my life as it is. I don't date and I don't have a cat and I don't screw around. I like my job and I live alone and I intend to keep it that way. Leave it at that. What security level are you cleared for?'

Having his knuckles rapped with such quiet force was a new experience for Drew. Senators got force-fed a steady diet of deference sickly sweet enough to give them all a kind of spiritual diabetes.

'Helen McDowell is the Chairwoman of the Oversight Committee. Her clearance is Umbra. That's several levels down from the President and his NSC adviser. I don't know and wouldn't tell you anyway what the President's security clearance level is called. In real life, the NSC hates giving sensitive information to anybody on the Hill. Even to us. We're not in the old boys' club and they think we leak like an overloaded Depends. And quite often we do. What's the kick in having a secret if people don't know you have one to keep? So if it gets down to McDowell and she wants to hand it out to the rest of the sitting members, the permission for her to do that has to come from the executive branch.'

'Like the President?'

'Not far from him, anyway.'

'So if what Gunther Krugman handed you has not been posted on SIGINT but it looked like a real Critic Flash . . . ?'

'And it did. I've seen enough. And I have a pretty good reason for believing it was real.'

'What reason?'

'Sorry.'

'Okay. Fine. But we can assume you weren't cleared to get it?'

'Yes. I think you're right.'

Thanks, Gunther.

'Which means . . .'

'Technically, I'm in violation of the Official Secrets Act.'

'The penalty for which is . . . ?'

'In these times? And a Gamma-level breach? Leavenworth.'

Luna's face showed the impact of that statement. Drew watched her and waited for the implication to become clear. She was a federal law-enforcement officer. Bound by oaths. Her next question gave Drew an intriguing insight into the way her mind worked.

'Britney Vogel asked you about this explosion in Mindanao?'

There it was. A very quick mind.

'She did.'

'Was there anything on the Critic Flash about it?'

'Sorry. Can't answer that.'

'I'll take that as a yes. Where is this document now?'

In my coat pocket, actually.

'Sorry again.'

'Which means it's probably in your coat pocket. If there was anything in it about a possible bombing in Mindanao that might be related to some sort of ongoing covert operation –'

'That's a hell of a stretch.'

'It fits the facts. And if this Critic Flash wasn't meant to be distributed, at least not to you, then you were being exposed to a terrible risk. A career-destroying risk. Why would Gunther Krugman compromise you like that? He's a good friend, isn't he?'

'I thought he was.'

'You need a lawyer. Today.'

Drew had already given that matter some thought.

'No. I don't. A lawyer's the last thing I need.'

'Christ, Senator! Why the hell not?'

'Because that's the weasel way. I'm an elected official of this government. I sit on a vital intelligence committee. If my country is facing a security crisis, my first move in response to that is not going to be to go leaping into my lawyer's arms and start squealing about my rights. I had no reason to think that this Critic Flash wasn't supposed to get to me. Krugman had delivered a lot of documents from the NSA and they were all legitimate. I've shown that flash to no one and talked about it to no one. I've done nothing wrong. I know this sounds like spin control, but my duty here is to help my country, not to stonewall it.'

The look Luna gave him was a mixture of respect and relief.

'You are actually serious? I mean, for real? Or do you think I'm wired and you're just saying this to impress Levi Sloane?'

Wired. It had never occurred to him.

'Are you?'

'Wired? No. Want me to prove it?'

With all my heart.

'No. No, I believe you.'

'What are you going to do now?'

'Obviously I'm going to have a talk with Sloane. After that – if there is an after – I have no idea. What are you going to do?'

'Me?'

'Yes. You. A federal agent. Sworn to uphold.'

'This has nothing to do with me. I'm not here to arrest you, if that's what you're worried about. I'll tell my section chief what you've told me. What he tells Sloane is up to him. I'm on overtime pay right now. They hate that. I've heard and seen too much already. They'll want me out of it. The pattern is to take low-level agents like me out of the loop if we get too involved. They'll likely send me home. I've got two weeks' leave coming. Hell, I might actually take some of it.'

She paused here. Sensing that there was something she wanted to say and she was trying to find a way to say it, Drew kept his mouth shut. Time passed. The light on the meadow changed, softening into a deeper yellow. The shadows pooling under the oaks and poplars were now running slowly across the tarmac like thin rivers of deep purple water. The soft wind freshened, stirring the long grass and sending a silky hiss through the bending rye. Her face was unreadable. Drew waited her out with a strange heat in his belly and a cold iron band tightening around his chest. After a timeless interval she threw her Davidoff down the road and turned to face him.

'Senator . . .'

'Drew. Call me Drew.'

'Why are we here?'

Drew knew what she meant. Why were they standing here at the intersection of two country roads in Maryland? What she was asking him now had nothing to do with her section chief. It was personal. For some demented reason, acting on God only knew what impulse, this woman wanted to help him. And the nonnegotiable reality was that Drew needed help badly. Confiding in people was not one of Drew's weaknesses. All his professional instincts warned him against it. If he answered her straight, then everything else would have to follow: Krugman's cryptic message. The lies of Abraham Olatunji. Alabaster Farms. He had come to believe that these things were all connected, link by iron link, and that if he followed this chain to the end, what he found there might be dangerous. If he told this woman any of it, he would in the end have to tell her all of it. Her face was bright with a strong clear intelligence and she waited for her answer with the kind of wary stillness you see in people who have lived through wars. She looked as if she expected to be hurt. If he involved her in this she probably would be hurt. There was some quality in her that invited trust. He needed to trust someone and she was right here in front of him. Maybe she could see a pattern here that he wasn't seeing. And in a way she was already involved. Maybe none of these reasons was really persuasive, but in the end that was how he sold it to himself. He started with Krugman and the St Regis Hotel.

Iligan City

Someone was speaking to Cole, leaning in very close. Cole looked away from the dead German's face and saw that a large man in a flowered shirt that was spotted with blood and dust had taken a knee beside him. The man looked familiar but Cole was having a hard time placing him. The man was saying a name and from the look on his hard ravaged face he was either extremely angry or extremely unhappy. The man spoke again, and although the sound was coming in through a kind of dense sonic veil made of white noise and crackling sparks Cole recognized his own name.

'Cole. It's Pike. Can you hear me?'

Cole rummaged around in the back of his mind and came up with the part of it that controlled his voice.

'Yes. I can hear you.'

The big man turned around and looked at four other men who were standing in the crowded hallway staring down at him, a narrow-hipped, big-shouldered black man with sad eyes; a second man, whipcord-lean with bleached-blond hair that hung down to his shoulders. The third man he knew vaguely . . . it was Ramiro Vasquez, of course. Not dead. Not a ghost. And a fourth man, a short iron-bound barrel of a man with skinny legs and arms so thickly muscled he had to carry them away from his torso. He was wearing a light tan two-button business suit over a deep blue shirt unbuttoned at the neck. His round rough face was weathered and needed to be shaved twice a day. His small round eyes were flat and cold. When Cole looked at him, blinking away the haze, the man's face hardened up like a lake freezing over. He stepped forward and knelt down beside Cole and Pike.

'Cole,' said Dean Krause, speaking softly. 'It's Dean.'

Cole blinked at him a couple of times. Yes. He knew him, Dean Krause – the only member of the unit recruited from the Navy, an ex-SEAL, therefore quite nuts. Terrible singing voice and a lousy driver. But a great trauma medic.

'Dean. Just when I really needed a seamstress.'

'He's out of it,' said Pike.

'He's in there,' said Krause. 'He's been drugged.'

'You're the medic, Dean,' said Vasquez. 'They broke us up when we got to triage. He says that's his ear in the box.'

Krause nodded once and turned back to Cole, reached out and gently lifted one of his lids. Cole let him.

'He's completely whacked,' said Krause, straightening up. 'He's got a skinful of meds. Look at his arm. They've shot him up with Demerol or maybe even morphine.'

Pike stayed next to Cole. He was looking at the bandage around his head. He reached out to touch it and Cole jerked away sharply.

'Leave it,' he said. 'Pike, where's Jesus Rizal?'

'I was thinking about that. We looked for him at the Blue Bird.'

'I think he set us up.'

'Set you up?' asked Burdette. 'How?'

'He knew enough to be on his way out of the bar when the place went up,' said Vasquez.

'How did you two get out?'

'Cole didn't like Jesus. We went outside to talk about getting him off the mission. We were across the street when Cole saw this little Moro guy on a motor scooter coming up Aguinaldo Street with a case of beer on the bars and his whole family up behind him. Guy drives the scooter right into the bar. Cole was halfway across the street when I got to him. I'm not real clear on the rest.'

'How are you?' asked Krause. Vasquez shrugged, touched the bandages on the side of his neck gently.

'I'm okay. Got a piece of shrapnel in the throat, missed my carotid by a millimeter. Nurse cut it out. Stings a bit. Also I'm pretty stiff from the concussion. I'm okay. I'm good to go.'

'You think Rizal did this?'

Vasquez looked uncertain. 'I think it's possible. Have you heard from him?'

'No. We cleared all our gear out of the hotel. There was no message from him. It could be he died in the explosion.'

Cole sat upright and shook his head a couple of times.

'If he turns up dead, then I'm wrong. If he turns up alive, we kill him. There's also a fat little guy in a Hawaiian shirt . . . ?'

Vasquez nodded.

'Yeah. His name was Butan Sabang. Rizal knew him. He was all over us and he left just before the explosion.'

'We can deal with this later,' said Pike. 'Can you walk?'

'We can't move him,' said Vasquez.

'This ship is packed with German MPs, Ramiro.

They're going down the levels checking everyone's ID. We can't leave him here.'

'Christ,' said Strackbein. 'We have to. Look at him.'

'Dean's right,' said Pike. 'As soon as the dust clears, the MPs and their Intelligence guys will go through this town street by street and room by room. We're gonna have to explain ourselves and we can't. He's coming with us.'

There was nothing to say to that. Pike stood up and took Cole by the arm. Cole pulled away.

'My ear. I need my ear.'

Pike took the small Styrofoam package from Cole's hands and opened it up. A bloody human ear lay on a small mound of melting ice. A little silver ring that pierced the lobe sparkled through the blood. Pink water sloshed around in the ice. Krause looked at the ear and then reached out and touched the bandage around Cole's head. Cole pulled away, raising an arm as if to ward off a blow. Vasquez and Strackbein turned away and walked a few paces down the hall. At the far end a small knot of uniformed men was working its way through the crowds, talking to everyone. He tapped Pike on the shoulder and Pike gave the German soldiers a hard look. Krause said something to reassure Cole and managed to lift up the bandage a few inches. A red mass of tissue and clotted blood showed in the cold hospital light. Krause leaned down and studied it carefully and then stood up again.

'Let me see the ear,' he said.

Pike handed him the box. Krause studied it.

'That's an ear, okay. It's just not his.'

'How do you know?' asked Burdette.

'He's already got two,' said Krause. 'That's all they give you on this planet. Cole, stand up. Cole!'

Cole staggered to his feet, half-pulled by Pike. Krause

called Strackbein over and handed him the Styrofoam box.

'Do something about the MPs. Give us some time.'

He and Vasquez and Pike began to frog-walk Cole up the hall away from the MPs. Strackbein looked at the ear and then at Chris Burdette. Three massive German MPs were walking towards them.

'Now what do we do?'

Burdette shrugged his shoulders.

'We could try flirting with them.'

Strackbein considered the three oncoming bruisers.

'Okay. You go first.'

Gideon

Four of his workers had stayed home from work this morning, three to bury a family member and one because he was dead. All killed at the Blue Bird. Or so they were claiming. Gideon would make sure they showed him valid death certificates to prove it or he would dock their pay. These mongrels were as lazy as Sikhs and nowhere near as honest. He had stayed in his office since he arrived at work this morning, trying to buffer his aching head from the howling of the turbines out in the generation hall. He was suffering terribly, and the absence of these workers had made his hangover even worse. Not that they cared about other people. They were selfish and low and working in Mindanao was a living hell. If it were not for his association with people of gravity he would have left this terrible island long ago and gone home to Indonesia, where his mother still lived. Now that his father was dead she would take him back if he wanted it; she had never judged him. True, there was the problem of his brothers. They were still at home running the family's computer service business, and they did not love Gideon the way his mother did. Perhaps the men with whom Gideon was now associated would help him with the problem of his

163

brothers. He leaned back in his chair and considered the bottle of Stolichnaya vodka that was locked away in the middle drawer of his big wooden desk.

His head was full of a dull, pounding stupidity, and his thoughts were as disconnected and random as his actions this morning. He had given the matter of the whereabouts of Jordan Kemp some disorderly attention, but he had made no progress. This worried him since he knew that in a little while Mr Gabriel would call him, and he *must* have something to show him. Mr Gabriel had made plain a palpable threat. He had sent his contact in Toronto an encrypted message, but it was night again there and the contact – whoever he was – never reported until morning had come back to North America.

North America. Gideon had never been there, although he had seen many American movies. His video collection was the envy of ... well, he had not made many friends here in Mindanao but he had once invited some of his more intelligent co-workers over to his flat to watch *Lawrence of Arabia,* and the one young boy who had finally shown up had been very impressed by Gideon's wonderful equipment.

Unfortunately some thief had stolen all of it three days later, and the boy never came back again. Still, before his DVD player had been stolen, and his big flat-screen television, Gideon had spent many hours listening to the way the English talked in movies like *Pride and Prejudice* and *Lawrence of Arabia.* He was especially fond of Peter O'Toole, and he was reasonably proud of the English accent he had acquired from the film. He also admired the way Peter O'Toole had become a great man in the middle of a squalid little foreign country by involving himself in great deeds, deeds of gravity and importance, out of

164

which a new world order would arise. These daydreams of a new world order brought him around again to the problem of Mr Gabriel and his impending call.

He looked at the telephone on his desk and then at the big computer that rested on a sideboard next to the desk. This computer was connected to the Lanao del Norte Power Corporation mainframe in Cotabato City, and from there broadband connections could be made through the Internet. Even voice connections using the computer's speakerphone. He had used this connection only a few times, because the connection was wireless – it traveled by microwave towers across the whole of western Mindanao – and Mr Gabriel had once told him that microwave transmissions were not reliable. Or safe. But there was a way to piggyback on the company's microwave feed, and no one would ever know. It was a secret way that Gideon had discovered when he worked for his father's company, and he had not even told Mr Gabriel about it. He had used it the day before yesterday to help Mr Gabriel – who must have been somewhere very far away by the number of relays involved – talk to a contact up in Cobraville, and nothing bad had happened to anyone.

It must be secure, because Mr Gabriel had most certainly made final plans for the bombing of the Blue Bird, and if anyone had been listening, then the bombing would never have happened. The Americans would certainly have stopped it. The fact that they did nothing *proved* that his method was secure. Mr Gabriel was a serious man, but he was no communications technician. Gideon was, and he knew his trade well. He looked at the big computer again and moved his dry lips across his dry teeth. His eyes were hot, and he felt a wave of sickness come over him again. Medicine was what he needed. A little vodka and some orange juice. If he had any orange juice.

The big computer was like a gateway that led to the whole world. Gideon knew how to travel through that gateway. There was no reason to wait for his contact in Toronto. Anyway Mister Gabriel had made his threat clear. He wanted an answer now. And Gideon would supply it. He could find this Mayo Clinic and ask someone there about Jordan Kemp's relatives. And these newspapers in Toronto. Newspapers stayed open all night long. Someone in one of these places would know Jordan Kemp. It would be necessary to be subtle and skillful. He would use his English accent. He would prove to Mr Gabriel that he was a valuable asset and a man of initiative. He would make the calls. And no vodka until after.

Levi Sloane

The dome of the Congress on the far shore was a
detached, ghostly sphere floating above a low bank of
pink-tinged fog as Drew brought the Escalade around a
long wide curve above the Anacostia River, deep in the
press of afternoon traffic, with Luna's black Crown
Victoria hanging in his rearview mirror fifty feet back, a
position she had held all the way from Beltsville. Beyond
her – six cars farther back – an unmarked navy-blue
Suburban was pulling up fast in the speed lane, radiating
official intent.

Drew's cell phone beeped and he picked it up.

'Drew, this is Luna.'

'Yes, ma'am.'

'You see the navy-blue Suburban just passing me now?'

'I do.'

'Levi Sloane's inside it; he wants you to take the next
exit and pull over in Anacostia Park.'

By this point the navy-blue Suburban had come abreast
of the Escalade and two hard-faced middle-aged white
men in dark-blue suits were staring at Drew through their
mirrored Ray-Bans.

'I see them, Luna. Where do they buy those
mustaches?'

'Eddie Bauer,' she said, laughing.

Luna broke off and Drew – now the middle vehicle in a three-car convoy – followed the Suburban around the exit curve and into the broad riverside park. The Suburban cruised through the parking area and then rode over the curb and down across the grass to an isolated spot right on the riverbanks. Drew parked the Escalade beside the Suburban, and as he climbed down, Luna pulled up a few yards away in the black Crown Victoria. Across the rolling lawn a group of picnickers stared at the gathering of very official-looking vehicles for a while until the two hard-faced men in the suits stared back at them long enough for them to find something much more interesting in the view of the Capitol across the river. The rear door of the Suburban popped open and Levi Sloane – bald-headed and slab-sided, the material of his suit straining to contain all that muscle and bone, with a thick black mustache and a pair of Ray-Bans right out of *Men in Black* – stepped out of the truck, his suit jacket flying open in the wind off the river to reveal a large black semi-auto pistol in a brown leather belt holster. The expression on his face was only a little short of grim, and when he took off his Ray-Bans there was a bleak look in his light brown eyes. He sent Luna a heated cautionary look before turning back to Drew.

'Senator, we need to talk.'

'Here I am.'

Sloane gave Luna another look, and she backed away a few yards with a sardonic smile. The other two men, silent and unsmiling, stood with their arms folded and stared out across the park at anyone who looked like their interest in the gathering might become impolite.

Sloane stepped in close enough for Drew to smell his

cologne – maybe Versace – and spoke in a low but carrying baritone growl that was barely this side of polite.

'You have that item with you, I hope?'

'I do,' said Drew, pulling it out of his pocket. Sloane folded it up without looking at it and slipped it into an inside coat pocket. Some of the tension and aggression left his blunt, forceful face. He even managed a smile, showing a set of uneven but very white teeth that made Drew think of a row of white marble tombstones in Arlington. It was a habit of Sloane's to toy with a large gold service ring he wore on the wedding-ring finger of his left hand, and it caught the light and glittered as they stood there side by side. The incised blue-on-gold crest of the NSA had been worn down by Sloane's nervous habit of rubbing it continually, but it was still legible.

'You handled yourself pretty well last night.'

'No, I didn't. I was pathetic.'

'So far the press has left it alone. You dealing with it?'

'No. Next question.'

'The CIA did a full backgrounder on this Dietrich Voss.'

'And . . . ?'

'No red flags. Graduated with a degree in engineering from Ohio State. Got a job designing computer surveillance systems and ended up with ADT in their system development section. Got bored. Quit. The FBI now thinks he took up B and E's and made a lot of money. He never got caught and he died last night. End of story.'

'I hope so.'

'You don't think so?'

'I think it pushes the envelope of coincidence. Let's leave it to one side for now. You want me to try explaining what went on this afternoon?'

Sloane gave Drew a long detached appraisal. Drew was aware that underneath Sloane's Southern manners there was a hard cold intelligence being focused on what he was about to say.

'If you think you can.'

Drew nodded and told the story of his meeting with Krugman at the Regis, simply and succinctly, withholding nothing factual, but he did keep to himself his underlying sense that Krugman had been trying to send Drew a particular warning, the nature of which had yet to become clear, even to Drew. Sloane listened to the narrative without expression or comment – his face altered only slightly when Drew reached the part where Abraham Olatunji was trying to persuade him that Cole Langan was on a bicycle trip in Thailand – but by the time Drew's story had brought them to the line of trees on the far side of the Alabaster Farm's fence line, no trace of Sloane's unreal smile remained on what was now a flat and openly unfriendly mask. In the silence – the long, considering silence – that followed, Drew held Sloane's look without offering an apology or an excuse.

After a time, Sloane seemed to relax.

'So you had no idea what the hell you were walking into?'

'Not at the time. I'm not a fool. By the response, the location is the site of one of our intelligence assets.'

'I can't confirm that.'

'You don't have to. You're here, aren't you?'

'And tell me again what you thought you'd accomplish by trespassing on that property?'

'I told you. My wife was concerned about Cole. I called the IMF office in New York and a man named Olatunji told me that Cole was in Thailand. But there was a background noise – a chopper – and when I heard the same sound –'

'You can ID various individual choppers by their sound?'

'No. Of course not – it was just a coincidence, but it was enough to make me curious about what was across the field.'

'A hunch? Just simple curiosity?'

'Essentially.'

'And you were at that location because Gunther Krugman wrote down the coordinates on a cigar wrapper?'

Drew smiled.

'Gunther can be sneaky.'

'Why do you think Krugman did all this?'

'I have no idea. Perhaps he's getting senile.'

'Is that what you think?'

'No. But it may be what I fear.'

'Your interest here is your son, I take it.'

'Without being able to speak to him, I have to admit to an irrational concern. I'd like to be able to reassure his mother.'

'And this Olatunji told you he was in Thailand?'

'Yes. Do you know the man?'

'No. Never heard of him. I can have the IMF office checked out, if you'd like. But I've never come across his name in any security sheet. Do you want me to have him vetted?'

'If he's running the IMF office in New York, I'm sure he's already been vetted by their own people.'

'You still think the IMF office was lying to you?'

Drew had already decided not to tell Sloane about his call to the Lotus Blossom Inn in Thailand, although if his suspicions were based on something more than paranoia, only a few agencies would have the technical resources to redirect his call to a false number. The NSA would have to be at the top of that list.

'I guess it seems highly unlikely.'

'You have no idea where Krugman is now?'

'None at all.'

'I left a message at your place last night.'

'I know. I was going to call you. Then things got a little hectic.'

Sloane glanced over at Luna, who was looking back at him with a certain focused attention, as if waiting for a signal.

'Look, Drew, about Cole, I might be able to get our embassy people in Bangkok to check this out. See if they can find out just where Cole is. If they can, we'll ask Cole to give you a call. How would that be? Would that ease your mind?'

It would sure as hell confirm that you know how to reach him.

'Yes, Levi, it would greatly ease my mind.'

'And you'll stop playing Drew Langan, International Man of Mystery?'

'I'm still concerned about Gunther Krugman's mental health.'

'Not as much as we are. Leave him to us.'

'You'll keep me informed?'

'I promise. And I'll see what we can do about getting you in touch with Cole. Where are you going now?'

'I missed my flight. I guess I'll take this truck to Harrisburg.'

'Alone?'

Drew looked around him.

'Yes. I seem to be a single man now.'

'How about Luna goes with you?'

'Luna? Why? You still think I need protecting?'

'Not anymore. I guess you proved that last night. But I think you could use some backup. How about it?'

Drew smiled.

'You think what I really need is a minder?'

This time Sloane's broad smile was perfectly convincing.

'Oh yes. Oh my yes. You sure as hell do.'

Down Range

The terminus of the Agus River Road
Ten miles southeast of Iligan City
Wednesday, August 20, 7:00 a.m. local time

Jesus Rizal was waiting for them at their jump-off point in the hills on the southeastern edge of Iligan City, standing in a jungle clearing beside a battered jeepney loaded with gear. They had more or less carried Cole through the back alleys and laneways of Iligan City in a nightmarish journey filled with the shrieking of sirens and the thud of heavy choppers pounding through a sky that had gradually changed from star-filled purple to deep green and then to a pale rose shot through with streaks of fire. A sea wind was blowing through the city, and it brought the stink of burned meat and charred wood with it.

During this surreal passage Cole had tried several times to explain his suspicions about Jesus Rizal and the aromatic lounge lizard to Pike and Krause – the two men who were more or less carrying him between them – but they wanted no talk from anyone, and every time he tried to bring it up Krause would tell him to shut up. After a while he had stopped trying and now that they had reached the jump-off point the pain was under control and he was reasonably clear in his mind. When he saw Jesus Rizal standing by the jeepney, Cole broke away from Pike and Krause and went at him with murder in his heart.

Rizal moved quickly backward and away from Cole.

'Stop him. I had nothing to do with it.'

Pike held Cole back while Vasquez came forward to confront Rizal. Rizal had pulled a heavy Browning pistol out of the small of his back and was holding it muzzle down at his side. His face was hard and no visible fear was in it. But it was slightly burned, and his eyebrows were gone. He had treated the burn with some sort of medical gel, and it gave his skin a greasy sheen. He had also changed his clothes and was wearing olive-drab army fatigues and a pair of shiny black jungle boots. Burdette and Strackbein and Krause moved a step to each side of Rizal, and now there were four heavy pistols out.

'Cole says you set us up,' said Vasquez.

Rizal nodded, never taking his eyes off Cole.

'I can understand that. But I did not.'

'Then why are you alive?' said Cole. 'Nobody got out of there. Nobody. Just you and the lounge lizard.'

Confusion flickered across Rizal's face.

'Lounge . . . What does that mean?'

'In that private booth. The chubby guy who came in – he smelled of perfume – shiny hair and his eyes made up. Remember?'

'Yes. I do. Gideon Sabang. One of Diego's relatives.'

'He was dogging us all night. Just before the explosion I saw him running east on Aguinaldo with one of your cousin's busboys. So he's in our booth, then he's outside it, he leaves seconds before the blast with one of your cousin's employees –'

'I know nothing about this. I was at the back. Gideon is a nothing – a fool – he only goes to the bar to pick up boys.'

'Why was he running away just before the explosion?'

'I don't know . . . but we will ask him.'

'You won't be around.'

'My cousin Diego is missing. His body has not been found. If I had known anything about this, would I have let him die? I went to the latrines. The latrines were not working. They had backed up and people were standing around in the filth and the sewage waiting for somebody to come. I could not wait. I have a bad bladder. I went out to the loading dock and pissed off the side. Then I turn and the wall hits my face. See? I am burned here.'

He stepped forward to let them look, and Pike's pistol came up in a blur. Vasquez stepped in and ripped the Browning out of Rizal's hand. Pike shoved the muzzle of the Colt up against Rizal's forehead. Rizal stiffened but stood his ground.

'A very timely piss,' said Ramiro Vasquez.

Rizal shrugged that off.

'Believe me or shoot. I will not beg.'

'Kill him,' said Cole, in a hard flat tone.

'Think for a minute,' said Rizal, fear flickering briefly across his flat face. 'Why would I want to betray you? If I knew about the bombing, why would I be there at all?'

'You were there because I'm your baby-sitter,' said Vasquez. 'You had no choice.'

'Even so if I am a traitor, what is the benefit to me if you and your friend are dead in this explosion?'

'Dead white meat,' said Cole. 'Isn't that what the terrorists want? Stupid white men are always better dead?'

'How about this,' said Krause. 'You knew about the bombing but you figured it wouldn't happen.'

'Why wouldn't it happen?'

'Because you thought we already knew about it and we wouldn't let it happen.'

'How would I know something like that?'

'There's been a lot of sloppy crosstalk coming out of Iligan,' said Cole, thinking about the Critic Flash. 'It might have been coming from someone you know. If you figured the conspiracy was blown, that we were going to stop the bombing, then the best way for you to play it would be to show up and pretend you knew nothing about it. You were sure there was no risk.'

'If that was how I was thinking, I was very wrong, wasn't I? And if you Americans already knew there was a chance that a bomb would go off in Iligan, why didn't you do something to stop it?'

That was a damned good question, and no good answer came immediately to anyone's mind. Everyone there who had read the Critic Flash had recognized that there was an imminent terror threat in Iligan City. And not one of them had done a thing to stop it. Telling yourself that it wasn't part of your mission was cold comfort in the face of so many civilian casualties. If they were engaged in a real War on Terror, stopping a terrible mass murder ought to have come in pretty high on the agenda, certainly higher than repairing an NSA relay monitor, no matter how strategic it was. And maybe Rizal was telling the truth. At Collections it was an operational mantra that the simplest explanation for a man's actions was usually the correct one: Rizal had showed up at the Blue Bird because he had no idea that terrorists were planning to blow it up. If he had, he'd have found some plausible way to get out of the meeting. He survived it because of blind luck, just the way Cole and Vasquez had survived it.

They all stared at him in a hostile silence, but it was clear to Rizal that his question had hit home. At the edge of the clearing a hot wet wind sighed in the heavy jungle, making the thick green canopy toss. Beyond the city the first golden light of the rising sun was lying on a faraway sea that looked like a meadow of summer rye, ruffled and gleaming. The men waited in silence while Rizal stared into the muzzle of Pike's Colt, his eyes wide and his mouth in a hard line. He was breathing through flared nostrils and his chest was pumping, but he was asking for nothing. He was ready to die or not to die. Pike was privately reconsidering the man.

'Fuck it,' said Cole. 'He comes with us.'

A soundless wave went through each man and the group broke up. They loaded what little they had in the battered jeepney – personal baggage, the satellite phone, the laptop, and Earl the plaster Buddha – and climbed in. Strackbein had already collected some basic jungle gear: water purification equipment, insect repellent, atropine, salt tablets, jungle boots, boxes of trail mix, dried beef, and several collapsible bags of fresh water. The men found what room there was and settled in as well as they could. Rizal stood at the side of the truck for a moment with his hand on the door. The men inside the bus waited for him and said nothing.

'If you were going to kill me it would make sense to do it deeper in the jungle. My body would not be found and my people would never know. I am not willing to go to my death like a fool.'

'We're not going to kill you,' said Cole.

'I just do not want to die like a pig.'

'Get in,' said Burdette. 'We're on the clock.'

'Yeah,' said Strackbein from the driver's seat. 'In or out?'

'In, then,' said Rizal, his burned forehead crinkling as a wide fatalistic smile cracked his face. He climbed into the passenger seat up front and pointed at the wall of thick jungle.

'There, between the two banyans – there's a riverbed. When they diverted the Agus for the power plant this channel ran dry. They used it for logging for several years and then forgot about it. My people keep it cleared. The canopy has grown over it, so we will not be seen from the air. It will take us past the power plant, then maybe twenty miles. It ends at the plateau beyond Agus Falls.'

'Then what?' asked Vasquez. Rizal shrugged.

'Then we hump it to Casey,' said Pike.

Cole lay back in the bench seat at the rear of the jeepney as Strackbein gunned the diesel engine and slipped the clutch. The bus jerked forward in a lurching shudder and then accelerated, the engine popping and crackling. He rode it up over a mound of rotting vegetation and broke through a screen of dead bamboo stalks. It was like driving into a tunnel filled with soft green light. The rutted track was mostly pebbles and crushed stone, but it was a reasonably smooth road that rose up in a sharp grade that curved away into the jungle, a road so narrow the hanging vines of banyan and the tangle of undergrowth brushed along the side of the bus as they moved along it. Strackbein pulled the bus a few yards into the narrow track and stopped it. Rizal got out and went back to the opening, where he used some of the broken brush to sweep away the signs of their tracks. Then he pulled the brush closed behind them and got back into the vehicle and they moved out. After three miles of a difficult uphill grind during which the men were too exhausted to speak, they reached a comparatively level stretch. Pike came back to the rear and stood looking down at Cole.

'How you doing?'

Cole touched a hand to the bandage over his right ear.

'You're sure there's an ear under this?'

'Yeah. It's ugly but it's still an ear.'

'Christ,' said Cole, sitting up with some difficulty, 'I remember looking at my face in a hospital mirror and all I could see was a mass of bloody flesh. I'm sure the nurse said my ear was gone.'

'Did she say it in French?'

Cole smiled at that. 'Yeah, I think so.'

'How's your French?'

'Usually pretty good. I guess I heard her wrong.'

'Guess you did. Strackbein says the satellite is almost directly overhead right now. You got a window of maybe twenty minutes. You want to check in with Collections?'

Cole looked at the laptop and the satellite phone.

'Through this canopy?'

'Better here than up-country. There's still a lot of radio activity in the sector around Iligan, so the techs on board the *Suffren* will have a hard time getting our position. You want me to set it up?'

'Yeah,' said Cole, looking forward to the driver's seat. In between Strackbein and Rizal he could see a patch of open track under an arch of deep green foliage mottled with sunlight. Little spears of sunlight came wavering down through the mist and dappled the floor of the track, making it look as if they were underwater. The tough little jeepney was laboring up the gentle grade, now and then spinning a back wheel. Burdette, Vasquez, and Krause were stretched out on a couple of benches, their feet on their packs, sound asleep. The frame creaked with every yard they gained. The roar of the diesel engine filled the interior and made his skull ache. And the heat was building, the steamy deadening heat of the deep jungle.

Pike was bent over by the laptop typing at the keyboard. After a moment the screen filled up with a deep blue light and he handed it to Cole.

Cole typed in his password and opened up the satellite link. Pike went to a window, slid it down, and held the phone out. Cole hit the Bluetooth connection and waited. And waited some more. It took over three minutes for the satellite link to respond, verify their encryption code, and contact the operations base. Eventually the laptop beeped and showed the LINK ESTABLISHED icon. Cole started the exchange by typing in his call sign:

– Six Actual this is Talaria.

The satellite delay, even for a fast-burst encrypted transmission, was still almost thirty seconds. Eventually the answer came back:

– Talaria this is Six Actual. Mission status.

– Mission status optimal.

This time the delay was longer. Cole could see the operator back at Collections turning to Levi Sloane and asking him what he should say. A long pause and then a rapid flow of letters:

– Urgent team leader confirm status re Red Bone. Red Bone has contacted New York office requesting status re explosion in Iligan. Please advise response.

Cole stared at the screen, literally stunned. Red Bone was their codeword for his father, Senator Drew Langan. Why the hell would his father think that Cole had been hurt in Mindanao? As far as his family was concerned, he was on a bike tour in Thailand. They had the IMF cover story in place. Didn't the man know that Thailand and Mindanao were 1,600 miles apart? Why was the interfering son of a bitch screwing around in his –

Well, he wasn't, was he? It would be his mother. Diana

was like that. If there had been an explosion in Seattle while he was in Denver she would call him just to make sure he hadn't been killed by a seal plummeting out of the sky. His father was trying to reassure her. And so far whatever he had heard from his IMF cover wasn't doing it.

— Six Actual compose e-mail and send to Red Bone in my name with specific reference to incident in Iligan.

— negative Talaria voice contact Red Bone indicated.

— negative Six Actual voice contact Red Bone not secure.

— repeat Talaria voice contact Red Bone strongly indicated.

Apparently Sloane didn't think his father was going to take an e-mail as proof of his son's condition. Why was the old man being so cagey? What the hell was going on in his head?

— Six Actual will comply. Contact number?

— contact number 202-434-9955 anytime. Urgent.

— Understood. Permission to use satellite phone?

— Permission granted. Query team leader?

— go ahead Six Actual.

— Red Bone detected immediate location Collections. Crossed security fence and approached perimeter line on foot at 1300 hours EDT August 19. Level one response local police. Diverted at scene. Explain.

The letters were English. He understood what was appearing on his screen in the sense that he recognized each individual letter and he could string the letters into the right words. It was only when he had the words all lined up together in the right order that the top of his skull seemed to come off. His father had found Collections?

First of all, how? And then why? The location of Collections in the heart of the Maryland countryside was one of the CIA's most closely guarded secrets. The entire complex was underground, from the air just another field of wheat. The base was being hardened and they were using a big lift chopper to bring in the ferro-concrete plates, but all the workers were fully vetted Army or CIA contractors. None of them would have given out the location.

Cole knew his father sat on the Intelligence Oversight Committee, but no one at the CIA would give anyone on that committee any information that would lead them to the base either. The committee was made up of elected senators, and history had proven that trusting a house full of senators with a secret was like trusting the O.J. jury with a cowboy boot full of warm piss. It had to be a coincidence. His fingers hovered over the first 'c' in 'coincidence,' but he could not hit the key. In the intelligence world there was no such thing as a coincidence. More letters scrolled across the screen.

– Repeat Talaria explain.

– Six Actual no possible explanation. Location of Farm compromised?

– Location not compromised but containment operation in place. Strongly recommend you break off mission and return base for debrief and investigation of security breach.

Sloane wanted them out of the field. Cole stared at the screen. There was only one hopeful word on it:

'Strongly recommend . . .'

Not 'ordered.'

Sloane was 'recommending' they break off the mission. Sloane had the power to *order* a pull out, and he wasn't using it. Which meant Cole was still the team leader and the call was being left in his hands.

– Talaria to Six Actual permission to charley mike.

– Six Actual to Talaria . . . wait one.

Cole sat back and stared at the pulsating blue screen. Now that Pakistan and Afghanistan were stabilizing, Southeast Asia was on its way to becoming a rallying point for terrorist operations. America needed that relay in working order, and if Cole pulled out they'd just have to mount another covert insertion next month, by that time into a sector on full alert for exactly that kind of action.

Another factor he had to consider: If he broke off and went home, it was probable that Sloane would never trust him with another mission. But if he stayed in-country and did the job, he'd be exonerated by his success. He looked at the other men in the jeepney. They had a say in this, and he would have to clear it with them. But first he had to get permission to stay. If the unit voted him down later, that was it. They'd go home. Two minutes were swept off the face of his Hamilton before the answer came back:

– Continue mission. Consider therapy.

He smiled at that. Sloane still had a sense of humor, anyway.

The screen flickered, and Pike turned in the window.

'You about done? The signal's getting intermittent.'

– Six Actual under circumstances do you still recommend direct voice contact between team leader and Red Bone?

– Talaria voice still contact strongly recommended.

They were asking him to call his own father, an unencrypted voice contact with him, a live call. It was crazy, operationally nuts.

'You got maybe four minutes, Cole,' said Pike.

– Heard and understood. Talaria breaking off.

– Roger Talaria. Status active.

The screen went blank as the data link was broken.

Cole closed the laptop, sat back on the bench, and stared out the side window at the crushing wall of green jungle that hemmed them in. The vines were sliding along the dripping window like snakes gliding over the glass, and the sound of them against the tin walls of the jeepney was very much like a nest of cobras hissing. It was a fever-dream image and it told him that there was still a lot of medication running through his veins. Pike sat down opposite him and leaned in.

'Trouble, sir?' he said in a level whisper.

'Oh yeah.'

'What kind?'

'Big kind. They want us to break off the mission.'

Pike's reaction was muted but intense.

'Break off? The fuck why?'

Cole looked at Pike for a few seconds, thinking about their long and uneven association. Then he told him what he had been told by Six Actual. Pike took it all in with nothing showing on his face. When Cole finished, Pike put his hands on his face and rubbed his cheeks slowly.

'If I get this right, Sloane wants you to make a real-time, unscrambled voice call to your father? In the field on a covert op?'

'Yes. That's right.'

'Sir, it could be they're testing you. If you warn him off they'll know something about you they didn't know before.'

'Yeah. That occurred to me.'

'This is the way Sloane wants to play it?'

'Looks like it.'

'Fucking rear-echelon officers. No offense, sir.'

'None taken.'

'Okay with you I run this by the rest of the guys?'

'What? The call?'

'No. That's your business. Whether we stay or pull out.'

'I wouldn't have it any other way.'

Pike nodded and then fell silent for a moment, staring down at the satellite phone in his hand. He held it up and squinted at the signal strength indicator.

'Whatever you gonna do about your father, you got maybe two minutes to do it.'

'No suggestions?'

'Burden of command, sir.'

'You're not afraid I'll say something stupid?'

'No, sir,' said Pike. 'I'm not.'

'Okay,' said Cole. 'Go talk to the guys. Give me the phone.'

Harrisburg

Northbound Interstate 83
Thirty miles south of Harrisburg, Pennsylvania
Tuesday, August 19, 8:30 p.m. local time

They were running northbound through the low dark hills
and the brooding scrublands that lined the Susquehanna
all the way upriver to Harrisburg. It was a hardscrabble
landscape of grimy mill towns and rotting wood-frame
houses separated by miles of empty strip malls and ruined
factories, but it was still Pennsylvania, and the homecoming feeling was strong in him as Drew pushed the
Cadillac up the interstate and listened to Luna Olvidado's
slow steady breathing beside him. The fading sideways
light lay on her sleeping face giving it an amber-tinted glow
that looked as if it came from inside the woman, and
the delicate lashes over her closed eyes stood out like fine
golden threads. All the wary hardness that was in her face
when she was awake softened while she slept. Unless her
life changed, the time would come when that hardness
would have taken such a hold in her that only one kind
of sleep would ever erase it. He looked away from her
and watched the oncoming black hills of the Second
Mountains, their oddly conical crests touched with fire
and the purple darkness pooling in the hollows of the
foothills.

In 1948, his father, Henry Langan, newly rich on

wartime steel, had built a massive Romanesque mansion made of red Pennsylvania sandstone on a high plateau overlooking the Susquehanna Valley and the city of Harrisburg. Right about now his father would be sitting in a deck chair on the colonnaded veranda that ran right across the front of the house, a prospect that gave him a fine view of the State Capitol along the river and the wide flat curve of the muddy fast-running Susquehanna.

He'd be watching the light change on the river and savoring a glass of Domecq sherry. One of his nurses would be next to him – they were usually young and pretty, with reflexes fast enough to keep the old man's hands out of their skirts and the flinty sense of humor required not to resent it – possibly reading aloud from the *Harrisburg Times*. Drew and Luna would be there by eight-thirty. What he was going to ask of his father was something he hadn't quite worked out yet. He was turning it over in his mind when his cell phone began to beep. He pulled it out of his suit pocket, not fast enough to stop the ringing from waking Luna. She straightened up in the seat and blinked at the landscape around them while Drew looked at the call display:

Out of area

'Langan.'

'Dad – it's Cole.'

The sound of his son's voice went through him like a warm wave, and the landscape blurred for a moment.

'Cole! Where are you? How are you? Are you okay?'

He could feel Luna's electric attention. She looked at him and then away. The connection was awful, full of rushing noise and static and the muttering pop of some kind of motor.

'I'm great. Having a good time in Thailand. They said

you were trying to reach me. What's the matter? Is Mom okay? Is it grandpa?'

'She's fine, Cole. So is the old man. Your mother was worried. I told her I'd call you. I've had some trouble getting in touch with you.'

The answer was delayed, and when Cole talked there was an echo following it that made his voice sound hollow and remote.

'I'm fine. Really. Why the calls? Why was she worried?'

'There was a bombing in the Philippines.'

Cole's laugh sounded tinny and harsh, like a crow's call.

'Jesus, Dad, the Philippines are sixteen hundred miles away. Can you still hear me? You there? The line sucks.'

'I can hear you. I'll tell her. Are you on your cell?'

'Yeah. The coverage here is lousy. Where are you?'

'Harrisburg. Going to stay with your grandfather for the recess. I hear an engine in the background. Where are you?'

'I'm on a bus. We're on our way to Bangkok.'

'When are you coming home?'

'Maybe a week. Look, Dad, I gotta go. The signal's fading.'

'I called the IMF in New York. What's the matter with those people? They gave me some phony number in Phuket –'

'Can't hear you. Signal's gone. Gotta go. I'll call you!'

'Cole –'

He was gone. Drew shut the phone off and looked at Luna. All the hardness was back in her face. In the slanting sunset light her eyes were a brooding dark green and hooded by deep shadows.

'That was Cole,' he said.

'I gathered. How is he?'

'He's fine. Sounded fine.'

'Good. That's wonderful.'

'Yes. Yes it is. I ought to call his mother.'

'Where is she?'

'In Paris. What time is it in Paris?'

Luna looked at her watch.

'I'm not sure. I think around three. Would she be in bed?'

In bed, yes. Alone was another question.

'I'll call her in the morning.'

Luna put her head back and watched the sun going down with half-closed eyes. Her voice, when she spoke, was tentative.

'So now what?'

Drew looked at her while he thought about his answer. She was wearing a tight black tee and dark-green pleated silk slacks the same shade as her eyes. She had on a pair of delicate black leather beach sandals, and a small black leather overnight bag was lying on the rear seat where she had thrown it when he picked her up at her flat in Crystal City. She looked wonderful, as if she had made a concerted effort to please him. A warm thought until he remembered that she was a federal agent who was reporting directly to Levi Sloane and that was the only reason she was in the car. Perhaps she was now thinking that Cole's phone call had altered that situation. Perhaps it had.

The relief that had come with it was rolling through him now, and the cold iron band that had been tightening around his chest had relaxed slightly. She could see the change in him and she smiled at that, an open-hearted smile that put creases around her eyes and two small moon-shaped crescents in the smooth, tanned skin on either side of her fine, rather delicate mouth.

'You look years younger.'

'Thanks. I feel it.'

She looked at her hands and then out at the highway.

'So you want to let it all drop?'

'You mean where Krugman went?'

'Yes. Wherever Krugman is and whatever he's up to, that's now Levi Sloane's problem. He's welcome to it. So what will you do?'

Drew was quiet for almost a mile. The traffic was building as they rolled into the suburbs of Harrisburg, and soon they were in a traffic jam on the approach to the main bridge over the broad, flat river. A golden light lay on the surface and reflections played on the face of the old Capitol building on the eastern bank. Luna waited him out in silence and with what seemed to Drew like a growing tautness in her body, as if she were braced for something.

'What would you do? In my place?'

'You have a home here in Harrisburg?'

'Not anymore. It's Diana's now. I mean, it's still technically where I live. But everything that was mine is in storage.'

'Where were you planning to stay tonight?'

'With my father.'

'Then my advice would be to go stay with your father and in the morning go fishing. Or hunting. Whatever it is wealthy senators do during the August recess. Forget about Gunther Krugman. He'll turn up or he won't. Let Levi Sloane worry about him. Walk away.'

'I can't.'

She made a hard slicing motion with her left hand.

'For Christ's sake, Drew. You're a US senator. Think about that. You have a career to consider. You're already on the list of –'

'The list of what?'

'The list of people who are pissing off the President.'

'I'm in the Los Angeles phone book?'

'You've heard from Cole. You know he's safe. So that's the end of it. You promised that to Sloane. You told him that you'd let him take care of Krugman. I heard you saying it.'

The traffic at the bridge picked up, and now they were rolling across the old steel structure. Langan family steel was in this bridge, and more of it was holding up the pylons along the Capitol grounds. Drew had an image of Gunther Krugman's fingers, the crushed and mutilated tips, the hard knots of his joints bent and twisted, and his father's cold silence when Drew asked what had happened.

'When I got to Washington, Krugman helped me in a hundred ways. He saw every trap coming. He made my career possible. When Cole wanted to join the Army, Krugman smoothed the way for him. Don't you think I owe the guy something?'

'You owe yourself something too. You think you don't have real enemies in D.C.?'

'What enemies are we talking about?'

'You think the agency spooks, the upper-echelon guys who got nailed by your Nine-Eleven committee aren't looking for payback?'

'What kind of payback?'

'I don't know,' she said. 'Maybe this kind.'

Dahlia Street

Lanao del Norte Power Authority
Maria Christina Falls Generating Station
Wednesday, August 20, 7:00 a.m. local time

Gideon made his first call at seven in the morning, using an Internet phone line rerouted through Oslo with a cutout in Hamburg and a masked server. The connection was broadband and he had buried it inside their digital microwave transmission the same way he had done it for Mr Gabriel yesterday. He felt confident and competent and just maybe a little fearful. He figured it was around eight in the evening in Toronto, Canada. Yesterday evening, a strange disorienting concept. The line rang four times and then it was picked up and a flat voice answered in a too-busy-for-this-crap kind of tone.

'*National Post.* Editorial.'

Gideon had been practicing his Peter O'Toole accent for several minutes while he stared out through the windows of his office at the huge glass wall of the turbine floor. He knew that Canada was a British country and they would have English accents. The walls were heavily misted by spray from the falls, and sunlight falling across the mist made it look as if the glass walls were coated in fine snow crystals. He had also taken a little bit of vodka to settle his nerves.

But only a little.

'Good evening. Jordan Kemp, please?'

'Who?'

'He's one of your reporters. Jordan Kemp?'

'Who's this?'

'My name is Holloway. I'm with Revenue Canada. Mr Kemp has a refund credit outstanding and we're trying to clear it from our computers. May I speak to him?'

'You say you're from Revenue Canada?'

'Yes. Clement Holloway's the name.'

'Bullshit.'

'Bullshit?'

'Bullshit. Revenue Canada's not called that anymore. It's Canada Customs and Revenue. Who the fuck is this?'

Gideon kept his equilibrium.

'You're right. I keep forgetting.'

'I wish we could. Anyway, there's no Jordan Kemp here. What are you, some kind of Goddamned bill collector?'

'Do you know how I could find him?'

'This is the second time one of you guys phoned asking for Jordan Kemp. I hate bill collectors more than I hate tax collectors. If I knew where he was, I wouldn't tell you. Who'd you say you were?'

'I'm only trying to find Mr Kemp.'

'Yeah? Well, I'm only hanging up on your lying ass.'

And the line went dead. Gideon stared at the screen and found that he was shaking just a little. What a rude set of bumpkins. Canada must be the motherland of louts. He would have to do better than that. He tapped out the numbers of the other Toronto paper, the *Morning Star*. The line rang and this time he got a young woman with the same flat adenoidal tone. He noticed that she did not have an English accent either. Canadians talked more like Americans, only their voices were pitched higher, and through the nose instead of the chest. He had not prepared a Canadian accent but he tried to soften his Peter O'Toole.

'*Morning Star.* Editorial.'

'Good evening. Can you connect me with Jordan Kemp?'

'Kemp? I don't think he works here anymore.'

Gideon listened as the young woman turned away from the phone and called out to someone who must have been on the far side of the country and got some echoing reply. She came back on.

'If you mean Jordan Kemp, he's a freelancer. Hasn't been around for a while. I think he's off sick or something. What?'

Someone was calling to her. Gideon heard Kemp's name.

'Okay . . . yeah. Look, who is this?'

'Holloway. Sterling Holloway.'

'Give me a break. Sterling Holloway's dead. Who is this? Is that you, Tony? What's with the Paki accent?'

'I'm with Canada Customs and Revenue. I assure you I'm not dead. Do you know how I can reach Mr Kemp?'

'You're working late. I thought all you government hamsters got put back in your cages at five.'

'Hamsters?'

'Look, sorry. Why do you want to talk to him?'

'Mr Kemp has a credit account and I'm trying to clear it. We've lost track of him.'

'A credit account? You mean RevCan is trying to give somebody some money back? That's a first.'

'Yes. I suppose it is.'

Gideon saw that he was going to have to come up with

a better cover story. Pretending to be a tax collector wasn't the best way to open doors in other people's hearts. But the woman's tone had changed.

'Hold on. One of the guys here used to work with him. I'll put you through to his desk.'

The line clicked and Gideon found himself listening to a recording of some young woman promising that her heart would go on. She had an amazing ability to hold on to a note and stretch it out very thin and then bang on it with something tinny. Gideon found himself hoping that her heart would not go on much longer. Then the song cut off abruptly and a harsh male voice was barking at him.

'Who's this?'

'Holloway. I'm with Canada Customs.'

'You're looking for Jordan Kemp?'

'Yes, I'm –'

'Well, I'm here to tell you that if you're trying to get some cash out of that guy you better bring a bench vise. He hasn't got a dime. Never did. Spent it as fast as it came in. And the poor bastard's dying. Why don't you leave him alone and go pick on somebody else.'

'But I'm not after money. He has a refund coming.'

'A refund? I didn't think he'd ever file a return. You guys are the Antichrist as far as he's concerned.'

'Do you know how we can reach him?'

'Last I heard Jordan was in chemo.'

'Chemo? Where is that?'

'Where is what?'

'Chemo?'

'It's a cancer cure. Who the hell is this again?'

'I'm sorry. We have a bad connection.'

'Yeah. You sound like you're on Pluto. Jordan got

196

prostate cancer. I figure he got it from the depleted uranium when he was covering the Iraq war. Dumb bastard was always sucking up to the American military. Look where it got him. I know he went to the Mayo Clinic and then I lost touch with him. We sent what was in his desk to a relative. You could try her. I got the address somewhere . . . Wait . . . Yeah . . . What we had we sent to a Laura Kennedy . . . Three six four Dahlia Street Northwest, Washington, D.C. . . . The zip is two zero zero one two . . . Got that? There's no number.'

'Yes. I have that. Thank you so much.'

'Yeah. Look, if you really do have some money for him, get it to him fast, okay. Last I heard he was in a bad way. Have a good one.'

Gideon was about to say thank you but the man was gone. A sudden people, obviously. Back in Jakarta it would have taken a four-hour conversation and two pots of tea to get halfway to the point. Gideon leaned back and looked at the address he had scrawled on his desk blotter. A feeling of expansive warmth blossomed in his belly and flowed upward into his chest and throat. He had found out what Mr Gabriel wanted to know without having to use this – what Mr Gabriel called an asset – in Canada. But he could do even better. He logged onto a website that showed him a selection of international telephone directories and clicked on Washington, D.C. Then he asked for a private listing under the name of Laura Kennedy. After a few seconds the answer came back: UNLISTED.

A small setback. But the program also allowed you to type in an address and it would search for a phone number connected to that address. He typed in 364 Dahlia Street, N.W., Washington, D.C. 20012 USA, and hit the search button. In a moment he had the answer, and he stared at it awhile trying to decide if it was good news:

WALTER REED ARMY MEDICAL CENTER

An Army hospital? Why would a Canadian freelance writer be staying in a US Army hospital? He searched for a phone number for Walter Reed and got 202-782-3501. He decided that this investigation was going well. It was a pleasure to excel at something, after so many disappointing years. An image formed in his mind, a falcon soaring above a field of crawling prey, circling and wheeling and coming closer and closer to his victim. He typed in the number and waited while his call went through. After a moment it rang and a silky-smooth female voice answered it on two.

'Walter Reed.'

'Good evening. I'm looking for a patient there?'

'Certainly. I'll transfer you to Registration. One moment.'

The line buzzed and another voice answered. These voices were very different from the Canadian voices, softer and more languid. He thought he would try a Canadian voice on this woman.

'Hello. I'm calling about a patient? His name is Kemp. Jordan Kemp. Can you tell me how he's doing?'

'What did you say the name was?'

'Kemp, ma'am. Jordan Kemp.'

'Just a moment.'

The line clicked a couple of times. He waited to see if the woman whose heart could go on was still going on here but all he got was some kind of atonal hum followed by a few harsh clicks. Then a man came on, another very deep voice, this time buttery and creamy.

'Hello, you're asking about Mr Kemp?'

'Yes, sir.'

'And you, sir, you would be . . . ?'

'Holloway. Sterling Holloway.'

'You're a relation, are you?'

'No, sir. I'm with Revenue Customs and Canada. We're trying to get in touch with Mister Kemp.'

'I see. Concerning what, sir?'

'We have a refund for him. He paid too much tax and we want to send him a refund.'

'What agency did you say you were with?'

'Canada Revenue and Customs.'

'Okay . . . Can you hold the line, Mister Holloway? This will take a few minutes.'

'Certainly.'

Hold the line. Gideon was the kind of man who would always hold the line. Men of importance and gravity always held the line, and Gideon was beginning to believe that he was a such a man.

In the event, he held the line for quite a while, and this time they did play music, Ravel's 'Bolero.' It was a piece of music he liked, and it helped to pass the time. Gideon did fidget a bit and around the fifteen-minute mark he poured a small splash of vodka into his coffee cup and sipped it delicately through pursed lips. At the sixteen-minute mark one of the Filipinos came in to ask for permission to discuss the fact that his paycheck was going to be docked for missing work because he had to bury what could be found of his wife, recently shredded at the Blue Bird, but Gideon gave him a black look and whisked him away with a gesture. He was still holding the line when the man with the buttery voice finally came back after a wait of – Gideon marked this down on his blotter because he intended to say something sharp to the man about the time he had been required to wait – seventeen minutes and thirty-eight seconds by the Casio with the red LED display on his left wrist.

'Mr Holloway?'

'Yes.'

'I'm sorry to keep you waiting. Mr Kemp was released from the hospital last week.'

'I see. Can you tell me where he is now?'

'As far as I understand it, he was going to the Far East.'

'Really?'

'Yes, sir. Mr Kemp is a writer. I think he was going to do some travel piece for a Canadian newspaper.'

'Oh ... well ... Do you have a number for him in ... wherever he is? We'd still like to reach him.'

'Sorry, sir. No idea. You have a great evening. Best of luck.'

Again a dead line. Did no one in the Americas ever say good-bye or goodnight? Just hang up the phone like thugs? Gideon was still regarding his screen and thinking unkind thoughts about the rudeness of Americans and Canadians when the black rotary phone on his desk began to buzz. He picked it up and heard the voice he expected. He said the secret things and then went out onto the turbine floor and down the clanking metal stairs again to the steel door marked:

ENGINEERING / NO ADMITTANCE

He stood in the narrow, cryptlike room surrounded by spinning dials and grinding gears and humming wheels and considered what he was going to say as he dialed the cell-phone number and waited for Mr Gabriel to answer. He felt odd, uncertain, a little deflated, as if he had made some sort of mistake or error, but he could not have said exactly what it was. Well, no matter. He had the information. If it was confusing, that was not his problem. He had done his work.

Camp Hill, Pennsylvania

Blue Mountain House
Camp Hill, Pennsylvania
Tuesday, August 19, 8:30 p.m. local time

Luna was still sitting beside him, maintaining her brooding silence, when Drew pulled the Cadillac up under the broad sandstone portico of his father's house and killed the engine. A warm yellow light came out through the cut-glass and wrought-iron doors of the mansion and dappled the flagstone driveway. The evening air smelled of freshly cut grass and the sharper tang of the cedars that lined the eastern edge of the lawn. The estate rolled rhythmically away to the edge of the overlook, a broad, rolling field of well-tended grass tinted purple violet by the evening light. Beyond the overlook the city of Harrisburg glimmered in the blue shadows cast by the mountains. Up here on the plateau the hum and clamor of riverside traffic and the steady rushing hiss of the fast-moving Susquehanna was only a gentle murmur in the distance. A breeze sighed through the oaks and cottonwoods that sheltered the big stone house, their leaves fluttering with a silvery light. Drew had grown up in this substantial old house. Its roots ran deep into the rocky ground of central Pennsylvania and the homecoming feeling was strong, oddly comforting. He looked over at Luna and offered a peacemaker's smile. After a moment of resistance, she softened and smiled back at him, the warm light from the doors lying on her right cheek and her hair.

'So this is home?'

'It is. For now, at any rate.'

'Very impressive.'

'Thanks. Are we still talking?'

She looked away at the entrance glass and then back at him.

'What are we looking for here?'

'As I said. My father and Gunther Krugman are very old friends. I'm going to ask my father for some advice. That's all.'

'How are you going to explain me?'

'Explain you? I'll tell him the truth.'

'Yes? And what's the truth?'

'You're my protection detail. It's the truth, isn't it?'

'Mostly. What about the B and E at your place?'

'I'd rather not say anything about that. Dad's an old man.'

A shadow moved behind the glass doors and a sudden shaft of bright light lit the interior of the truck. Drew looked up and saw his father's black silhouette framed in the open doorway. He popped the door, got out, and opened Luna's door for her. She slipped out and followed him up the broad, flat stone stairs, looking tentative, even nervous. His father came out onto the landing and stood under the portico lamp, his face shadowed and a soft light on his shoulders.

Luna saw a frail but clear-eyed elderly man who had once been very strong; not a tall man, but standing straight, with his shoulders back, and a flat belly. He was wearing charcoal-gray pleated slacks and a pale blue shirt, polished black slippers. An attractive young brown-haired woman who managed to look both sunny and sensible in a pair of blue jeans and a red plaid shirt open at the neck was watching them from the hallway, a slight smile on her face, obviously staying out of the way.

'Drew, welcome home,' said Henry Langan, his voice still strong and deep, with only a bit of a quaver in it. Drew came up the stairs and hugged the old man hard, feeling the dry bones in him where solid plates of muscle used to be, smelling the lime-scented bay rum the old man always wore. The earthy smell of a Cuban cigar hung about him, and there was sherry on his breath. His father stepped back and looked at Drew in the lamplight, his weathered face lined and his deep-set gray eyes bright.

Drew saw his son, Cole, in the old man's face, the same bumpy, uneven bones and the hard jaw and the uncompromising mouth that was capable of such a warm open-hearted smile. As he always had, Henry Langan saw his long-dead wife in Drew's fine-boned face, and felt the deep dull pain of that loss again the way hard old men who have grown sentimental with their years sometimes do.

'Damn, son, you look like hell. And who's this?'

Drew turned as Luna came up. Before he could introduce her she smiled carefully at the old man and offered her hand.

'I'm Luna Olvidado, sir. It's a pleasure.'

His father's angular face softened as he studied her in the light, and he shot Drew a short, sharp sidelong look of appraisal and amusement. His father, although no fool for a flirt or a huntress, admired certain kinds of women openly. He took her arm and floated them both gracefully into the house on a river of compliments, introduced them to Andrea Collier, the auburn-haired young woman in the background, who gave them a brief but incandescent smile and disappeared up the stone staircase that led to a colonnaded landing.

Henry Langan – still talking amiably and with particular attention to Luna – walked them through the round central hall lined with carved wooden panels and on into a large, low-ceilinged, and stone-floored room where three large and heavily padded emerald-green leather sofas were arranged on a faded Persian carpet in front of a complicated stone fireplace. It was a Frank Lloyd Wright kind of room, with a beamed wooden roof, lit with mission-style stained-glass lamps and filled with a soft, warm light the color of a whiskey and soda. It was a warm-hearted and intelligent room, filled with the calm that a quiet mind can bring; Luna liked the old man for it.

Drew's father spent a few moments at a long mahogany buffet and then brought over a silver tray with three heavy crystal glasses of pale gold scotch over ice. They shared a ceremonial toast to Drew's return, and then a young Asian man, who was introduced to them as Cornel, came in with a tray full of small roast-beef sandwiches. He set the tray down on a low mahogany table in front of Luna and left the room. Luna sat in silence and listened while the two men talked quietly and softly about unimportant things – family concerns – for a few moments. Her attention drifted – she was suddenly very tired. She became aware of silence and then Drew was touching her hand. She blinked at him.

'Luna, would you like to turn in?'

Both men were watching her, Drew with concern and his father with an amused, even a cynical, smile.

'No. Not at all. I'm sorry. I was wandering.'

'We are boring this poor woman,' said the old man.

There was a note in his voice that had not been there before; some element in it – perhaps of coldness – put her on guard. The old man now had an air of watchful expectancy, and the tenor of the room had altered. He lifted his glass, sipped it, and set it down on the table in front of him in a way that seemed conclusive, as if a small but important ritual had just come to an end and another one was about to begin. He leaned back in the sofa and regarded them both with a somber face and a cold light in his gray eyes.

'I think you two have come here with a story. Perhaps now is the time to tell it.'

Luna and Drew exchanged a look that brought a thin smile to the old man's pale face. Drew set his drink down, took a moment to gather himself, and laid it all out for his father, the same way he had laid it out for Luna that afternoon. Henry Langan was a gifted listener and heard the story through with only a brief question now and then to draw out a detail that he felt he had not adequately understood. The process took about fifteen minutes, and at the end of it Henry's expression was stony. Luna recalled that Drew's father had been a military intelligence officer in the war. That man was in the room now. He leaned forward and lifted the watery scotch but did not drink. He sat with his head down and studied the ice in the glass.

'Drew, you're a damned fool.'

Drew said nothing in reply, since there wasn't much to say.

'I don't hold with your views. You know it. But in your own dim, well-meaning way you do act as a restraint on some of the pushier hawks in D.C. Your influence depends upon your probity. You convey the impression of a man who can be trusted with secrets. And you threw all of that away this afternoon. You'll very likely be thrown off your senate committee for what you've done this afternoon. I hope that whatever part Gunther Krugman played in this sorry outcome will prove justified. I have nothing more to say about that. You've always gone your own way, and you've made a nice career for yourself. It was yours to ruin. But I have a more immediate concern. Ms Olvidado?'

'Luna, please, sir.'

The old man gave her a hard direct look that felt like a blow.

'Why are you here?'

'Officially, I'm with the senator as part of his protection detail. But you certainly know that's not all of it. I would like to say that I'm not just here as Levi Sloane's agent. I am, but that's not all of it. I admire Senator Langan. I even agree with some of his feelings about our foreign policy. Even security drones have opinions. I think what he does is good for the country. I think he's a good man. We need more like him in government. So I guess I just don't want him misunderstood.'

'By Levi Sloane, you mean?'

'Yes. And by the rest of them.'

'So, because you admire him, you agreed to be an informant?'

'I don't like that term.'

'Who does?'

'I was assigned to protect him. When Drew –' She sent him a look that had some heat in it. 'When the Senator started getting tricky with his Secret Service escort, it put us all on guard. He looked like a man with troubles. Sometimes those troubles can be a sign that he's been compromised by something personal, something that could be used to force him to give out information. We watch for that kind of thing in everybody on the Hill. It's routine. I'm sure you already know that. Then Drew shows up at a highly classified, top-secret site and that sets off a whole rainbow of alerts.'

'And do you know what facility is located at that site?'

Luna shook her head with some force.

'No. I don't. But it's not hard to infer from their extreme reaction that it's directly related to national security operations.'

'Intimately related,' said Henry. 'And what happened then?'

'My section chief had a talk with Levi Sloane. They were going to saddle Drew with some kind of surveillance. That was automatic. I offered to do it myself. I said I was already on the scene and Drew trusted me. They took me up on it. I have nothing to apologize for. If anybody was going to be watching him, I thought it should be someone who wasn't hostile. Everybody knows there's tension between the Oversight Committee and the NSC. Drew's made a name for himself resisting . . .'

'I think he calls them "foreign adventures"?'

'Yes. Foreign adventures. Covert operations. Secret wars. And that's made him a lot of enemies down in Langley —'

'And on Pennsylvania Avenue,' said Drew.

'Yes. It has.'

Henry gave Drew a heavy look.

'What do *you* want to do about this woman?'

Drew looked at Luna, a look she met straight on.

'I knew they'd have to put someone on my case. Luna was a natural for the job. If I have to have a minder, I'd rather it was someone who wasn't holding a grudge because I sat on a committee that deep-fried all of her dearest friends. Luna's a smart woman and I'd like her to stay. I'd like her to hear whatever you've got to say about this situation. Obviously, we need some good advice.'

'He's right, sir,' said Luna. 'And the best advice you could give him is to persuade him to leave this entire issue alone. He's already agreed to let Levi Sloane look into what happened to Krugman. Now he's apparently going back on that agreement. If he does, I'll have to tell Sloane, and at that point I don't know what will happen. Your son might be placed in what we call "protective custody" – held incommunicado until the security issues are dealt with. There are serious consequences here. I know you were in Intelligence yourself. You know what they are. I'm asking you to tell him to let this go.'

'I don't have that kind of power over my son. And I'm not persuaded that leaving all this to Levi Sloane is necessarily the right course of action for him.'

'Why not?'

'Krugman has compromised him badly. He is already under intense suspicion. If we leave the investigation entirely up to them – to Sloane and the rest of the security establishment – we have no way of countering any subsequent allegations. Krugman dragged my son into this. Until we know exactly why a man of his experience found it necessary to do that, it would be dangerous to step out of the picture.'

'It's more dangerous to stay in it.'

'Perhaps,' said Henry Langan. 'Either way, we're in trouble. We'll have to see. Drew, do you have this Critic Flash with you?'

'No. Levi Sloane took it back.'

'But it contained a specific reference to this bombing in

Iligan City? So close that when Diana told you there'd been an explosion in the Philippines you automatically assumed it was Iligan?'

'Yes.'

'And then you tried to contact Cole? Why? He was sixteen hundred miles away. Or didn't you believe that?'

'I did. Initially.'

'And now?'

'He called me. On my cell. He said he was in Thailand.'

'So you have said. And safe? Unhurt?'

'He said he was fine. He sounded a bit stressed. I figured he was tired. He was on a bus headed for Bangkok. I think.'

'You think? You don't believe him? You think he's lying?'

'Dad, when was the last time you talked to Cole?'

'Last spring. He stayed here for a week.'

'Have you ever asked him exactly what it is he does for the IMF? When I called the New York office –'

'You felt you had been transferred to another location.'

'Yes. And then they lied to me about the hotel in Thailand.'

'So you believe.'

'They *were* lying. I get lied to every day. I know the signs.'

'So do I. Which is why I never ask Cole what he does for the IMF. I don't like being lied to either.'

Camp Casey

A mass of low, steel-gray cloud heavy with the monsoon was pooling westward out of the wet green hills, hardening the sky into a concrete ceiling stained with black oily streaks. They could smell the coming rain in the air itself, a hot dank scent like an old root cellar. Sudden forks of lightning flickered through the cloud cover and the sound of distant thunder rumbled around the mist-shrouded valley. They were spread out on a ridge overlooking the long, narrow valley that contained the vine-covered shacks and barrack huts that used to be a US Army training camp. There were eleven buildings in all, each one an island to itself, shuttered and sinking into decay, its roof fallen in and the jungle sprouting from the gaps.

They deployed along the ridge and spent the last few minutes watching for any sign of life; so far, nothing but a flock of herons flapping heavily through the rain and a disconsolate-looking outcast boar. Pike gave the valley one more pass through the binoculars and signaled the all-clear to the rest of the unit. Looking like ghosts in the mist, the men rose up out of the damp sawgrass that coated the ridge and began the long walk down the slope. Halfway down the sky broke open on them once again.

Over their heads the palm trees began to sway and bend and the fronds lashed like whips. Half-blinded by streaming water, they ran the last few feet to the door of the old HQ – the only building that still had a roof – Pike booted the door open – they filed in, cursing, like generations of infantry troops long gone, cursing the monsoon and cursing the rot and damning the jungle itself.

Jesus Rizal – still wary and nervous – put his back up against the rotting wall and watched skittishly as the rest of the men dropped their gear and leaned themselves up against it. Cole saw the humming tension in the man; if he was going to get canceled this was a good place for it. Rizal sensed Cole's attention and tried for a friendly smile.

'You should not trust the floor,' he said. 'After so many years, the boards are mostly held together by dirt.'

Cole looked at Rizal, thinking, How would he know that?

'So am I,' said Chris Burdette, rubbing his face with a soaked T-shirt, streaks of blood running down his thorn-scratched face. 'That was a deeply nasty hump. Piece-of-shit jeepney, Loman.'

'You're welcome,' said Strackbein, in a low growl.

'Leave him alone, Chris,' snapped Ramiro Vasquez.

In spite of Chris Burdette's good-natured bitching, the little jeepney had done them proud, grinding its way past the Maria Christina power station and another eighteen miles all the way to the Agus River Plateau before it blew a rod and promptly set itself on fire. They had managed to get the fire out before it reached their gear, and they left the vehicle there at the end of the logging run, smoldering away under a heap of vegetation. The subsequent hump to Camp Casey had been about as bad as they all expected it to be. For Cole the only advantage had been that the long slog through the dense jungle had completely cleared his head, and the intermittent rain had been a kind of soothing balm for his burning ear. He had lost the bandage a couple of miles back and was beginning to hope that he would one day be able to hear through his ear again. He looked around at the exhausted men lying against their gear. He felt the same way.

Pike rooted around in his duffel bag and came up with some energy bars. He tossed them around to the rest of the unit and ripped the plastic off his with his teeth. Burdette watched him devour the bar in two bites, Pike's jaw muscles bunching as he stared into nothing.

'What you thinking about, Pike?'

Pike glanced over at him, and Cole saw a great distance in Pike's eyes, as if he were looking back at Cole from another time. Pike's slow grin finally appeared and his eyes lost some of their chill.

'This rain. This jungle. Reminds me of old times.'

'Vietnam?' asked Vasquez.

Pike nodded. Vasquez smiled at him.

'Miss it, do you?'

'A little.'

'What do you miss most?'

'Having an enemy you could depend on.'

'What does that mean?'

'You could depend on the NVA to do what made sense. You know, from a war-fighting point of view? You could hate them, yeah, but you could also count on them.'

'You don't think we're doing any good here?' asked Cole.

'What did we do about the Blue Bird?'

'What were we supposed to do? It wasn't our job.'

Pike looked at Cole.

'We should have done something. Why did Sloane let us download that Critic Flash if we weren't going to do anything about it? He controls who gets them. What was he thinking?'

'What did that thing really tell us, Pike? Something bad was going to happen somewhere in northern Mindanao? What were we supposed to do about that?'

'So you really did know that something was going to happen?' said Rizal. They all turned to look at him.

'Yes,' said Cole. 'We had some warning.'

'Yet you did nothing?'

'We've been over this already, Jesus.'

'But if you let things like that happen often enough, even if the reasons are strong, don't you stop being good men?'

No one answered him. They fell into a long introspective silence. Pike had a point: Why had Sloane let them see that Critic Flash? What was Sloane thinking? Was it a warning? Or was it a test? Was he checking for a security leak? If someone had warned Barrakha and he called it off, would Sloane then be looking hard at a short list of people who had actually *seen* the Critic Flash? It was a classic counterintelligence move – leak something vital, something true – leak it deliberately to a small number of people – see who comes up with it on the other side, and work backward to find your leak. The hell with this line of thought. Cole decided to leave the ethical struggle to the rear-echelon people; they could afford to be detached. The best thing Cole could do for this unit was to get this job done fast and get them all out alive.

Another sound came through the drumming of the rain on the roof and the thunder in the valley. A deeper sound, steady and rhythmic. All the men looked up through the gaps in the roof and listened with their mouths open and their throats working. The steady beat grew until it seemed to be hammering the air all around them. Krause moved to the hole in the wall that used to be a window and craned upward. The sound gradually diminished. He came back to Cole with a worried expression.

'A German chopper,' said Vasquez. 'A one oh five. They're still flying those ugly pigs. Even in this rain.'

'Loman,' Cole said, calling across to the soaked heap of clothes that marked the man's position. 'You got the map box?'

'I do,' said Strackbein, raising his head and staring at Cole.

'Bring it here, okay?'

Strackbein got into a crouch and duck-walked across the floorboards, which creaked alarmingly under his boots. He handed Cole a small, flat, gray metal box. Cole gave Rizal a hard look and the man slipped away a few yards. Cole punched a code into the keypad and the box popped open. A small but detailed map lay inside it. Cole handed the map to Krause, who held it up to a shaft of dim light coming in through the window.

'I think we can find this,' he said.

'Okay. Take Burdette. I think he needs some air.'

Krause nodded and moved off to tap Burdette. They gathered some gear – a trench tool and a small pry bar – and slipped out into the sheeting rain. Cole gestured to Pike. The big man seemed to rouse himself with an effort from a morose private rumination.

'Got the phone?'

'I do,' he said, lifting a waterproof case.

'It's satellite time. How's the power?'

'Should be okay for a short one. You want the laptop?'

'Yeah. Then go keep Jesus company.'

Pike handed him the communications kit and shuffled over to Rizal, who was slumped in a far corner. Cole booted the laptop and set the satellite phone on a section of dry floor with the antenna pointing at a gap in the ruined roof. He typed in a short text message and hit SEND. In forty-five seconds the screen opened.

– Six Actual to Talaria – situation?

– Situation nominal en route ETA six hours.

– Any casualties?

– Negative. Anything to report?

– Affirmative – confirm intercept relay function test still reading intermittently – note – inquiry reached Walter Reed re cover ID Kemp. Originated Maria Christina power plant this day.

Christ. Somebody *else* was poking around in their business?

– Six Actual – result of trace?

– Talaria NSA reverse trace and voice analysis revealed ID assistant plant manager Maria Christina station – Indonesian national Butuan Sabang – AKA Gideon – male Filipino – single – born Manila moved to Jakarta – age 39 5 feet 4 inches 160 pounds – black hair – brown eyes – graduated Jakarta Technical University – computer technician – communications specialist – multiple hits for sex offenses in Jakarta, Singapore, and Thailand – no known terror links.

Butuan Sabang. Diego's cousin, pronounced harmless by Jesus Rizal.

– Six Actual Kemp ID compromised?

– Possible Kemp ID compromised. Abort mission?

– Six Actual ETA target 6 hours – completion of mission and extraction of unit 20 hours maximum.

– Your call Talaria.

– Action re Barrakha and Sabang?

– Talaria mission comes first. Secondaries optional.

– Roger Six Actual Talaria out.

– Roger Talaria – CYA and Good Luck.

Cole shut the link down and stowed the gear away. He sat back and considered Jesus Rizal for a while. Rizal had found something fascinating in the floorboards and was busily staring it down. Pike was sitting right next to him and staring back at Cole. Ramiro Vasquez was watching Cole's face too, along with Loman Strackbein. When Vasquez was sure he had Cole's attention, he shifted his gaze to Rizal and then back, lifted a hand, and made a knife of it, drawing it across his throat. Cole shook his head briefly and Vasquez shrugged. Loman Strackbein smiled an inward smile, put his head back against the wall and closed his eyes. Pike shifted his weight – sighing – and settled back against his pack. Jesus Rizal kept his head down.

They all waited in a drumming silence for another thirty minutes, and then the hut door opened again. Burdette and Krause came in with a pelting rain at their backs, carrying a long, flat wooden box still coated in mud, their faces red with the effort, strained muscles popping. They set it down with a bang on the groaning floorboards, and the men gathered around to watch while Chris Burdette – his chest still heaving – used the little pry bar to crack the seals. The lid popped up with a brief hiss of pressurized air that smelled of gun oil and cold steel.

Inside the case – wrapped in clear plastic and covered with silicon grease – lay several gleaming M-16s, several sealed cases stencil-marked 5.56 MILITARY BALL, spare magazines, some small olive-drab plastic cleaning kits, and two Colt .45s that looked brand new, complete with spare magazines, holsters, and two hundred rounds of hollow-point. Something entirely unexpected, for a combat field cache – a Barrett 82A1 – a 29-pound, 60-inch long semi-automatic sniper rifle that loaded a .50-caliber round. Against his better judgment – hell, against all common sense – Cole claimed it, motivated by nothing more complicated than sheer unadulterated gun lust. Under the Barrett he found a box of match-grade Browning rounds and two spare box mags. He dragged it away to clean it, like a lion with a gazelle's carcass. No one objected – he'd have to carry it.

And there was one more item – a long angular weapon that looked something like an overweight barracuda; a Marine Corps rebuild of the classic M-60 machine gun, now tagged the M-60 E-3. Under the gun there were eight glittering brass belts of 7.62 ammunition, coiled in and around each other like a nest of golden cobras. Pike looked down at the 60 with the pale light of old wars in his ravaged face. He reached into the box and lifted the 60 out as lovingly as if it had been a bronze spearhead found in the rubble of Carthage. 'This,' he said in a low growl, 'is mine.'

'And welcome to it,' said Dean Krause, extracting one of the M-16s and carrying it over to a corner. Strackbein lifted out another M-16 and stripped the plastic cover away. Vasquez rummaged through the case with a dis-tracted, even a reluctant air, and finally selected an M-79 40-millimeter grenade launcher – a sawed-off-shotgun look-alike called a bloop gun because of the sound it made when it fired off a round – along with several bandoliers of high-explosive and flechette rounds.

'Why take that?' asked Pike. Vasquez shrugged, smiled.

'It's light. And whatever I manage to hit will know it.'

Jesus Rizal was the last man standing over the open crate, somehow managing to look furtive and avid at the same time. Cole saw the expression and told him to take one of the M-16s. The relief that flooded into his face – and the raw greed to possess the weapon – made him look like a hungry child. Rizal pounced on one, gathered up some magazines and a box of military ball, took his rifle to another corner and began to field strip it. Watching him work, Cole gave the man a couple of marks for competence; he knew what he was doing and he was doing it quickly.

Vasquez was watching him too.

'Little bastard knows the piece, anyway,' said Ramiro, softly.

'He does.'

Over in his corner, Pike Zeigler already had the M-60 broken down and the barrel off. He held it up to his eye and pointed it at a window. The interior gleamed like quicksilver and the mathematical perfection of the rifling inside it seemed to pull him in. He set the barrel down gently and went to work on the receiver with ferociously affectionate concentration, his face rapt, his hands quick and sure.

Cole looked at Vasquez, thinking about his injuries.

'You okay, Ramiro?'

Vasquez nodded.

'Yeah. Stings a bit, and my head's still ringing. But I'm good to go. How about you?'

'I'm starting to get some hearing back. Got your piece ready?'

Vasquez hefted the rifle and smiled. There's nothing like a loaded assault rifle and extra magazines to brighten the gloomiest day.

'Locked and loaded.'

'Then take Chris and Dean and go do a walk-about.'

'In this rain?'

'Remember? War is an outdoor sport.'

'That it is,' said Vasquez. He swiveled on his knee and got Burdette's attention; Burdette sighed theatrically, tapped Krause, and both men got to their feet, gathered their gear, and slipped out into the downpour. Cole went over to Pike.

'Earl's done his job. Take him somewhere private and break him up. Put the relay in plastic and keep it close. The rest of the hump is worse than this morning.'

Pike nodded and moved off with the duffel bag. Cole signaled to Rizal and the little man came back over, carrying his rifle, his expression calm but cautious. He had sensed a change in Cole's attitude since the contact with Sloane; he had good instincts. Cole was ready and willing to see the man in a new light.

'We were talking about your priest.'

Rizal nodded.

'Okay. You know why we're here?'

'I know what you have told me. You want to get information about some people in the area around Cobraville.'

'We're interested in two people. One is a man called Hamidullah Barrakha. He's an Al Qaeda contact man – a money man and a recruiter – we think he might be somewhere around Cobraville.'

Rizal shook his head, some of his confidence returning.

'We all know this Barrakha. He calls himself Mr Gabriel,

after the angel. Our people have been hunting him since last year. He is protected by the Moro Liberation guerrillas. It is said he brings in the money from Yemen. Many of the village headmen – the Bukidno, the Tausug, the Manguindanao – they take money from Barrakha to keep him protected. When he comes into Mindanao, he stays up in the hills above Lake Lanao. But he has never been seen anywhere near Cobraville. Father Constantin would know. He would have told me.'

Cole let that slide for now.

'And the other man?' asked Rizal.

Cole told him about the trace-back to the power station, and the identity of the man running the desk. Rizal took it in with widening eyes and a slow anger began to burn in his blistered face.

'Gideon Sabang works for Barrakha?'

'That's what it looks like.'

'Then we must kill him.'

'It's on my list.'

Rizal stopped to work something out, and Cole waited for him to do that, watching him carefully. Rizal looked up again.

'You are aware there is difficulty around the power station?'

'What sort of difficulty?'

'The hydroelectric plant had to be built up in the Islamic regions. It is powered by the run-off from Lake Lanao, and Lake Lanao is almost a sacred thing in the hearts of the Marawi peoples who live along it. They fish from it, sail on it. Their water comes from it. When the Iligan Power Commission came to divert the head-waters of the Agus, there was fighting. The Moro tribes-men killed many of the Filipino workers who were trying to build the plant. The army had to go in. There is still bad blood, but most people are accepting it.'

'What changed their minds?'

'Iligan Power decided to send free electricity from the station back up the grid to Marawi and the villages around the lake.'

'Sounds like a good idea.'

'Maybe. Although there are coal-fired power companies in Davao and Cotobato province who were very upset that they lost that business. Most of Mindanao gets its power from coal-fired plants run by foreign corporations. Sweden and Germany are the main ones. Those contracts are worth billions of dollars. The Maria Christina plant is one of the first hydroelectric plants in all of Mindanao. An American company built it for the US government. It was a free gift from the United States to the people of northern Mindanao. It is now the only plant completely owned by the people themselves and not by a foreign country.'

'So, if the people own the plant, why all the resentment?'

'As I have said, the Maranao people of Lake Lanao are strongly Islamic. They do not love the Christians of Zamboanga, and Iligan City too has many Christians. And they have been taught to hate Americans. The plant is American. Sometimes religion is a more powerful motivator than self-interest. There have been many attempts to sabotage Maria Christina. More in the last few months. Two months ago someone tried to float a bamboo raft filled with *plastique* into one of the intake channels, but it was stopped by the steel gates that screen the entrance ports. If it had not been stopped by the gates – it exploded against them, but they have been replaced – had it gone off – it would have blown up the station and perhaps even the dam itself. Iligan City would have been flooded. Thousands would have died. There is a lot of security around the plant now – German infantry and light armor – and the legionnaires patrol the length of the Agus.'

'I get all this. But what's the connection with Gideon Sabang?'

Rizal shrugged, an oddly Italian gesture. 'You're certain that Gideon is connected to the terrorists?'

'They traced a call all the way back to him. Voice ID.'

'How did they have a record of his voice to compare it?'

Cole was vague, partly because he had no idea. 'Other sources. The NSA monitors a lot of traffic.'

Rizal nodded but seemed unconvinced.

'What's the problem?' Cole said.

'I am . . . worried.'

'Okay. Tell me why.'

'Since the plant is of such importance to Iligan and there has been so much resentment from the Islamic peoples upriver, we have hired only reliable Christians to work there. But to manage the plant we have had to hire a few specialists with the technical skills.'

'I hear you saying "we"?'

'My cousin Diego –'

'The guy who owned the Blue Bird.'

'Yes. He owned the Blue Bird, with some others, but it was not what he did full time. He was an official in Iligan with many other duties. One of them was to sit on the board that runs the power plant, Iligan City Power Commission. In that capacity they had to review and approve all non-Filipino applicants for work in the power commission. This included a detailed background check.'

'Who did the background checks?'

'The Army of the Philippines. Interpol. It depended upon the country from which the applicant was emigrating. But it all ended up with our own police. The Iligan City police department coordinated all background checks, and the chief himself had to sign off on every applicant. It was a very vital process, because the plant is critical to the survival of Iligan City, and Iligan City is the financial center of Christian Mindanao. The Islamic regions up-country are poverty-stricken. The only way to bring them to accept the presence of Christians anywhere in Mindanao is to improve their living standards. So the power plant is right at the center of that effort.'

'Who is the chief of police?'

Rizal was having trouble with the implications of his answer.

'Also my cousin. Diego. Diego D'Aquino.'

'Busy guy.'

'It is Mindanao. Our ways are complicated. Clans, families. They do not share power. There is much ... cooperation.'

'Do you think Diego knew that Gideon Sabang was a mole?'

Rizal said nothing for almost a minute.

'It is possible.'

'Why?'

'Because no one has found Diego's body yet. His wife, yes, and his daughter. But no one has found him. Or the body of his son Benito. Some people say they both left just before the bombing. Before what you have told me, I would not have believed that.'

'But now?'

'Now I do not know.'

Camp Hill, Pennsylvania

Blue Mountain House
Camp Hill, Pennsylvania
Tuesday, August 19, 9:30 p.m. local time

'Why would Cole lie to you about the IMF?'

'If I asked him, he would have to. So I never asked him.'

'Cole works for the ... the NSA? The CIA? One of those?'

'I believe Luna thinks so?'

Luna nodded.

'I think Cole Langan's connected to some aspect of the intelligence network. It's the only plausible explanation for what Krugman did to Drew. I mean, if you accept that he meant the family no harm. Which personally I don't.'

The old man stood up and gathered their glasses, walked across to mix them fresh drinks. As he worked he spoke over his shoulder.

'This Critic Flash? You've gone over it?'

'I have. Several hundred times.'

'And your conclusions?'

'I've come to a few. First, there was a clear indication in it that a terrorist group – Abu Sayaf or Al Qaeda, I don't really know – but a terror operation was being planned for Iligan City. It involved a man named Hamidullah Barrakha and another unknown man who was possibly a

Filipino. And this turned out to be accurate since, that very same night, the Blue Bird was blown up. Nothing had been done – that I could see – to stop it.'

'And from this you deduced . . . ?'

'The Critic Flash was released in the early afternoon. The explosion in Iligan took place hours later. There was plenty of time to put boots on the ground in Iligan and try to stop the attack. Yet nothing was done –'

'You can't know that,' said Luna.

'True. But what the hell is the NSC and the whole intelligence network for if it isn't about stopping that kind of thing?'

Drew's father was prepared to follow the argument through.

'So if we assume that our intelligence people suspected –'

'Let's say expected.'

'Expected that a terrorist act was imminent in Iligan, and did nothing to stop it – what conclusions do you draw from this?'

'There's only one reason to allow something like that to happen. To protect an ongoing operation that would be endangered if the enemy knew we could intercept his messages. They were embedded in a digital microwave transmission from a power station above Iligan. That's a highly sophisticated method of communication, and Barrakha must have had a great deal of confidence in it to talk about a terrorist operation so openly on it. Yet it was intercepted anyway. If the NSA wanted to go on using this intercept, and getting the same kind of high-quality signals intelligence, they couldn't act on the information directly. They have to create some other plausible explanation for the failure of the bombing. They didn't have much time. So, to protect their intercept relay, they chose to do nothing.'

'The Zimmerman telegram,' said his father.

'Yes. Exactly. The Zimmerman telegram.'

'What the hell is the Zimmerman telegram?' asked Luna.

Drew's father stood up and walked over to one of his bookshelves, opened the stained-glass doors, and retrieved a framed document. He handed it to Luna.

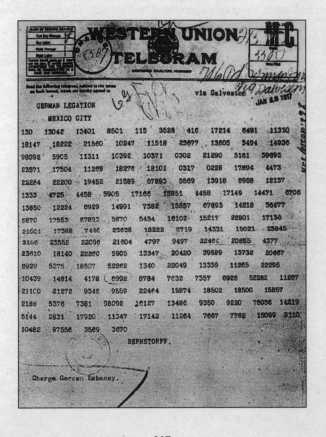

'Okay ... it's some sort of cipher?' said Luna. 'On a Western Union telegram dated January nineteenth, 1917. Sent to the German legation in Mexico City by someone named Bernstorff. What does it mean?'

'Turn the frame over,' said Drew, who had heard this story often. His father had even made him try to work out the cipher code, as a mental exercise, when he was eleven. It took him three weeks, and in the end Gunther Krugman had secretly slipped him the key. Luna flipped the frame and saw a sheet of paper glued to the back.

TELEGRAM RECEIVED
January 19, 1917
=====================

We intend to begin on the first of February unrestricted submarine warfare. We shall endeavor in spite of this to keep the United States of America neutral. In the event of this not succeeding, we make Mexico a proposal of alliance on the following basis: make war together, make peace together, generous financial support and an understanding on our part that Mexico is to recover the lost territory in Texas, New Mexico, and Arizona. The settlement in detail is left to you. You will inform the President of Mexico of the above most secretly as soon as the outbreak of war with the United States is certain and add the suggestion that he should on his own initiative invite Japan to immediate adherence and at the same time mediate between Japan and ourselves. Please call the President's attention to the fact that the ruthless deployment of our submarines now offers the prospect of compelling England in a few months to make peace.

SIGNED, ZIMMERMAN.

'Christ,' said Luna. 'I've never heard of this.'

'Well it's taught in every intelligence training course,' said Henry. 'It's actually the first page in the history of international US intelligence, in a way of speaking. Europe was bleeding itself into World War One, but Woodrow Wilson had been elected on the slogan "He Kept Us Out of War." He intended to keep it that way. However, the British blockade was hurting the Germans badly. The Germans had pledged not to use submarines against civilians or noncombatants – it was called the Sussex Pledge – but in early 1917 they broke it. The US then severed diplomatic relations with Germany. So, in January of the same year, this coded telegram from Zimmerman, the German Foreign Minister, sent to the German ambassador in Mexico, was intercepted and deciphered by British cryptographers.'

'And the Brits promptly told Wilson, right?' said Luna

'Hardly. First of all, it was to their advantage that the US take some serious hits from the Germans. It would force Wilson to change his neutral stand and get the Americans into the war. But what was more important to the British was that the Germans did not find out the Brits had broken the German codes. They were in a terrible war; they needed that advantage. They didn't tell Wilson about this German plan until they had worked out a way to convince the Germans there was a spy in the Mexican government. The Germans were fooled into thinking that this unknown double-agent had leaked the translation to the English. The Brits protected their code-breaking operation. They finally told us on February twenty-fourth, 1917. It was a wake-up call. In April, Wilson and the Congress declared war on Germany. The Zimmerman telegram woke America up to the hard realities of the covert world. We were never the same after it. Symbolically, that was when the American intelligence service was born. With the Zimmerman telegram.'

'And we're still doing it,' said Luna. 'Just like the Brits did in 1917. We're letting innocent soldiers and civilians die in Iligan to protect our intelligence resources? Is that it?'

'There's no way of knowing if this bombing could have been prevented,' said Henry. 'And our way of life is under attack. It's a hard world. That's the way it is. Tell me, Drew, was there anything else in this Critic Flash that caught your attention? Anything at all?'

'Yes. Parts of the conversation between Barrakha and this unknown Filipino were tagged "inaudible." There was a comment from the reader that the intercept relay they had in place was failing.'

'Really? So we have a malfunctioning relay and this relay is positioned deep inside UN-controlled DMZ called – if I remember the reports – the Iligan Line.'

'Yes. It runs from Iligan all the way southeast to Lake Lanao. The relay would be concealed somewhere in the vicinity of the microwave transmitter chain between Lake Lanao and the power station. On high peaks, in towers. Line of sight, probably.'

'Yet this hidden relay is vital? It must be repaired?'

'I'm sure the NSA thinks so. It's their stock in trade.'

'And this is not a repair job that would usually be entrusted to some local asset?'

'I doubt it.'

'They'd have to send in a covert unit? An American unit?'

'Jesus, Dad. Is that what you think Cole is doing?'

'I am merely speculating. Getting angry isn't helpful. In

any event, we can prove nothing. Nor would we care to try. It does perhaps explain Krugman's intervention.'

'How?'

'You're not going to like this.'

'I haven't liked much since I went to bed last night.'

'I believe Gunther Krugman recruited Cole for the CIA.'

'Krugman? He'd do that?'

'Why not? It's important work. Vital to the nation. An honorable pursuit. Cole quit the army suddenly, didn't he?'

'Yes.'

'In the middle of a very successful career as a combat officer? A decorated war hero? You didn't wonder why?'

'Not really. I was too relieved to worry about it. I guess I assumed he didn't like combat.'

'Few people do. Who got Cole the job at the IMF?'

'According to Cole, Gunther Krugman.'

Henry raised the glass.

'I rest my case.'

'This is what I suspected all along,' said Luna. 'What I don't get is why Krugman had to drag Drew into it.'

'I think there's a reasonable explanation.'

'I'd love to hear it,' said Luna.

'What would be the logical response if my hapless son here had managed to accidentally endanger a covert operation? Especially a politically sensitive covert operation inside a UN-controlled DMZ?'

'They'd pull the unit,' said Luna. 'Immediately. Get them out.'

'Abort the mission?'

'Damn right they would,' said Drew. 'But why would Gunther want the mission aborted in the first place?'

'I would only be guessing.'

'Then please guess.'

'Understand me. This interpretation is only valid if Cole Langan is actually one of the people involved in the operation. I think the facts support that interpretation. Look at the sequence of events. You are a United States senator, and you somehow come into possession of a Critic Flash that is directly connected with an ongoing covert operation that involves your own son. The fact that Gunther felt obliged to hand it to you personally supports the idea that, in the normal run of events, you would not have been allowed to see this particular Critic Flash. If this Flash did actually contain an oblique reference to a mission that involved your own son, it seems highly unlikely that the NSC would have wanted you to get it. But here you are in possession of it nevertheless. Now. If you then do anything to convince the CIA that you know something specific about the mission – and you are on the record as being opposed to covert operations in general – then they would assume it has been blown, and the only safe thing to do would be to pull the team out. Cancel it.'

'I can see that. But why would Krugman want this mission canceled? Even if Cole is involved. He's part of that whole culture. Why would he sandbag something he supports so completely?'

'It may be that Gunther came into information that convinced him the mission was compromised.'

'Compromised?' said Luna. 'You mean blown?'

'Yes. I mean blown. But even if it was, Drew, remember it's possible that Krugman's ruse was successful, and that the mission has been pulled out of Mindanao already.'

'If he thought it was compromised, why wouldn't he

just tell the CIA that? Why risk Cole's life and Drew's career?' asked Luna.

'Perhaps he tried and was not believed.'

'Forgive me, sir, but that's ridiculous on the face of it. Levi Sloane and Gunther Krugman are old friends. It looks like Levi Sloane is directly connected to this operation –'

'As Deputy Chief of Operations, he'd have to be –'

'Right, sir. So all Krugman would have to do is show Sloane what he felt was proof that the mission had been blown, and that would be an end to it. Levi Sloane is an experienced controller. He'd never let a mission be compromised. He'd pull them right out.'

'Perhaps. But *proof* of such a thing is hardly ever available. It becomes a judgment call. Covert operations, once set in play, develop a certain momentum. Reputations are on the line. Careers. And there are always risks in any operation. The men in the field are often very reluctant to break off the mission. And they're men who are quite willing to take terrible risks for their country. Look at those anonymous stars on the wall at Langley. People die. Information still has to come in. This is an ugly war. Chances will be taken.'

Luna was still not convinced.

'All of this is so damned convoluted. Krugman thinks a covert mission has been compromised. Levi Sloane doesn't believe him. So he goes to Drew. But he doesn't *tell* Drew anything useful. He just fills him up with a lot of cryptic jargon and sends him off to sink his career. Why not just tell Drew outright? Here's the mission. Your kid's on it. This is why I think it's compromised. These are the bad guys. Let's you and me go and tell Levi Sloane to get Cole out of there.'

Henry nodded. 'Your point is well taken. That is what Krugman would have done if he actually knew what you are accusing him of knowing. I don't think we can estimate how much of this Krugman should have told Drew. We don't know what he was certain of and what he only suspected. I think he was still putting his case together. But if Cole was in danger and Sloane needed more proof before he'd do anything about that, Krugman may have decided that he could not wait. So he put Drew into the game and hoped for the right outcome.'

'I can accept that Gunther Krugman might have done all this for a good reason,' said Luna. 'What I can't understand is why he went to all this trouble only to step right off the planet? Why do that?'

'He may not have done it. It may have been done to him.'

'You think he was abducted?' said Luna.

'I think nothing.'

'What does all this mean? For Cole?' asked Drew.

'I say again, this is all speculation. It *could* mean that Cole has unknowingly engaged in a covert mission where some of the elements are not what they seem. These operational uncertainties greatly increase the risks inherent in the mission.'

'I hear you telling me that Cole may have walked into a trap.'

The frail old man looked pained and answered with reluctance. 'Yes. That is another way of stating the matter.'

'Well, what the hell are we going to do about it?'

'That's clear, at least,' said Luna. 'You do nothing. It's up to Levi Sloane to find Gunther Krugman.'

Henry was shaking his head. 'I doubt very much that Sloane will be able to do that.'

'But why?' asked Drew, his patience failing.

'Because I haven't heard from him. Not a word. In the normal run we speak often and e-mail each other almost weekly. If our hypothesis is correct, he would have been in touch with me as soon as he heard about the explosion in Iligan City. He greatly admired Cole. At the very least he would have told me directly that he had some reason to believe that my grandson was in a dangerous situation.'

'Forgive me, Dad, but do you think Gunther hasn't let you in on this because of his concerns for your . . . your health?'

'In other words, he would have kept me out of it because I'm a frail, doddering old fart? That sort of thing? If I were totally senile I could hardly have done worse than you have. So, to continue, I have heard nothing from Gunther since early last week, and that was to discuss a fishing trip in the Adirondacks.'

'Which tells you what?' asked Luna.

'It tells me that he is unable to communicate.'

'He's being held?'

'That's one possibility, Miss.'

'Not the CIA or the NSA. They're the ones who are tearing D.C. apart looking for him right now.'

'That could be a diversion, Luna,' said Drew.

She shook her head and spoke with some force.

'No. I know that game, Drew. I know when they're panicking. The effort I'm seeing, you only see when the security threat is serious. It's no bluff. They don't have him.'

'What's the other possibility, Dad?' asked Drew.

'That he's already been dealt with.'

'You mean he's dead?' said Luna.

'Luna contends – persuasively – that our officials do

not have him. I believe she's right. But some group or organization had a strong motive to silence him. However, to kidnap and detain a man as highly placed, as visible, as Gunther Krugman would be needlessly risky. The simplest thing to do would be to kill him. That is what I fear may have happened. The efficiency with which it has been accomplished – no signs of forcible entry at the hotel, according to Luna, no signs of any struggle, the absence of a corpse – all of these factors suggest a foreign intelligence agency. A very sophisticated agency. There are only a few nations that have such a capacity and who would be prepared to use terminal force against a highly respected and well-known United States citizen.'

'What agencies?' asked Luna. 'Al Qaeda? Hamas?'

Henry Langan made a gesture of dismissal, his face bleak.

'Those thugs? September Eleventh was the peak of their reach. Now they are on the run all over the world. They may manage one or two more attacks on American assets in the Middle East or Southeast Asia, but a surgical hit in the middle of D.C. is beyond them. And Hamas and Hezbollah are reduced to strapping explosives to death-intoxicated teenage hysterics.'

'Then whom?'

'The Pakistanis could do it. The British. The French. The Germans. Some of the Balkan states have pretty efficient networks. The Russians still, although they have fewer resources these days.'

'The British are our allies.'

'Yes. For now. I'm only thinking of agencies with the skills required. The best people in the world for this sort of covert overseas sanction work are of course with the Mossad.'

'The Israelis would never kill an American, Mr Langan. We're their closest allies. It would never happen.'

'Really, Luna? Tell that to the men who died on the *Liberty*.'

'The *Liberty?*'

'Yes. It happened during the Six-day War. On the eighth of June, 1967, around ten in the morning – a fine sunny day with unlimited visibility – the Israelis attacked without the slightest provocation a United States naval vessel cruising – unarmed, I might add – a few miles off the coast of Israel. She was the USS *Liberty*. She was clearly flagged – the Stars and Stripes flying at her masthead – the photographs show it plainly – and her hull numbers, GTR Five, visible. The name USS *Liberty* was painted in large black letters on her hull. An Israeli reconnaissance aircraft called a NORD circled the ship several times, close enough to risk clipping the mast. The sailors waved to the pilot, who waved back and smiled. Then he flew off.'

Here the old man paused, recalling the times.

'At ten the assault began with Dassault Mirages. They strafed and bombed and napalmed the ship repeatedly in spite of desperate attempts by the radio officers to reach the Israeli pilots. The air assault lasted four hours, and at the end of it the USS *Liberty* was a flaming hulk adrift in the eastern Med. She had eight hundred holes in her superstructure and in her hull. The decks were running with blood. They were not finished with her, however. Before they flew off, the Israeli Mirages strafed and sank every lifeboat in the water. Then Motor Torpedo Boat two zero three came in to finish her. Two hundred and fifty-three men died.'

'But . . . why? Why would they attack us?'

'The *Liberty* was an NSA Surveillance ship,' said Drew. 'She was monitoring the fighting off a town called El Arish. The Israelis had too many Egyptian prisoners to handle. So they lined them up in a mosque and started shooting them. They have admitted to as much quite recently. The *Liberty* was capable of picking up incriminating radio transmissions from the Israeli commanders. They in fact were not doing any such thing. However the Israelis knew exactly what the *Liberty* was – the hull letters GTR stood for "General Technical Research," and she was clearly listed as an electronic surveillance vessel in *Jane's Fighting Ships* that year – so they sank her just in case. America has allies, Luna. She has no real friends.'

'But ... why isn't this generally known? Johnson was the President then. Why didn't he do something?'

'He did. He gave orders that the entire affair was to be hushed up. Suppressed. He told Robert McNamara that any protective air cover for the ruined ship was to be recalled. When Admiral Geis, the commander of the Sixth Fleet, protested, Johnson came on the line personally. He said – and here I'm quoting – he didn't give a horse's right testicle if the fucking ship sank with all hands. He wasn't going to embarrass his allies.'

'His allies? You mean Israel?'

'Yes.'

'Why would he want to protect Israel?'

'He was afraid that the presence of a US naval vessel would give the Arabs a reason to accuse the United States of helping Israel in the Six-day War. It was easier – politically – to let the ship burn and forget it ever happened. He was also up for reelection the next year and he needed the support of pro-Israeli Americans, which he wasn't going to get if it held Israel to account for this atrocity. The commander of the ship, Bill McGonagle, was awarded the Congressional Medal of Honor for what he did to save his ship that day. This is the nation's highest military honor. Normally an award like this takes place in the White House. The President pins it on the man himself. Bill McGonagle got his in a secret ceremony at the Washington Navy Yard – a stinking little scrap yard next to the Anacostia River. Before he approved the award, Johnson even asked the Israelis if they had any objections. Fortunately for Bill, they said it was okay to give him his medal.'

'And no one demanded that the Israelis explain it?'

'There have been many private lawsuits. The official Israeli position is that their fighters mistook the ship for an Egyptian troop transport called *El Quseir*. That ship – a corroded rust-bucket – was tied up at Alexandria two hundred and fifty miles away. You can compare the two ships. I have the photos filed somewhere. The ships are completely different. And to suggest that Israeli intelligence didn't know exactly where the *El Quseir* was when they were planning the war is simply absurd on the face of it. No. The attack was deliberate. When the survivors of the *Liberty* tried to get some media attention for their lawsuit the Israelis launched a PR campaign that blatantly accused the crew members of anti-Semitism. That was the end of it.'

'Jesus,' said Luna, after a pause, 'what a planet.'

'This is the way the game is played. We have not been without sin ourselves. At the end of the First Gulf War we invited the Kurds and the Shi'ite Moslems to rise up against Saddam. Then we decided that Saddam was better than another Iranian ayatollah ruling in Iraq, so we called off the air support and told Saddam he could do what he wanted to the Swamp Arabs and the Kurds. He promptly killed a hundred thousand people. He massacred the children and the mothers and the fathers and we stood aside to let him do it. They died in their own blood – cursing the Americans who betrayed them – while New York City held a ticker-tape parade for the troops.'

He looked at Luna, a pale cold light in his eyes.

'Tell me then, Luna, how are we better than the Israelis? There are no lasting loyalties in the global dynamic. There are only transient accommodations. No, alliances outlive their usefulness –'

He stopped suddenly, fatigue draining the blood from his face. The cold ferocity that had animated him slipped slowly away. He looked blue and weak and his right hand began to shake. Cornel materialized from the kitchen with a glass and three cylindrical blue caplets, which Henry accepted with a nod and took immediately. He said something inaudible to Cornel, who went to the sideboard and mixed him a fresh scotch. He brought it back to Henry and sat down next to him on the sofa. Henry's color came back.

'Good lad. Thank you.'

Cornel ducked his head briefly and said something polite in a strong Parisian accent. A brief smile crossed his solemn, childlike face, his teeth very white against his coffee-colored skin.

'Cornel comes to us via your wife, Diana,' said Henry. 'He met her at one of Mitzi's affairs in Paris. Diana sent me a letter about him, very complimentary. He's staying with us for the summer. Helping Andrea cope with me.'

'It's my pleasure, sir,' said Cornel, looking shy.

'Going to the Juilliard in the fall,' said Henry.

'Yes, sir. Is there anything else I can do?'

'No. Thank you. I'm fine now. You go on. Tell Andrea I'll be up late. I'll put myself to bed. There's a good lad.'

Cornel got up and left the room; the three of them sat together in a careful silence for a long time before Drew came over to his father. He touched the old man's hand; it was damp and cold and trembled very slightly.

'You okay, Dad? Too much talk?'

His father stirred and looked at him with a thin smile.

'Son, you need to know something. I was working with Gunther Krugman. A kind of partnership. Informal.'

'You were in business with him?'

Henry nodded sadly, as if resigned to an admission of guilt.

'For a while. Krugman was doing consulting work for foreign governments. Lobbyists. Foreign corporations. Arranging meetings. That sort of thing. Occasionally I gave him the benefit of my intelligence experience. I introduced him to some people in the utilities business in Europe. Connections. It seemed harmless and I admit I enjoyed being useful. I liked being back in the game.'

Luna stepped in.

'Mr Langan, do you know of any projects Krugman was involved in that might be connected to what's going on in Mindanao?'

'No. But that's why I brought this up. I know where you might start looking. Cape Vincent. Gunther keeps a safe house there. He told me about it last year and I was up to see it a couple of months ago. He said if anything ever went haywire in any of our projects – or if he died and I wanted to tie up our loose ends – I should go up there. He didn't want his files ransacked by the wrong people. Newspapers, that kind of thing. Details he didn't want retailed around D.C. for the amusement of the media. Krugman has acted for many of the most powerful people in Washington. He felt he owed them his discretion. If he ever died or was in any way incapacitated I was supposed to go up and sanitize everything. I'm his executor. If he kept any records that would help you in this thing that's where they'd be.'

'That's a long drive into upstate New York.'

'Then take the chopper.'

'The chopper?' asked Luna.

'Is it fuelled?' asked Drew.

'I'll have them top it up.'

'You people have your own chopper?'

The entire fuselage of the chopper was vibrating in a steady teeth-rattling rhythm that she could feel all the way up her spine and into her skull. When she tried to talk, her voice came out with a quaver in it that made her sound like a cartoon character. Drew held the cyclic steady in his right hand and backed off on the twist throttle of the collective in his left hand a couple of notches. The beat of the rotors softened slightly. The sound inside the cabin became bearable and the vibration backed off. Her face was tinted a soft amber in the glow of the instrument panel. He leaned to his left in the pilot's chair and asked her to repeat the question. Beyond the windscreen the town of Binghamton lay spread out in a complex grid of shimmering light. Overhead a yellow moon streaked with cirrus kept a gliding pace with them and a single cold star glittered in the black night. In the glow from the instrument panel Luna's fine-boned face was remarkable for a look of fixed rigidity that, in another woman, Drew might have taken for stark terror.

'When did you learn to fly this pig?'

'I started out as a pilot. And it's not a pig. It's a classic Huey chopper. An American icon. Dad paid for my course when I was in school. When I got out of Harvard I wanted to go work in South America. You know. Fly medevac missions for sick people. Take them out of the bush and into a hospital. I had a job lined up with the UN to work for one of their CIDA agencies in Venezuela.'

'You? A medevac pilot?'

'Yeah. Me. Why not?'

'You're just so senatorial. What happened?'

Drew shook his head and tapped the side of his headphones.

'Say again?'

'So why didn't you go?'

'The job disappeared. I asked them why. They just said I wasn't qualified. After that I tried with three other agencies. No luck.'

'The job just disappeared? Who disappeared it?'

'Who do you think?'

'Not your father?'

'I could never prove it. But who else had the clout?'

'Why wouldn't he want you to do it? After all, he paid for your lessons. Why not let you go?'

The altimeter needle was dropping. Drew twisted the throttle and pushed the cyclic forward. The whine of the turboshaft grew louder and the wind rushing over the screen rose in pitch as their airspeed increased. Underneath them Binghamton was drifting away southward and up ahead they could just make out the lights of Syracuse, a pale yellow glow on the horizon.

'Steel. Steel is the family business. We're not a public company. Dad wanted to keep it that way, and to do that he needed a family member to take over. I was it. I helped him run the Harrisburg operation for a few years and then he put me in charge of our steel polishing plant in Scranton.'

'What happened?'

'The year after I got there the union voted for a strike.'

'Really? The great American sport. Then what?'

'I sided with them. Walked the picket line myself.'

'You picketed your own company? The one you owned?'

'I guess I was getting even. And being a smart-ass. They did have a good case. Sort of.'

'How did your dad take it?'

'Fired my sorry ass. Flew up to Scranton and walked out into the picket lines and fired me right there on Live Eye at Five. Had two security guards frog-march me off the property. Wonderful video.'

'I never knew this.'

'I thought you knew everything about me.'

'Only the evil bad stuff. What did you do?'

'Do? What all good Democrats do. I played the class struggle. Headlines all over the US Scion of the House of Steel Defies Evil Tycoon Dad. I went to work for union causes. Got pretty well-known on the state level. The Democrats asked me to run for junior senator. My opponent was saddled with the last recession. Steel towns were dying all over Pennsylvania. The Rust Belt was wide open for us. A lot of the voters figured I'd be able to bring back the steel contracts. I won in a landslide. The rest is parody.'

'You can be quite amusing. I know you take your job a lot more seriously than you let on. How far to Cape Vincent?'

'From Harrisburg? Two hundred and seventy miles

direct. But we have to fly around Binghamton and refuel in Syracuse. The Huey only has an effective range of two hundred and fifty miles. I've got a pad reserved at the airport. We'll touch down and refuel. Then go.'

'What are we going to do when we get there?'

'Krugman's memory is in that house.'

'I mean how are we going to get inside it?'

'We have the security codes.'

'So what? We plan to enter without Krugman's permission.'

'Not really. Dad's the executor for Gunther's estate.'

'That only counts if his will has been probated. Until we know he's dead this is still a very dicey entry. What if we get caught?'

'You're a law enforcement officer?'

'I'm a high-grade security guard, Drew. Anyway, even the FBI needs a warrant. You'll get us arrested by some local cops.'

'How about "exigent circumstances"?'

'Hah! I'm not going to fry my career by helping you break into a house in the middle of the night in some rural backwater in upstate New York. Think of something else.'

'You could call your boss. Levi Sloane won't need a warrant.'

Luna fell into an uneasy silence. Drew shot her a look.

'You have called him, haven't you?'

'Not yet.'

'Why not?'

'Partly because it's late and I'd only get the duty desk. Partly because I want to have something substantial to tell him.'

'What else?'

Luna said nothing for a while. Drew waited her out.

'Okay. Maybe I'm worried about what Sloane will do with the information.'

'Why?'

'You and Sloane want two different things. You want to know if your son –'

'This isn't about my son. Cole's a grown-up. He is where he is because he wants to be there. I've had my own life manipulated by my father. I'm not going to do that to my son.'

'Okay. I stand corrected. But you want to find out if this unit is in danger, and Levi Sloane has other priorities. If the alternative is a major international uproar with the UN leading the pack, he might be just as happy to see it all go away.'

'You really think that?'

'I think it's possible.'

'It would be a bad move. My family has a lot of resources. It's not safe to piss off my dad either. He's the vengeful type.'

'Just how much money does your family have?'

'I have no idea. Billions. It's not mine, anyway. It's Dad's.'

Luna made a sound just this side of a contemptuous snort.

'Right. How'd you get this chopper? Your paper route?'

'It's not mine either. It's war surplus. Dad got it dirt cheap.'

'Define cheap.'

'I'm not sure. Including the rebuild, around two million.'

'Jesus. Two million is cheap? You know how long a normal person has to work to make two million dollars?'

'On Wall Street, about a half an hour. It's all relative.'
Drew paused. 'What did you think of my father?'

'I liked him. No. I didn't like him. I admired him.'

'I know exactly what you mean.'

'He has a long memory.'

'Most of it filled with things he's trying to forget. He hasn't seen a truly happy sunrise since my mother died.'

'I can understand that. What did he think of your wife?'

Drew flinched at the mention of Diana.

'Damn. What time is it?'

'Around two thirty.'

'Look, I can't take my hands off the controls. Can you do something for me?'

'Forget it. If you need to pee just land the damned chopper.'

'I have to call Diana. My cell phone is in the pocket of my jacket. Will you call her in Paris and tell her that Cole's all right?'

'Me? Call your wife? She hates me, in case you don't know. You've got a radio in that Buck Rogers headset, don't you? You call her. Have the air traffic operator patch you through.'

She had a point. Drew got Syracuse GCA tower on the line and got a patch through to Mitzi's flat in Paris. The line rang several times and then he was listening to Mitzi Gallant's whiskey baritone explaining in mutilated pidgin-French that she and the marvelous Diana were out having an early breakfast of croissants-and-mimosas so do leave a message, darlings. Drew gritted his teeth and spoke exactly fifteen words, six to tell Diana that he'd heard from Cole and he was fine and nine more which were probably not going to improve his relationship with Mitzi Gallant. Or with his wife either, for that matter. Luna listened to Drew's part of the communication and laughed at the message he finally left.

'You have a wonderful gift for invective. I had no idea.'

'Thanks. Diana's friends bring out the best in me. Why would you say that Diana hated you? She never said a word against you.'

More silence from Luna. Finally, she spoke.

'She knew I was on to her. We all were, but the rest of the unit was just a bunch of guys and she knew how to handle men. Me she really hated. I was asking you what your father thought of her.'

'They got along well. Dad relates to attractive women with brains. What do you mean she knew you were on to her?'

'I knew she was sleeping around. It made her nervous. She tried to get me transferred. Didn't you know?'

'No. I didn't. I'm sorry.'

Another silence. Then another unusual question.

'So what happened with your wife, anyway?'

'It's complicated.'

'Tell me about it. It'll take my mind off this hellish ride.'

'We met in New York. At a party for Bill Clinton. Diana was a fund-raiser, knew everyone in New York. Her family was originally from Albany. Shipping. Lots of money. She was what my father calls "a big-shouldered broad." Knew how to drink and when to shut up. Good storyteller. Great listener. Funny. Smart. Brave.'

'Sounds like a dream girl. What went wrong?'

'She had fidelity issues.'

Luna laughed, a short hard bark that ended in a sigh.

'Fidelity issues? I love it when you talk like that. I'll admit she puzzled me. She had a good marriage. At least it looked like that to us. Being on a Secret Service detail is a barrier to any kind of permanent relationship. Bodyguards are just observers. Life goes on around us. We're just furniture with guns. In the meantime we have a ringside seat for a lot of domestic decay. It can get you down, seeing how dedicated people are to making each other completely miserable. So when you see someone willfully screw up what looks like a happy marriage to a pretty decent guy for thrills, it sort of depresses you. I thought your wife was a fool.'

Drew tried to keep his reaction small enough not to spook her.

'That's the nicest thing you've ever said to me.'

It was the wrong thing so say. As far as it was possible to erect a wall of silence inside a helicopter, Luna had hers up in a heartbeat.

'Yeah? Then let's just drop the subject, okay?'

Drew glanced at her. It was like looking at a still photo. The hardness was back in her face and the lockdown on tight. He just did not get her at all. The woman was crazier than Diana. He flew for a while in a bruised silence while the shimmering field of light that was Binghamton slipped far away into the southwest. Up ahead a few country roads showed against the velvet blackness as a spidery webwork of glowing beads on pale yellow ribbons. Cars and trucks crawled over the webs pushing twin cones of light into the darkness. Red glitters followed them. To the west and far above them the strobe light in the belly of a passenger jet blinked rapidly as it flew into the east. In a couple of hours the pilots would see the sun rising up out of Europe. It would be morning in Paris and Diana would be having her croissants au chocolat with Mitzi in a sidewalk café on a sunlit boulevard lined with linden trees. Beyond Europe lay Asia – now gliding into the early afternoon – and beyond Asia the setting sun would be glimmering on the South China Sea, making the vast empty expanse look like a sheet of embossed gold leaf. And somewhere in the South China Sea on the mountainous green island of Mindanao now rolling into the twilight his son was walking through a jungle clearing on a mission that could end up killing him. He had to think of something else. He looked at Luna again.

'I don't get you. You just spent twenty minutes grilling me about my family and my marriage and when I say something that sounds like a compliment you slam my fingers in the car door.'

'What makes it your business?'

'You made it my business. You signed on.'

'I signed on to help keep you safe. And to keep Levi Sloane advised. I did not sign on to babble on about my hopes and dreams like some teenage bimbette on MTV.'

'I'm not trying to crack you open. I'm just interested.'

'You're not? You just want to know my hopes and dreams, right? Well fuck my hopes and dreams.'

'You never married? Never wanted children.'

'Christ, no. I loathe children. Nasty squalling little brutes. Sewage out one end and puke from the other. I'd rather keep an ant farm. I told you: I don't have a cat and I don't have a boyfriend and I don't like women either. What I do like is my job. And I intend to keep it. I'm a blue-collar federal gunslinger – check that – a *Latina* gunslinger – working a protection detail. Any one of us in the service gets involved with the people we're assigned to, we end up not only disgraced but unemployable. Listen to me, Drew. We're not involved, and if you keep pressing it, I'll take the next chopper out and you can deal with whoever Sloane replaces me with. One of the reasons I like you is that you never made an out-of-line move on me.'

'I won't. But we're both single, aren't we? It's not immoral to be attracted to a woman like you. It's a pretty human emotion.'

'Look, you're a good-looking guy – in your own way – and you could make a plausible run at all kinds of women. But you never crossed the line with me. You've never done anything low. I admire you for that.'

'I thought about it. That night at O'Hare . . . ?'

'Sure, I remember. We were both a little tanked. I knew what you were thinking. I half expected you to show up at my hotel-room door. But you didn't. That impressed me.'

'Don't be too impressed. I thought about it for quite a while.'

Luna was about to answer when his cell phone rang. She jerked at the shrill metallic beeping and Drew knew that whatever she was going to say had fluttered off into the irretrievable night. The moment was gone, blown away by a Goddamned cell phone. He was sure he had turned the damned thing off. The phone shrilled like a car alarm, sending an electric jolt through them both. He couldn't take his hands off the controls – do that for even a second and the chopper plummets out of the sky like a gut-shot goose. Luna fumbled in his jacket and pulled the phone out.

'Hello?'

'Hello. Who the fuck is this? Where's Langan?'

A harsh female voice, full of smoke and whiskey.

'This is the Secret Service. Who the fuck are you?'

'Helen Claiborne McDowell is who the fuck I am, missy.'

Luna jerked at that and looked at Drew.

'Who is it?' he asked. Luna told him.

'Oh shit. What the hell does she want?'

'Ma'am, Senator Langan cannot take the call right now.'

'Why the fuck not? And what's that damned noise?'

The woman was angry. Perhaps also very drunk. But angry.

'Ma'am, we're in a chopper. Senator Langan's flying it.'

'Okay. Figures. Where the hell are you?'

'Where are we? We're in the air over Binghamton, ma'am.'

'Why the hell are you in the – Who're you again, missy?'

'My name is Luna Olvidado. I'm part of the senator's security detail. My badge number is –'

'I don't need your badge number. Give our boy a message.'

'Yes, ma'am. Go ahead.'

'Tell him he's off the fucking Intelligence Committee.'

'Ma'am –'

'Tell him!'

Luna put the phone down.

'Drew – she says you're fired.'

'Fired? Like fuck I'm fired! Ask her the fuck why.'

Luna did, editing his query slightly.

'Why? Look, missy, I'm up here in the Goddamned Front Range on what was supposed to be a hunting trip and I get a call from the Goddamned National Security Adviser, who tells me all about Senator Langan's attempt to enter a security zone –'

'Ma'am, I was with him. What security zone?'

'Ask him if he's ever heard of the Special Collections Service.'

Luna relayed the question. Drew shook his head.

'Well they sure as hell heard of *him*. They run all the Signals Intelligence work for the NSA. They do the hardware repairs. They go into foreign countries to set up the gear. They break into –'

'Ma'am, you're on a cell phone.'

'What?'

'You're speaking on a cell phone. There's no security.'

'Jeez, a junior senator from some rust-belt shanty-town shoved way up there in the nation's colon starts to fuck around with issues of national fucking security and – never mind – tell him he's been suspended. Tell the media he's got the mumps or SARS or the Goddamned shingles. I don't care. He's gone. Have a nice flight.'

The line cut off. Luna stared down at the phone.

'What did she say?'

'Well ... I think I can safely say that she was disappointed.'

Cobraville

After an endless struggle through dense jungle under the driving monsoon, they came in the failing light of evening to the edge of the palm line and looked down onto the flat shining rice paddies where the village of Cobraville lay, almost five hundred yards away: It was a random-looking cluster of brown, grass-covered lodges gathered in a wavering circle along the banks of a large, slow-moving, gray river matted with floating islands of lotus. Curtains of rain swept and wavered across the tall grass of the clearing, shredding the gun-metal surfaces of the paddies and pattering hard droplets across the river.

Cole tugged out his binoculars and gave the village a scan. It was much bigger than it had looked on their NIMA charts, over a hundred large octagonal huts – solid-looking and well-maintained – made of hardwood poles held together with stripped vinework, skillfully sided and thatched in sawgrass and palm fronds, arranged in meandering clusters along the river's edge. Thin plumes of pale blue smoke rose up from many of the huts, bending sideways under the driving rain. The only people visible were a large group of naked brown children chasing a hoop through a mud puddle next to a large open-sided stable roofed in sawgrass. He could see the broad, coal-colored backs of a herd of water buffalo – called carabao in the Philippines – crowded in a tight press under the shelter.

Next to the stable he could make out what looked like a double row of large oil-drum latrines under a shelter. The latrines were an unusual addition – possibly the sanitary influence of this Jesuit priest, Constantin Desaix. It had not been Cole's experience that remote jungle villages in the Third World devoted a lot of effort to effective sewage management. Cole saw a single wooden building of obviously European make at one edge of the central clearing, a long rectangular construction a hundred feet long feet by forty feet wide, made of planks of mahogany and roofed with corrugated iron. Blinds made of bundled sticks covered two rows of glassed-in windows. This extraordinarily expensive building had to be the medical clinic.

The building had a military sharpness to it which contrasted with the careless, almost accidental disposition of the rest of Cobraville. A flagstaff had been set into a concrete base at the entrance to the wooden building. The French tricolor flag hung limply from the head of the staff, water streaming off it and pooling around the base.

A veranda had been built out from the entrance, sheltered by a roof of bamboo stalks covered with palm fronds. An elderly man was sitting on this veranda, wearing faded tan slacks and a military-looking shirt with shoulder tabs and watch pockets, leaning back on a wooden chair tilted back against the wall, his booted feet resting on the railing, smoking a pipe. He was very thin and looked as if he was made out of the same kind of hardwood sticks that held the veranda together. Cole felt a motion at his right side and turned to see Jesus Rizal squatting beside him and grinning widely, the skin around his eyes still raw and his burns showing raw and livid.

'That is Constantin. We are fortunate he is here.'

'How do you want to handle this?'

Rizal swelled visibly with this signal of Cole's trust. 'If you permit, I will go down to him.'

'Is he expecting you?'

Rizal shook his head firmly. 'No. I did not think it wise to talk about our visit. But we are friends, and he is used to my unexpected arrivals. I will go down alone and prepare him for you. If that is all right?'

'Wait here.'

Cole moved off down the tree line until he reached Ramiro Vasquez's position. Vasquez had his back up against a towering banyan. His shirt was pulled up and he was using a lighter to burn a tiger-striped brown leech about five inches long off his flat muscular belly. A thin ribbon of blood ran out from under the leech and trickled down into his belt. Vasquez looked up as Cole sat down beside him and smiled broadly. He plucked the writhing leech off his belly – it let go with a sucking pop – and offered it to Cole.

'Escargot? Fresh today?'

'Jesus, Ramiro – get that thing away from me.'

Vasquez threw it into the bush with a rapid flick.

'No problem. You've probably got a bunch of your own anyway. What's the plan?'

'The plan is you and Rizal are going to go down there and talk to the priest. If everything looks okay, we'll follow you down.'

Vasquez shrugged, a gesture of fatalistic acceptance.

'And if they butcher us like pigs before you can stop them?'

'I'll write a very strong letter of protest to the UN.'

'With really really big words?'

'If necessary I'm prepared to use the word "exsanguinated."'

'Yow. What does it mean?'

'You probably don't want to know.'

'What do we do if this all goes batshit?'

'Follow the drill. We hook up back at Camp Casey and call for an extraction.'

'What's our recognition signal?'

'Jupiter. Just signal Jupiter.'

'Why Jupiter?'

'Why not?'

'Okay, boss. Give us a kiss and I'm off.'

'Go fuck yourself.'

'If only we could all be happy just fucking ourselves. This world would be a better place. Come on, Jesus. Let's go see the man.'

Vasquez and Rizal broke through the brush and moved out down the slope, leaving a silvery trail in the tall wet grass. Cole, Strackbein, Krause, and Burdette all pulled back into the tree line and covered them with their rifles. As the two figures reached the bottom of the slope and walked out along one of the berms that enclosed the rice paddies, a bell began to chime from somewhere deep in Cobraville. The sound of it floated across the fields, a clear ringing.

Cole watched the man on the veranda through the binoculars as he stood up and stepped out from under the shelter of the veranda. Rizal lifted a hand, and Cole heard him calling out to the priest in French. The priest waved back, a slow languid gesture. People started to come out from the huts, women and men and children, streaming out now, slender brown-skinned figures wearing bright green headscarves and deep red sarongs that contrasted vividly with the gray-green of the sawgrass and the dull brown of the huts.

Cole and the men watched as Rizal and Vasquez reached the edge of the village. The priest met them there and they stood in the rain together. Rizal said something to the priest, and the priest reached out to shake Vasquez's hand as some of the villagers gathered around, a crowd now numbering close to fifty. They could hear a low murmur of excited talk – the laughter of village girls, high and bell-like – coming faintly through the hissing rain. A few more minutes passed during which the three little figures in front of the clinic talked quietly and then Jesus Rizal stepped back from the group and waved toward the ridge. All the small brown faces turned to look up toward their position. Cole cursed softly. Rizal's voice came floating up to them:

'It's all right. Come down.'

'Looks like the dinks want a parley,' said Pike. 'We going in?'

Cole said nothing for a full minute. The rain pattered around them and a curtain of mist moved across the slope stirring the tips of the sawgrass. No one spoke. Finally Cole stood up and handed his Barrett .50 to Dean Krause.

'No. Just me. Anything goes wrong . . .'

'Charley mike?' said Pike.

'Yeah,' said Cole, tapping the Barrett .50.

'Finish it.'

The Jesuit priest came forward out of the crowd of villagers to meet Cole at the base of the grassy slope. Cole watched the man as he came up into the sawgrass; he was a taller man than he looked in the long lens, over six feet and still holding himself erect, his shoulders back, the expression on his creased and weather-beaten face closed and wary. He reached Cole and extended a long-fingered hand.

'Welcome to Cobraville. I am Constantin Desaix.'

Cole took the old man's hand. His skin was soft and his hands supple, a surgeon's hands, and the light in his deep brown eyes was clear and watchful. He was heavily lined around the eyes – so much so that when he smiled his eyes were wreathed and half-hidden in folds of parchment-colored skin. His beard was snowy white and carefully combed, his long white shoulder-length hair shining with a silvery light and flowing back from a strong-boned, extraordinarily handsome face, a beaklike promontory of a nose – very French – and a good, well-defined jawline, a hard line of a mouth with creases around it that looked grim and deeply cut. He carried himself like a soldier, with some of the vanity and self-regard that Cole had seen in Pentagon brass and senior field officers, the residue of sustained rank and unnaturally prolonged privilege. His voice was rich and deep, his accent an almost unrecognizably thick southern French, a kind of muttering growl that started in his chest. The smile he gave Cole was still careful, but slightly more friendly.

'It's a pleasure, Father Desaix.'

'How am I to call you?'

'My name is Kemp. Please call me Jordan.'

The priest smiled at the name with a trace of wry humor in his eyes, and then his expression changed and his look became sharper.

'You are hurt here,' he said, reaching out to touch the right side of Cole's head and the bloody mess around his ear. Cole shied away from the priest's hand reflexively and then allowed the old man to examine it. He leaned in with a look of professional curiosity and then made a kind of humming sound that came from deep in his chest.

'You must let me clean that. And a good dressing is required.'

This in a tone that did not encourage negotiation. Desaix turned to walk them into the growing crowd of villagers who waited for them in the clearing, patiently enduring the driving rain, a group that now numbered almost a hundred people, muscular hard-faced young men in pantaloons with machetes strapped to their bodies and AK-47's slung around their shoulders, a number of gnarled shaven-headed old crones with sunken lips and hard black eyes, perhaps thirty naked children from infants at the breast to awkward teenagers, and a small unified cadre of well-built middle-aged men who stared at the newcomers with blank unfriendly faces and lips set in lines of suspicion that bordered on open hostility. The village felt like what it was – a civilian town inside a very dangerous war zone.

Vasquez and Rizal watched Cole approach, Rizal with an anxious expression – as if he were afraid that Cole would not treat the priest with sufficient respect – and Vasquez with a slightly cynical smile on his fine-boned face. A short, barrel-bodied, brown-skinned old man stepped up to Cole and made a brief bow. He was wearing a bright red linen vest and a sagging dirty cotton sarong-skirt wrapped around bony hips and legs as thin as a heron's. His teeth were filed into points tipped with tiny silver cones. His eyes were red-rimmed and almost hidden behind thick lids, and the expression in his dried-out walnut face was unreadable. Around his waist was a dirty scarlet sash, and inside the sash was the beaten silver scabbard of a long, bone-handled knife. He had a necklace made of what looked like finger bones, some bright white and others as yellow as antique ivory. He had an indefinable air of layered, implacable cruelty.

Cole thought about Krause, Pike, Strackbein, and Burdette far up on the ridge line and felt the welcome presence of their guns at his back. Rizal stepped forward to meet the man, gave him a deep bow, and raised his hands – palms together and fingertips steepled – and touched his forehead. The old man returned the salute in a way that struck Cole as dismissive, never taking his eyes off Cole himself, and stood there with his arms folded while Rizal made a long speech in what Cole presumed was the Samal dialect, after which the wizened old gnome began what Cole soon realized was a welcoming speech in the same language, high-pitched and musical and filled with a glottal clicking sound that reminded him of wooden bells.

Jesus Rizal, his expression grave and his bearing stiff, translated as he spoke, speaking softly in a manner that mixed respect with a degree of cautious mistrust.

'This is the O'Onta, Dak Prai. He is the headman.'

The headman spoke in this urgent ceremonial drone for several long minutes, unmindful of the driving rain, during which the crowd fell into a reverential silence and Cole found himself the center of curious attention for a group of young village girls – presumably the headman's wives – all wearing vivid green pantaloons and tight cotton blouses soaked through with the rain. Their eyes were all the same soft golden brown and their skin – the skin of all the natives in the little group – was a light tan color with a silken sheen in it as if they had all been lightly powdered with gold dust. Even in the downpour the old man smelled bitterly of stale sweat and oil of cloves.

Dak Prai came to an abrupt halt. Everyone stared at Cole expectantly. Cole made his bow, touching his joined palms to his forehead. Immediately a trill of high-pitched laughter ran through the women. Constantin Desaix and Jesus Rizal grinned at him as well. Vasquez smiled a smile that did not soften his cynical look in the slightest. The headman's wrinkled face congealed into a fistlike contortion of scars and creases and he showed Cole all of his teeth.

'You have given him a woman's bow,' said Desaix.

'Next time do not raise your palms so high,' said Rizal.

Cole nodded several times and tried a few words in Tagalog – *maraming salamat ho – ako si Jordan* – but the effect was startling – a ripple of general shock ran through the entire village, followed by a general burst of excited and – to Cole's ears angry – chatter.

Rizal said something in Samal to calm them and turned to Cole with a warning in his eyes.

'It's best not to speak Filipino here. They have a little English. The Maranao and the Moro speak Tagalog, so these people have learned to mistrust anyone who uses the language. I've explained that you were merely trying to be polite.'

The priest nodded in strong agreement.

'We never speak that tongue here. Let's go into the clinic.'

Cole and the others stood a little apart as Desaix addressed the villager and reaped a bouquet of bright white smiles from the gathering of women and children. The headman frowned darkly while Desaix spoke to the group – the look he was giving Desaix struck Cole as little short of murderous – but he seemed ready to regard the formal introductions as fittingly concluded. He clicked and bonged something that sounded final at Cole, showed him his teeth again in a feral snarl, then turned abruptly and brushed his way through the crowd, which gave way respectfully, even fearfully as he passed.

The villagers dispersed and followed him away in the direction of the their own huts on the far side of the clearing. A rising wind stirred the French flag into a flapping frenzy, and a sheet of hard rain pelted them as Desaix led them up the stairs of the clinic and onto the little bamboo-covered veranda. Desaix stopped at the heavy mahogany doors of the clinic and spoke directly to Cole.

'Your men on the ridge. Will they come down?'

Rizal and Vasquez kept their faces blank and left the answer to Cole. Desaix watched this exchange with a grim smile.

'Cobraville lives under threat. Last week the Moros took eight of our children while they bathed downriver, and the five young girls who were with them. Dak Prai himself has lost two sons by his best wife. We knew you were coming when you passed the defile and came out into the highlands. The men knew Jesus, so you were able to pass without being confronted. Mr Kemp is a *nom de guerre,* of course. I understand the necessity. Monsieur Rizal and I have an old understanding about the work his people are doing. If you mean these villagers no harm, your men are welcome to come down and share a warm meal. I have some Beaujolais, and Marie Claire has already begun a very fine bourguignon. Lamb, I am afraid, not the proper beef. But hot fresh bread and mangoes. Brandy and coffee. Something to smoke. We are dry and warm inside. There is no reason for your people to suffer a night watch in this dreadful monsoon. And it is not safe for them to stay out during the night. Not at all safe.'

Cole nodded at Vasquez, who stepped away and pulled a small handset out of his back pocket. He spoke quietly into it and they all heard Pike Zeigler's voice crackling in reply. They stood and waited as the rest of the unit rose up on the ridge line, slung their weapons, and came down the long grassy slope, hunched against the rain and their heads bowed. Cole watched Pike as he came down the hillside behind the others. He had the M-60 in both hands, and from a hundred yards out Cole could tell that his finger was inside the trigger guard. Even in the dull and fading twilight and through the gliding mist the long brass belts of 7.62 that hung around his shoulders glimmered with golden light.

When the men reached the veranda, Cole could also see from his harsh, fixed expression that Pike Zeigler was not at all happy to have been called down from the ridge. Pike shook hands roughly, unsmilingly, with the old priest, and Cole had the feeling that something instantaneous seemed to pass between the two men as they stood face to face under the drumming roof of the shelter, the mutual and hostile recognition of two incompatible minds.

A familiar sound rumbled through the night sky under the constant rattle of the rain and the gusting winds, a steady mechanical drumming that was felt in the chest more than it was heard. They all looked up into the black night sky as the sound rose into a deep syncopated thrumming – peaked – and seemed to float gradually away into the south towards the hidden reaches of Lake Lanao. They never saw the chopper itself, only the heavy bass beating of its passage. Desaix waited until the sound had faded completely away and then turned to look at the taut wet faces of Cole's men standing around him, their weapons at the ready.

'The Germans make a helicopter patrol. It happens every evening around this time, raining or not. But they always stay above the clouds if they can. Still we like to hear them out there. The people feel it will frighten the Moros and help keep them away.'

'What about ground patrols?' asked Chris Burdette.

Desaix shrugged and lifted his hands.

'A column of legionnaires made a sweep through here last night. They were very tense. They spoke of this bombing down in Iligan and asked the villagers many questions. Then they left – that way – back towards their camp at Maria Christina Falls.'

'How many men?' asked Krause.

'A full platoon. All well-armed.'

'Air support?'

'Only a German helicopter. One of their one-oh-fives.'

'Is there a routine?'

'No. They come and go without a warning. But we do not expect to see them again in Cobraville for a while. Dak Prai told them about the missing children and the girls, and they said they would send some of their people to go and look for them in Marawi. With the Moros. We should not stand in the light, however. Let us go inside.'

The priest did not ask Cole's men to stack their arms on the veranda, and Cole did not make the offer. He opened the great wooden doors wide and they stood in the warmth and the yellow light streaming from the warm sparsely furnished interior with the rich spicy smell of hot beef stew flowing out of the hallway.

With the rain lashing sideways across his battered

face, Pike hesitated on the landing and studied the comfortable-looking space inside, a large low-roofed rectangular room lined with windows shuttered by wicker blinds, off to one side a row of empty cots made up with military crispness, draped in mosquito netting, and in the center a charcoal fire burning in a stone fireplace under a hanging tin chimney, with several ancient wicker chairs and even a spindly rocker arranged around the fire. An office desk littered with paper was set just inside the door, lit by a gas lantern. The building smelled of antiseptic and lye soap and hot coffee. It was a welcoming room bearing the promise of hot food and comfort. Cole and Pike stood side by side in the open door as Father Desaix led the rest of them into the clinic. At a nod from the priest, a very pretty young Samal girl in a gauzy white smock – Marie Claire, Cole presumed – set herself about the business of drinks and robes for them all to wear while they dried their clothes.

Cole waited for Pike – understanding the man's fears, angry with him anyway – and Pike shot Cole one fierce sidelong look full of accusation and disapproval. Then he went inside with the others, his boots sounding heavily on the plank floor, carrying theM-60 at port arms, the heavy belts of 7.62 clanking like armor.

Cole sensed something behind him in the dark. He turned in the doorway and saw a solitary figure standing alone in the clearing, caught in the shaft of light from the open doors. It was Dak Prai, the headman, alone in the glittering yellow rain, standing with his feet apart and his heavy body braced against the rushing wind, staring up at Cole through the tunnel of flickering yellow light. On his face was a feral, Stone Age look that contained nothing recognizably human. Cole held the headman's look for a full minute and then the little figure stepped out of the shaft of light and melted into the surrounding night.

Cape Vincent

Bell UH-IH helicopter Tripoli
Altitude 65 feet – speed 5 knots
Cape Vincent, New York
Wednesday, August 20, 6:00 a.m. local time

The sidelong light from the rising sun lay full on the broad
sweep of the deep blue St Lawrence River to the north,
and the heat of it was strong on Drew's right cheek. Luna
shaded her eyes with her hand and watched as Drew
lowered the shuddering chopper toward a wide green
lawn surrounding an old cedar-roofed farmhouse lined
with tall oaks and maples. The rotor wash was flattening
the long grass and making the heavy boughs of the
trees heave and sway wildly. Their leaves showed silvery
white and lashed back and forth as the heavy machine
settled slowly, kicking up clouds of pale blossoms and
seedlings that whirlwinded around the chopper like a
spiraling swarm of bees. Drew pulled back on the cyclic
and the machine went into a classic flare. Luna felt the
struts touch down, lift, and then settle firmly onto the
earth. Her heart slowed and the relief that ran through
her was as intense as it was familiar. Drew flicked off
several switches, and the Lycoming engine shut down.
The machine rocked gently as the rotors flickered and
strobed and the metal frame groaned.

Drew pulled his headset off and stretched his arms

out. His shoulders ached from the strain of flying the Huey. He lifted his feet off the tail-rotor control pedals for the first time in hours and flexed both his hands. Holding the cyclic in your right hand and the collective in your left – in what is literally a death grip – has a price. And the constant vibration of the rotors works its way through your skeleton until all your bones feel soft. Flying a Huey over distance is like spending several hours trapped in an airborne Nautilus machine that will only stay airborne if you keep on pumping out bicep curls.

Luna watched with a less than sympathetic expression as he tried to work the ache out of his body. It hadn't been her idea to take the chopper in the first place. The Cadillac was just fine with her.

'Why is there no autopilot in these stupid things?'

'I'm it. Hueys don't belong in the air.'

Drew popped the door and eased himself out like an arthritic old codger. Luna slipped gracefully out of her side with all the oiled flexibility of youth. They crab-walked – needlessly but reflexively – out from under the 24-foot reach of the turning rotors through morning dew still wet on the long grass. The old white-painted clapboard house was shuttered and sealed. The screened-in porch that ran all the way around the low rambling construction sagged a little under the memory of eighty years of snow and falling leaves. But the steps that led up to the front door were solid, and new paint was on the trim around the screen door. They stopped at the bottom of the stairs and looked around the property. It was ringed on three sides by a thick forest of mixed hardwood with a scattering of dense, dark-green pines. The north side was open to the wide reach of the river with a few slender lodgepole pines marking the stony banks. The summer lay on the grounds in full bloom, and early morning bees were zipping from blossom to blossom in a wildflower garden by the lane.

The air was sweet and lazy and held a little tang in it from the great rolling expanse of the St Lawrence streaming past the property. They could see its shining surface through the standing pines, the whitecaps churning in it, showing like diamonds against the deep blue-green troughs. On the far side of the wide channel lay Wolf Island and beyond that the mainland of Canada. The place had an end-of-the-line feeling, as if they had come to the roof of America, to the last old place in the country. Cape Vincent had the weight of the eighteenth century in it, a last bastion of the forest-heavy darkness of early America. Standing there together under the sagging awning, breathing in the rich loamy smell of grass and flowers and the heat of late summer, listening to the soft wind in the oaks and the rushing murmur of the big river, it was easy to feel some of the peace that Gunther Krugman had looked for here.

Drew pulled himself out of a reverie with some difficulty – he desperately needed some coffee – and turned to face the old screen door. Beyond the door a highly polished wooden-floored porch held a few spindly rockers. The interior wall was shuttered. The boards looked new, freshly painted. There was a crisp nautical feel to the house, like a fine old wooden schooner maintained Bristol-fashion.

'Well,' said Luna, 'what now?'

'We go in. Unless you still want to wait for Levi Sloane to get up here with a warrant?'

'No. I'll fill him in when – and if – we find out anything useful. But can we just take a minute to review here?'

'Sure.'

'What if we're wrong? What if Cole really is on a bicycle trip through Thailand? What if Gunther Krugman is off on a bender in the Canadian Rockies and we're three minutes away from being arrested for B and E by a couple of no-neck bruisers from the local PD?'

'And what if my dad is totally crackers?'

'That too.'

'Why'd I get fired, then?'

'Because Gunther Krugman tricked you into it. You can talk your way back onto the committee, can't you?'

'I'm not sure I want to. I'm getting a little sick of the secret world. There are better things for senators to do with their time than trying to monitor a conspiracy of professional liars. I'm ready to trade with somebody whose delusions are still operational. Mine are all shot. And we won't know if we're wrong about any of this unless we open this door and try to find out.'

Luna looked at him steadily for a while and then she reached into the back of her slacks and pulled out a lean, compact black semi-automatic pistol and worked the slide. Drew stared at it.

'How long have you had that thing on you?'

'Always.'

'Doesn't it hurt?'

'Only when I shoot somebody with it. That stings a bit.'

'You think we need it?'

'Better to have it and not need it than need it and not have it. Aren't you glad you had yours? You still have it, by the way?'

'No. The cops took it with them. They said I'd get it back after the DA decided about laying a charge. Got a credit card?'

'I don't think we'll have to check in.'

'Just gimme one.'

Luna took out her badge case and handed Drew a gold Amex card. Drew looked at the card and then at Luna.

'Okay, it's my Secret Service credit card. Don't give me a hard time. We still have to pay for the personal stuff. Okay?'

Drew used the card to flip open a small drop latch, and the screen door swung back on rusted hinges. Luna turned to look behind them. No one around at all. Beyond the trees they could see a distant steeple, white with a gold-painted cross shining in the morning sun: the town of Cape Vincent, two miles away down the shoreline road.

Drew crossed the creaking hardwood boards and stopped in front of the main door. Although it was painted white and looked quite ordinary, it was obvious when you got close to it that it wasn't made of wood. It was a solid plate of steel set into an iron frame. The walls that looked like old wooden clapboards painted white were actually fairly new aluminum panels. Drew had a feeling that if he pried one off he'd find solid stone behind it. What looked to be an eighteenth-century wood-framed cottage was actually a solid little fortress made of steel and stone. Drew hesitated and then knocked on the door several times. It was like thumping on a vault.

'You thought someone would answer?' asked Luna.

'I was hoping we'd find Gunther here.'

'We may yet. How do we get in?'

Drew walked over to one of the boarded-up windows and ran his hand along the underside of the sill. Half-way down the board he stopped and felt a small keypad. He got down on one knee and punched in a series of letters and numbers. A tiny red light blinked green and the front door popped open as if it had been spring-loaded.

'Neat,' said Luna, raising the pistol and pulling the door open. She led them into the cool darkness of the house. An alarm panel inside the front door beeped once and a green LED flickered on. The house smelled of wood polish. The sharp scent of log fires and cigar smoke floated in the air. The main room was lined in dark-stained pine boards. Two large sofas in warm plaids were arranged around a fieldstone fireplace set into a wall filled with books and framed photographs. A gleaming percussion-cap Hawken rifle lay in a rack over the mantel, hammer down in the old-fashioned way. Beyond the main room there was a small galley kitchen, and a couple of doors on either side of the fireplace wall led into two bedrooms, both furnished in the same masculine style as the main room, twin beds and dressers and sash windows bolted down and covered with thin steel bars, through which they could see tall trees swaying in a rising wind. The place had the feel of rooms that have not been used in a long time. They checked the entire house out in a minute – despite the outward appearance of size, it was an oddly cramped place – and ended up in the kitchen, Luna leaning on the counter and Drew standing in front of an open and depressingly barren fridge hoping to find something that he could persuade himself was coffee. He found a tin of Arabica behind a couple of juice cans and popped the lid. The rich sharp scent filled the kitchen, and he set about brewing a ten-cup pot while Luna wandered around the house one more time.

She came back when the coffee was ready.

'Lovely spot,' said Luna, 'but I don't see anything useful.'

'Walk around again. It'll come to you.'

'I'm a bodyguard, not a real-estate agent.'

'Place seem a little small to you?'

Luna went back out into the main room and turned around several times. Drew followed her out with two cups of black coffee steaming in his hands. He handed one to Luna.

'Walk it off from the fireplace to the front windows.'

Luna did.

'It feels . . . I don't know. Short.'

'Right. So do the bedrooms.'

Luna walked into the wood-paneled hallway that led to the bedroom on the right of the fireplace wall and ran her hand along the paneling, tapping and pressing. Drew followed her in and watched while she went over both bedrooms. She found nothing.

'This isn't fair. You already know.'

'Yeah,' said Drew. 'Watch.'

He went back out into the narrow wooden hall and took a small remote out of his pocket. He pressed the button and ran the remote over a seam in the wall paneling. The paneling cracked unevenly along what looked like a seam in the wood grain, and then it glided back into a recess in the wall with a smooth hydraulic whir and they were looking at a room about ten feet by twelve. It was clearly an office, with a large, antique banker's desk with a leather top, an old wooden swivel chair with a worn green leather cushion. A large black Dell desktop computer with a flat-screen monitor looked out of place in the forties feel of the office.

The shelves were lined with three-ring binders and stacked with old copies of *Foreign Affairs* and *The Economist*. Against the rear wall rows of brown metal file boxes had been stacked three high. A complete twenty-volume set of the unabridged *Oxford English Dictionary* was within arm's reach of the office chair. An old green-glass banker's lamp with a highly polished brass base was set to the right of the computer. Although crowded and filled with books and papers, the room was orderly and squared away. The only thing on the desk aside from the lamp and the big black computer was a large green-leather notebook, closed, neatly lined up with the edge of the blotter. A fat-bodied solid-gold fountain pen lay next to the blotter. The smell of Krugman's cigars was thick and harsh in the little room. Drew looked for a switch and found one next to a stack of *Jane's Intelligence Review* copies. He flicked it up, and a hidden fan began to whir softly. He sat down at the desk – feeling like a thief – and turned the computer on. The screen filled with a soft blue light and a small, red-lettered message appeared in the middle of it:

ENTER PASSWORD

'Oh jolly,' said Luna. 'Here we go.'

Drew gave her a look.

'Dad gave me the code. I'm not a complete idiot, Luna.'

'Hey. I never thought you were a complete idiot.'

Drew pulled a sheet out of his shirt pocket and typed in a long series of letters and numbers. He got it wrong three times, but on the fourth attempt the screen flickered and he was at Krugman's desktop screen looking at a series of program icons.

'Try his e-mail first,' said Luna.

Drew clicked onto his MAIL icon. The AOL entry screen popped open and asked him for another password.

Drew blinked at the screen for a while.

'You don't have his e-mail password?' asked Luna.

'I wasn't expecting to need one.'

'Great. What do we do now?'

'I'm open to suggestions.'

'You could bash the keyboard repeatedly with your head.'

'You're beginning to wear on me, Luna.'

'Try your first name.'

'Why?'

'Just try it.'

'That's not going to work. It's too obvious.'

'How do you know? I'll bet Krugman expected you to end up here. I'll bet he counted on it, if things went wrong. Just try it.'

Drew did.

PASSWORD INCORRECT

'Try your last name, then.'

'Krugman's an ex-spook, Luna. He wouldn't be that obvious.'

'Try it anyway.'

Drew tried his last name.

PASSWORD ACCEPTED

Luna, mercifully, said nothing.

Drew clicked on the YOU'VE GOT MAIL tab and the mail screen opened up. It seemed Krugman was a very popular guy.

'Man,' said Drew. 'There has to be eighty e-mails there.'

Luna leaned over him to run her finger down the screen. Drew hated it when people touched the screens of monitors with their fingers. It always left greasy little marks that drove him nuts. But she smelled quite wonderful. He inhaled her deeply, trying not to let her hear him. He was not completely successful.

'What . . . are . . . you . . . doing?'

'Nothing. Really. I'm just breathing.'

'No you're not. You're snuffling at me.'

'I am not.'

'You are too. Stop it. Most of these look like they're from the same address. Try the most recent one.'

Drew clicked on an e-mail from ls_scss@mil.gov dated the previous morning around eight.

GUNTHER:

  IF THIS RELATES TO TALARIA MOST URGENT YOU CONTACT US IMMEDIATELY. LEVI

'What's Talaria?' asked Luna.

'No idea. Whatever it is they're now ready to listen to him about it. Typical. How about you search for anything on his hard drive containing the word "Talaria" and I'll go through his papers?'

'Sure. Let me in there.'

Luna sat down at the computer and started up a hard-drive file search program. The search screen began to flicker through all the files and programs on the main drive. She switched back to the AOL screen and started to work her way through Krugman's most recent e-mails. Most were business-related, messages from lawyers and registered lobbyists. She knew a few of the names, but none of them seemed remarkable and they all predated his disappearance by several days. She was about to open up the archived files of old mail when the search screen popped open:

Hard drive search for 'Talaria' complete: one file found
Cobraville.aol.mail (e-mail document 2145/08/10)

She double-clicked on it and the Word program started up. In a moment she was looking at a short single-spaced paragraph.

Kohl_Keune at Sternhagen confirms decrypt:

'Source informs us that he has items ready for the market that if made available will greatly improve hotel security. Competition concerns in hotel business will require visit to secure client interests. Composition of force not yet decided upon. DAQ confirms Talaria. Timeline NA. Urgent.'

Forwarded to LS Saturday August 10
no response to date / no action taken to date

She hit PRINT and the HP printer on the side table began to chatter out the document. She leaned over to pick it out of the tray and handed the sheet to Drew. He started to read it, and Luna turned back to the screen. At that point a clear male voice announced – in a chirpy computerized tenor – 'You've got mail' and Luna jumped a yard.
'Okay. This is odd,' she said. 'He just got an e-mail.'
'Who's it from?'
'This is too weird. It looks like it's from Krugman.'
Drew leaned down and studied the screen.

GKrugman@gsoro.intertec.org

'What's the time marker?'
'I have to open it to see.'
'Then open it.'

'There's an attachment.'

'So.'

'What if the attachment has a virus?'

'Risks have to be taken. He's got McAfee. Open the thing.'

Luna hesitated with the cursor hovering over the e-mail. Then she clicked on the OPEN tab. It contained one sentence.

Unknown male – Sternhagen / MPEG.

No signature. The time marker indicated that the e-mail had been sent on Wednesday, August 20, at 0715 hours.

'Drew. This was literally sent minutes ago.'

'Sent to Krugman's AOL account by Krugman from another domain. Before you do anything else, see if the anti-virus program can tell you what computer sent this e-mail.'

'How do I do that?'

Drew clicked on the McAfee program and selected Visual Trace. A screen popped up with word "pinging." In a moment they had an ISP address:

Giovanni Soro Institute. 335 East 48th Street. New York.

'God. Maybe he really is still alive. Try the attachment.'

Luna clicked on OPEN. The server showed them a file description: kohl_keune/Sternhagen.MPEG.

'An MPEG is a digital film clip. See if you can get it.'

Luna clicked on DOWNLOAD FILE. A bar graphic began to inch across the screen, along with an estimated time for the download to complete. Next to it was a message:

TIME TO DELETION: 30:00:00

The numbers began to tick off in tenths of a second.

'Oh hell. What now? Does it sterilize all the hamsters in a fifty-mile radius or something?'

'No. But you're going to have to download that file in a hurry.'

Luna clicked on DOWNLOAD NOW. Drew began opening drawers and pulling out boxes.

'What are you looking for?'

'A writable disk. A CD. Help me.'

Luna and Drew scrambled around the drawers and the boxes until Luna came up with a plastic container full of blank CDs. Drew slipped it into the CD burner and closed it.

'As soon as it loads, copy the file to the CD burner.'

The download screen showed them an estimated download time of thirty minutes. The clock in the upper right hand was preset for thirty minutes. The download bar started a maddeningly slow crawl from left to right. Drew silently cursed all rural phone lines.

'Are we going to make it?'

'I don't know. Whoever sent this –'

'You don't think it was Krugman?'

'I don't know. Have you ever seen anything like this before?'

Luna shook her head. 'No. But computers aren't a big part of what we do. This feels like some sort of spook program.'

'Look, can you stay on this? I'll go through some of these file boxes and see if I can find a reference to something called Talaria.'

'What if I screw it up?'

'Would you rather sling these boxes around?'

'No. You're the guy. Go do the grunt work.'

In a few seconds she was lost in concentration. Drew watched her face illuminated by the screen for a few moments and then turned to confront the wall of papers and the file boxes piled up in the corners. He picked up one marked TAB–TUNGUSKA and laid it down on the corner of the desk. It was a box of hanging file folders listed alphabetically, starting with the name TABULATE and going all the way to TUNGUSKA. Drew recognized the name; it was the location of an asteroid strike in Siberia early in the last century.

He flipped through the files looking for TALARIA. Nothing at all. He then examined each individual file in the box. Nothing that looked useful. He picked up a box labeled AARON–AZUL and opened it up. A bright square of yellow sunlight that had been lying on the floor of the hallway outside the office worked its way slowly up the wall. Now and then he glanced at the slow-moving download bar on the screen and tried not to throw something at it.

'How much download time do we have?'

'Ten minutes.'

'And on the clock?'

'Thirty-two seconds to spare. Thirty-one.'

Eight minutes later she said, 'Drew, come here.'

Drew was on the floor, his back up against the rows of file boxes, surrounded by a litter of papers and files. His face was drawn and weary and he needed a shave. He looked like hell. Luna didn't point this out to him because she suspected she didn't look a lot better.

'I don't think I can get up.'

She came over and offered him a hand. He took it and she pulled him to his feet.

'Look at this.'

She placed a fingertip on a small icon in the lower right-hand edge, half-hidden in the task bar. A tiny telephone.

'That wasn't on a few minutes ago.'

She moved the cursor over to it and a pop-up read:

INSTANT MESSAGING ACTIVE

'What's that?'

Drew looked at the download bar. It was almost complete.

'It's the AOL Messenger icon. I think we're being monitored.'

The download bar registered 98 percent complete. The clock had sixty-three seconds left. They stood and watched the bar in silence.

It finally hit the end of the line and the pop-up said:

DOWNLOAD COMPLETE

WRITING TO CD-RW DRIVE

The CD drive began to hum. The clock hit 00:00 and a message came up: DELETING HARD DRIVE. One by one all of Krugman's e-mails began to vanish off the list. As they were clearing a small square screen appeared in the upper right of the AOL screen:

INSTANT MESSENGER: IM CHAT (CATO)

CATO: Hello . . .

'That . . . is flat out creepy,' said Luna. 'Who is it? Krugman?'

'I have no idea.'

'Should we answer it?'

'How should I know?'

CATO: Hello . . . please respond . . .

They stood there transfixed for almost thirty seconds. The CD writer stopped and the screen reported DISC COPY COMPLETE. Drew popped the drawer and scooped up the CD. Icons were now disappearing all across Krugman's desktop screen.

CATO: Hello . . . please identify . . .

'Now's a great time to show some leadership, Drew.'

'Ask him to identify himself first.'

Luna began to type.

Who are you?

CATO: Krugman.

'Jesus,' said Luna. 'It looks like he is alive.'

A second message appeared almost instantly:

CATO: Who was Conjurado?

'What does that mean?' asked Luna.

'He's asking me to prove who I am. Tell him Conjurado was a horse. My first. Krugman was there when my dad gave him to me.'

'Conjurado? You mean the Spanish for conspirator?'

'Yes. Type it in.'

Conjurado was a horse.

The instant she hit the last 'e' the chat screen went blank. The hard drive continued to spin, and a pop-up message read: SHUTTING DOWN. They both watched the screen with a growing sense of panic. After a wait of almost twenty seconds the screen reappeared with this brief message:

Kohl Keune at 212-355-9955.
I fear you can trust no one else. Krugman.

The screen flickered and went black. Luna pressed the reboot button. The entire machine was dead. She sat back and stared at the screen for a moment and then looked up at Drew.

'Now what do we do?'

'That's a New York City area code. The Giovanni Soro

Institute is right there in Midtown. Obviously we should go to New York.'

'I think we should talk to Levi Sloane.'

'I think we should do both.'

Iligan City

They were waiting for him when he got home. Gideon opened the door to his two-room flat on Fortaliza Street, and the first thing he noticed was the harsh reek of sweat. He walked into the room with his arms loaded, groceries and a paper sack with two bottles of Stolichnaya vodka. The men were sitting in his camp chairs and facing the door. Neither man had any weapons visible. Gideon stopped in the open door with his mouth open. They looked back at him with flat unfriendly expressions, a young Maranao with tribal tattoos on his cheeks, dressed in a white shirt and jeans, and an older man – cheeks unshaven and a small threadbare goatee, a narrow jackal's face, and small hard black eyes, wearing a dirty and wrinkled business suit that had started out years ago in some sky-blue tint, an open-necked shirt that had not been white for many weeks, and sandals. He did not know either of them. The young Maranao stood up and closed the door behind Gideon and stayed there, facing him. The older man – he had a Middle Eastern look – remained where he was, his hands in his lap, erect, his attitude one of tension and aggression.

'Who are –'

'Shut up,' said the man with the jackal's face. The Maranao youth pushed Gideon toward the bed and sat him down on it. Gideon slouched there with his groceries still in his arms. The Maranao took the bags away and set them on the dresser next to his computer. He pulled out one of the bottles of vodka and showed it to the bearded man. The man's face hardened up and he showed Gideon teeth that were dirty and uneven. An open window behind the seated man poured hot damp air into the room and blew the man's acrid sweat smell across to Gideon. He looked at Gideon with simmering dislike.

'You are drinking?'

Mr Gabriel. This is Mr Gabriel.

'No. Yes. Only after work. You are Mr Gabriel?'

'Yes. Ibrahim, pour Mr Sabang a drink.'

'I don't want a drink. It is a pleasure –'

Mr Gabriel held up a leathery hand with a pale yellow palm and Gideon closed his mouth, accidentally biting the inside of his cheek. The pain was sharp and searing, but he tried not to react to it. His eyes watered a little. The boy called Ibrahim selected a filthy glass from Gideon's dresser and filled it with warm vodka. He handed the glass to Gideon. His eyes were flat and small and black and nothing at all was in them. They could have been the glass-button eyes of a doll.

'Drink,' said Mr Gabriel.

Gideon put the glass to his mouth. The edge of it rattled against his teeth. He filled his mouth with the vodka and choked it down. It burned his throat. Mr Gabriel watched him drink with an expression of extreme disgust, as if he were watching a man defile himself. Gideon put the glass down on the wooden floor and straightened up again. Mr Gabriel moved in his chair, making it creak. From the open window street noises floated up and Gideon could see a light rain drifting like a gauze curtain across the rooftops on the other side of Fortaliza Street. His gaze returned to Mr Gabriel, and he swallowed, his throat convulsing. He could hear his own heart. It was making a high throbbing noise he had never heard it make before.

'Tell me,' said Mr Gabriel, in a quiet voice, Arabic, guttural, '. . . about Jordan Kemp.'

'Sir, I have already –'

'I know. Tell me again.'

Gideon made an effort to show some dignity. He was a man of importance and Mr Gabriel had no reason to be . . . like this.

'Well, I have done what was needed. My information is that Mr Kemp was very sick and now he is better. I believe he is in Iligan City. I saw him at the Blue Bird. It might be that he is dead.'

'It might be that he is dead.'

The flat toneless repetition was unnerving.

'I do not know this. But I did see him there. Although he did not look very sick. He was with Jesus Rizal. He is the cousin of –'

'We know who he is. Tell me, exactly how did you obtain this information concerning Mr Jordan Kemp?'

'How did . . . I . . . I used the channels.'

'What channels?' Mister Gabriel drew the word out, putting weight on it, and his eyes bore into Gideon. Gideon's unease grew and he worked to hide it. He had nothing to worry about. He had only done his job.

'The computer.'

'This one?' said Mr Gabriel, inclining his head toward the dresser.

'No.'

'No? The one at work, perhaps?'

'Yes. It is much more powerful.'

'I see,' said Mister Gabriel, and to Gideon he seemed pleased at what he was hearing. Gideon found some air and got it into his lungs.

'You have used this method before?'

'Yes, sir.'

'When?'

'I ... helped you to speak with – I do not know, of course, who you spoke with. I only used the conduit. I did not listen.'

'Of course,' said Mister Gabriel. 'You did not listen. Tell me, Gideon ... do you know a man named Yusef al Ashrami?'

'Yusef ... ?'

'Yusef al Ashrami. The name is known to you?'

'No. It is not.'

'May I tell you who he was?'

'Please.'

'When I was a boy in Yemen he was my father's cousin's son. We played together in my father's gardens and later we went to the same schools. Even to the Sorbonne. Do you know the Sorbonne, Gideon? It is in Paris. Have you ever been to Paris? No? You should have gone to Paris. Those were great times in Paris.'

Mr Gabriel stopped talking here while some emotion rippled across his face. He gave Gideon the impression of a man suffering a chronic pain. The bones of his face stood out clearly and two white spots formed on his cheeks. He reached into the pocket of his wrinkled pale blue suit jacket and withdrew a small blue plastic cylinder. He held it to his mouth and pressed a plunger on the top, inhaling twice, two short sharp gasps. He put the metal cylinder away and the white spots over his cheeks grew more pink. He leaned back in the chair and crossed his legs. Gideon saw that he wore sandals, thick, with black rubber soles, and he had no socks on. His insteps were rubbed raw by the straps. The black hairs on his lower legs were coarse, like wires.

'Well, you do not know Yusef, as you say, and that is the way it is. Ibrahim, show him the picture.'

Ibrahim pulled a thin white envelope out of his back pocket and slipped a small photograph out of it. He handed it to Gideon. It was a color shot of a middle-aged man with dark skin and a beard. He was lying on his back on some sort of metal table. He had no shirt on and the muscles of his neck were standing out like tight cords. His eyes were wide open and the edges of his mouth were pulled back in a terrible contraction of agony. Even in the still photo Gideon felt he could hear the echo of a shriek. It was a photograph of a man in unthinkable pain. Gideon studied the photograph longer than he needed to in an attempt to delay the hands of the clock that were turning on the face of the bedside alarm next to his elbow. Finally he set the photo down with care on the tangled coverlet of his bed.

Mr Gabriel glanced at Ibrahim and the boy picked up the photo and carried it over to Mr Gabriel, who took it with reverence and stared down at it for a while. Then he spoke again, still staring at the photo.

'So . . . this is Yusef. He works for us, Gideon. He is one of our co-workers. One of your co-workers. You can see that he is undergoing some sort of . . . unpleasantness. Do you wonder what sort of unpleasantness he is undergoing? Shall I tell you?'

Gideon said nothing. The clock at his side had stopped.

'First he has been stripped naked. They have laid him on this metal table – a part of which you can see here underneath him – and they have tied him down with straps. The straps are padded so as not to cut into him. You cannot see them but they are there. Next he has been given an injection, like a medicine. I will not bore you with the names, but the effect is to keep the heart beating under whatever strain it may be feeling and also to elevate the senses of the subject. To . . . clarify and heighten the physical responses. You understand? Everything is slowed down and everything is available to the man now. Whatever is happening he will experience it with a newborn baby's intensity. His universe is now wide, infinite. Then they begin.'

'Who are they?' Gideon could not stop the question.

'They?' said Mr Gabriel, smiling. 'They are the Americans. This is what the Americans routinely do to our people. This is being done to Yusef right now. Do you wonder how this photograph has reached me all the way from America? It was e-mailed by the Americans to my mother in Yemen. My mother then e-mailed it to our home office in Karachi. From there it was e-mailed to me. Is not the technology of the Ferenghi marvelous? When your dear friend may be tortured in this way and a photograph of it actually happening may be sent all the way around the globe – bouncing – bouncing – bouncing – like a child's ball off the skin of the planet – and arriving here in the hotel. But I haven't told you what they are doing. I will tell you, yes?'

'Yes,' said Gideon, and Mr Gabriel told him. It took a few minutes, and as he listened to Mr Gabriel's soft voice the words began to run together, and the images they carried sank deeply into him and he drifted in a kind of waking dream. Then Mr Gabriel stopped talking and Gideon came back to the little room and the open window and the traffic noise and children's voices coming up from Fortaliza Street.

'And the wonderful thing about all of this is that Yusef will not die from what they do. No. Not at all. Can you believe it? There is hardly any evidence. Only a few tiny hemorrhages in the whites of the eyes and some anal bleeding. When it is over Yusef will have told them anything, and yet even he could not prove later that he had ever been touched. It would all be in his memory. Nowhere else. So then it is impossible for Yusef to ever go home again with honorable scars to prove he has been tortured and to explain a little why he had betrayed his friends. So he must stay with the Americans after all, since he knows he cannot go back to his friends ever again. And soon he will talk without the need of the torture. He will talk freely and in the end he may even come to think that he loves the Americans because they have not tortured him in a very long time. What do you think of that?'

Unable to think of anything else to do, Gideon nodded.

'So,' said Mr Gabriel, putting the photograph away and sitting up in the chair. 'Do you want to know how the Americans found out where Yusef was living?'

Gideon was sure he did not want to know. He was certain. But Gideon knew that Mr Gabriel was not really asking a question.

'It seems that someone from here – in Mindanao – got onto a computer and started phoning various companies and people around the world looking for a man. He named the man. Jordan Kemp was the name. Now, you have heard of a thing called the National Security Agency? Yes, of course. Now the National Security Agency listens to . . .' He made a globe-encompassing gesture, his arms widespread . . . 'Everything! Wonderful, is it not! They listen to . . . everything . . . and they take notes, Gideon. Yes, they take notes! The devils. Think of this! And their computer takes notes. It listens for special words. Special names, Gideon. Names such as Jordan Kemp. And one of the notes they took was of someone talking to a news-paperman in a place called Toronto. This is in Canada. Canada is a very little country with some very naive and gullible people running it, so many of our co-workers are able to go there and help our work. Your work. Our work, Gideon.'

Gideon nodded. He was afraid to ask for water. He reached down and picked up the glass of vodka and drained it.

'Yes. Our work. So one of the newspaper people who got this call remembered that he had gotten a call very much like it – about this man Jordan Kemp – only a few days before. So he said so to the man who was asking this time. And this comment, Gideon – this saying of the name Jordan Kemp twice in such a short time, it was heard. And acted upon. The National Security Agency – that is what they call it, the NSA – then used a computer to find out – this is amazing – everyone who had called this newspaper in the days before. And then they used another computer to trace the source of every one of these calls. And one of these calls came from an office of the Canadian government itself. The Department of Immigration. And the man from this Department of Immigration in Ottawa was named Jorge Esquivez, who was a Canadian citizen who had emigrated to Canada from Brazil many years before. But Jorge Esquivez was not who he seemed to be, and after some looking and some asking the

Americans told the Canadians to bring Jorge Esquivez to a place called Niagara Falls, where Mr Esquivez was handed over to the Americans. I'll bet you can figure out who Mr Esquivez was?'

'It was Yusef?'

'Yes. Very good. It was Yusef. Yusef had gotten himself a very good job inside the Canadian government itself and he was able to use the government's own computers to find out ... whatever we needed. And now we do not have Yusef anymore. But that is not the best part. Do you want the best part?'

Gideon held himself quite still.

'Okay ... after making all these calls, Gideon – and letting the Americans hear the words "Jordan Kemp" – you then called an American Army hospital in Washington called the Walter Reed hospital. Do you remember that?'

'Yes,' said Gideon, his stomach rolling.

'Good. And do you remember having to wait awhile for your answer? I don't remember you telling me about this, so perhaps you forgot about it. But it seems that you were required to – I think they call it "hold the line"? Did you hold the line?'

'Yes.'

'And how long did you hold the line?'

'I ... maybe a couple of minutes. No more?'

'Well, what harm could come from that? True?'

'None. Sir, I used many tricks to fool the –'

'Tricks to fool the Americans. Yes. Still I am sorry to tell you that your tricks were not good enough and the Americans were able to follow you all the way back through the telephone lines and the microwave transmitters – you can almost see them, crawling up these electronic tunnels like swift little rats – following the scent

293

of Gideon Sabang – until they reach the computer on your desk at the power station and they pop out onto your desk and run around on it with their noses twitching. Did you see them, Gideon? When these American rats popped out of your screen?'

'I . . . made a mistake. I can fix it?'

'Tell me, Gideon, why do you think you are still alive?'

The Adirondacks

Bell UH-IH helicopter Tripoli
The Adirondacks, New York
Wednesday, August 20, 11:00 a.m. local time

The blue-green rolling peaks of the Adirondack chain lay spread out under them; at this elevation – very close to their flight ceiling in this thick summer heat – the mountains lay spread out in a magnificent sweep of coiling hills with slender creeks and rivers running in their deep valleys like thin silvery ribbons in the sunlight. The sky was a heart-lifting luminous blue and clear of all but a few high-flying streamers of cirrus cloud. They had banked around the gray peak of Little Moose Mountain, its rocky crest breaking free of the dark-green tree line like a gray whale bursting out of a rolling ocean, and now the sloping green bulk of the Big Range Mountain was filling up the windscreen.

To Luna's left, a long slender spearhead of deep blue with a glimmering of reflected sunlight lay in between two peaks, and she could see a tiny white triangle slicing across the surface of the lake, a sailboat heeled over hard, cutting a white, lacy trough in the water like a glass cutter being drawn over a mirror – another, safer world, she thought, as she watched the tiny craft cutting through the rippled wavelets – music on the stereo – the cold drinks going round – people laughing and talking – happily oblivious to the outer world . . .

She found the line of thought painful and looked away to the southwest, to the cluster of high mountains all around them, some of them almost level with their chopper. The ancient Adirondacks gave away slowly to a range of more rounded hills that eventually disappeared entirely into a lambent violet haze. A smudge of yellow smoke floating on the southern horizon with a smear of grimy black underneath it marked the suburbs of Albany, a hundred miles away. The Huey was thrumming gently, and the muted whine of the turbine had seeped quietly into the background of Luna's consciousness. The constant rhythmic vibration of the chopper had lulled her into a kind of surreal calm, a component of which she recognized as simple physical exhaustion, and her head was nodding slightly as her eyes began to close. Sleep . . . slow and sweet . . . her head fell forward and she sagged in her harness. Time passed – she had no idea how long, although it could only have been a few minutes. She became dimly aware of Drew shifting restlessly in the pilot's chair – and then the engine noise changed, the machine went into a slow but definite bank, and there was a strong warm light shining on her face – she saw the red blood-tint of her closed eyelids – and opened her eyes, blinking.

'What's happening?'

'Got a chopper up ahead,' said Drew, indicating the haze that rode along the horizon line. 'That fat black dot.'

Luna strained to see what Drew was seeing and finally managed to make out what looked like an enormous black bumblebee hovering in the shining air about a half-mile away. To her untrained eye it seemed to be almost on a level with them, but motionless. A silvery disc of light flickered above the fuselage, and a thin plume of blue smoke trailed behind it, lacy, a transparent smear against the sky.

'Can you see any markings?' asked Luna.

'No. He's got the sun behind him. Probably a forestry chopper. This is fire season. They do patrols over the high country looking for smoke. Don't worry. He'll shear off. He can see us too.'

'What kind of helicopter is it?'

Drew squinted into the glare.

'Looks like a Bell Jet Ranger. I think.'

'Are we supposed to talk to it?'

'We can. If it will make you feel better.'

Drew flicked the radio band over to air-to-air and pulled his mike around to the front.

'Unidentified Rotary, this is Bell Huey *Tripoli* on your quarter about two thousand yards. Come in.'

In his headset the sound of the broadband hissed like wind in the trees. He heard a thin clicking and then silence. This was not the usual response, and his attention centered on it fully as he watched the chopper hang there in the bright midmorning light; leaner, faster, infinitely more maneuverable than his ancient Huey. He repeated the call again, putting some force into it.

'Rotary bearing zero niner seven, this is a Bell Huey. We're about a half-mile to your southwest. Just want to give you a heads-up. We're inbound to Albany on your port quarter. Come back?'

Silence. Drew squinted at the black shape and saw it tilt forward slightly and begin to pull some air. The distant machine was rising now, and a shimmer of sunlight ran over its belly as it ascended. It leveled off about a hundred feet higher than their machine – moving rapidly now – and looked to her to be closing in quickly. Luna watched it with a thickening lump in her throat.

'Is he coming after us?'

The tension in her voice was contagious and Drew felt his own heart jump and his throat constrict slightly.

'Rotary, this is the Huey. You are closing on us. Please alter bearing or altitude. Current course will bring you right on us.'

Silence.

The chopper had gained considerable air speed now and was less than six hundred yards out. The sun was still behind it and all Drew could make of the machine was a black silhouette.

'Drew . . .'

'I see him. Guy must have his radio on the wrong frequency. You strapped in?'

'Strapped in? Yes. Why –'

'I'm maybe going to make a little move here.'

The unknown chopper was now less than three hundred yards away, and on a course that would take it right overhead, with what looked to Luna to be a damn small margin for error. Sunlight shimmered in its rotors, making it look like a flying chain saw. Now the whine of its engine came through the cabin walls and the beat of its rotors thrummed in the air all around them. Luna tightened her harness and eased her Berretta out of her belt holster. Drew was watching the chopper closing in with narrowed eyes and his mouth tight and angry.

'What . . . is . . . this . . . asshole . . . ?'

The unknown chopper slowed suddenly, flaring. Drew held the Huey steady as the other helicopter changed its aspect and began to move in a parallel course on their left side, less than a hundred yards away and about fifty feet higher.

Out of the glare of the sun now, Drew was able to confirm it as a Bell Jet Ranger, navy blue, with private markings: CVX993365H. He could see a white-faced man in the pilot's chair, aviator sunglasses and a black ball cap and a large handlebar mustache, staring back at him through the windscreen with no discernible expression; a look of flat emotionless appraisal. Drew tried to raise the chopper again: 'Rotary, this is the Huey *Tripoli*. Identify. You are exceeding air space restrictions and I will file against you.'

Silence.

The blue chopper was now moving southeast along their course, a little higher, less than fifty yards off Luna's window. Luna pulled her side-screen back and tried to wave them off. The pilot stared back at them for about thirty seconds, a hard-looking face past middle age, with pockmarked, flabby cheeks and a slash for a mouth.

'What is this guy's major malfunction –'

The blue chopper abruptly flared again and swept upward in a rapid rising arc, now crossing almost directly over them. Luna craned her head to follow the flight path of the machine. It was now almost directly above them. She watched as the starboard panel slid back and now there was a black figure in the open bay, leaning out, something in his hand ... long – dangling it – the sun glinting –

'Drew – he's got a chain. I think he's going to –'

Drew pitched the Huey into a wild right slide and dropped a hundred feet in a second, the rotors slamming through the thickening air and the turbine winding out into a hysterical shriek. The green mountains wheeled crazily in front of them – earth and then sky then earth – Luna felt her harness cutting brutally into her left side. She braced herself on the bulkhead with her left hand and twisted in her seat, frantically looking for the other chopper, her head swiveling and electric blue panic beginning to slither through her mind.

'Can you see him?' Drew shouted over the howl of the turbine and the hammering rotors.

'No. I – yes. He's right behind us.'

'Hang on. I'm going in low.'

'Low! There's a very big planet down there. All done up in earth tones. You can't miss it.'

'We can't stay up here. That Jet Ranger can fly loops around us. He can max out at three hundred knots. We can't outrun him. He drops that chain into our rotors we have four thousand feet to fall. We have to go down.'

'Down to where? They can still catch us down there.'

'They'll have to work for it. Hang on.'

Drew put the chopper into a steep dive, and her view abruptly filled up with a wall of green pines that seemed to rush up at them, getting more detailed every second. Wind streamed around the screen and howled past her open side screen. Luna twisted around and caught a fleeting glimpse of the big blue chopper – almost on their tail rotor – two men inside the cabin staring back at her with cold expressionless faces – something shiny and glittering was trailing from its right side that flailed and lashed in the slipstream – a length of heavy steel chain almost twenty feet long –

'You're right. He's trying to drop that chain into the rotors.'

'I know it,' said Drew, watching the ground flying up at the screen, feeling the cyclic jumping in his hand, gripping the collective so hard his fingers were numb, keeping an eye on the altimeter and the RPM gauge. They dropped through the air like a shot bird, falling so fast the air pressure change made their ears ache. The earth flew up at them, and Drew pulled back on the cyclic, the chopper shuddering and jolting, bucking like a reined-in horse. Treetops wheeled below them.

In a few heart-stopping seconds they were racing sideways over a narrowing river valley lined with sharp lodgepole pines. They looked like green spikes rising out of sheer rock faces. He was less than three hundred feet off their tips and dropping fast. He could see the shadow of the Huey flickering over the pines below him, a huge black shape like a stingray gliding over a green ocean. A second shadow flowed over the same trees, less than fifty feet behind, its shape fluttering and skimming over the spikes of pines fifty feet below them, with one long black snake lashing under it. Drew could feel the beat of its rotors and hear the deeper drone of the Jet Ranger's engines over the high skirling whine of the Huey.

A black cloud of crows exploded out of a lightning-struck pine up ahead, and he flew through the rising flock at a hundred miles an hour, flinching away instinctively as one fluttering black shape loomed close – slammed sickeningly into the windscreen in a smear of bright red and black sticky feathers – the solid thud of the impact shook the cabin and a spidery crack spread itself like a fork of silvery lightning across the Plexiglas in front of Luna's white shocked face. She stuck her head out the side screen and saw the Jet Ranger closing in about fifty feet off their rotors. She popped her harness, braced herself in the seat, and stuck her Beretta out the side window, trying to steady her sights on the underbelly of the Jet Ranger.

She saw the co-pilot staring down at her through a clear panel below his knees.

His mouth opened just as she squeezed the trigger – seven rounds slammed out and the pistol bucked wildly – out of the corner of her right eye she was aware of the bright golden rounds flying away and the glitter of sunlight on them as they tumbled into the air and disappeared against the blurred wall of trees under her right arm – two tiny white spots seemed to splatter against that clear panel and she saw the co-pilot jerk his feet away –

And then the Huey lurched drunkenly to the left as Drew put it into a steep banking turn and the green valley underneath them rose up around them. She was now looking at a river flowing swiftly over rounded black rocks – close enough to see each individual wavelet – she caught a fleeting image of a steel-blue trout hovering in a pool of clear-running water – she looked up ahead and saw a narrowing gap where two mountains bordering the long twisting valley squeezed it into a narrowing gorge filled with white water. The gorge snaked left and then cut right again – straightening now – hard sunlight baking one craggy gray rock face and the other – moss-covered and dripping with lichen – hidden in a deep blue-black shadow.

Drew dropped the chopper down hard until it was skimming at speed less than ten feet off the surface of the river – they could hear the booming echo of their own rotors now – thundering back at them from the rock face – and their own shadow flickered beneath them like a banner of rippling black silk gliding over the churning white water of the river – their rotor wash left a wake of foaming spray behind them and the trees on the banks lashed silvery-white as they boomed past – a deer with her

ears laid back and her white tail flashing bounded away
from a steep bank and flashed into the forest – a blur of
tawny light and one soft brown eye looking wild – Drew's
face was white and his shoulders ached from fighting
the cyclic, and his right knee was jerking spasmodically as
he held the tail rotor in line – and they heard three sharp
clear cracks like cold branches breaking in the dead of
winter – three holes filled with sunlight punched themselves through the cabin roof less than two feet away from
Luna's head.

'They're shooting at us!' Luna shouted.

'You think? Go shoot back!'

'Can you hold this damn breadbox steady?'

'I'll do what I can. If you open that bay door be careful.'

Luna gave him a hard look – how much worse can this
get? – slipped out of the harness – and then stumbled back
into the passenger cabin. The canyon walls had closed
in tight and all Drew could do was torque the chopper
through its racing curves as the granite cliffs blurred past
him on either side. His head was full of numbers – he had
more lift because he was riding his own rotor wash – but
the rotors had a radial sweep of twenty-four feet – if he so
much as clipped a root at this speed, the fiberglass blades
would tear themselves to pieces in less than a second – the
whole shuddering mass would cartwheel down the canyon
like a runaway freight – caroming off the rock walls –
JP 5 spilling out from ruptured tanks – they would end
in a fireball.

Drew's main calculation was that the Jet Ranger pilot
now hounding his tail was a reasonable guy – maybe just a
mercenary – who wanted to come out of this insane
action alive even more than Drew did. He had no time
to think about who these guys were – a problem for the

survivors to deal with. He heard Luna working the bay door latch and was suddenly aware of a burst of white noise and wind rush, and the cabin filled up with the clean tangy scent of lodgepole pines and spring water.

He spared a second to glance back and saw Luna silhouetted in the open bay door, her black pistol in her hand. As he watched she extended the pistol, steadied, and then squeezed off four shots in a steady even rhythm. He turned to look back out the windscreen and saw three bright red spheres hanging in midair about a thousand yards up the canyon, seeming to float weightlessly. As he watched, a quick beam of sunlight played across an almost invisible silver thread.

'Luna!'

Her voice came back faintly, blown away by the roar of the wind and the echo of rotors thudding off the canyon walls.

'What?'

'What's he doing?'

Luna looked up and saw the blue chopper less than twenty feet back and a little above them. The co-pilot's chair was empty, and someone was leaning out the port passenger door with a rifle in his left hand, struggling with the slipstream.

'Waddya think? He's trying to kill us, you idiot.'

The red spheres were eight hundred yards away and closing –

'Shoot at the pilot. Distract him –'

– Five hundred yards –

Luna reloaded the Beretta and aimed it at the chopper.

'What the –'

– Four hard cracks slammed around in the cabin –

'fuck –'

304

– Two hundred yards –

– four more percussive booms and Luna saw the pilot flinch – glaring whitely at her with his mouth a black slash – don't like that do you? – you miserable son of a bitch – five more sharp cracks –

'– do you *think* I'm doing?'

Two more rounds out and Luna saw her last round glance off the curved Plexiglas windscreen of the Jet Ranger and had the intense satisfaction of seeing the pilot duck and the chopper wobble on its headlong race down the canyon – she was cursing the featherweight nine-millimeter Beretta and fumbling for her last magazine – a heavy rifle round cracked past her head at the speed of sound – followed by a deep echoing boom – she stuck her head through the open bay and saw the co-pilot leaning out the door with his rifle –

– one hundred yards –

She punched the magazine home, kicked the slide, steadied the Beretta on the black figure –

– fifty yards –

Had the shooter in the notch – wavering – two red dots and a third just a little off the line – steady now –

– ten yards –

Squeezing –

A silver band flickered over her head – three bright red spheres flashed over the chopper's roof – held together by a band of heavy silver cable – barely skimmed the rotors of the Huey and caught the Jet Ranger on the spinning driveshaft just under the rotors – Drew heard the bowstring twang over the roar of the turbine – heard Luna yelling, 'Holy shit' – and then a following concussive blast struck the tail rotor – the pedals jumped and jolted under his feet – he fought the shuddering cyclic and twisted the collective throttle hard – the juddering Huey leaped suddenly upward – bellowing – rotors thundering – the canyon walls dropped away abruptly and they soared far up into a pale sky streaked with paintbrush and horsetail cirrus.

Drew leveled the chopper at five hundred feet off the sloping green shoulder of Big Range Mountain and banked gently into the east. Luna came forward – her face pale and her expression fixed – and buckled herself into the co-pilot's chair. Drew wheeled out over the canyon again and they followed the rising plume of oily black smoke back up the river for a half mile until they found the wreckage, scattered for a hundred yards along the gorge.

The tail rotor assembly was lying in shallow white water, sheared off behind the cabin, the river already changing its course around this new obstruction, and cold clear water running through the shredded aluminum hull. He brought the Huey to a slow glide and then into a hover taxi that rattled the old fuselage and vibrated through their bones. Luna felt the deep rhythm of the machine and under it the fluttering percussion of her own heart inside its cage of bones.

They passed by a sheared-off spar of thick, white pine with something hanging from its broken spear-point, the upper torso of a man, still wearing a Kevlar vest. Below the vest a stringy rope of pale blue intestines fluttered in their prop wash and a spray of red blood drops glittered like rubies in the bright clear air where the sunlight caught them. A hundred yards farther up they floated across the cabin itself, crushed like a blue eggshell and smoldering blackly.

A small fire was burning inside what was left of the shell, and something manlike was crumpled up against the roof, arm splayed and a stunned white face staring up at them through the gap. Drew brought the machine to a hover about ten feet off the wreck, the downwash pressing the smoke away in a black circle. The flames brightened and flared, and the manlike shape lifted a crisping blackened arm toward them as the flames reached his legs.

He began to writhe, looking like an animal in a leg-hold trap, and his burning face twisted, his mouth became a black hole in his face. They could hear the thin high cry above the sound of their rotors, a terrible cutting edge inside it. The sound rose beyond their hearing.

Luna unhooked her belt and went back to the bay door while Drew held the chopper steady. He heard her calling to him.

'Lower . . . That's it . . . Hold it.'

He held it there, balancing all the warring forces, feeling the machine beating under his hands and humming in his bones like a living thing. A pause. Waiting. Then three quick shots – three hard clear percussive slams inside the vibrating cabin – and Luna came silently back to her seat. He lifted the chopper into the sky again.

At four thousand feet he looked over at her. She was staring straight ahead at a point somewhere out there on the horizon line. The sun moved through the cabin as he banked into the east toward New York, and three clear shafts of smoky yellow light lanced downward from the roof. Luna looked down at the cabin floor and watched as three tiny ovals of hard sunlight moved in unison over the studded steel plating and finally stopped in between their seats.

Drew brought the chopper up to full power and moved the cyclic forward. The rotors bit into the air and the machine tilted as their airspeed climbed. After a very long while she reached out and touched Drew on his left shoulder, resting her hand there, feeling the hard muscle and bone underneath his jacket, the uneven rise and shuddering fall of his unsteady breathing.

Cobraville

Cole stood at one of the high sash-windows of Father Desaix's clinic and watched as the sudden tropical night came down over the village. Impenetrable darkness seemed to flow down from the surrounding jungle and pool itself through the village, until all that he could make out in the darkness was the pale yellow glimmer of lanterns inside the village huts, and here and there the bright flicker of a charcoal fire burning in a brazier, a tiny red glimmer seen dimly through a solid wall of rain. The monsoon had increased to a drumming thunder on the corrugated iron roof, and the wind whipped at the palm fronds that towered over the village, filling the surrounding blackness with the lashing of loose thatch and the groaning creak of the palm trunks.

The air was steamy, fetid, stinking of river rot and sewage from the overrun latrines and the bullock sheds. Beyond the wall of falling water he could just make out the rattle and patter of the rain on the back of the big brown river and the hissing rush of the current sliding through the islands of lotus that lay on its surface. Fat droplets hurled themselves against the rippled glass of the window or rattled against the bamboo shutters, and then ran downward in a writhing tangle of slithering rivulets.

Through the wooden floorboards he felt the rumble of the clinic's ancient gas generator, powering the yellow lights that ran down the roof-beam, as well as the priest's few jungle indulgences: a medical monitor, a pump, the shrouded machinery of a little OR he had walled off at the rear of the clinic, a small boxy fridge clanking wheezily in a corner of his open kitchen, the reading light above his double hammock, a two-way radio on a bamboo sideboard, the yard-sale lamps he had moved to light the long wooden table around which the rest of his men were sitting on frail wooden chairs, leaning back from their dinners, sated, filled up with Marie Claire's spicy bourguignon – the scent of which still filled the long dimly lit hall – small squat, shot glasses filled with brandy resting in front of them. They looked boneless with fatigue, their unshaven faces hard in the downlight. The smoke from a selection of stale, acrid cheroots rose up from the little gathering and lay curling against the wooden rafters, lost in the upper darkness of the peaked roof. Music was playing quietly on an ancient turntable, a scratchy thirty-three that wobbled on the turning disc and gave the music – something lush and deep over which a single eloquent violin mourned an unknown but piercing loss – a quavering, reedy undertone that reminded Cole for some demented reason of a squalid smoke-filled Hamburg nightclub where he had once spent ten days and nights waiting for a man who later turned up facedown and bloated into a waxy obscenity in a reeking industrial canal a mile south of the Kaltenbrunner Gate.

Cole turned away from the window as the girl came up to him: Marie Claire, the priest's – what? Acolyte? Servant? Assistant? Mistress? He had no idea. Their relationship seemed ambiguous, and the priest had shown no inclination to define it. The young woman had a full, almost overripe brown body imperfectly covered by a translucent white smock dress made of some sort of gauzy fabric, with a square, open neck that ended just above the lush swelling of her breasts. In her deep golden-brown eyes Cole could see a kind of challenge, a readiness to defy judgment, and under that a considerable amount of adolescent heat. Smelling of sweat and cloves, she bobbled liquidly in front of him, and held out a kaleidoscopic tray filled with slices of mango, pineapple, lime, kiwi, even bloodred oranges. Drew smiled and took a crescent of mango. She showed him her impossibly white teeth and a flash of pink tongue as she smiled and said, in a tone that literally purred, her accent very French:

'Father asks if you will not take some brandy with him?'

Cole came back and took his chair at the end of the long table, catching a look of contained urgency from Pike over the edge of Pike's shot glass as he took a short sharp jolt and set it back down on the boards, a little too firmly. Father Desaix – from his position as host at the head of the table – leaned forward into the light, cupping his hands around a fat green bottle of Remy Martin, his craggy face already bright with drink; yet his eyes were still clear and cold, his manner alert, his trim beard glinting silver in the half-lit gloom.

'I have been telling your sergeant he is an enthusiast.'

Cole glanced at Pike and then around the table as the rest of the men looked back at him – Burdette with a lazy off-center smile and a cheroot smoldering at his fingertips; Dean Krause leaning back with his hands folded across his belly and his blunt uncomplicated face composed, apparently at ease but quietly watchful; Strackbein wearing his arched left eyebrow a little high and looking cynically amused – keeping, as always, his personal distance; Ramiro Vasquez sprawled lazily back in his chair, one knee braced against the table, gently swirling a glass of brandy in his hand and watching Cole with detached amusement; and Jesus Rizal, flushed with too much food and stolidly intent on his brandy glass, which he had found to his growing dismay had a tendency to empty much too fast and which at the moment urgently required a refill. Cole looked back at Father Desaix, gave him a bow over his glass, and downed the fiery brandy in a single shot. It burned inside his throat and flamed up in his blood, driving away his fatigue.

'My sergeant?' he said, raising an eyebrow like Strackbein.

The priest pulled unsteadily on his cheroot and exhaled a blue plume, smiling broadly at Cole through the haze.

'I speak too frankly. But there can be no doubt. In all armies the sergeants are as one man, the hard rock at the center. I ask no names.'

Cole nodded, his glance shifting momentarily to Jesus, who flicked his eyes away and found something fascinating in his empty shot glass. The man had talked, Cole knew. But how much?

'You look troubled,' said the priest, reading Cole's look.

'I do?'

'You must endeavor to relax more. The jungle rewards stillness. I do not mean to preach,' he said, lifting his glass and draining it, reaching unsteadily for the green bottle. 'I mean only that we who work in the old places of the world, the outposts beyond civilization, most particularly in these remote jungle villages, must take care not to become rigid, too focused on the importance of our mission ... for example Mother Teresa. You know of her, yes?'

'We do,' said Strackbein. 'She's now considered a saint.'

'She was a viper,' said Desaix, waving his glass carelessly, spilling his brandy. 'A terrible woman. I visited her once, on a delegation from the Vatican. These poor Calcutta lepers under her care, she refused to give them anything to ease their pain. Dragged their lives out to the uttermost pitch. She refused to change, even after a plea from the Pope himself to ameliorate. Pain-killers. Palliatives. She closed her face like a fist, those cruel jaws clamping shut, those hard little black eyes. She said that their suffering was an offering to God. I wondered at her. We all did, and soon left her, leering at us through a filthy window as our train lurched out of Calcutta, her acolytes clustered around her in their dirty blue frocks and their clumping black shoes.'

'We're told,' said Strackbein, 'that God requires the suffering of the world. In penance. And for the salvation of our souls.'

'So we are endlessly told,' said Desaix, nodding. 'I often wonder why God is represented to us as a deity so addicted to suffering. God as a *connoisseur* of human grief. Such a God would truly be a monster, if He existed at all.'

'That's not my God,' said Cole, a lapsed Episcopalian.

Desaix made a gesture of resignation, sighing.

'Sometimes I am ashamed of what we Catholics have made out of our God, a brooding old dweller in the cathedral apse, a grudge-holder demanding our praise, our shameless supplications, these mewling, self-hating entreaties – the store-bought incense, our mumbled pleas ... We are told that we can speak to God only through the saints – through Jesus – that insipid cocotte with his simpering, vacant smile, those watery eyes – the cartoon heart crowned with thorns – entreaties channeled through the Cult of the Virgin – idolatry, abject submission, self-hatred. This farcical Pope, preaching alms for the poor while he squats in his city of gold, his rancid soul bought and paid for by those fundamentalist thugs in Opus Dei.'

'You don't believe in God,' said Krause, enjoying not only the old man's raving arias but also the ironic possibilities provided by an honestly atheistic priest. Desaix flared his rheumy red eyes at him and smiled hugely, showing teeth like old yellow bones in red earth.

'I am merely a Jesuit,' he said. 'We are not required to believe in God. Only to serve Him. If you want to see true *belief,* go to the Islamic world and see what belief has done there. This Barrakha – he is also an enthusiast, drunk on belief – I have told you that last week he – or his Moros – kidnapped five of our village children – came down on them while they were fishing in the shallows only a mile from here – took three of the young women as well. Butchered an old man sent to find them and left him strung up in a durian tree.'

'Why?' asked Strackbein. 'What does he want with children?'

'He doesn't want the children. He wants our despair – he wants us to strike out – to run berserk in the market-places of Iligan and Cotobato and Marawi – and so justify our extermination. Why does he seek this? Because we are not believers. Therefore we must be eradicated. All the great movements of the world require this sacrament of death. You were in Vietnam, sergeant, were you not?'

Pike jerked at that, and then gave him a sullen nod.

'I thought as much. You have the visage – the face. You know the country around Can Tho, Sergeant? The Mouths of the Mekong?'

Pike nodded again.

'A wonderful misted land, very much like a paradise. Sheltered in palms, the Mekong flowing timelessly along beside, bringing the corpses out of Phnom Penh. Our family had a plantation there, back in the years before the Viet Minh, even before the Japanese. Somewhere here I have the photographs . . . After the massacre at Dien Bien Phu, the Viet Minh came to our plantation and told our people, the villagers who lived around our plantation, that they were to be reeducated – that they had lived too long with us, the Europeans, to be true citizens of the new people's republic. We were to be left alone, *la famille* Desaix, because it was necessary to have the plantation be productive – but the villagers had to be transformed. Naturally, the elders resisted. So what did the Viet Minh require? They proposed a demonstration of their new orthodoxy. This demonstration consisted in requiring of each mother of more than one child to select the one who would be beheaded the next morning. If she made no selection, or offered herself – many did and were obliged at once – I will never forget the crack of the ax as it slices through a young mother's outstretched neck, the leaping blood, the head like a gourd falling . . .'

He paused, and ran an unsteady hand across his eyes as the men watched him, Pike with a fixed intensity.

'As I have said – belief – enthusiastic energetic expansive belief – always requires sustained campaigns of ceremonial brutality. That is how the killers are exalted. They kill in order to become divine, to achieve the coldness that they see in God. Hussein's Ba'athists said they used torture and killing to bring their brothers to their true selves, of which they were ignorant. We Jesuits made our name during the Great Inquisition. We tortured to purify. This great sin lies at the heart of all religions, in their early pride, in the genetic code of their origins. They sanctify themselves with the blood of others, the more innocent the better. Mother Teresa limited herself to merely prolonging the pain of lepers upon whom she fed her vanity, so of course she is regarded as a saint. Perhaps for her forbearance. But in the early days of Christ our Lord, we required genuine martyrs. Death alone could exalt. Mere suffering was not enough. We required the sacrament of slaughter. You were an agent of this slaughter yourself, Sergeant, in the war? In your war? You would agree?'

'I killed my enemies.'

'No. Of course. I do not assault your honor. I merely make the point. You killed your enemies in defense of your country, of the interests of your country. Then, in defense of those interests, it became necessary to leave, and the people who remained – on the rooftops of Saigon – pushed over the fences at your embassy – barred from the carriers – thrown from the helicopters as you ran away – your allies and supporters – where was their rescue? Their reward? Their dream of liberty? They were led to the killing fields, the reeducation camps, to the bloody stone wall pitted with bullet holes. I recall hearing your Secretary McNamara say that their allies had to be "sacrificed." In the context of our discussion, a telling word, no?'

'If it's all for nothing,' snorted Pike. 'what are you doing here?'

'I had nothing else to do. My family was gone. Our

plantation burned, overrun. Ruin. So I left all that behind for the Order, for Paris and the Sorbonne, and so came finally to Mindanao. Now I serve the people of Cobraville, and if God is in the people of Cobraville – which I often doubt – then I serve Him, do I not? Whom do you serve?'

Enough of this, Cole decided. They had a mission to finish.

'Father, as Jesus may have told you, we have an interest in this man Barrakha. Jesus tells us you might be able to help. Is he right?'

'I know very little. Barrakha is a careful man. He is known in the hills as Mr Gabriel, after the archangel. Dak Prai has a man among the Bukidno who believes he is out of the country right now.'

'Any idea where?'

'The rumor is that he was in Germany. It had to do with money, with someone in the money business there. Now he is coming back, but no one knows when or how. It is said he has a young European child with him, a sick child. Barrakha needed asthma medicine for him. Barrakha is also an asthmatic. He suffers from it often. That is how we manage to hear about him. The only place he can get good asthma medicine is from Iligan City. There is someone down in Iligan who buys it for him, and it is sent to Marawi with Bukidno runners.'

'When Barrakha's in the country, where does he usually stay?'

'In Marawi. He is seen there often, according to Dak Prai's man. At a beach café on Lake Lanao. But if you hope to find him there, you should think of another plan. The Bukidno and the other tribes have created a cordon around Marawi. Even a patrol as small as yours would never get through. Last month Dak Prai heard that some

Bukidno men were coming through to Marawi. He sent six of the best men in the village into the jungle to follow them, to find their secret way. Only one of them came back, and he was cut. His orchids sliced off and fed to a dog while he watched. He was let go so he could come back and tell us. No one can get through to Marawi now.'

'How often does Barrakha need this medicine?'

'Every few weeks. He has to order it often because it is hard to keep it cool in this climate, so it decays. And there is only one kind that helps him. It is called Therafine. It is made in France. Last week a carton of Therafine inhalers was stolen from the hospital ship in the harbor at Iligan. I believe that it is being held for Barrakha's return.'

'Which could be soon?'

'It is not safe for him to stay away for long. He is the leader. Without him the tribes fight each other. Old grudges come back to the surface. Affairs of *maratabat* – of face and honor – are revisited. The men who guard him are mercenaries, and mercenaries must be paid.'

Marie Claire drifted in from the outer darkness and leaned into the glow of the table to clear away their dishes. Her dress opened and showed the table her breasts, the pale belly beneath them. The priest regarded her with obvious hunger. Cole found that hard to watch.

'Okay. That's helpful, Father. And thanks very much for the dinner. We may be coming back this way tomorrow. Maybe we can work something out together.'

'If we can help you find Barrakha, we will.'

'Then I think it's time we pulled out.'

'So do I,' said Burdette, who had been silent all through the meal. 'But first I'd like to hit the latrines.'

'Me too,' said Vasquez.

'They are down by the bullock sheds,' said the priest.

'Jesus, show them the way. Be careful. There are kraits.'

Burdette and Vasquez stalked across the wooden floors, Rizal tottering drunkenly along behind them. When the doors opened, the rushing sound of the monsoon filled the room and the scent of jungle poured in on a warm wet wind. When they left the room an uneasy silence descended, as Pike brooded darkly and Marie Claire moved around the table. Krause and Strackbein watched her – Krause with obvious appreciation, Strackbein with a kindly but disinterested expression, and he then considered the old man at the head of the table. Desaix felt his look and smiled disarmingly.

'You admire her? My little Marie Claire?'

Strackbein grinned tightly at him. 'Only in a professional way. She reminds me of someone.'

'Who?' asked Desaix, a wary expression rising in his face. Marie Claire stepped away from the warm circle of light and seemed to stand still just beyond it, waiting. The priest grew suddenly still.

'She looks exactly like one of Dak Prai's wives. The same golden eyes. The same face. The same body. Is she related to him?'

'All the villagers look like Dak Prai, and Dak Prai looks like all the villagers,' said Desaix. 'The Samal do not breed with strangers.'

'Maybe,' said Strackbein. 'I was just wondering.'

'Wondering what?'

'What she is to you?' asked Pike Zeigler, his latent suspicion breaking through, spurred by his instinctive distrust of the man. The priest reacted to his accusatory tone as if Pike had struck him. He stared at Pike in a long tense silence, during which Pike's expression hardened into open contempt. Desaix tried to break the mood with a short barking laugh: 'Marie Claire is my wife, of course.'

'I see,' said Strackbein. 'And Dak Prai's daughter?'

'You are an observant man, sir. Marie Claire is Dak Prai's daughter by his third wife. Our marriage is blessed by the whole village. Are you going to preach at me?'

Strackbein said nothing, but Cole recalled the murderous look on Dak Prai's face as he stood alone in the rain.

'How does Dak Prai feel about it?' Cole asked.

'He is deeply honored. I am highly regarded in Cobraville.'

'What about your vow of chastity?' asked Strackbein.

'Are you a married man?'

'Not currently.'

'But you have loved?'

'Yes.'

'And you, Sergeant?'

'I've been married. I loved her. She died.'

'You do not strike me as a man who has really loved.'

'That's really going to keep me up nights.'

'And you, sir?' looking at Dean Krause.

'No. Not anymore.'

'No. You are all solitary men. This of course comes with your trade. I am an old man now, and my order has released me from the vows. Many good priests take a woman after a lifetime of celibacy. There is nothing in God's law to forbid it and nothing in the Order to prohibit it. Chastity is a choice for us, not an obligation. Marie Claire and I are properly married. And God himself has sanctified marriage.'

'The god you don't believe in?' asked Strackbein

Desaix bristled.

'For you to sit at my table and lecture me about what is and what is not correct in God's eye seems presumptuous.'

Strackbein looked into the darkness where Marie Claire was standing, rigid, arms crossed over her breasts, frozen in place. The priest followed Strackbein's look, grunted angrily, and lurched away from the table, his face turning bright red. She backed quickly away as he approached her, turning her head. He raised a hand – held it – looked at Pike – at all of them – and a shudder passed through him. He came back to the table, collapsed into the chair, passing a shaking hand over his face. He looked up at Cole and Pike and Strackbein.

'You beat this girl?' asked Pike.

'No. I correct her.'

Pike held his look and said nothing for a while, and then looked at Cole, the meaning in that look quite plain. Cole and Strackbein pushed their chairs away and stood up.

'Loman, go find out what's keeping Burdette and Vasquez.'

Strackbein gave the priest a last flat look, picked up his gear, and went out the doors. The priest stayed seated, head down, his hands around the dark green bottle of Remy Martin. Cole watched the old man, wondering what kind of intelligence use could be made of him. Very likely none. He was unstable, possibly a drunk. But the information about Barrakha's Therafine supply was worth the visit. Cole held the big Barrett .50 in his hands, the weight of it, the warm steel and the bulk, oddly, reassuringly solid and reliably material after the old priest's 'philosophy.' Marie Claire stepped out of the darkness and stood beside the old man, looking at Cole across the table.

'He will sleep now. He always does, after such a dinner.'

'Does he beat you?' asked Pike

She shrugged.

'No more than Dak Prai.'

'Why are you with him?' asked Krause.

Another fatalistic shrug.

'Dak Prai's wife knew that Dak Prai wanted me. She sold me to this man. I went willingly. She would have put a krait in my bed one night. He is not so bad. He is old – I look up at the fans turning on the ceiling. It is soon over. He has electricity, too. No one else has that in Cobraville.'

'Why not?' asked Pike. 'The grid runs all the way to Marawi.'

The priest got to his feet, swayed slightly, looked at Marie Claire reproachfully, and stumbled away in the direction of a curtained-off enclosure. Marie Claire watched him walking away with a look of detached amusement.

'Father Desaix wishes us to remain true to our ways. He says it makes us pure, and that God loves us better because we have not given up the old ways. He says electricity brings evil with it, that electricity is the great destroyer. Are you going to find Hamidullah Barrakha? If you do will you kill him for us?'

'We're going to try,' said Cole.

The doors opened and Jesus Rizal came back into the room – looking haggard but slightly more sober – followed by Strackbein, Burdette, and Vasquez.

'Hear that?' asked Burdette. A sound penetrated the drumming of the rain on the roof – a distant heavy thumping, uneven, rolling, deep in the earth itself – the men looked at each other.

'That's no chopper,' said Pike.

'No,' said Krause. 'That's small arms, machine guns. Mortars. That's a real firefight.'

A muted thud shook the boards under them, followed by a prolonged chattering rattle, like a string of fire-crackers, ending abruptly. They heard the sound of voices – the young men of the village stirring – and in the middle distance an old woman began to complain bitterly, her voice harsh and shrill, cut off by a blow.

They gathered up their gear – Pike gave Marie Claire one final look – she smiled back at him – and then they went out into the night, the heavy doors slamming shut behind them. Around them the village lodges were dark, shuttered, closed, all their lanterns out. The night air was pulsing with the shock waves, with the rolling pop-pop-pop, and the ground-pounding thump of distant guns. The men of the village were out, AKs shouldered, setting up a perimeter. More gunfire crackled in the distance, and flashes like sheet lightning lit up the night sky in the south. The village men gave way as Cole reached their line, their faces closed, their AKs averted only far enough to avoid giving offense or provoking a fight. No one said good-bye.

They moved through the line of villagers in a combat file, reached the bank, and crossed the broad, flat, waist-high river with their weapons lifted high, trailing streamers of lotus, the muddy water warm as blood, and came up to the edge of the jungle on the southern bank, the lock-and-load line. High above the trees a necklace of bright green fire lanced into the sky from some hidden anti-aircraft gun and an answering ribbon of red tracers poured back down into the jungle from an unseen source above the racing clouds. They pulled back the bolts, smacked in the maga-zines, chambered their rounds, tightened the slings, and made final adjustments to packs and gear. No one spoke. There was really nothing to say. Pike looked at Cole, who nodded. Burdette, on point, sighed and pushed a path through the matted vines. The jungle gave way before them and then closed in behind them like an emerald-green snake, pulling them into itself.

Manhattan

Bell UH-IH helicopter Tripoli
Altitude 1,000 feet – speed 30 knots
The East River, New York City
Wednesday, August 20, 2:00 p.m. local time

The winds that were whipping the East River into white-capped waves that looked a lot like shark's teeth were also banging the Huey around cruelly as they descended through the hot damp air toward the 34th Street Heliport. They were running south – and, in Luna's opinion, very damn low – almost skimming the broad blue river, having dipped suddenly – sickeningly – after clearing the 59th Street Bridge. She glanced at Drew, expecting to see her own fear reflected there, but his haggard unshaven face was calm, relaxed, almost happy, although his mouth was set in a hard line and a muscle jumped in his left cheek. She studied the streak of silver-gray hair at his temple and decided that he had aged perceptibly in twenty-four hours. She sighed and looked past him at the huge glass wall of the United Nations gliding by as the chopper headed for a landing pad the size of a dessert plate a thousand yards down on the eastern bank, next to the stream of cars pouring up and down the FDR.

Up ahead on her left, the container yards of Greenpoint lay in a dusty pool of light and the wharves sticking out like spokes into the river had curling wakes of white water flowing from their tips. In front of her the towers and peaks of Lower Manhattan rose up massively inside a pale jaundiced haze, dim blue-black canyons in between. Luna looked briefly – with a sharp, familiar pang in her chest – at the looming rectangular absence in the Manhattan skyline, where the memory-mirage of the World Trade Center hovered eternally over the city, a sorrow-filled, ghost-haunted space floating in the luminous summer air. The Williamsburg and the Manhattan lay across the East River like tollgates, sharp-edged black shadows, angular and ugly. A small flotilla of diamond-shaped sails carved a rippled sea-lane northward toward Roosevelt Island, trailing white foam. Past the Brooklyn Bridge – sunlight racing up the fanlike strands – the broad blue river curved away, passing out of sight behind the Battery. In the distance a vague pearlescent light lay over Gravesend, the Atlantic beyond it a thin crescent of beaten copper lying along the horizon.

The rotor tone changed, the turbine howled, and New York City climbed up around her, shouldering out the sun, and now the heliport pad was spinning crazily as she watched the ground racing up at them through the Plexiglas panel at her feet. The chopper turned slowly into the west – the river spreading before her – the machine dropped – settled – the struts took their weight, and they were down. Drew released the cyclic and the collective and flicked the engine cutoff switch on the forward panel. The machine rocked on its struts, slowing, the beat subsiding. Through the windscreen the disc of the whirling rotors altered and became two single blades turning slowly. Drew leaned back in the seat, stretched mightily, and pointed over his right shoulder at a small knot of official-looking men dressed in federal blue suits –

ties flying in the river wind and hard expressionless faces —
waiting at the gates like bill collectors.

'Company.'

She twisted around to look.

'Levi Sloane. I don't know the others.'

'What do we tell him?'

'I don't know,' said Luna. 'Let's see what he has to say.'

A man in a ball cap, his tan windbreaker flapping
like a loose sail, tapped politely on Drew's side panel,
holding up a clipboard. They climbed out, Drew still in
his blue pin-stripe with his laptop and his briefcase, Luna
carrying her black leather overnight bag and looking
apprehensively toward the waiting officials. Drew gave
the ground-crew chief his credit card, signed off on the
storage agreement, and they walked out across the platform toward the exit gate with the wind whipping around
them and their hair wild. Levi Sloane stepped forward out
of the group and met them a few yards before the gate.

'Drew, I'm afraid I have some rough news.'

Drew stood still, the wind whipping his hair and pulling
at his jacket, buffeting him. His stomach tightened and his
chest grew cold.

'Is it Cole?'

A wary look passed over Sloane's face and then cleared.

'No, your son's fine. Far as I know. It's your father.'

'My father?'

'Yes sir. He's in Harrisburg Central right now.'

'Is he all right?'

Sloane's glance bounced briefly off Luna and came back
to Drew. She could see him hardening himself and knew
in her heart what Sloane was about to say.

'No, Drew. He's not. They're saying it was an
embolism.'

The world took a huge staggering tilt to the left – then abruptly righted itself. Drew heard his own voice, hollow, unnaturally soft.

'An embolism . . . how . . . his heart?'

'No, sir. It appears to have been a stroke.'

Drew involuntarily stepped a few paces back. His right leg began to shake at the knee and he looked dazedly around for something to sit on. Luna took his arm and steered him to a luggage rack. He stared up at Sloane, and the three men behind him, seeing them now for the obvious FBI agents they were. His vision blurred and he fought to clear it, his throat closing.

'Are you telling me my father is dead?'

Levi put a hand on Drew's shoulder. Luna stood close beside him, both looking at Drew with worry, concern, even apprehension.

'I'm sorry, Drew. We all are. I don't know what to say.'

'Who found him?' asked Luna.

Sloane retrieved a note pad and held it out, squinting.

'A Deacon Holyrood. Your father was supposed to play golf with him in the morning. He knocked on the door, no answer. Got worried and called the Harrisburg PD. They found him in the master bedroom. Died in his sleep, Drew. The responders said he looked peaceful. No pain at all.'

Drew focused on Sloane, his face changing.

'Dad had people taking care of him. Where were they?'

'People? I thought he lived alone? The cops say the house was empty. Deserted. No sign that anyone else had ever lived there.'

Luna stepped in, her manner now quite official.

'There was a young man staying with Mr Langan,' said Luna, looking away from the pain in Drew's face, steeling herself against it. 'Cornel ... something. Mid-twenties, five feet eight, maybe a hundred and fifty pounds, long black hair, Asian features, golden-brown eyes, light tan skin. Clean-shaven, no visible marks or scars. Spoke with a distinct French accent, said he was going to the Juilliard in the fall. A dancer.'

Sloane shook his head.

'No one like that on the scene.'

'And a woman, early twenties. Andrea Collier. Short brown hair, feather cut, medium build, maybe five-two, one fifteen. Shoulders like a swimmer, brown eyes, coffee-colored skin. Where was she?'

'There was no one else in the house, according to the Harrisburg PD. The only room that looked lived in was Henry Langan's. According to the first officers it looked like he lived alone, and simply died in his sleep.'

'Are they doing an autopsy?'

Sloane shook his head.

'They haven't got one planned. His own doctor examined him at the scene. His heart was like a brown paper bag, he had diabetes, sclerotic ...' He saw the look on both their faces. 'Maybe they better do an autopsy?'

'An autopsy is a very good idea.'

Sloane turned to the men standing behind him and waved them forward, two young white men, solid, blank-faced, with short-cropped hair, and an older man, hawk-faced, with shaggy white hair and bushy eyebrows, a sallow liverish expression, sad distant eyes, the demeanor of a funeral director. The older man offered Drew a bony hand.

'I'm Harry Pruitt, Senator Langan. Local agent in charge. This is Agent Hayward Canning and his partner Cab Stackhouse. We're sorry to intrude ...'

Pruitt's rote speech tapered off as he took in the mood of the people in front of him. His attention seemed to narrow, focus, a concentrated intelligence showing in his desiccated face.

'Harry,' said Sloane, 'Henry Langan's death is beginning to look a little more complicated. Drew says his father had people taking care of him. Now they're nowhere around. Missing.'

'Who were they?'

Sloane told him about the two house guests, both gone. Pruitt asked for details, and while he listened one of his young partners wrote the descriptions down and the other stared at Drew without expression, the flat robotic negation of any human emotion that they seem to hire them for before they even get sent to the Academy. Harry Pruitt listened – asked a couple of pointed questions – seemed unmoved, skeptical – but grimly prepared to go through a number of useless motions for a senator.

'Well, Senator, we're here to do what we can. I can't tell you how sorry I am about this. We're gonna do everything possible. Miss Olvidado, can you spare us a minute?'

Drew stood up, a little unsteadily. Sloane took Drew gently by the arm and walked him away from the rest of the men. As they walked, Sloane sent Luna a hard look full of meaning.

'Tell them what you can. You follow?'

'I do, sir.'

She walked over to the FBI men and they closed around her in a tight attentive knot. Drew watched them begin an earnest discussion, their words inaudible, their faces unreadable, Luna at the center, straight-backed and contained. Sloane stopped them about fifteen feet away and spoke in a low urgent tone.

'I got a letter from Gunther Krugman this morning.'

'When was it sent?'

'We're working on that. It's recent. In it he says he set you up, that you had no idea that the document was not cleared for release.'

'I didn't. I told you that yesterday. You told me to leave it to you, to go home and forget about it. Now my father is dead.'

'We don't know that he was murdered, Drew. We don't know if there's any connection at all. This whole thing is getting out of . . .'

Sloane's run of words seemed to trail away as Drew's mind went inexorably back to the idea of his dead father. The effort of concentration was maddening. He wanted them all to go away and leave him to sit by the river. He wanted to take the Huey right now and fly it back to Harrisburg. More than anything else he wanted to see his father one last time. There was the house, the estate. He would need a military funeral. Would Arlington take him? Find this Cornel kid. Call Diana . . . he became aware that Sloane was speaking more forcefully, his voice almost a bark:

'Drew! You need to get a grip here.'

Drew gathered himself, willing the voices in his head to shut up, forcing his grief down. He even managed a ghastly smile.

'Levi, I have a question. Is my son working for the CIA?'

Sloane hesitated, looking briefly at the FBI agents gathered around Luna, leaning in close, the wind whipping at their clothes.

'Yes. He is.'

'Is he in Mindanao right now?'

Sloane looked pained.

'Senator, you know how dangerous this stuff is.'

'Tell me what you can.'

Sloane stared hard at Drew, assessing the risk, the man.

'Okay . . . Cole works for a branch of the CIA called –'

'The Special Collections Service.'

That rocked him; Drew savored the effect.

'How did you know that?'

'Helen McDowell told me about it. Just before she kicked me off the Oversight Committee.'

Sloane's face reddened and then cleared.

'The stupid old bitch.'

'My sentiments exactly. What about this Collections group?'

'They freelance for the NSA. Installing SIGINT monitors wherever the NSA wants one. Anywhere in the world – Iran, Syria, North Korea, Pakistan – anywhere the NSA thinks it should have one. When they break down –'

'Like in Mindanao?'

'Yes. Like in Mindanao.'

'Was an NSA surveillance relay in Mindanao failing?'

Sloane nodded absently, his mind racing ahead.

'Yes. At least, that was the reading they got from the SIGINT techs. Like I said, when they break down, no matter what's happening, people like Cole go in and fix them. That's where he is right now.'

'Isn't Mindanao a UN peacekeeping zone?'

'Yes. That's the damned problem. This stunt of Krugman's brought a lot of attention – if somebody leaks a hint of this to the United Nations, we'd have France, Germany, Russia howling blue murder at the General Assembly. Worse, we'd lose some of the newer coalition members – the Balkan states – not to mention what they'd make of it in the European Union.'

'Do we still care?'

Sloane frowned into the wind off the river.

'The official line these days is mend the bridges – Iraq is expensive. We'd like some other nations to carry some weight. And we do want to maintain our ties with the old Eastern Bloc countries – Poland in particular. England has taken a stand on our side. A blown CIA mission in a UN area would cause a hell of a row in Whitehall. The government could collapse. Lose England and we have few friends with any real muscle. These days we need all the friends we can get.'

'Is the mission blown?'

'Blown? Not yet, anyway. The controllers are in constant touch with them. The mission is – it's almost complete. They'll be out of Mindanao in twenty-four hours. Tops. The thing is –'

'Are you holding Gunther Krugman now?'

Sloane shook his head, his face hardening.

'Hell no. That's why I'm talking to you. Do you think I'd be standing here having a heart attack if I knew where the hell the old bastard is? What about you? Do you have any idea where he is?'

Krugman's warning came drifting back.

I fear you can trust no one.

'No. No idea at all.'

'Any leads?'

'Nothing.'

'You were in Harrisburg last night, right?'

'Yes. Luna and I.'

'So she told me this morning. Finally. She also said you got a bunch of data out of Krugman's safe house

333

in Cape Vincent. I'd like to have all of it. Right now.'

'It's all in my briefcase. But I have something to say. I'm not going to say one word about any of this – no matter what happens, as long as what happens to that unit is in the line of duty. Cole is a grown man and what he chooses to do with his life is his own damned business. I'm on your side that far.'

'What if this mission gets into serious trouble?'

'Define serious trouble.'

'Let's say this mission becomes a problem for American intelligence. The existence of it, I mean. Not just a problem for some bosses, but a real political disaster?'

'You do what you have to do. I trust you to do it well. Lie your asses off with my blessing. So long as you get your guys out of there. The CIA ought to be able to arrange an extraction from a place as chaotic as Mindanao. But if you abandon those troops to rot in some Third World prison without a reason that I find pretty convincing, I'll make it my business to nail you for it.'

'You'd go to the media?'

'Fuck the media. I'd take this to the President himself.'

Sloane's face hardened up, closed down.

'It ever occur to you that those men in Mindanao would bitterly resent your interference? They signed on to do a dangerous job. A job nobody wants to do and everybody wants to have done. Mission deniability is part of their job. And the job is a lot more important than whatever the hell it is you senators do. Sometimes missions go sour and people are lost. You use your position to embarrass the intelligence service and the President, from what I've heard about your son, he'd never speak to you again. He'd see you as a traitor.'

'It's not about my son. America can take a little heat

from the UN. It's not going to ruin the country. If that unit needs help, I expect our intelligence agencies to do everything in their power to see that they all get out alive.'

'What else?'

'I get the hell out of the way and you find out if my father was murdered – look for this Cornel kid. Dad said he had a letter from my wife, Diana – I'll give you her number in Paris. Do that and you won't have to worry about me anymore.'

'I want whatever you got out of Krugman's files.'

'You'll have it all.'

'Anything else?'

'Is Luna in trouble with you?'

'I would have liked to hear from her more often.'

'Answer the question.'

'I think her loyalties are a little screwed up.'

'She withheld nothing from you.'

'She took her own sweet time getting it to me.'

'So she is in trouble.'

'She needs to reexamine her priorities.'

'You see Luna keeps her job.'

'I can't promise you that.'

'Yes you can.'

Sloane stared hard back at him and Drew held the look.

'All right,' he said, grudgingly, 'I'll do what I can.'

'No. You'll succeed.'

'I'm not her boss.'

'You have all the muscle it takes. I don't expect her to stay on my detail. I understand that. But I don't want her posted to some backwater assignment with her career in the dead-letter box. She gets real work somewhere, honorable work. Something worthy of her.'

'You're asking a hell of a lot.'

'I'm offering a hell of a lot.'

'And you leave the rest to us? Mindanao, Krugman?'

'I promise.'

'Your word?'

'My word.'

Sloane stood in the hot wind off the river for a while, his face unreadable. Then he put out his hand and Drew shook it once, hard. They looked over at the FBI men, at Luna standing apart now, her arms crossed over her chest, her face pale and her expression one of nervous apprehension.

'Drew, is there anything you can tell us that would help us figure out who's doing what to whom here?'

Drew was quiet for a time.

. . . trust no one . . .

'You know the Big Range mountain, up in the Adirondacks?'

'Yeah. I fish there, with my kids, on Indian Lake.'

'You know the gorge that runs along the eastern slope?'

'I've seen it.'

'There's a chopper down there. A navy-blue Jet Ranger.'

He reached into his pocket and pulled out a scrap of paper and handed it to Sloane: C V X 9 9 3 3 6 5 H.

'Those numbers were painted on her fuselage. There were two guys inside it. White guys, middle-aged, looked military. They intercepted us at four thousand feet just northwest of Big Range Mountain and tried to drop twenty feet of chain through our rotors.'

That rocked Sloane.

'Jesus. What happened?'

'I took the Huey low – nap of the earth – and they chased us. Halfway up the gorge they hooked a power line and crashed.'

'Holy shit. Both dead?'

'Eventually.'

'Why didn't Luna tell me that when it happened?'

'You're not going to like my answer.'

'I can handle it.'

'How did this chopper know where to find us?'

Sloane worked that out in a second.

'You think – because she called me when you were leaving Cape Vincent – you think somebody on my end leaked it?'

'Who knew where we were? Who knew what kind of chopper I was flying? They weren't just drifting around New York State hoping to run into us. They were right in our flight path, waiting. The only person Luna called was you.'

'Did you have your cell phone on?'

'Yes.'

'So anybody who knew your cell number could have gotten a fix on your position.'

'Anybody with access to the Blackbird trace system. And a cell-phone fix wouldn't have told them that I was in a Huey chopper four thousand feet in the air over the Adirondacks.'

'Hueys have a limited range. You had to refuel. People would have seen you, wouldn't they?'

Drew looked uncertain.

'Yes . . . you have a point.'

'Did you use the Huey's radio?'

'Yes. Once. I patched a call through the Syracuse tower.'

'You would have had to ID your airframe.'

'I did.'

'So anyone around the Syracuse tower would have known who was flying that Huey. Anybody in upper New

York State with a police scanner could have heard you making the call. That's a lot of people. Did you refill after Cape Vincent?'

'Yes. We topped up at an airfield near Black River.'

'So a lot of people could have known where you were headed?'

'Yes. I'd have to say you're right.'

'Hear me. My guys are not traitors.'

'Okay . . . I apologize. You might get your forensic guys to look over the decking just to the left of the pilot seat. There'll be three big rounds in there. Probably mashed out of all recognition, but you can try. The rifle may still be in the wreckage of the other chopper. If not, you'll find it along the gorge somewhere.'

'They fired at you?'

'Three times. Big-caliber rifle. I don't know how they missed the rotors.'

'What did Luna do about that?'

'She fired back.'

'With that little service Beretta of hers?'

'Yes. She handled herself very well. Saved my life. She deserves a citation. Or a medal.'

'I'll send a crew up there. You going to go back to Harrisburg?'

'I should. I'm the executor.'

'You know there'll be a formal forensic autopsy now. If anything turns up, that will bring in the Harrisburg PD and maybe the FBI if the search for these two kids goes interstate. If you're thinking funeral you can forget that. Sorry, but they'll hold on to your father's body for days. Maybe weeks . . .'

'Arrangements need to be made. He had a lot of friends.'

'So you're going back to Harrisburg anyway?'

Soon. But not yet.

'Yeah. I need some sleep. We'll go back tomorrow.'

'We? Luna and you?'

'She's still a Secret Service agent, isn't she? I'd like to hold on to her for a few more days, that's all. Then you can have her reassigned. I'm still a senator. Two nights ago I had to shoot a man who had broken into my house. Today two men in a navy-blue Bell Jet Ranger tried to kill me. I'd say that rated an escort, wouldn't you?'

'It rates a whole protective detail. Maybe a safe house. Movement restricted. Travel in a convoy. Armed guards in black Suburbans. Air cover. How about that?'

'No. Just her.'

'If anything happens to you, she'll get the blame.'

'I'll sign a release. You can say I refused your offer.'

'Yes,' he said, frowning, nervously toying with his worn gold NSA service ring while Drew watched him. 'You sure as hell will.'

SAIC Harry Pruitt and his two FBI partners, Canning and Stackhouse, insisted on dropping them off in front of the Beekman Towers Hotel at First and 49th Street. Pruitt sat in the back with them and grilled them politely all the way up First Avenue, stopping only once, to stare bleakly, with a censorious frown, out the side window as they rolled past the United Nations building. All the flags were out on the staffs, fluttering and whipping in the wind that always seems to be blowing up First. Canning was at the wheel, Stackhouse beside him, and Luna found herself staring at the backs of their necks and wondering how they found shirts to fit. Agent Pruitt smelled of wintergreen mints and cologne, and his voice when he finally spoke was as soft as sleep.

'Why do we allow them to stay, I wonder?'

Drew stirred himself out of a leaden weariness and stared out the window at the bank of flags lashing in the hot dusty wind, at the glass wall towering behind it, and the black limos lined up along the curved driveway, the solid blank-faced men in blue suits and white earpieces milling around the plaza.

'You mean the United Nations?'

Pruitt turned to look at Drew, his white eyebrows raised.

'It was only your rhetorical question, Senator. I don't mind them having a clubhouse. I just don't want it in New York. And sir, I must say, they do suck up the man-hours, of course – the Second Undersecretary from Burkina Faso needs a driver to pick up his child at daycare – the Permanent Attaché from Canada has lost his brief-case – the second son of the third wife to the Caliph of Mali objects to a search of his highness' person at La Guardia – you're staying at the Beekman, are you?'

Drew nodded, and the Crown Victoria swerved sharply to the curb and bumped against it. Luna – habit over-turning fatigue – popped out and jogged around to take Drew's door as Pruitt slid over and saw them out onto the sidewalk. He leaned out the open door and grinned up at them both, an old cop's look, knowing, searching.

'Anything else the agency can do for you?'

Drew looked down at the man, his skull pounding.

'Just find out what killed my father.'

'Or who?'

Contact

Two miles south of Cobraville
Lanao del Norte, Mindanao
Thursday, August 21, 3:00 a.m. local time

All night long the fighting deep in the southern jungles grew in intensity and the black sky above the canopy flickered with the orange lightning of heavy artillery. The air quivered with the thump and thud of guns and the deep rib-rattling vibrato of German choppers circling over an unseen enemy down by the shores of Lake Lanao. Now and then a high ripping sound, like fabric being torn, would carry over the hiss and rattle of the rain – someone in a gunship chopper pouring minigun fire down into an enemy concentration only the gunner could see. Each man felt the strangeness of it, the unreality of walking so near to a firefight that had nothing at all to do with him.

Up at point they could hear the hacking of Burdette's machete and his low intermittent curses as he laid into a difficult bush as if it were his particular enemy. Cole – in the middle of the line – bitterly regretting his tactically useless Barrett .50 – had sunk into the grim and dogged consideration of Jesus Rizal's dim shape a few yards in front of him. By Cole's reckoning – he was navigating by the glow of a small GPS transmitter strapped to his wrist – they were within a hundred yards of the big banyan tree where the SIGINT transmitter had been placed. A red sensor beside the pale blue glow of the GPS receiver pulsed rapidly, growing stronger. The relay was less than fifty yards away. He pulled out the Radio Shack walkie-talkie Pike had bought in Iligan City and pressed the CALL button. The tinny metallic beep sounded alien and unreal in the dense living jungle, and Chris Burdette's hoarse whisper came back sounding hollow, his breathing coming in short hard gasps as he hacked a trail through the thick jungle ahead of them.

'Yes, boss.'

'Chris, I'm showing our target at less than fifty yards.'

A silence – then his voice again.

'Can't see much in this dark. I think I can make out a big tree a ways up the trail here, up against the clouds. Huge.'

'A banyan?'

'Christ – who knows from trees? Big sucker.'

'Okay – take us in.'

Cole clicked off, and waited, on one knee with the Barrett at port arms, until he sensed the dim shadow of Ramiro Vasquez looming up in the darkness. His voice came out of the blackness – low and wary: 'Cole?'

'It's me, Ramiro. We're almost there.'

Vasquez settled in beside him, his M-79 clanking and the belted grenades crisscrossing his chest glimmering faintly in the phosphorescence. He smelled of gun grease and running sweat. A series of deep thudding booms reverberated through the jungle and the clouds overhead glowed bright blue and then faded into a dim flickering red.

'Hell of a firefight,' said Vasquez. 'Sorry to miss it.'

'I'm not,' said Cole. 'We're almost there. Move up and give Chris some cover. Pike still pulling drag?'

'No. He handed off to Loman. He and Krause will be up presently.'

'Okay. I'll wait here. You move on up, help Chris set up a perimeter – and Ramiro?'

'Yes, sir.'

'Keep Jesus close, will you?'

'Sure. Why?'

'He's about to find out why we came here. He'll know the location of a critical intelligence asset. So he's not staying in Mindanao. He's coming back to the States with us.'

'You still don't trust him?'

'I search my soul for charity, Ramiro, I really do.'

'There are easier ways of handling the problem.'

'Maybe. I keep thinking about what he said back at the trailhead, about trying not to become too much like the people we're fighting. I don't want to kill a man just to simplify my workload.'

'Fine by me. I'll keep him in my back pocket.'

Vasquez moved soundlessly off toward the trailhead. A few seconds later Pike and Krause materialized by his side, so softly that Cole jumped a little as they settled down next to him.

'We're almost there. I'm gonna move up. Tell Loman.'

Pike's head moved in the dark and Cole patted his meaty shoulder, moving off up the trail, lugging his damned Barrett. He found Chris Burdette and Ramiro Vasquez about forty yards up – or rather, they found him – Cole almost ran onto Burdette's bayonet as he pushed through a tangle of liana vines and came into a small clearing around the base of a towering banyan that stretched up through the layers of canopy and lost itself in the blackness above. Burdette held something out in his hand

and Cole fumbled in the dark for it; a can of something liquid.

'What's this?'

'Thirty-three. Sorry it's not cold.'

'You packed in beer?'

Burdette sounded a little hurt.

'Only a six-pack.'

'Where's Jesus?'

'In the bush across the way.'

Cole heard a muffled groan, and then a sigh.

'His innards are tending outwardly,' said Burdette.

Pike and Krause slipped into the clearing, followed by Loman Strackbein. Strackbein settled down beside Burdette and Cole, sighing heavily. Cole reached out for Strackbein's hand and placed the can of what was left of the warm beer into it. They could dimly see Strackbein's arm move inside what seemed to be a slightly brighter darkness. A very distant morning – a strictly theoretical concept down in this green hell – was rolling up from somewhere out in the South Pacific, and in time they would be able to see a hand held very close to the face.

Strackbein took a long pull, drained the can, crumpled it, and shoved it into his pack. His head turned in the dark and they all saw a streak of pale white show in his face as he smiled, inhaled deeply, and then the smile disappeared abruptly.

'What is that fucking awful smell?'

Vasquez nodded toward the brush where Jesus Rizal was still moaning and retching.

'Our boy Jesus is unwell.'

'That's not it,' said Strackbein. 'It smells like corpses.'

They all pulled in a long breath. He was right. The smell of death, of corruption, although faint, seemed to drift down on them with the rain. Cole pulled in the scent again with a huffing noise.

'No. Not corpses. There must be a stand of durian around.'

'Man,' said Vasquez. 'Why would God make a plant that smelled like a rotting corpse?'

They heard a clumsy stirring in the brush, and Jesus Rizal made his groping way across the clearing toward the sound of their voices. He stopped in front of them, sniffing rapidly.

'I wouldn't do that,' said Krause.

Rizal's black shape shrugged in the dark.

'Durians, I think. Rotting durians. They taste best when they smell like this. You soon get used to the odor.'

Strackbein got to his feet.

'Between you and the durians, Jesus, I think I'm going to go climb a tree. You got the thingummy, Pike?'

Pike, a few feet away, staring outward into the impenetrable black night, his M-60 at the ready, reached into his pack, and extracted a black box about eight inches by twelve. Strackbein reached out a fumbling hand, felt for Pike's reaching hand, and took the module, along with a small plastic tool kit and one of the Radio Shack walkie-talkies. As he straightened again, a long peal of machine-gun fire – a steady chunking rhythm – sounded in the middle distance.

'That's a sixty,' said Pike, a whisper out of the night. 'Do the Frogs have sixties?'

'No,' answered Vasquez.

'The Germans don't either,' said Cole. 'You sure that was a sixty?'

He couldn't see Pike's contemptuous glare. 'I know a pig when I hear one,' he said, out of the darkness. The weapon sounded again – a rapid percussive beat with an underlying pounding metallic clang – and then the firing cut off abruptly. In the following silence they heard a big German chopper circling – not far away – it gradually moved off, the beat of the rotors fading into the south. Gone. Nothing at all but the rain and the wind.

'Sounds like the fight's over,' said Vasquez. 'Loman, go get this done. The stink here is killing me.'

The unit spread out around the little clearing and took up a silent watch, weapons at the ready. Cole kept Jesus close. At the base of the banyan, Strackbein strapped on some lineman spurs and shouldered the small kit bag. He slipped on a pair of leather gloves, shoved a .45 into his belt, and laid his left hand on one of the gnarled trunks of the banyan's base, feeling the texture of the bark.

Then he moved, a liquid powerful climb, easy and graceful. Cole, watching him, saw only a slim black shape that seemed to glide upward, spiderlike. In a few moments Strackbein was a formless shadow moving swiftly into the upper darkness. Cole found himself staring up into the blackness of the giant banyan, its dimly seen limbs twining and interlacing hypnotically as they soared up through the dripping jungle toward the unseen canopy a hundred feet above his head. In a short while Strackbein's shape was lost inside that tangled network. Cole looked away at the surrounding jungle, at the blackness that seemed to press in against his eyes, sighed quietly, and waited, listening to Rizal's steady shallow breathing a few feet away, fighting the decaying corpse-stink that lay thickly on the damp air, that filled his throat with a choking poisoned sweetness in every breath he took.

Time passed.

The rain slowed to a steady drip-drip that smacked

against the broad flat leaf of some nearby plant. The Barrett .50 lay heavy in his grip, wet and blood-warm, smelling of grease and steel. In a while Cole became aware of a dim gray light beginning to sift down from the upper darkness; a shape nearby that had been nothing but a thin black line against a deeper black gradually became the delicate arching stem of a nameless fern. He held his hand up in front of his face, turned it, and saw a pale shape floating there in front of him. He turned, and now he was just able to make out the low mounded form of Rizal, lying on a bed of ferns a few feet away, the black bar of his rifle muzzle sticking out. Across the clearing, a misty hollow gradually filling with ghostly gray shapes in the gathering light, he could just make out Pike's broad back, crossed with heavy belts of 7.62 ammo. Morning was finally coming.

What was keeping Strackbein?

He looked upward into the dim tangle, and now he could see vague shapes in the upper branches – large gourdlike objects trailing a beard of ropy vines that hung downward from it – suspended from the outstretched branches fifty, eighty feet off the ground. Wasp nest? Giant cocoons? He had a terrible vision of a spider-silk cocoon suddenly ripping open and a million tiny tarantulas pouring down on him from the upper branches of the banyan. It was a nasty image and it sent an electric shiver of instinctive loathing up his spine. Nerves jangling, he fumbled for the radio and thumbed the CALL button.

Far overhead he heard the tinny beeping of Strackbein's receiver, and then Strackbein's voice, a whisper in the speaker:

'Almost done here – just have to test the old unit.'

'Roger that. Any trouble?'

'Just the Goddamned stink. At least the light's getting better.'

'Still dark as a dragon's colon down here.'

'You should see it from up here. I'm sticking right out of the canopy. Looks like the monsoon is breaking up. I can just make out the microwave tower above Marawi. This one big tree. Must be –'

Strackbein's voice cut off.

'What is it?'

'Cole? I just did a circuit test on the old unit. There's nothing wrong with it. Hold on a minute.'

'What do you mean?'

Cole stared upward as the light of the coming morning grew, straining for a glimpse of Strackbein at the top.

'Boss, I think we've been had. There's a jamming unit attached to this thing. I couldn't see it until I got the back off.'

'A jamming unit?'

'Yeah. It's right here by the processor. Very nice work. Looks German.'

'Are you saying the original unit was okay?'

'I'd have to get it on a bench. But this little jammer would have made the output intermittent. Wait, I'm coming –'

'Loman, have you turned on the new relay yet?'

'Yes. Fifteen minutes ago –'

'Shut it down.'

'Shut it down?'

'Yes. Set the destruct timer and get the hell out of –'

They all heard the rising beat of a chopper – the sound seeming to come from all around them – closing in fast – and another close behind it. Rizal was on his feet, staring up, his pockmarked face wet with sweat, his brown eyes widening. Pike was up too, his 60 elevated. Vasquez, Burdette, and Krause stayed in position, their weapons aimed out at the surrounding jungle, now filling with the milky light of early morning that was streaming down through the misty air from the canopy –

'Cole, there's two one oh fives coming right at us!'

'Blow the unit, Loman. Get out of there now!'

The steaming air of the jungle was vibrating with the beat of big choppers, coming in low. They all heard a rapid rustling of branches, leaves swaying, some flying loose, the solid thunk-thunk-thunk of Strackbein's spurs as he punched his way back down the huge trunk. Cole craned upward and now he could see him as he burst through a thicket of tangled upper branches – the hanging seed pods began to sway obscenely as Strackbein worked his way down – there was a sharp crack as the explosive in the NSA module blew the surveillance relay into fragments – and then the pounding vibration of heavy rotors was right above them and the old tree began to sway from the downwash of rotor wind – the leaves lashing wildly as if in a gale – and they all saw the broad belly of the chopper through the churning branches – German markings white against the green-and-black pattern – it moved heavily, turning slowly – Cole looked up at Strackbein – he was hanging from a limb eighty feet from the ground, his legs dangling, his black face staring down at them –

'Move it Loman – move it!' Cole shouted.

The chopper came lower – a hard metallic voice boomed out of a loudspeaker in the belly, the sound echoing around the jungle – a harsh German voice barking a warning –

'ATTENZION! *Lassen Sie ihre Waffen fallen!*'

Strackbein was moving again –

'ATTENZION!!'

– No more talk: the gunner opened up with his chain-gun, and the steamy air was immediately shredded by an ear-splitting ripping snarl – cut leaves fluttered and flew – two of the pods burst into shreds and a shower of tiny red sparks tumbled downward through the branches – spiders – tiny red spiders in the millions – more pods burst as the column of minigun fire swept through them – one broke free and tumbled earthwards, smacking a branch – turning – more spiders raining downward – a stream of minigun fire stitched across the wet red earth of the clearing inches from Burdette's right leg, dirt spouting up with each impact, the belly of the big chopper shuddering as the weapon sprayed the jungle floor. The tumbling pod struck the ground with a solid meaty thud. Cole saw – in that zone of heightened perception that can only be found under fire – a seething mound of infinitely small spiders spreading out over the jungle floor like spilling sand – the column of fire traversed again – spent minigun cartridges, a golden rain of shining brass cylinders, began to rattle down through the torn branches. Cole saw Strackbein clinging to the trunk of the banyan as the ribbon of tracer rounds played all around him – literally ripping the tree to shreds.

'Loman – keep moving – Loman!'

The minigun stitched a path of fire across the clearing – a steady rippling downpour of heavy rounds – a sizzling line of bright fire punched across the mud inches from Cole's face as he dragged the Barrett into cover. He looked back and saw Pike Zeigler raising the 60 – pointing it into the sky –

'Pike! Hold your fire!'

Pike's wet face turned to him, his expression wild, the look of cold murder in his face – more rounds hammered into the dirt as the gunner marched his line of fire through a killing mechanical grid – the gunner up there was firing blind now – trying to kill anything living under the canopy – Strackbein could not move without being touched by that solid stream of fire – Cole saw him pressing his face, his whole body, under the shelter of a heavy tree limb – Pike lowered the weapon, hunched his shoulders like a man running through a rain shower, and bulled his way into the dense brush, landing next to Cole with a thump that drove the breath from his body.

'They're going to kill him!'

'We do not engage these guys!' Cole shouted over the beat of the chopper, an order meant for all of them. He looked around to see where his men were and saw Jesus Rizal running fast, already fifty yards away. Vasquez, seeing him at the same time as Cole, shouldered his piece and took off in pursuit. Cole snagged him by the shirt.

'He set us up. I need him alive.'

'Why alive?'

'He's was Sloane's personal pick. I want to know why.'

'Okay. If he lets me,' said Vasquez, straining to go.

'If we get separated, we meet at Camp Casey!'

'I know. Call sign Jupiter.'

Vasquez gave him a quick sideways grin, and then he too flashed into the brush and disappeared.

Cole looked up at the tree again.

'Loman, you have to move!' shouted Pike, his face white.

'I'm trying –' Strackbein called down to them above the noise of the chain gun. More fire – as if the gunner could hear Strackbein's voice – the terrible red tracers slicing the air inches from his hunched shoulder – Pike was close to hysteria –

'Boss, let me fire back!'

The heavy chopper rose up, still firing, the big round belly turning against the ragged opening it had torn in the jungle canopy, and then the firing stopped abruptly. Slowly, ponderously, like a whale moving through a sea of streaming clouds, another German 105 chopper moved into the opening and four heavy lines snaked liquidly down through the canopy and dangled into the clearing, their ends jumping and lashing.

'They're gonna abseil in,' Krause said, in an urgent whisper. 'If we're not going to engage them, Cole, we need to move out now!'

Strackbein was moving again – but jerkily. Cole, staring upward into the atticlike upper reaches of the tree – saw blood running down Strackbein's left leg, the black fabric of his jeans torn away – raw flesh showing, and a pink arc of thigh bone. He was so damn far away – overhead the abseil lines were being shipped inboard. Cole saw an arm reach out and clutch it, a shape slipping out of the open bay. He looked back at Strackbein – Strackbein was looking directly at him, his face wet with sweat and his eyes very white – 'GO GO GO!' – he shouted it down at them – now men were on the hanging lines – Cole sent Strackbein one last look and Strackbein raised his hand – Cole grabbed Pike by the arm.

'Move out. Go! Now!'

Gideon

Everything looked the same, yet none of it was at all familiar to him as he inched his painful way – like a man filled with broken glass – across the broad polished stone turbine floor toward his office. The turbines were spinning in their cradles like iron tops, and a deep humming vibration shook the entire building. The great hall sounded to Gideon like a hive of giant bees. Through the glass wall that made up one whole side of the station the cataract of the Maria Christina Falls bounded endlessly, a streaming river of white water over which floated a silvery mist with a faint rainbow hovering in its center. The sun – looking brand new after the gray roof of the monsoon had dissipated – was resting on the shoulder of the mountain to the east, and its slanting rays were just touching the edges of the canyon inside which lay the generating station, perched on the ledge fifty feet above the cataract, the entire building shaking with the force of the water running deep in its heart; creaming white and green water that flowed massively into the two square maws of the intake ports upstream, racing down through tunnels carved into the rock that led the water – in a narrowing vault that channeled its force – onto the steel propellers under each of the five turbines – a thing of great power and beauty.

But Gideon could see only Mr Gabriel's cold wet face as it hovered upside down above him, moving in and out of the hard white light of an overhead bulb, and the Maranao boy – Ibrahim – only a voice in the background. How long he had suffered in this pain he could not have said, but eventually it had lessened and softened and then receded, pulling back down the long shoreline of his rising consciousness. Then he was lying naked in a puddle of his own fluids on a steel tray as warm as his blood and Mr Gabriel was asking him – over and over – if Gideon understood what was to be done and when it was to be done and how it was to be done – over and over and over – a metronome endlessly ticking.

Gideon had worked very hard at getting the details right, because he had grasped the central implication of Mr Gabriel's plans: For them to work as he was describing, it would be necessary for Gideon to be alive, and it was this thought to which he clung as his mind swam into and out of the light that floated behind Mr Gabriel's hovering face. When he was finally able to repeat the instructions word for word, Ibrahim – out of sight down at the end of the steel bed – had done something that sent a warm flood of blessed relief coursing through his veins, and sleep took him down a very long way. When he woke he was lying in his own bed in his little flat on Fortaliza Street, and if it had not been for the tiny red dots that floated in the whites of his eyes and the blood between his legs he would have imagined himself waking from a terrible dream. But it had not been a dream. Now he was awake and present and inching his way across the humming turbine floor toward his familiar office, carrying with him the secret burden of one last important service for Mr Gabriel.

Cobraville

Cobraville
Lanao del Norte Province, Mindanao
Thursday, August 21, 8:15 a.m. local time

A wind out of the north brought a new scent to them, the tang of smoke from burning wood, drifting down into the still-wet jungle to sear their throats and lungs as they jogged through the last of the mahogany trees that led to the edge of the river. The sound of pursuit behind them had long ago faded to a few hoarse shouts that grew ever more distant. A mile back, a German 105 had hammered overhead; low, moving north, moving fast. It had skimmed the tops of the trees almost right over them but it had not slowed, and the rotor wash had swept through them like a traveling cyclone, whipping up the dead growth around their feet and tugging at their wet clothes. They reached the river's edge where it curved around Cobraville, their lungs aching, legs trembling, a few minutes after eight. There they came to a halt, just inside the tree line, with Pike guarding their rear, Burdette and Krause taking the right and left of their line, and Cole in the middle, the unit spread out along thirty yards of river bank and well dug in. Across the broad brown back of the running river, across the drifting lotus islands, more smoke was churning inside a wet north wind, piling itself into a spreading cloud that lay over the village; above this, the rising sun was burning off the mist. The village itself lay in the clear light that comes after a monsoon, and the men watched the village in a stunned silence, because Cobraville was burning.

'What happened?' asked Pike, in a ragged whisper, moving up beside Cole, and staring across the river at the village. Every hut was in flames, some of them already reduced to smoldering piles of ash, others still burning yellow and red and blue against a background pall of thick black smoke. Bodies were lying everywhere – men, women, babies like broken fruit – in the clearings, crowded into heaps against a fallen hut, cut down in the open while running for the tree line. A slaughter. Not one living thing – not a dog – moved anywhere.

Father Desaix's clinic was a ruin, gutted already, its roof fallen in and the bamboo porch – a quirky survival – now standing as the entrance to a black pit filled with the fire-twisted skeletons of a row of hospital beds. A dead carabao, its belly exploded and a river of bright blood streaming from its mouth, lay in a round, black heap, legs jutting stiffly, a few yards from the base of the flagpole, at the top of which the French flag still fluttered, singed black around the edges.

'The Moro? Abu Sayaf? Barrakha's people? I don't know. How could this happen just three miles from us?'

Pike shrugged.

'It was night. The monsoon. We couldn't have heard this under the firefight down by Lake Lanao, and that went on all night.'

'We can't stay here,' said Krause, a few yards off. 'The Germans will see this smoke. We have to keep moving.'

'We need to find Vasquez,' said Cole. 'And Rizal.'

'Have you tried their radios?' asked Krause.

'Yeah. Nothing.'

'Vasquez knows the fallback point,' said Pike. 'We go there and wait for him. When we hook up, we find out what the Krauts are doing with Strackbein and we go in and get him out. Right, Cole?'

Getting Loman Strackbein away from the Germans – if he was still alive – was going to be a decision made a lot further up the chain of command than Cole Langan. Cole was about to tell Pike this when they all heard the sound of a chopper closing in, its direction hard to read, the syncopated bass-drum beat echoing off the far hills and reverberating through the shallow valley. The sound grew, and then they saw it – a German 105. It swept across the tree line to the north and slowed above the village, its rotor wash swirling the black smoke into several tornadoes and fanning the dying flames into new life. The gunship descended, banked sharply, and did a slow tree-top run all around the perimeter of the village, its gun ports open, a heavily built trooper manning a chain-gun visible in the open bay door. Cole and his unit pulled back into the cover and flattened as it boomed overhead and then passed on to the hills to the north, where it banked again and came back, flared and settled into the clearing, sending curling walls of black smoke spiraling into the sky, where the rising sun caught them and tinted the smoke blood red and amber.

'This,' said Pike, invisible in the bush, 'is not good.'

The chopper settled onto its struts and men began pouring out of the bay – nine German infantry troops. Cole recognized one of the German soldiers, the kid with the perfume-model looks swilling a tankard of brown ale in front of his chanting friends in the lobby of the Milan that first afternoon. Two men in civilian clothes, wearing the blue armband of the United Nations, emerged from the belly, carrying medical gear. They jogged toward the nearest huddle of bodies while the German troopers fanned out across the ruined village in teams, weapons at the ready. Two of them – young blond men in fatigues, their jungle boots shining black – headed straight for the river.

'I am definitely open to suggestions,' whispered Burdette.

A big man with officer's tabs on his fatigues stepped out of the pilot's hatch and walked around to the open bay. They could see movement inside the chopper – silhouettes against the slanting light – and then the officer stepped back onto the grass and an infantry troop appeared on the ledge, someone close behind him.

The trooper stepped down – turned – and dragged Loman Strackbein – handcuffed, a gaping wound in his left thigh bleeding – out of the bay, and threw him onto the ground. A wave of silent shock ran through Cole's men, and he felt Pike's coiling attention as they watched the big trooper drag Strackbein toward the flagpole and dump him at the base. The trooper stepped back and steadied his weapon on Strackbein's upturned face, while the officer walked over to the two civilians and stood there, obviously talking about the prisoner. The two German troops who were coming toward them stopped about fifty yards away to look at something lying dead in the long grass.

'What's your rule book say about this, Cole?'

Cole looked back at Pike, at Pike's cold expression.

'Loman knows the drill.'

'We just gonna leave him here?'

Cole said nothing. Pike leaned in close.

'We were set up, Cole. They waltzed us in and waltzed us out like a Broadway musical. Somebody warned the Krauts. They were waiting for us. Either Rizal or that priest ratted us out. This rat-fuck mission is over.'

The two German troopers turned and shouted something to the officer, who said something in reply and began to walk down toward their position. Pike steadied the 60 on a mound, and placed the sights on the officer's chest as he came towards the two soldiers. Cole put a hand on his forearm, feeling the deep, wire-tight vibration there.

'Not yet, Pike.'

The officer reached the men, knelt down, and rose up again with the naked body of a young child in his arms. He hefted it and turned back toward the village, followed by the two troopers. He reached the base of the flagpole, knelt down, and laid the child gently at Strackbein's feet. Then he stood up – pulled out a pistol – and leveled it at Strackbein's face. Pike – who had tracked the officer all the way back – grunted, as if he'd been struck.

Cole pushed the muzzle down, dragged the Barrett sniper rifle around, popped the forward bipod open, and took a prone brace by the lip of the bank, snugging the butt tight into his shoulder; he worked the bolt, the oiled machinery gliding inside the steel frame as it scooped a .50-caliber round out of the box mag and locked it into the firing chamber. Cole put his right eye to the telescopic sight, and the tiny figures around the base of the flagpole seemed to leap into full size. He laid the cross-hairs over the officer's temple, and held them there. They could hear the officer's voice carrying faintly across the open terrain; harsh, staccato, full of accusation. In the shining circle of the sight, Cole watched as Strackbein spoke – his manner calm – saying something to the officer that did not reach them as they all waited in silence five hundred yards away, in the dim sunlight-dappled green of the jungle's edge. The officer seemed to listen to whatever it was that Strackbein was saying – Cole could see the man clearly in his scope, a shimmering disk of pulsating air surrounding a thick-faced, darkly tanned man with a broad black mustache and a shaved head, the weapon in his out-stretched hand some sort of Glock. He had the pistol aimed right at Strackbein's forehead, his finger still outside the trigger guard. Cole moved the cross-hairs to track the man as he took a step closer to Strackbein, shouting something in German.

Cole could feel Pike's tension – so close it stirred the hairs on his forearm – the heat of Pike's body next to his. Pike was holding the binoculars now, his jaw muscles bunched, watching the officer with the pistol. Cole's world narrowed down to this luminous disk of light float-ing in his right eye, the man contained within its bright circle, the serrated etching of the trigger blade cutting into his index finger, aware of the tiny movements of the sear and the ratchet deep inside the frame, the reassuring weight of the weapon in his arms, the heat in his belly that came up from the jungle floor under him, the solid con-tact of the padded rifle butt against his shoulder, and Pike Zeigler burning at his right hand. Cole knew in his heart what he was going to do if that officer put his finger inside the trigger guard of his pistol.

'What the fuck –' whispered Pike.

Cole moved his eye away from the scope and looked where Pike was pointing, at a flicker of white cloth above the tree line on the far side of the valley. He shifted the Barrett and watched as a thin figure in blood-stained, tan clothing tottered to his feet, waving a scrap of white cloth at the people down in the village. A high, reedy, quavering voice called out, and the officer gestured to two soldiers nearby to go and meet him.

'Christ,' Cole said, staring. 'That's Desaix!'

'He's alone,' said Pike, watching him come down.

The priest's face was burned, and half his beard was charred away. One shoulder was wet with fresh blood and he staggered as he came down the hill. He reached the soldiers, and now they were standing in a knot, Desaix's arms waving as he talked, his gestures large and angry, his outrage audible at two hundred yards.

One of the UN medics ran up with a medical kit, and as he reached them Desaix collapsed into the grass at the bottom of the hill. The men bent over him, helped him to his feet. He staggered free and began to lurch unsteadily toward the flagpole, where Strackbein lay in handcuffs, watching him closely. The officer with the pistol stood silently and watched the priest coming, his pistol never wavering from Strackbein's face. The priest reached the man, and they could hear his voice now – raised, angry, a rapid stream of French – the German officer listening – Cole steadied the Barrett on the officer again and watched as the two men had what looked like an angry confrontation – the officer turned suddenly to the guard and spoke to him – the guard stepped forward and dragged Strackbein to his knees – Cole's finger tightened around the blade of the trigger – Desaix stepped in between them and turned to face Strackbein. Strackbein lifted his head and seemed to look straight into Cole's right eye – his mouth was moving – Cole focused on Strackbein's lips – the words seemed to form inside Cole's skull –

Shoot – the – priest.

Cole shifted the sights – centered on Desaix's red face – and then they all heard a sharp, distant crack. It rolled around the village and lost itself in the tree line. The priest turned away.

Cole moved the sight to the officer –

'The Kraut officer just shot Loman!' said Pike, in a flat voice.

Cole steadied the sight on the officer's head, squeezed – the big Barrett bucked in his grip – the muzzle-brake flared smoke and blue fire. In the luminous disk the officer's head exploded. The boom of the heavy sniper weapon tumbled around the clearing and heads came up everywhere – white faces showing – men dropped to the ground. The officer, now headless, still holding the Glock, tottered a step and crumpled onto the ground.

Cole shifted the sight, passing over the splayed-out shape of Loman Strackbein lying on the muddy ground, and found Constantin Desaix staggering clumsily away toward the ruin of his clinic. Cole steadied on him, and then jerked away as Pike opened up with the 60 right at his ear. Cole lost the priest, shifted again, looking for a target, and saw Strackbein's guard squatting with his rifle raised. Cole drilled him through the upper chest. The man's body tumbled, cut nearly in two, his HK rifle flying through the air.

Puffs of pale smoke marked the troopers in the long grass as they fired back. A humming burr in Cole's good ear as a rifle round thrummed past inches from his head. He worked the bolt again and heard lighter, ratcheting fire coming from Burdette's position as he opened up with the M-16. Then more outgoing fire from the left, as Krause did the same. Three of the Germans were down, olive-drab heaps, bloody red against the bright green of the grass; and now a man was running for the chopper, three quick strides before he was wrapped inside a cloud of churning earth as Pike's 60 found his range. Cole moved the weapon, raking it over the field, searching for a target. There was a flicker of movement to the far right, and he saw a trooper kneeling with a LAWS at his shoulder, the perfume model. Cole could make out the drops of sweat on his cheek, the wrinkle of concentration as he steadied the reticule plate of the LAWS.

Cole put a round right down the muzzle of the rocket launcher, and the boy disappeared inside a volcanic eruption of bright red blood, bits of earth, a section of skull. He saw a flayed forearm whirling away like a thrown stick.

'Chopper!' someone was shouting – Cole's ears were ringing from the muzzle blast of the Barrett and the steady chatter of Pike's 60 right beside his head.

'Where?'

Krause was urgently pointing to the east. Cole saw a black oval hovering above the tree line, a German gunship closing in fast – its rotors a shimmering disk of light over its squat, insectlike windshield – rocket pods under the weapons rack – coming in low out of the rising sun. Cole ejected the box magazine, slammed in the spare, raised the Barrett – vaguely aware of incoming rounds hissing and zipping – blades of grass and fern shredding around his head as the troopers who were still alive concentrated their fire – a halo of red flame shimmered around one of the weapon pods as the gunship fired a rocket – it lanced across the shimmering air, a silvery spear surrounded by a visible blur of air, and screamed over Cole's head into the dense jungle behind him.

A deafening blast and the sound of a mahogany tree falling. Cole had his sights centered on the rounded

Plexiglas dome where the pilot would be sitting – he heard a meaty whack as a round came in and a chuffing grunt from one of his men – he steadied the sight – squeezed – the Barrett kicked heavily back, and a star-shaped hole appeared in the chopper's windscreen.

The chopper flared – sliding – and then one of it rotors clipped a tree and the blade shattered. The machine shook crazily as the other rotors tore themselves to pieces, and then it glided sideways down an invisible ledge of thick air, hit the tree line, tumbled, and exploded in a rising, churning ball of black smoke and red fire. A push of air swept by them as the shock wave rolled outwards. Pike was calling his name.

He looked down, and saw Pike holding Dean Krause in his arms – Krause's hard, blunt face set against the pain and his eyes wide open, his mouth a thin line holding back a groan, his right hand pressed down over a bubbling red pool low on his right side. Cole dropped down to a knee beside Pike as Burdette – firing his M-16 at the troopers still alive in the clearing – came up the line and crouched beside them. The firing from the village stopped abruptly, and in the silence they heard a building roar – faint but growing – very high in the clouds.

'They've called in air,' said Krause. 'Leave me. Get out.'

Far away in the northern sky they saw two silvery sparks, Mirages, caught in the sun – coming in fast. Down in the village the three troopers still alive were lying in the long grass, face down, with their arms crossed over their heads. Cole nodded to Pike, who slung the 60 around his back, got onto a knee, and lifted Krause up in his arms – Krause's face twisted in pain – Burdette policed up Krause's gear – Cole took one last look at Strackbein's body – and they slipped back into the jungle. A few long, silent seconds passed, and then two Mirage jets streaked in on a rolling crest of thunder and laid down eight tumbling, silver canisters that sprouted into eight pillars of billowing fire. They erupted sequentially along the far bank – one red column after another – and set the jungle on fire.

New York

First Avenue was a shadowed canyon, but high overhead the last traces of twilight had turned the western sky
into mother-of-pearl. Drew stood at the window and
stared down the long, glittering traffic stream pouring up
First Avenue. A convoy of yellow cabs was coming up out
of the underpass by the United Nations. Lights were on
all over the East Side, and the skyscrapers of lower
Manhattan were black rectangles against the twilight, the
office windows blazing in the clear evening air like square-
cut diamonds. His father's voice played quietly in his
head – no particular story – just the comforting burr of
his voice, as if it were being heard by a young boy half-
asleep in another room. Shaved, showered, dressed in a
light-blue dress shirt and a pair of black slacks, Drew
stood barefoot on the soft carpet and thought about what
he would find back in Harrisburg the next day. Beyond
the half-open bedroom door he heard the muted rush of
the shower running, and a green-apple scent of shampoo
and soap came wafting out through the doorway on a
warm, damp cloud.

Although they had already placed a call to the person –
Kohl Keune – that Krugman had named in his e-mail –

six rings, and then his voice mail – a thick German accent – but so far, no callback – Drew was edging toward a decision to leave the welfare of Cole's unit up to Levi Sloane. He had done what he could – put the man on guard – motivated him to protect Cole, and to keep the Secret Service from punishing Luna as well. He had to place his final trust in Cole himself, in his skills as a combat leader. Cole knew the mission might be compromised; he'd take steps to protect himself and his crew. Cole would get out of Mindanao alive; Drew had to believe that.

The reverberations surrounding his father's death had changed everything, had shifted all his priorities. He had called the Harrisburg police, who told him the FBI had already taken over the case, that a nationwide search was now on for Andrea Collier – so far without results – and that a Thai national named Cornel Chulalonkorn, holding a student visa to Juilliard, had been admitted to the United States on July 17, after arriving at O'Hare on a direct flight from Paris.

Cornel Chulalonkorn had taken a connecting flight to Harrisburg, and had given as his contact address in the United States Drew's father's home at Camp Hill. Drew's wife, Diana, had been contacted by the Sûreté in Paris, and she had confirmed that she knew Cornel vaguely – had met him at one of Mitzi Gallant's parties – but that she had no idea that Cornel was staying with Drew's father in Harrisburg, and had certainly never written him a letter of introduction to Henry Langan. In the meantime, a forensic autopsy on his father's body was already underway. No matter the outcome, his place was back in Harrisburg, dealing with the estate and maintaining the family business.

He still had options. Although he had turned over the material he and Luna had found at Krugman's Cape Vincent house to Levi Sloane, he hadn't told Sloane that they had first copied it into his laptop. Nor had he given Sloane a copy of the MPEG they had downloaded, although he hadn't told Luna that yet. He had no solid reason for withholding it. But he kept it back.

They had already looked at the MPEG. It turned out to be a short video – taken at some distance, through the waving branches of a flowering tree – that showed a pillow-shaped, puffy-looking man in his early sixties – beautifully turned out in a dove-gray suit – sitting at a sun-lit boardwalk café, sipping at a tiny espresso cup, his soft, pink hands holding it daintily, his round, fat face beaming with jovial charm at a woman sitting opposite him, her back turned to the camera, her long blond hair falling around her bare shoulders.

The man was leaning forward over his rounded belly and talking to the woman, his full lips slightly wet-looking, his manner that of a self-satisfied businessman enjoying a long, liquid lunch with a beautiful girl. In the background, three tall spires rocked beyond a sea wall, some sort of eighteenth-century sailing vessel, flying the Union Jack. Pennants fluttered in the bright midday light, and people – obvious tourists, from their Banana Republic shorts and their floppy canvas sun-hats, their fanny packs cinched in under their bulging bellies, trailed by strings of equally fat children like flocks of overstuffed ducklings – ambled around a broad, piazza-like square: Drew had recognized the South Street Seaport immediately. The video ran for about thirty-five seconds – a telephoto lens – zooming in at the end on this unknown fat man's moist-looking face as he completed what must have been a fairly long commentary addressed to the woman, whose face was never seen.

Watching the man's mouth moving – the video ran in total silence – both Drew and Luna got the intuitive impression that the man wasn't speaking in English. Luna had commented that, whoever he was, the body language of the woman with him suggested that she was either drugged, or suffering from near-fatal boredom. Drew had copied a digital slice of the film with the background visible, and then run it off on the hotel's printer; a snapshot of an unknown man sitting in the sun, radiating smug contentment.

He heard a cell phone ringing in the bedroom, and Luna's soft step as she came out of the shower to answer her phone. He watched the traffic streaming northward and the lights changing in the long, canyonlike avenue, listening to her muffled voice as she spoke into the phone; a muted, but apparently intense conversation, and then the thump of the phone hitting the bed. Luna – wrapped in a white terry robe, her hair in a white towel, and her skin scrubbed and shining – came out into the living room, still dewy and fragrant from her shower. Drew turned away from the window with what he hoped was going to be a witty and charming comment, and stopped dead when he saw her scalded-looking face.

'What is it?'

She blinked at him. Her robe, slightly open, revealed a livid tracery of deep purple and red scars above the swelling of her breasts – a pulpy, bruised-looking network of tissue that led downward under the terry robe. She saw his shocked look, and pulled the robe around her convulsively with her left hand. Drew once again noticed the vivid, raw-looking burn that covered the back of her left hand and slithered like a pale pink snake all the way up to her left elbow.

Luna came over to him, close enough for him to breathe in her soapy green-apple scent, her green eyes filled with warning.

'That was Levi. He says to turn on CNN.'

Drew's chest tightened, and a chill seemed to rise up from his chest and flood out around his neck and shoulders. He nodded, and walked over to the huge, flat-screen Sony in the French Provincial armoire. Bracing himself, he flicked the remote. The television blipped on, and he was looking at Aaron Brown's sad-eyed, quietly intelligent face –

'– much more we can say about this, except to promise you we're going to stay with this breaking story –'

At the bottom of the screen, a subtitle read:

BREAKING NEWS –
POWER PLANT BOMBED IN THE PHILIPPINES

' – hard times in this UN peacekeeping zone, made all the tougher by the devastating explosion thirty minutes ago at the Maria Christina power plant a few miles upriver from Iligan – we have no video of that yet, but you'll see it as soon as we can get it – early reports from the scene are that the entire plant was destroyed by a powerful explosive, and that the dam that held back the waters of the reservoir was severely damaged. Initial reports are that up to twenty workers may have been killed. UN officials are saying that the explosive was apparently placed on a raft, and then floated into one of the huge intake ports above the station. Blame for the explosion has been placed on an allegedly disgruntled employee, who is currently missing, and who may have snuck into the plant in the early hours, and raised the automated steel gates which were designed to prevent this kind of attack. The guards stationed around the plant had all been pulled off to support German peacekeepers, who were involved in an all-night firefight up around the Lake Lanao region. It seems this unidentified employee took advantage of their absence to open the gates and let the raft enter the intake tunnels. Power to the whole region has been cut off totally, from Iligan all the way to the town of Marawi, thirty-five miles away at Lake Lanao. We are told that, had the dam given way, the city of Iligan, already mourning the loss of so many in that terrorist bombing at the Blue Bird and struggling with a power blackout, might have been facing a flood that could have killed thousands more, and devastated an already suffering city –'

Drew shut the television off.

They stood there a while, staring numbly at the black screen. Out on First, sirens blared and horns complained. Drew looked down and saw a chain of black Suburbans – red police lights flashing – butting through the traffic, escorting a long black Lincoln Town Car northward toward the 59th Street Bridge. He turned back to Luna.

'What did Levi say about this?'

She gathered herself, making an effort.

'He told us to stay put. Anyway, this has gone beyond anything we can do. And what good would it do? Sloane swears that they've got a submarine on the way from Guam to take Cole's unit off, if they can get to a beach –'

There was a strong triple knock at the door. They exchanged glances – Luna went back into the bedroom, came out with her Beretta in her hand and walked over to the door, where a large lens in the panel showed a fish-eye image of whoever was outside. She studied it for a second, and turned around to Drew with an odd look, puzzled and alarmed.

'I think they're cops.'

'Federal?'

'No. They look like NYPD.'

More knocking; emphatic, official. Impatient.

'I'll handle this,' said Drew.

'Not without me,' said Luna, stiffening. She pulled the robe tighter, and went over to sit down in one of the wing-backs. Drew opened the door on two men, both of them in well-cut Italian suits, one in silky gray, the other a soft golden brown. The older man had a rounded, muscular jaw; a thick, powerful body barely contained by his extremely expensive silk suit; and quick, intelligent brown eyes. He was holding up a gleaming gold shield. His partner was a young Italian-looking man, with a lot of wavy black hair, very broad shoulders, narrow hips, oddly short legs that looked slightly bowed, intense black eyes that looked sleepy, but were not.

'Senator Langan?' asked the older man in a deep carrying voice, his accent pure Bronx.

'Yes. What's the problem?'

'I'm Detective Vernon Geberth. This is my partner, Sergeant Lou Gambatti. May we have a moment, sir? I apologize for the hour.'

'Certainly. Come in.'

Drew stepped away, and the two men came into the suite. Both of them looked at Luna sitting upright in her chair, and Drew was aware of Luna's scent, the green-apple scent of her shampoo, still floating in the air of the living room.

'Luna, these men are from the NYPD. This is Luna Olvidado.'

'"Forgotten Moon"?' said Gambatti, clearly an instant admirer.

'What're you? Berlitz? Zip it, Lou. Sorry, ma'am.'

Luna nodded once, her expression neutral. Drew did not identify her official status. Detective Geberth, obviously impressed, introduced himself and his partner with a touch of chivalric flair. Drew found that he had not yet arrived at an immediate dislike of the man, which was not his pattern with law enforcement. They both stood for a moment in the center of the room, and looked around as if they were thinking of buying the furniture. Drew asked them to sit down. They sat, but he stayed standing.

'Okay. How can I help?'

'First of all,' said Geberth, 'we hear your father died recently. We're sorry about that. He was a Marine, if I'm right. I was in the Navy myself –'

'How did you know he was dead?'

'We had a reason to run your name in NCIC, and the FBI called us back when our query showed up on their computer. An Agent Pruitt. He told us your father had died. Like I said, sorry to be bugging you at a time like this.'

'Are you here about my father?'

Geberth and Gambatti – Drew figured the NYPD paired them for the alliterative bounce of their names – looked at each other and then at Drew; it was like having two gundogs stare at you, the same soulful look masking the same predatory intensity.

'You called a number earlier this evening –'

Gambatti flipped open a steno notebook and read the numbers – 212-355-9955 – off in a monotone, while Geberth watched Drew's face closely. When he had finished, Geberth went smoothly on.

'You called that number about two hours ago. Can you tell us why you were calling it?'

'Can you tell me why you're asking?' said Drew, but he was only stalling to give himself some time to think. He was afraid he already knew the answer to that question. Geberth, perhaps sensing this delaying tactic, became a little less friendly.

'I'd appreciate an answer first, Senator.'

'Okay. Fair enough. I was calling a man named Kohl Keune. I don't know him personally. I was referred to him by a family friend in connection with a project I'm currently involved in. I was told that Mr Keune might be in a position to give me some help.'

'What kind of project would that be?' asked Geberth.

'Is it necessary for you to know?'

Geberth gave him a broad, predatory smile.

'I like to know all sorts of things. It's an occupational disease.'

'I'm looking for a man.'

'Are you? There's a lot of that going around. What man?'

'His name –' Drew suppressed the 'was' – 'is Gunther Krugman. He's an old family friend, and we're having some trouble locating him. The family is concerned. He's an old man and . . .'

'The family is concerned. I see. Would this be the same Gunther Krugman that the Feds are currently ripping up most of the northeastern seaboard looking for?'

Drew gave himself points for always following a golden rule: Never tell a lie to a big city cop. He smiled back at him.

'Yes. That's the man.'

Geberth, surprised at Drew's straightforward admission, relaxed visibly. Drew found himself liking the man. Gambatti was a cipher, but then this was Geberth's show. He was gold-shield homicide.

'Well, I wish you all the luck in finding him, sir. But if you were hoping for some help from this Kohl Keune guy, then I have some bad news for you. We got him on a slab down the street a few blocks in Bellevue, at the ME's office. I can see by your face that this doesn't surprise you all that much.'

'No. I'm afraid it doesn't. Where did you find him?'

'Just around the corner, as a matter of fact.'

'Around the corner? On Forty-eighth Street, maybe?'

'Yeah,' said Geberth, beaming at him. 'That's right.'

'At three-thirty-five West Forty-eighth Street, to be precise?'

Gambatti and Geberth exchanged a look, and Geberth came back to Drew with the light of the hunt shining in his soft brown eyes and an expression of cynical amusement marking his strong face.

'You confessing, Senator?'

'You found him at a place called the Giovanni Soro Institute?'

'Exactly right.'

'How long had he been dead?'

'Suppose you tell us how long you've been in town?'

'I flew into the Thirty-fourth Street Heliport at two o'clock this afternoon. I was met there by a man named Levi Sloane, who works for the National Security Agency, and by three FBI agents, Special Agent in Charge Harry Pruitt and his partners, I think their names were Canning and Stackhouse.'

'And before, you – Are you a pilot?'

'Yes.'

'What were you flying, by the way?'

'A Bell Huey.'

'No shit. A real Huey? With the avionic rebuild?'

'Yes.'

'Man. Is it still there? I'd love to see it.'

'I think the NSA may have taken it by now.'

Geberth looked a little disappointed, then he brightened.

'And before you flew – was it a rental?'

'No. I own it.'

'Lucky man. I used to fly them in the Navy. So, before you flew in on your very own Huey, can you tell us where you were?'

'I was in Harrisburg, Pennsylvania, last night, and in Cape Vincent this morning.'

Geberth glanced across the room at Luna.

'You got some corroboration on that?'

'I do. Miss Olvidado was with me.'

'Well, I gotta thank you for being direct, Senator. Fact is, we figure Mr Keune was killed sometime in the morning.'

'This morning?'

'Yeah. The ME figures maybe eight or nine at the latest.'

'How did he die?'

Geberth's face altered. Nothing visible, but it was as if he had put on a mask that was an exact replica of his real face.

'It was ugly, sir. He'd been tortured. Looks like that went on a while. Nobody heard a thing, but this is New York. Somebody was trying very hard to get something out of him. I don't know if they got what they wanted.

The office looked like a slaughterhouse. You're wondering how we got to you?'

'Because I called?'

'Well, that too. But there was a computer in his office. It was still turned on, and we searched the drive. The guys at One Police – the geeks – found an encrypted program that they tell me was designed to send a message out automatically once some sort of remote key had been entered. A reference to some sort of horse called a Conjurado. The message went out at around seven A.M.'

'"Conjurado" means trickster,' said Gambatti.

'Thanks for the latest translation, Lou. Remind me to get you some duct tape later. They traced the link to a computer at a private house in upstate New York. A place called Cape Vincent. The New York State boys did a little digging for us, and found out that the house was deeded to your father, Henry Langan, to be held in trust by the Giovanni Soro Corporation. We don't know who owns that corporation yet. We searched the Henry Langan link on NCIC and came up the fact that he had died, and that the FBI had been talking to you here in New York. So you can see why we were interested when our vic gets a phone call from you. Now, you just now told us you were in Cape Vincent this morning. Around what time?'

'We got there at six, I think.'

'And left when?'

'Around ten.'

'So you were in the house this morning?'

'That's right.'

'And you got the message?'

'Yes. I did.'

'And what was in the message?'

'I wish I could tell you.'

Geberth smiled at him, not kindly.

'And why can't you?'

'You know I'm on the Senate Intelligence Committee?'

'Actually, we heard you used to be on it.'

That rocked Drew, which seemed to amuse Geberth.

'Gossip is a terrible thing, Senator. And the Feds are the worst. We've been told that Helen McDowell turfed you out of the committee yesterday. So that sort of makes it easier for you to tell us what was in that message. Because, you see, we sort of figure that whatever was in the message might help us figure out who killed Mr Keune. You following me?'

'I've been as straight as I can be about all of this.'

'That you have.'

'But what was in the message – that relates directly to a matter of national security –'

'The last refuge,' said Gambatti, in a sneering tone.

Luna was now watching Drew with greatly heightened interest and a clear warning in her eyes.

'Of national security – and if I were to reveal the content of the message I'd very likely be under arrest ten minutes later.'

Geberth blinked at him slowly.

'You know something, Senator ... I am inclined to believe you. I think it could be you're a stand-up guy, and I'm gonna take a chance on you. How about we do this? You cast your mind back over this message. Is there anything in it that you *can* tell me that might help us figure out who whacked the unfortunate Mr Keune?'

Drew looked at the man, who returned the look with self-contained gravity.

'Maybe. But I have a question.'

'Everybody has a question. Let's hear yours.'

'Can you tell me what Keune did for a living?'

'Yeah. He was a security consultant. He worked for a security company based in Berlin, called Sternhagen. Very big in Europe, offices in England, and all over. We talked to Sternhagen, and they say he was working on a contract with a private client. Wouldn't say what the job was. We know Keune used to be with German intelligence – I forget what they call themselves – and he retired last year to go to work for this Sternhagen outfit. He's some kind of crypto expert – also does surveillance – that sort of thing. Now, how about my problem?'

'Okay . . . I think, based on what I saw in that message – what I can tell you about it – is that it's possible that whoever kidnapped or killed Gunther Krugman are the same people who killed Kohl Keune.'

Geberth groaned softly. Luna got up and searched through Drew's suit jacket until she found a box of his Davidoffs. They all watched her as she lit one and blew the smoke out, leaning forward in the chair, her legs crossed above the knee, the robe falling away slightly. Geberth thought of Marlene Dietrich. Gambatti thought of Sharon Stone. Drew thought of wrath and retribution. He was going to hear about this later, but he was grateful for her present silence.

Geberth came back to Drew.

'So this is a federal gig, then?'

'Fucking peachy,' said Gambatti. 'They'll come in and jerk it out, and we'll never find out who the hell did what to whom?'

'That depends,' said Drew.

'On what?' asked Geberth.

'I have a situation, and I need some help with it. I'll tell you what my situation is. If you can do one thing for me,

I'll do what I can to see that the Feds don't shut you out.'

A wary look crept across Geberth's blunt features.

'Sounds ducky. If you can pull it off.'

'This morning, while we were flying in from Cape Vincent, two men in a Bell Ranger chopper tried to drop a chain through our rotors. At four thousand feet.'

'Jesus,' said Geberth, shooting a glance at Luna, who kept her face as uninformative as she could manage. 'How?'

Drew told him the story, leaving out Luna's part. When he finished, the detectives were seeing them both in a new light.

'You went low? In an old Huey? Trying to outrun a Jet Ranger?'

'My point is, the two men in that chopper? The timing is right for them to have been killing your victim this morning. Right now, the NSA will have people up there at the scene. If you can get someone from the state cops to help you out, you may be able to get an ID on the two men in that chopper or maybe get a trace on the airframe numbers. Got a pen? The serial numbers on the chopper, were C V X nine nine three three five H. No other markings. See what they get you. After that, it's up to you to keep the case.'

'This Levi Sloane guy, how's he gonna feel about you giving us this information?'

'I'd rather you didn't tell him where you got it.'

Luna stubbed her Davidoff out with unnecessary force. Since he wasn't wearing a welder's mask, Drew avoided direct eye contact with her. Geberth was quiet for a time, clearly working out an angle.

'Okay ... I got some friends in the state CID. If a chopper went down in the Adirondacks, that's their jurisdiction. If I tell them it's maybe related to a homicide here in New York, they won't let the NSA keep them off the scene. If they can ID these guys or the chopper, we can work it backwards, and see if this Jet Ranger took off from anywhere close to New York. Yeah. I like it. This works for me.'

'I'm happy to help. Now you can do something for me.'

'Okay,' said Geberth, his wary look coming back.

Drew walked over to the computer desk and picked up the color printout of the unknown fat man in Kohl Keune's MPEG. He handed it to Geberth, who stared at it with an unhappy expression.

'Who's this mook?'

'I don't know. This was taken at the South Street Seaport. I think it's recent. We need to know who this man is.'

'And that's where I come in?'

'Yes.'

Geberth looked down at the shot, shaking his head ruefully.

'Ah jeez.'

Mindanao

They went directly north, back through the vine-choked valley of tears that they had taken the day before – at least it was downhill this time – carrying Krause on a liana-vine litter between Pike and Cole – eventually stumbling out of it onto a plateau wearing a thick coat of elephant grass, where a distant glimpse of the blue ocean rolling under white cumulus clouds and a puzzling column of black smoke rising from the site of the Maria Christina Power Station tantalized them but answered no questions – plunging into the jungle again, and down the green slope of a whale-backed mountain that led – after more struggle – into a palm grove a few miles south of Camp Casey – seventeen miles in all, most of it covered at a dead run, carrying the limp bulk of Dean Krause.

They stopped for brief intervals to catch their breath, drink whatever water could be found inside the upturned leaves of lianas or in the cusps of unknown flowers, and to change Krause's bandage. Then on again, a jingling jog-trot with their breath coming in short sharp gasps, their guns slamming against their ribs, their legs quivering, and in the air all around the beat of unseen choppers sifting the jungle canopy looking for them, and far overhead, Mirage fighters cruising, a thunderous rumble from two thousand feet up.

At two o'clock – his legs turning to spaghetti, and his injured ear throbbing painfully – Cole called a halt under a royal palm at the edge of a descending river bed, where a trickle of muddy water was carrying what was left of the monsoon floods down toward Iligan City. They lay Krause down carefully on a bed of ferns and then collapsed, chests heaving, with their backs up against the rough round pillar of the royal palm. Krause – his skin gray and covered with beads of sweat – blinked up at the sky through the fan of palm leaves, his lips pale blue.

'Leave me here,' he said, in a hoarse croak.

Pike wiped Krause's lips with his sleeve. Chris Burdette found a coconut shell and scooped up some brown water from the stream, brought it over to Pike, and handed it to him. Pike put a strong, long-fingered hand under Krause's head, and held the coconut to his cracked lips. Krause swallowed, coughed, tensed immediately – his face twisted – and Pike put a hand on Krause's bloody, matted bandage.

Fresh blood was already seeping through it.

'We're not going to leave you here,' said Burdette.

'No,' said Pike. 'Nobody else gets left behind.'

'I'm a medic,' said Krause, struggling for air. 'You're not. The round punched through the abdominal wall, maybe hit some intestine. If I was bad hurt, I'd have bled out by now. But I'm going to go septic, if I'm right about the intestines, and I'm going to need some really strong antibiotics pretty damn soon. And that round can't stay in me. If you leave me here, I'll give you a decent lead and then light a fire. That'll bring the choppers. I'll be on that hospital ship fifteen minutes later.'

'You saw what they did to Loman,' said Pike.

'That was in the heat of the moment. And we made sure they all paid for it. Way I see it, they'll want to keep us alive just to figure out who the hell we are. I'll die anyway, if you don't leave me here.'

'They'll grill you.'

'I've been grilled before. I've got a legend. I can take it – and you can't carry me all the way to Iligan. If you leave me for the Krauts, at least you guys have a chance of getting out. Just leave me the forty-five. I'll figure out what to do with it later.'

Cole stared down at Krause, tapped Pike on the shoulder, and they both stepped away while Chris Burdette bent down to change Krause's bandage again.

'We still have the satellite. How about an extraction?'

'We're an embarrassment,' said Pike. 'If we use the satellite phone, we let them know exactly where we are. Not to mention the Krauts, who'll have all their electronics on. Yeah, our guys may come and get us. But our orders were no contact. We lit up seven troopers at least – one of them an officer – plus maybe two UN civilians. If we contact Collections, do you really think that they're gonna be happy to hear that we're still alive?'

Pike was right about that. Cole had to agree with him. By the terms of their oath, it was their duty to evade capture, or to die if necessary, to protect the secrecy of the mission. Other agents had done it, put a bullet in their heads just as the secret police kicked in the safe-house door. Unlike Pike, Cole still believed in Sloane. He was a decent man and good controller, and he had a long record of honorable service, decorated many times for heroism back when he was a field agent. But everybody in the CIA knew what was expected of them all when it came down to mission secrecy. It was part of the job.

Chris Burdette, who had done what he could for Krause, his piratical face growing more and more solemn as he worked at the blue-edged circle where the round had punched in, looked up from Krause's pale staring face with a ragged smile.

'So death turns out to be our fallback position after all?'

'Fuck that,' said Krause, struggling to a sitting position. 'It's easy for you guys to talk about dying. And if we all die, whose gonna go back to the States and see to it we all don't get stuck with this psycho-baby-killer tag? We all got family, friends in the service, people who will remember us. Is this how you want to be remembered? Not me. You guys stay alive, there's still a chance. Hook up with Vasquez at Casey, and get the hell out of this country. Tell the real story.'

Everyone was looking at him now, in silence.

'Look, here's what's going to happen. I'm going down to that hospital ship and get my belly fixed. Since I don't think I can crawl down to the ship, I'm gonna draw the UN guys up here to me. How will I do that? Cole leaves me the satellite phone. The walkie-talkies have a range of, what? Three – maybe four miles? I give you time to get to the extreme range of the radios, then I dial up Collections and I arrange an extraction for you guys. I get the details, I radio them to you. You commence to bug out at speed. You find Vasquez at Casey, do your escape and evasion thing. You're all miles away before the Krauts zero in on me and send a chopper.'

They all considered Krause's blue face, his white lips. They knew in their hearts that carrying him any farther would probably kill him anyway. Krause was right, but Pike wasn't ready to accept it yet.

'What if Sloane doesn't send in a sub? What if he gets the Navy to zero a cruise in on your ass and light you up?' asked Pike.

'Then I go up in a cloud of glory. You're still a long way out of range. Stay alive. Get out of this place. Find Sloane and put it to him.'

Cole shook his head.

'I don't buy Sloane as a traitor.'

'I do,' said Pike.

'I'll grant you he's lost his touch. He's no traitor.'

'Maybe he is, maybe he isn't,' said Krause. 'I'm still right. Either way, you do it my way and live, or do it your way and end up in a prisoner's box at The Hague right next to me. Enough talk. Shut up and go.'

'Jeez,' said Burdette. 'I love it when you're masterful.'

'You know I'm right,' said Krause. 'It's time.'

He was. And it was.

They all shook hands with him, said a few private words, and then they moved out – gear policed up, and on their way in two minutes. Cole stopped a few yards away, down the river bed, and looked back up the line at Dean Krause, propped against a palm.

Krause smiled back at him gently. Cole turned away with a stone in his heart, and moved off down the slope. Krause watched them for a long time, until they disappeared into a gathering mist.

New York City

The phone shrilled at him. Drew sat up in a daze, throwing off the blanket, and picked up the phone. The hard white light of morning was streaming in through the eastern windows.

'Hello.'

'Senator. This is Vernon Geberth. You sound like I woke you. I been up all night, and I lose track of the time. Did I wake you?'

Drew sat up straight, reached for a cigarette, fired it up.

'No. No you didn't,' he lied; a reflex. For reasons buried in the human heart, no one likes to admit to being asleep when the phone rings. Across the room, the bedroom door opened and Luna stood there, drawn curtains darkening the room behind her. She was wearing the same white robe, and as she stepped into a shaft of sunlight coming in through the window she filled up the room with light.

'Any word on your dad yet?' Geberth was asking.

'My dad?'

Of course. His father was dead. Grief flooded back up into his chest, and he forced it down. 'My dad. Nothing yet. No call.'

'Okay. Good luck on it. We got a NCIC notice asking the department to look out for this Cornel Chulalonkorn character, and I saw the reference to your dad. I hope they nail this mutt.'

'Thank you, Detective. How did you do at the chopper site?'

'You were right about the Feds crawling all over it. My buddy with State says he's never seen that many Ray-Bans and gunfighter mustaches since he busted a fetish bar in Lackawanna. But he bulled his way into it. He didn't get much other than tentative ID's on the dead guys. You want them?'

Drew, surprised, said he did.

'Okay. The chopper was a rental from an agency in Albany. It was rented by two accredited pilots named Werner Schliemann and Heinz Graz. Both German nationals. The agent at the airport said these two mutts were in one hell of a hurry. Paid the deposit and in the air inside of fifteen minutes. Less than two hours before they tried to kill you over the Adirondacks, so they were really hot on your trail. It also means they knew exactly where you were going to be, so, as they say, govern your ass accordingly. The credit card used was personal, but they traced it back to that German security company, Sternhagen. On unpaid leave from the company, for reasons nobody knows. Sternhagen denies any knowledge of what they were doing chasing you around upstate New York with a tow chain, but my guy managed to get copies of the dead guys' prints off the spooks working the crash scene, and we typed them for matches at the Kohl Keune crime scene. As we say in the detective game, bingo! So I owe you big for this one.'

'They matched?'

'They did. Anyway, it looks like our killers are dead courtesy of the United States Senate, for which I thank you. I got a query.'

'Yes?'

'My buddy with the Staties says one of these guys had three nine-mill rounds in his chest. Nice grouping. You do that?'

'No.'

'Miss Forgotten Moon, maybe?'

'Perhaps.'

'No offense, chief, but she puzzled me. So I ran her.'

Drew looked at Luna, who glanced away, and then came back.

'Okay. I'm interested.'

'I figured her for Secret Service.'

'I can understand that.'

'Ah, she's right there, hah?'

'That's a possibility.'

'I'll make this short. I got a guy at the Feebs, and he pulled her seven-twenty. Not much there but her civil service rating. She's making about twice what a Secret Service agent would pull down. There's also a contact tag on NCIC. About a year ago, she got pulled over for speeding on the Bruckner by one of our harness guys. She tinned him, and he let her go. He wrote up the contact as "interagency courtesy." The ID she tinned him with was NSA.'

'I'd want to see that file for myself.'

'I like you, Senator, but we're not on those kinda terms.'

'I find this extremely difficult to believe.'

'You don't want to hear this, that's okay with me.'

'Why all the energy?'

'Like I said. I owe you. I followed up.'

'I'm listening. Anything else?'

'How long she been on your protection detail?'

Six months. Longer. What did this mean?

'Not long.'

'Long enough, right? Look, you watch yourself, hah?'

'I will. Did you get more than just the names of these guys?'

'No. All the Feds would give me is they're German nationals, in here on work visas – they entered on a Lufthansa flight into JFK last week – and that they're ex-German army. I think I can close the Kohl Keune case anyway, but I'll never know the whole story. Or will I?'

'If I ever find out, I'll tell you.'

'You staying on this thing?'

'Yes. I have to.'

'You got *cojones*, chief. My advice is to keep Miss Forgotten Moon nearby. Like the Don says, you keep your friends close and your enemies closer. Oh, wait – I did a facial recognition scan on that mook in your photo. It turns out he's on our C and E registry.'

'C and E?'

'Consular and Embassy. They all get a photo ID, so they can show it to our guys when they're telling them sorry-I-backed-over-your-mom-coming-out-of-D'Agostino's-but-I-got-diplomatic-immunity-so-fuck-off. His name's Eisenstadt. Gerhardt Eisenstadt. Drives a big silver Benz, diplomatic plates. German citizen – you notice there's a lot of Krauts in this case – seventy-two years old, Berlin address, works as – I love this shit – Junior Undersecretary for International Trade and Development at the United Nations. New York address is two-forty-nine East Seventy-seventh Street, a townhouse.

According to his CV, he oversees foreign aid and something called "infrastructure development" in Southeast Asia. Funny little footnote here – his kid went missing in Berlin two days ago. Filed a missing persons with Interpol. That's how I saw it – the computer brings up any agency reference connected to his name. This seem strange to you?'

'How do you mean?'

'I mean, the guy loses his son – files with Interpol – and yet here he is in New York, twenty-four hours later – we dated your shot from the tall ship in the background. She's the *Flying Childers*. She was only in town three days, and he just got into New York two days ago. So his kid goes missing, and he promptly flies off to New York, and here he is having a drink at the South Street Seaport, all fat and jolly. It just strikes me weird. Anyway, this stuff any use to you?'

'Yes. It is.'

'Well then, I got to run. I owe you for this. Most people with your kind of muscle wouldn't have opened the door to us without having the Supreme Court hiding in the bathroom. Instead, you gave me the collar. You still got my card? Anything I can ever do, you call.'

The line went dead.

And promptly rang again.

'Senator Langan? This is Britney Vogel.'

'Britney. How did you know I was here?'

'You always stay at the Beekman when you're in New York. Do you remember what we talked about at the airport?'

'You were going to wait for me to call you.'

'I was. But something's come up here at the paper, and I wanted to warn you about it. Off the record.'

Luna padded barefoot across the rug and placed a coffee on the low table in front of him. She stood there, her green eyes troubled. Drew mouthed the word Britney Vogel at her and she frowned, then ran a finger across her throat, shaking her head vigorously. Drew held up a hand, picked up the cup, and sipped at the coffee – rich and black – trying to anticipate Britney and keep his balance.

'You on your cell phone?'

'Yes. Why?'

'Call me back on a landline.'

A silence while Britney worked that out.

'Okay. I'll call you right back.'

Mindanao

The long valley that held what was left of Camp Casey looked like a great green bowl filled to the brim with pale blue mist. The tops of the taller palms pierced the surface of this mist like drowned trees rising out of a mountain lake. A heavy stillness was on the valley, and they lay there along the tree line for several minutes, trying to sense the presence of something – anything – in the camp below them. No wind stirred the palms, and the only sound was the steady drip-drip of heavy dew falling off the leaves around them, a sound like a clock ticking. Finally, Chris Burdette shifted closer to Cole, moving through the bending grasses with a soft, hissing sound. He leaned in close to Cole's good ear, and spoke in a soft whisper. His breath smelled of mint and beer. Where was he getting the beer?

'Whaddya think, boss?'

Cole glanced over at Pike, who was lying a few feet away, looking down into the thickening mist along the barrel of his 60.

'I think it looks hinky.'

'Hinky?'

'Yeah. Hinky.'

'You know, I never could figure out where that word came from. "Hinky." It makes no sense. It has no entomological roots.'

'Thanks for the diversion, Chris. And it's "etymological."'

'You wanna use the radio?'

'You mean call down, see if Ramiro is there?'

'That's the general thrust of my argument.'

'No. I don't.'

Pike took his eyes off the barrel sights and looked across at them through a screen of wet vines.

'Can't see a thing. Somebody's gonna have to go down there.'

'Somebody like me, perchance?' said Burdette.

'Perchance?' said Pike.

'Somebody like you,' said Cole.

'There's nobody like me.'

'Okay, then you specifically.'

Burdette stripped off his gear belt and rifle, and rolled over onto his back, did a press check on his pistol and lay there for a moment, staring up at the sky, a thin wash of wet gray cloud drifting at the canopy level. Beyond that there was the palest shade of blue. The fog was low and local, and it seemed odd to him that somewhere else in this miserable island there was sunshine and blue water and people having tall cold drinks in a dockside cantina. He gave some thought to another line of work, and decided against it. He was a one-trick pony, and he knew it.

'Okay. What was the call sign again?'

'Jupiter.'

'Why Jupiter?'

'Why not?'

'Okay,' he said, rolling over and gliding away down the hillside, moving on his belly through the tall wet grass.

They watched him until he faded into a dark gray blur against the soft wet green. In a moment he was gone into the mist, and the dripping silence came back.

'That boy moves well,' said Pike.

'I think he has some alligator in him.'

'I'd buy that,' said Pike.

Time passed. The mist rose up out of the valley and began to spill out into the tree line. They lay there and watched it as it rose to the height of the canopy, and now it was as if they were lying at the bottom of a cloudy lake. Neither man moved or spoke while Cole watched forty minutes and thirty-eight seconds tick off on the red dial of his digital wristwatch. Pike stiffened, and hissed at Cole. They both heard the faintest gliding rustle. It was coming from down the slope right in front of them. They stared into the fog. Cole became aware that he was not breathing, and he pulled in several slow breaths to ease his adrenaline rush and calm himself for battle, if it came. A disembodied whisper drifted out of the fog.

'Jupiter.'

'Come ahead,' said Cole, steadying the muzzle of his Colt on the space where the sound had come from. The tall grass split, and Chris Burdette glided back into the tree line.

'Ramiro's there.'

'You left him?' said Pike.

'Yeah.'

'Is he dead?'

'No. He's sitting there in the same cabin where we bivouacked before. Has his M-16 on his lap. Looks alone. Looks okay.'

'Did he see you?'

'Nobody sees me.'

'Why didn't you bring him out?'

'He has his rifle on his lap. His head is down. He's breathing soft, but he's not looking up. It's like he's meditating. In a trance.'

'For fuck's sake, Chris,' said Pike.

'His rifle?'

'Yeah?'

'Well, there's no magazine in it.'

'What?' said Cole.

'You heard me. There's no magazine in his rifle.'

'And he's holding it in his lap.'

'Yeah. Like he wanted me to see it.'

Cole was silent for a time.

'The last time we saw this valley, there was a boar working it. And herons. A whole whack of herons live here. You hearing them?'

No one said anything for a while, until Pike said, 'Shit.'

'Now what?' said Burdette.

'Nothing,' said Cole. 'We wait.'

'We should go down there and get him out,' said Pike.

'No,' said Burdette. 'Cole's right. We wait. These UN troopers are green. If they're here in this valley, they'll do something stupid.'

The stillness came back, stronger and thicker than before. The mist closed in around them while they listened to the jungle pressing in on them. The mist gathered on the thick leaves overhead, pooling into the central veins and dripping off the tips. They fell to earth with a soft, ticking sound. Ten minutes passed this way. Fifteen.

Then they heard a soft chuffing noise from across the valley.

'The boar?' said Pike, in a hoarse croak.

'No,' said Burdette. 'Somebody sneezed.'

Another faint chuffing sound, cut off abruptly. Then a low, murmuring vibration. Sound traveled well in the damp air, the way it would underwater. It seemed to come from the far side of the valley.

'Somebody's got his sergeant ripping him up,' said Pike.

'They're here,' said Cole. 'You sure they didn't see you?'

'If they had infrared? Maybe. But they'd be on us by now.'

'Unless they're waiting for all of us to show up,' said Burdette.

'That's true,' said Cole.

'What's it gonna be?' said Pike.

Cole was picturing the valley in his mind, how he would lay out his troops to contain the camp. Let someone in, but never let him out.

'They'd need a platoon at least.'

'Yeah,' said Pike. 'Fire teams on the far ridge.'

'OPs down the slope.'

Cole, picturing the valley in his mind, pointed out into the mist.

'There.' He moved his hand. 'And there.'

'Spread out,' said Burdette.

'In this soup.'

'Youngsters,' said Pike. 'Scared. Itching to rock and roll.'

Cole looked at his watch, then at the two men.

'We do what you're thinking, Boss,' said Burdette, 'we got a good chance of getting ripped up in the crossfire.'

'Fuck that,' said Pike. 'It worked real good in Eye Corps.'

'That,' said Burdette, 'was a long time ago.'

'This blue-on-blue shit never changes, Chris.'

'Okay,' said Cole. 'Chris, you know the way. You go down, take a position near the cabin. Stay low. When the shit starts, you go in. Take out whoever's sitting on Vasquez. Give Vasquez a full magazine, and you two kill anything that comes at you. We hook up on the northern slope fifty meters into the tree line. Call sign is Jupiter. Pike, you take the far slope. I'll take these guys dead ahead. How long you want?'

'Gimme seven minutes,' said Pike.

Cole glanced at his watch.

'Okay. Seven. Go.'

Burdette slipped back down the slope. Cole went at an angle, low, his Barrett at port arms, the wet grass slipping and sliding across his shins. A tall shape loomed in the mist, a royal palm. He padded by it, the ground under his feet slick and uneven. The hill sloped off to his left, and he followed it down, moving into a patch of brush. He could only see a few feet in front of him now. Trees and vines materialized before him, and he slipped through them, a soundless, shapeless ghost. His breathing was slow and steady, and he was fully and completely alive. In his belly he felt a rising fire, and the heat spread out across his chest and shoulders, warming him. In his throat an artery pulsed, gently. Fifty yards down the grade and now the ground leveled off, and he was entering a stand of royal palms. They rose up, leaning crazily, and disappeared into the mist overhead. He took a knee and looked at his watch. A figure stood up in front of him.

'*Du bist* —'

Cole pivoted on his right leg, his left leg extended, and kicked the man's feet out from under him. The soldier went down with a huffing thud and Cole was on his chest, his knee in the man's hard belly, his left hand shoving the man's chin upward – feeling the slick wet of his hot skin and the rasp of his beard – his K-Bar in his right. He forced the man's head back brutally with his left hand, and sliced deeply through his neck – left to right – a spray of bright red blood – oddly vivid in the half-light – shot out of the man's opened gullet. A hot, wet, warm exhalation burst from the man's gaping windpipe, and Cole could smell the man's last meal – some sort of spiced meat washed down with beer – the soldier's body arched and went rigid as Cole held him down, and the blood spurted from his severed jugular. Damp, hot air hissed from his opened throat, and Cole felt the blood on his left wrist as warm as salt water. Then the soldier went limp, and Cole sat back at the man's booted feet, looking around him into the fog. He heard the faint pulsing sound of the man's arterial blood pumping out, slower now, and softer. Then it stopped, and the immense stillness was back. He looked at his watch.

Ten seconds . . . five . . . now.

He got onto one knee and steadied the Barrett, taking a blind sight on the far ridge, invisible in the fog bank. He fired into that fog, seeing the muzzle flash reflected in thousands of tiny droplets of water, dazzling, and the massive boom of the rifle kicking in his hands sounded muffled, oddly distant. From his right he heard the sudden bass chatter of Pike's 60, and the ripping, tearing sound the rounds made as they cut through the jungle. From all around the ridge line came a sudden hailstorm of answering fire – flickers of red tracers slicing through the fog – they arced and sizzled through the wet air above his head. Now more fire was coming from the farther ridge as the troopers opened up, their tracer fire interlocking and crisscrossing the outgoing fire from the ridge line just above Cole's head.

He heard a hoarse cry, in German – and shouts came out of the fog bank, now near, now far away, and the thudding of boots as men came racing down the hillside. He pulled back into the palm grove as a line of men – heavy-booted, their gear jingling – lumbered past his position – fifteen yards past him, and they ran full into a wall of friendly fire coming from the other ridge and got cut to pieces – more heavy syncopated chatter from Pike's 60 – and over that the metallic clatter of a Heckler rifle – several Hecklers firing now in a mad minute – now all of them – and then the solid thump of a mortar round, and a bright red flare showed in the tattered mist on the far side of the valley – another and another – and the voices of men, some in pain, others angry – panicking – the tracer fire from the ridge cut back across his position, as a trooper up there traversed his machine gun, firing blindly into the roiling fog bank.

Cole scrambled up the slope, moving directly under the bright red spouting of the gunner's muzzle flare. The machine gun rattled to a stop – Cole popped up and fired two heavy rounds into the machine-gun position, and heard a man's voice – thin, young, in mortal pain – cut off in a bubbling moan, and Cole loped into the machine-gun post. A young German trooper was on his back with his shoulder shot through – just a wet, red, gaping hole where his left arm had been. His legs were moving in a jerky spastic manner, and his wide blue eyes were staring up at Cole, an intense bright blue against the flecks of blood spattered across his face. His mouth was working, his lips white, and his teeth red with blood. Cole stood over him for a moment – raised the rifle, and steadied it on the young boy's face –

'*Bitte! Nicht –*'

'Loman Strackbein,' Cole said, and squeezed the trigger. More fire from down in the valley – the sizzling, popping crackle of small arms, and under it, the heavy metallic thudding of Pike's M-60 – Cole turned away from the dead German soldier, and plunged back down the slope and out into the valley.

New York City

While Drew and Luna waited for Britney Vogel to call back, he spent a while telling Luna what he had heard about this man named Gerhardt Eisenstadt. He said nothing about what Vernon Geberth had told him about her. Luna had immediately picked up the phone to call Levi Sloane. Drew had stopped her. She took it badly. Now, they were both sitting in a cold silence heavy with unresolved anger, waiting, while the sound of morning traffic building on First Avenue drifted up from the street and the light changed in the room.

Fifteen minutes of this cold silence, and then the phone rang.

'Okay. It's me. I'm on a pay phone.'

'Good. What did you want to tell me?'

'Well – let me set this up for you – you're aware of this massacre in Mindanao?'

'You mean the dance club? The Blue Bird?'

'No. This was a village. It was called Cobraville. Some group went through it, shooting everybody. Men, women, children. Even the animals. Over a hundred people are dead, including some UN peacekeepers. It's on CNN right now. I can see it in a store window.'

Drew sat up straight. Luna started to speak, but he held a finger to his lips, and she waited in grim silence.

'On CNN? Hold on a minute.'

Luna went across and turned the television on, hitting MUTE as she did so. In a moment they were both looking at a grainy, hand-held video taken from a helicopter – early morning somewhere in Mindanao – green mountains rolling away into a blue distance – a line of burning palms near a broad brown river – a blackened, smoldering village, limp, torn bodies scattered everywhere – a water buffalo, belly-burst and swollen, stiff-legged, lying beside a burned-out building, a scorched French tricolor whipping madly on a staff as the chopper flew over it. At its base, a muscular young black man lying on his back, knees twisted, his brains obviously shot out, and next to that, the headless corpse of what looked like an infantry soldier, still clutching a pistol. The video panned to a group of stunned-looking German soldiers walking around with video cameras, and some UN medics with blue armbands. Bodies were being gathered up in litters.

'Okay. I've got it on.'

'This is going to sound pretty weird, but there's a black man who was killed at the scene of this massacre, and the UN investigators are saying that this man is suspected of being one of the people who committed the massacre. There's also a Jesuit priest on the scene by the name of Constantin Desaix. Apparently, he was running a medical clinic there, and he's saying the massacre was carried out by a unit of American soldiers dressed in civilian clothes. Says he saw it happen, but there was nothing he could do.'

'He says he *saw* it happen? Saw the Americans doing it?'

'That's his story.'

'He's lying. Who is he anyway?'

'I don't know.'

'Can you try to find out?'

'I can do a LexisNexis on him.'

'Will you? If you get it, e-mail me what you find?'

'I will. About this Strackbein guy, the UN is saying he checked into a hotel in Iligan a couple of days before, under some phony name. They've linked him to four other men who checked into the same place – the Milan Hotel – around the same time. The Filipino police went back over the still pictures taken by their security cameras at the ferry docks where people come in, and I'm hearing that they have shots of three of them. They've identified one of men in these shots as Jordan Kemp. They say he presented a Canadian passport in that name –'

'How'd they ID this Strackbein guy?'

'They're not saying. It sounds like they have an informant.'

'Who has the story, Britney?'

'It hasn't been assigned yet. Everybody's just standing around switching between CNN and Al Jazeera. If anybody gets it it'll be –'

'Can you get it?'

'I can try. I'll have to have some persuasive reason.'

'Tell me the worst of it.'

'The UN has established that a Jordan Kemp once worked as a journalist for one of the Toronto papers. Among other things, he covered the Iraq War for the *Morning Star,* as an embedded reporter. Here's the thing. He was embedded with a unit of the Third Infantry Division. Isn't that the unit your son served in? And the people at the Toronto paper are saying that the picture of Jordan Kemp that the UN is showing on Al Jazeera isn't really Jordan Kemp.'

'Have you seen these security-camera shots?'

'Yes. That's why I'm calling you. The man they're calling Jordan Kemp looks a lot like your son, Cole. Is that possible?'

'I don't know. Have you told anyone yet?'

'No. What do you want me to do?'

'Can you get the story?'

'There's only one way. I tell my editor that I recognize who the man in the picture really is. Then I tell him I have you as my source. I'll get the assignment. I'm willing to give you some time.'

'Time for what?'

'Time to figure out what the hell is going on.'

'How much time?'

'Can I tell him that you'll give me an exclusive?'

Luna was watching his face. He could promise whatever he wanted. It didn't matter. If this was the thing that Krugman had been trying to warn him about, it had already happened.

'Yes. You can.'

'Then I'll hold it as long as I can.'

'Can I get a day?'

'Maybe. I'll have to do some dancing.'

'Thank you, Britney.'

'I'll be here.'

'Good. Stay off your cell phone, Britney.'

'Why?'

'The Feds have been tapping it since Krugman vanished.'

Silence.

'Okay then. I'll be in touch.'

'Take care.'

With great difficulty, Drew found the control required

to set the phone down gently in the cradle. He leaned back in the sofa and looked up at Luna. He told her what Britney had told him. When he was finished, she looked back at him with a flat hostility that he had never seen in her face before.

'Have you lost your mind, Drew? First the NYPD, and now Britney Vogel. Sloane will crucify us both.'

Drew rubbed his face, feeling his stubble, a certain numbness flowing up from his belly and spreading outwards across his chest. He looked so wretched that her expression softened. She reached out and touched his knee in silence. Drew patted her hand, and she immediately jerked it away, reaching for another Davidoff.

'We're calling Sloane, Drew. We have no choice.'

Drew nodded, but did not move. They looked at each other in a long, heavy silence for a time. Drew sat forward, stared at his hands.

'Can I ask you something, Luna?'

'Certainly.'

'Who works out an agent's cover?'

'How would I know?' she said, exhaling a blue cloud that drifted into a shaft of sunlight. 'You were on the Intelligence panel. If you don't know, I'll ask Sloane when I'm talking to him. Which will be when this cigarette is done. Right?'

'The controller works out an agent's cover?'

'I would think so.'

'And Levi Sloane is Cole's mission controller.'

'Yes. I think we've established that.'

'So Levi Sloane gave Cole a cover story with a large, smoking hole drilled right through the middle of it. Why would he do that?'

Luna pulled on the cigarette while Drew watched her.

That this was a delaying ploy was clear to both of them. The question was why she was doing it, and what she was thinking. She was here as Levi Sloane's contact. The truth was, she worked for him, not with Drew.

'Are you saying that you think Levi Sloane is a traitor? Because his record is nothing short of brilliant. That's why he is where he is.'

'Who knew I had that Critic Flash?'

'Krugman. Levi may have suspected it later.'

'Geberth made a comment that there were a lot of Germans in this thing. Gerhardt Eisenstadt. Kohl Keune. Those two German agents in the chopper, Schliemann and Graz –'

'Gunther Krugman.'

'Yes. Another German. And the guy I shot. Dietrich Voss.'

'Voss was ID'd by the D.C. cops.'

'If my memory serves, that D.C. detective said they got the ID from the Feds. So all Packett knew about Dietrich Voss was what he got from a federal agency.'

'That agency was the FBI.'

'So what? Robert Hanssen was an FBI agent.'

'What's next? A hat made out of tin foil? Aliens are talking to you through your dental fillings? Don't be an ass, Drew.'

'I told Sloane I was going to see my father in Harrisburg. We leave him around midnight, and he's dead by the morning.'

'He was an old man, Drew.'

'You called Sloane when we were leaving Cape Vincent. And you told him where we were going.'

'Of course.'

'And halfway to New York, two German agents are

waiting for us in a Jet Ranger over the Adirondacks. German agents who it looks like had just finished murdering Gunther Krugman's guy in New York. Krugman hands me a secret document and disappears later that night. Somebody with a German name breaks into my house in Georgetown the same night. He tries to kill me. My father dies next. Then Kohl Keune in New York. Anybody following up on Krugman's disappearance has the life expectancy of a fruit fly.'

'Whatever your drug is, I'll take two.'

'Who assigned you to go on the road with me?'

'My boss at Secret Service HQ.'

'Didn't you think assigning a Secret Service agent to work as a liaison for a controller in the NSA was a bit unusual?'

'Maybe. But I was already involved.'

'Who asked him to assign you to me?'

She hesitated.

'Sloane did.'

'His name keeps coming up, doesn't it? Somebody's engaged in a cleanup operation, and it's being run by an experienced spook. Levi Sloane is an experienced spook, Luna. This spook knew where we were going, and how, and who we were seeing when we got there. Levi Sloane had all of that information because he made sure you were along to give it to him. There's no other explanation that fits.'

'A lot of people knew we were up in that chopper. Levi said so himself, according to you. Ground crew in Syracuse. In Black River, where we refueled. Plus, you used the air-to-ground radio to call Diana in Paris. Anybody with a scanner would have picked that up. You even got a call from McDowell, and I told her we were flying over Binghamton. None of this points to Levi. This is nuts, Drew.'

'I need to know who Dietrich Voss was working for.'

'They told you that. He's a professional thief.'

'So I've been told.'

'The CIA confirmed it! Drew, this is deeply crazy. You're tired. Your father has just died. You've been up for days.'

'Go to the window, Luna. Draw the drapes.'

Luna looked puzzled.

'What drapes? These ones?'

She looked at the open window next to them, the sun streaming in through the gauzy curtains blowing in the wind off the East River. The blackout drapes that were closed in the bedroom were wide open here in the living room, and sunlight was streaming in.

'Yeah. Stand up, go over, close the drapes.'

'You go close the damn drapes. For Christ's sake, Drew.'

'Okay.'

Drew stood up and moved toward the window. Half-way there, Luna jumped up and caught his arm, stopping him hard.

'No. Don't do it.'

'Why not?'

'I'm your bodyguard. People have already tried to kill you. You shouldn't be standing in front of any windows.'

'I've got nothing to worry about. The people who were trying to kill me are all dead. Isn't that right?'

Luna said nothing, standing in very close, looking up at him. Her green eyes were filled with a dark light.

'Drew, come away from the window. Please.'

He let her draw him away. She went to the window and

pulled the blackout curtains closed, plunging the room into darkness. Only a thin shaft of hard light came slicing through the drapes. It lay on the Persian carpet between them like a shard of broken glass.

'Who was Dietrich Voss, Luna?'

Luna said nothing, but she looked away from him.

'I don't know.'

'Why was my protection unit pulled off that night?'

'Because they sent that Dwayne David Canmore freak off to a loony bin in Allenwood. We all got reassigned.'

'When you met me in that field near Beltsville, you told me you had two weeks' vacation coming. When was it supposed to start?'

'That morning.'

'But instead, you got sent out to track me down?'

'I was the last agent to see you.'

'Who sent you?'

'I told you. My boss.'

'Who gave the orders to pull off my protection unit?'

'Who else? My boss.'

'I'm going to ask you again. Who was Dietrich Voss?'

Luna walked away and reached for his Davidoffs again. Drew watched her light up. The flaring match lit up a troubled face, a deeply unhappy face. She inhaled the smoke and blew it out.

'Truth time, Luna. Either tell me, or leave.'

Luna studied his face for a while. Drew held her eyes and said nothing. Finally, she sighed and sat down, and the mood shifted.

'He was a thief. I don't know his real name. He did a lot of work for the CIA. They provided his screen. Levi Sloane sent him.'

'You knew about this?'

'Not until later.'

'How much later?'

'Last night. When I took his call.'

Everything that occurred to Drew to say was not easily said. But Luna could read his face fairly well by now, and she looked away from what was in it. Drew let the betrayal slide. She had admitted to being an informant. She had not admitted to working against him. Yet.

'Sloane sent him. Why did he try to kill me?'

'Levi doesn't think he did. He thinks you panicked.'

'He came at me with a knife. He was sent to kill me.'

'No he wasn't. He was after your laptop and that Critic Flash.'

'I'm governed by the Secrets Act. All Sloane had to do was send over two agents and confiscate everything I had.'

'He explained that.'

'He explained why he sent a man to kill me? That must have been some seriously snazzy explanation. I'd love to hear it.'

'He said that if they sent out an official team to present you with an entry warrant, then all of D.C. would find out what Krugman had given you. If any of the other agencies found out that Krugman had been able to intercept and download a Critic Flash –'

'Krugman stole the flash?'

'Yes. He used his Gamma access to download it from the NSA mainframe a few minutes after it was received.'

'He was waiting for it to come in? That means he knew where it was going to come from?'

'Yes. Somehow he did.'

That changed everything.

'Was Gunther Krugman a spy?'

'Levi thinks so.'

'For whom?'

'We don't know yet.'

'Does he think I'm a spy?'

'No. But he thinks you might be a security leak.'

'And what do you think?'

'I think it's possible you're being manipulated.'

'By Krugman?'

'Yes.'

'It's just as possible that Levi Sloane is a traitor.'

'He isn't.'

'You're sure of this?'

'Absolutely. His record is –'

'You know his record?'

'Everybody does.'

'Everybody in the NSA.'

Luna said nothing for a while.

'How long have you been on my detail?'

'How long? I don't know. Six, seven months.'

'What did you do before that?'

'What?'

'Whose detail were you on?'

'What is this all about, Drew?'

'Can't remember?'

'Where are you going with this?'

'You ever spend time in Walter Reed?'

Luna drew the robe tighter around her.

'Yes.'

'You're pretty badly burned, aren't you?'

She stared at him, trying to read him. Her face was a mask and her look had become cold, remote, full of wary antagonism.

'Yes. I was burned. In an accident.'

'What sort of accident?'

'None of your fucking buiness. It was a long time ago.'

'Rickett said you were burned trying to pull a child out of a burning car.'

'Rickett should learn to keep his mouth shut.'

'Is it true?'

'Yes.'

'Is that why you're through with love?'

That was so low and outside that it visibly rocked her. Drew felt a twinge of self-hatred. It felt familiar and he found he could take a little more. He wanted what he wanted out of this woman right now.

'That,' she said, her eyes shining, 'is a rotten thing to ask me.'

Drew shrugged that off, hardening his face.

'I thought all Secret Service agents had to be in top physical condition. How is it that someone with the kind of burns you have could qualify for high-level protection work?'

A glittering tear carved a shining line down her cheek. The green of her eyes intensified and her face grew even paler. Drew had cut her deeply and he knew it but he said nothing.

'You can be a real shit, can't you? I do my job. I'm healing. You have no –'

'Yet you were cleared for service in D.C.?'

'My injuries were not sustained on the job.'

'That's not my point.'

'I was hurt just after I got out of Glynco. I was on my way to my first assignment. I got a leave of absence. I needed some reconstructive surgery. It took a while. It cost a lot of money.'

'Did the Secret Service pay for that?'

'What does that have to do with anything?'

414

'So you paid for it?'

'Yes. I wasn't hurt on the job, so the service would not pay for it. I asked them several times and the answer was always the same.'

'Who would have made a decision like that?'

'Not Levi Sloane, if that's where you're going.'

'Then who?'

'I don't know. What does this have to do with anything?'

'I'm trying to figure you out.'

'Well don't. There's nothing here to figure. If this is about my injuries, I was cleared for service after a year of rehab. You better have some reason for this other than some sleazy need to hear about my poor burned-away body. Would you like to see it, Drew? Is that was this is about. Because I can show you it right now.'

Luna stood up and undid the belt that held her robe together, her face a white mask and a look of hatred and pain in her eyes.

'No,' said Drew. 'Please don't.'

'Then get to your point.'

'Why were you put on my detail?'

'I was in the pool. I drew your detail.'

'Nothing more?'

Luna seemed to come to the end of some internal road.

'Is all of this from that cop?'

'Geberth? Yes. Some of it anyway.'

'How could he get access to my records?'

'He wouldn't say. So . . . ?'

'Yes. I work for Levi Sloane.'

'You're with the NSA? Not Secret Service?'

'Yes.'

'And he put you on my detail six months ago?'

'Yes.'

'Why?'

'Your association with Gunther Krugman. And your position on the Intelligence Committee made you a person of interest.'

'So you reported to Sloane how often?'

'Not often.'

'Who I was seeing? When? What was said?'

'Yes.'

'Including whatever conversations I had with Gunther Krugman?'

'Yes. Particularly those. I told you. It's possible that Gunther Krugman is a spy. He was in close contact with you. Leaks were happening. A few of his missions went very wrong. People were getting killed, in Prague and Tehran, in Paraguay and Waziristan. We're all trying to figure out why. Information is obviously getting out. Who could it be? Well, you're on the Intelligence Committee and Krugman has Gamma-level access. So Levi wanted that situation monitored. He wanted to know who Krugman was seeing.'

'Did you tell Sloane that I'd met with Krugman at the Regis that night? And that he gave me an envelope from the NSA?'

'Yes. I got the briefing from Dale Rickett.'

'Who told Rickett to break off my protection detail that night?'

'I did.'

'On whose orders?'

A pause. Drew waited her out.

'Levi Sloane. He wanted a clear field for Dietrich Voss.'

'CNN is talking about a man named Loman Strackbein. Does that name mean anything to you?'

416

Luna's face hardened up, and she said nothing.

'Is he a member of this Special Collections Unit that Sloane is running? Is he NSA?'

'No.'

'No what?'

'No, he's not a member of the NSA.'

'Is he CIA?'

Nothing from her.

'Luna, the UN has his name. Where did they get it?'

'I don't know.'

'Do you know who he is?'

She inhaled on the Davidoff and crushed it out.

'Yes. I do.'

'Who else knows who he is?'

'Levi Sloane. Most of the operational side of the NSA.'

'You still think Levi Sloane is a stand-up?'

'I know he is. Are you?'

'I'm no spy. And I'm not the leak in this case.'

'As far as you know.'

'Are you a stand-up, Luna?'

'You know I am.'

'I hear you telling me.'

'It's the truth. And so is Levi Sloane.'

'Is he? Care to put him to a test?'

Mindanao

Quinalang Point – two miles north of Iligan City
Northern coast of Mindanao
Thursday, August 21, 10:00 p.m. local time

Like an immense gray shark, the USS *Hadley* broke the shimmering surface of Quinalang Bay with two hundred and fifteen feet under her long, angular keel, as the last of the twilight seeped out of the western sky. White water creamed in two continuous folding waves away from her blunt cutwater, and air vented from her float stacks with a hissing chuff as she glided through the water. The forward tower hatch clanged open, and her commander, an old Navy fireplug by the name of Truman Canaday, climbed laboriously up the ladder, the rheumatism in his right knee troubling him more than usual. He reached the con and raised his glasses, scanning the narrow white strip of beach, the coconut palm forest beyond it, and the glimmering stretch of sea between the ship and the shore. A small black oblong bobbed in the rollers, less than a hundred feet from the hull. He turned and called back down the shaft.

'All ahead, stop!'

The deep vibration of her engines stopped, and the long, lean shape slipped through the hissing water in a burbling silence. A team of sailors swarmed up the hatch and ran down along the forward hull, carrying ropes and medical gear. A lookout scanned the skyline, looking for Mirages or a French patrol boat, seeing only the uneven wavering line of the horizon, and the tentative glimmers of the first evening stars. The little cockle-shell skimmer made its clumsy way toward the sloping hull of the submarine, dark shapes working inside her, a pair of oars plying the surf without much grace or coordination.

'Lubbers,' said the commander, in a low voice. His XO muttered something in agreement, and they stood there together in the conning tower with their nerves jumping, willing the little craft more speed than she could ever have hoped to show; but it only took four minutes for the boat to bump into the hull of the *Hadley*, and muffled voices to call from the swelling rollers as the boat bobbed and butted by her side. Canaday watched as lines were tossed and dark figures hauled themselves up.

The cockleshell wherry – double-prowed, with a large red eye painted on the forward bow – drifted clear. The sailors and the men from the boat ran back toward the tower and climbed the ladder, their boots making the steel ring, their breathing audible in the still evening air. Canaday gave the sky one last look – he hadn't seen stars since Guam – and stepped back to give the men room to step out onto the deck. In the red light from the open hatchway, Canaday saw a heavy-bodied older man with a soldier's battered face, and another who looked like a heroin-addicted surfer, a seamed, haggard face and long, stringy bleached-blond hair held back by a piratical black ribbon.

Both men saluted crisply, and Canaday snapped one off in return, forcing a smile, secretly disapproving of their scruffy clothes and their general air of mercenary disorder.

'I thought there were five of you to come off,' he barked.

Pike looked at Chris Burdette, and then back at the captain.

'We're it,' he said. 'Nobody else made it out.'

Rudi

The townhouse was a pale granite slab rising for three storeys above a leafy side street, near upper Third. Two Corinthian pillars that supported the façade had a slapped-on look that clashed with the Art Deco cleanness of the granite face. The door was solid steel, and painted dark green. A highly polished brass plaque set into the middle of it read, in simple but impressive Roman letters:

GERHARDT EISENSTADT

Luna Olvidado, wearing a severe charcoal-gray suit jacket over a short, but rigidly pleated matching skirt, pressed the brass button under the plaque. From deep inside the building they heard a soft mellow bell ringing discreetly. As she waited at the top of the stairs, she turned and looked down at Drew, who was leaning on a gleaming, black Crown Victoria with tinted windows. He was wearing a navy-blue pin-stripe suit, a stiff white shirt, and a blue silk tie. He returned her look and waited, his arms folded across his chest, a dark blue business envelope in his left hand. After a minute, a voice came through the speaker grill, a woman's voice, young, with a strong German accent.

'Yes. Who is it?'

'Secret Service. We're here to see Mr Eisenstadt.'

'Who?'

'The Secret Service, ma'am,' said Luna, in an official tone.

'What is it about?'

'Mr Eisenstadt reported a missing child. Interpol handed the case to us, and we're here to follow up. Open the door please.'

'Just a minute.'

Another wait, followed by the sound of heavy locks being turned on the other side of the door. It opened, and a stunning young blond woman was standing in the doorway, her eyes full of some strong emotion. She was wearing a well-cut, pale gray Armani dress that Luna had seen last week on a model on the back page of *The New York Times Magazine*. The cool air that flowed out from the softly lit hallway behind her carried her scent, a mix of Hadrian by Annick Goutal and white wine. At the far end of the long, wood-paneled hallway, a fat man in rumpled gray suit pants and a pale blue business shirt stood bathed in the warm glow of a Tiffany ceiling lamp. His face was red, and even from this distance he looked damp and nervous. The woman held onto the doorknob, and her grip on it was strong enough to whiten her knuckles. Luna showed the woman her Secret Service badge. She leaned in to read it, squinting.

'May we come in?'

'Of course.'

She stepped aside as Luna turned to look at Drew. He pushed himself off the Crown Victoria and came up the stairs after Luna, following her inside the townhouse. The woman closed the door, and the street noises ceased abruptly. From somewhere deep in the house they heard the sound of a Strauss waltz floating in the scented air.

'This is Drew Langan, my partner. Are you Mrs Eisenstadt?'

'Yes. I am.'

She turned and gestured to the fat man at the other end of the hall, who seemed to be rooted to his spot.

'This is my husband, Gerhardt. Gerhardt, these people are here about Rudi.'

Eisenstadt got himself moving with a visible effort, and formed his fleshy features into a rigid caricature of innocent concern as he came forward with a fat pink hand held out in front of his belly like a dying pet. Luna took the cold soft thing and shook it. He did not offer it to Drew, who kept his hands at his side, the navy-blue envelope deliberately prominent, and his expression appropriately official.

'Hildi tells me you are here about Rudi?'

The question was addressed to Luna. Eisenstadt seemed to sense that she was the person in charge.

'Yes.'

'He has been found?'

'Can we sit down somewhere, Mr Eisenstadt?'

'We were just about to go out,' said Eisenstadt.

Luna looked at his wrinkled pants, and then at his stockinged feet. He had the rumpled, frowsy look of a man who had just gotten up from a couch in front of a television. The lie hung in the air between them for a while.

'Gerhardt, this is about Rudi,' said Hildi, in a tight voice.

'Of course. Please come into the sitting room.'

He led them into a high-ceilinged living area with a large, white marble fireplace and several lurid French Provincial chairs done in bright red and green patterns of

Thai silk. Hildi hovered in the doorway as they sat down and faced each other.

'May I get you something to drink? Some wine?'

'That would be fine,' said Luna. 'Thanks.'

Hildi left the doorway with palpable relief, and they all sat there in a silence that Luna allowed to become difficult. Eisenstadt, visibly uneasy, broke it before she did, as Luna had intended him to.

'So – this is about my son?'

Luna turned to Drew, who handed her the navy-blue envelope. She put it down on the table, and left it there. The crest of the National Security Agency glimmered in the downlight like a bright gold coin. Eisenstadt found it difficult to take his eyes off it.

Luna pulled out a notebook and flipped it open.

'Yes. You reported him missing in Berlin two days ago.'

'Yes. It was terrible. He was on his way home from school. He is only eight years old. We have searched and searched –'

'He is asthmatic, we understand,' said Luna, pretending to read this from her notebook.

'Yes. He must have his puffer. We are sick with worry.'

'Are you,' said Luna, looking up from her notebook, and holding his gaze. 'Then why are you here in New York, sir?'

'What?'

'Your son went missing in Berlin. You and your wife –'

Hildi came in with a sterling tray and four tall crystal glasses filled with cold white wine. She offered them in turn to Luna and Drew and Eisenstadt, and then took hers. She sat down heavily on a chair near the door, the smell of peach schnapps very strong on her breath. Her face was pink, and her cheeks were flushed. Luna went on.

'Your son went missing in Berlin last Tuesday, and yet you and your wife flew to New York on Wednesday. Can you tell us why?'

Eisenstadt stared at her for a while, and then collected himself.

'I am the Undersecretary for International Trade and Development at the United Nations' – this was said in the kind of voice usually reserved for ceremonial incantations, as if the words had the power to ward off evil – 'and my personal tragedy cannot be allowed to affect my work. Too many lives in the Third World depend upon my ... my work. Look, you are here to tell me about my son. Have you found him? Do you know where he is?'

'You reported his disappearance to Interpol. Did you take any other steps to investigate his disappearance?'

'Other steps ... ?'

'Yes. Other steps.'

'We did,' said Hildi. Eisenstadt flinched, but said nothing. Hildi stared at him defiantly for a second, and then turned to Luna.

'We hired investigators.'

'Hildi –'

'Just a moment, Mr Eisenstadt. What sort of investigators, ma'am?'

'Private investigators. A very good firm.'

'What firm, ma'am?'

'A German company,' said Eisenstadt, shooting a vicious look at Hildi, who recoiled from it. 'All ex-Securizdat men.'

'Sternhagen,' said Luna, without emphasis, as if clarifying a minor point before moving on to more important things. Eisenstadt grew quite still, and they could see a hunted look coming into his eyes.

'Sternhagen? No. Of course not Sternhagen. How did you –'

'Sternhagen is a company of interest to us,' said Luna, as if that explained it, which it did not.

'But we . . .' Eisenstadt's voice trailed off as he considered the implications. Luna reached for the envelope, and pulled out three sheets of computer paper. She picked one up, read it in silence, and then put it down again. Eisenstadt, who was used to the German version of authority, was effectively silenced by the gesture.

'Your duties as the Junior Undersecretary' – she stressed the word 'junior' – 'involve matters of infrastructure and development in Southeast Asia?'

'Yes. Of course. What does this have to do with the disappearance of my little boy? I have to tell you that –'

'So you're aware of what happened at the Maria Christina hydroelectric station in northern Mindanao?'

He paled visibly. Drew's chest, which had been bound by iron hoops for the last fifteen minutes, began to relax, and his tension was replaced by a developing anger. If Luna saw the same emotion in the man, she gave no sign.

'Such a tragedy. That is why I have had to return to New York in spite of my son's disappearance. This crisis in Mindanao – decisions will have to be made. Iligan City has no power. It must be rerouted from coal plants in the south. In the meantime, the monsoon will return, and the pumps must operate. In the hospitals, people are dying from the heat. There are many people injured in that terror bombing of the disco a few days before. My responsibility –'

'Will you be in charge of repairing this facility?'

'No. Not directly. The United Nations will of course

recommend steps. We are an advisory body only. Individual nations will decide what particular corporations will undertake to rebuild the plant. But what does this have to do with my son?'

'We're looking into motives, sir.'

'Motives?'

'For the abduction of your son. This advisory capacity you hold. How often are your recommendations accepted?'

'How . . . well, it is usual . . . almost always.'

'So your decision carries a great deal of influence.'

'Of course.'

'Do you recommend specific companies for the contracts to rebuild power stations?'

'No. As I said –'

'Who built the Maria Christina plant?'

'Who . . . I think it was a company called Consolidated Power Systems.'

'A German company?'

'No. American. The Maria Christina power plant construction was funded by a grant from the US government. They selected Consolidated Power to build it for them. All costs were paid by your government.'

'But now that plant is gone?'

'Yes. Totally destroyed. A tragedy.'

'And your committee will help decide who will rebuild it?'

Eisenstadt hesitated, his throat working.

'Not necessarily. There are issues involved. Procedural issues.'

'Are there other power plants operating in Mindanao?'

'I really don't see –'

'As I said, we're looking at motivations.'

'This is rather far afield.'

'Do you know of other plants in the region?'

'Of course. We oversaw the construction of three of them.'

'We . . . ?'

'I mean the United Nations.'

'Who built those plants, sir?'

'I think it was . . . yes, it was KSB.'

'KSB?'

'Koenigsburg Stadtlander Bundt SA.'

'A German company?'

'No. Global. But their head offices are in Berlin.'

'You're from Berlin yourself, aren't you, sir?'

'Yes. We have a lovely –'

'So, your committee recommended a German firm to run power plants in Mindanao?'

'I only took on the portfolio two years ago. I had no influence over that decision. It was made long before my time.'

'How many plants does KSB run?'

'They have many plants. More than thirty. All through Southeast Asia. Coal-fired, even a nuclear one is planned for Mindanao, and if it is successful they will bid on three more in Luzon. They are very skilled, very experienced at this sort of thing.'

'These are all for-profit enterprises?'

'Naturally. Costs are well within the UN guidelines, of course.'

'Is KSB a public corporation?'

'Yes.'

'Do you own shares in KSB, sir?'

Eisenstadt got to his feet, his face reddening.

'This is intolerable. I have diplomatic – I will *not*

be interrogated in my own home. I will contact your superiors.'

'Is it possible, sir, that your son was abducted in order to influence your recommendations in this area?'

Hildi stood up and left the room. Eisenstadt stared at Luna.

'What . . . do you have any reason to think that?'

'Do you?'

'Do I? No one has contacted me! How would I possibly . . . ?'

His voice trailed off as Luna pulled the second sheet of paper off the table. Under it was a photograph of Hamidullah Barrakha printed out from Drew's laptop. She lifted the sheet and began to read it in silence, totally ignoring Eisenstadt. Drew watched the man staring down at Barrakha's face, and knew in his heart that they had just nailed Gerhardt Eisenstadt's hand to a door. Luna looked up from her notes and smiled at Gerhardt Eisenstadt.

'It was just a theory, sir.'

'A theory?'

'Yes. Well, I think we've taken up enough of your time. We'll be in touch very soon. We'd appreciate it if you could stay in town until we clear this up. Will that be a problem?'

'Stay in town? I have no plans to leave. But . . .'

Eisenstadt's wet face collapsed along hidden fault lines as he stared at Luna through his glasses. Luna got to her feet, gathered her papers, and nodded to Drew. Drew stood up and walked to the hallway door. The Eisenstadts stared at them as they prepared to leave, obviously in distress.

'You are going?'

Luna looked at him over her sheaf of papers.

'Yes, sir. Thank you for your help.'

Eisenstadt followed them to the front door, visibly suppressing a strong desire to babble a series of questions. They both shook hands with him, and went out into the twilight and down the stone stairs. The door closed behind them with a solid thump, and the sound of steel bolts being energetically shot home. They reached the Crown Victoria and climbed into it, Drew behind the wheel. They pulled out into the traffic and turned south onto Second Avenue. Drew drove the car a couple of blocks, made a right onto Seventy-fourth. In a few minutes, they were back on Eisenstadt's street, a few doors down. Drew parked the car, shut off the lights, and settled back into the leather seat.

'Well?' said Luna.

'You rattled him down to his slippers, Luna. You opened him up like a Chinese fan. It was absolutely inspired. The stuff about his kid being abducted to influence his decision? I thought he'd pass out. Where did that come from?'

'Nowhere. A shot in the dark.'

'Well, it was brilliant. Do you think it's true?'

'How would I know? I doubt it.'

'It hit him hard. I saw his face when you said it, and it went right through him. They said their kid's asthmatic? This Rudi kid.'

'Yes. Poor kid. I wonder if he's still alive.'

'Barrakha's an asthmatic too. Why did you hit Eisenstadt with the picture of Barrakha?'

'I was just throwing things at him, and hoping something would stick. If he has a guilty conscience – then he'll see a pattern, where we only see details.'

'Think about it, Luna, Eisenstadt lives in Berlin.

Eisenstadt sits on a committee that controls UN-financed infrastructure in Southeast Asia. Barrakha's file has him connected to Berlin-based terror cells. Next, we hear that Barrakha has moved his operations to Mindanao. The Maria Christina power plant gets blown up. That's now in Eisenstadt's territory. Eisenstadt and Barrakha. Luna, what if Eisenstadt knew that the Maria Christina plant was going to be hit?'

'The only person who had any idea the plant was going to be bombed was Barrakha. You really think someone as security-obsessed as Hamidullah Barrakha is going to risk his entire network by talking to a feckless poofter like Gerhardt Eisenstadt?'

'Poofter?'

'I heard it on *Masterpiece Theatre*.'

'Great word. No, now that you say it, there's no way Barrakha would be able to trust a guy like Eisenstadt. He's just too soft.'

'Yes. He is ... if you were going to use him for anything, you'd have to have some way of ...'

'Controlling him?'

'Yes. Some way of making sure he kept his mouth –'

'Shut? Like taking his son?'

'Blackmail?'

'You mean extortion. Do what's needed, or your son dies. Yes, extortion would be one way to keep him focused.'

'But on what?'

'Yeah. That's the thing. On what.'

'Drew, didn't Eisenstadt tell us that he had to come to New York to deal with the aftermath of the Maria Christina explosion?'

'Yes?'

'Well, he left Berlin on Wednesday morning, and the plant was blown up twenty-four hours later.'

'You're right. So that's a lie. A stupid one, too. What made you run the Sternhagen name on him?'

'I wanted to see his reaction.'

'I think he blew a vasectomy clip. Honestly, Luna, that was brilliant. You should have been a trial lawyer.'

'That's not necessarily a compliment.'

'Luna. He's into something rotten. I can feel it.'

'You know, Sloane will have already ID'd Eisenstadt from that video clip we got at Krugman's house. He's going to be working this same connection right now. What about that?'

Drew shook his head.

'He doesn't have that video.'

'Yes he does. You gave it to him yesterday, along with all the rest of the stuff. Didn't you?'

'No. I kept the MPEG.'

The news seemed to stun her into silence. Drew watched the emotions that ran across her hard-planed, drawn-looking face; shock, sudden insight, and, in a very short time, anger.

'Sloane doesn't even know about it?'

'Not unless you told him.'

'I didn't bring it up. I assumed he had a copy. So you withheld information in an ongoing counterintelligence operation?'

'I guess I did.'

'And Sloane has no idea that you've ID'd Eisenstadt?'

'Not from me, anyway. Geberth might have told him.'

'When he finds out you held information back, he's going to blow more than a vasectomy clip, Drew. He'll come after you with everything he's got. He's been warning you off ever since this thing started, and here you are, still in it up to your second chin.'

'Second chin? I have a second chin?'

'I agree that Eisenstadt is probably up to something. It might even be something that involves Barrakha and his missing kid. Whatever it is, I don't see how it in any way connects to Levi Sloane.'

'You tell Sloane we're at Cape Vincent, and we're flying to New York to see a guy named Kohl Keune. Two guys working for Sternhagen promptly kill Kohl Keune, and then intercept us over the Adirondacks. That connects Sloane to Sternhagen, and Sternhagen connects to Eisenstadt, who could connect to Barrakha.'

'We've already been over this ground. This is all just wild speculation. What's in it for Sloane?'

'I haven't a clue. But why wouldn't he pull Cole's unit out of Mindanao? Why did he ignore Krugman's warnings? They turned out to be pretty damned accurate.'

'Your father said that it was possible that Cole refused to abandon the mission. You still haven't told me what would motivate a decorated counterintelligence agent to conspire with a terrorist.'

Drew fell silent, and Luna could see she had hit home.

'I told you. This Sloane stuff is simply fucked in the head.'

'I have to say, Luna, under stress, your language skills really deteriorate.'

'Not as much as your ability to reason. If you want to know who I'd be taking a hard look at in this thing, it would be another German. Gunther Krugman. He's all over this.'

'Maybe. I do wonder why Eisenstadt is still alive.'

'Why?'

'If I were feeling heat about a scam I was running, he's the first guy I'd take out of the picture. The fact that he's still here means he's too important to kill. But why?'

Drew's face changed.

'I know why. Because whatever it is they're working on hasn't happened yet. He's still needed. That's why he's still alive.'

'God, Drew. What color is the sky in your world?'

'Olive drab, with streaks of crimson. You're still with me on this stunt?'

'I'm willing to be around when you have to admit to being a paranoid lunatic. Actually, I'm really looking forward to that.'

'Fair enough.'

They fell into an uneasy silence while a passing RMP slowed down long enough to give the two of them a look-over as it rolled by, a black female harness cop with cold black eyes and a lollipop in her mouth staring at them as the unit drifted alongside. And then it picked up speed, made a left at the corner, and disappeared down Second.

'That unit comes back,' said Luna, 'we'll have a problem.'

'Why?'

'They slowed down long enough to get our plates. Maybe Eisenstadt called the cops on us.'

'Called the cops on a Secret Service agent?'

'He saw a badge. These days you can get them on eBay.'

'If they come back, just can them.'

'Can them?'

'You know. Show them your badge.'

'You mean tin them.'

'Yeah. That's it. Tin them.'

'Drew, it's important for you to remember that one

day all of this will be over, and you'll have to go back to your home planet. How long are we going to sit here?'

'Until somebody shows up. Or until Eisenstadt makes a move.'

'That's another problem. What makes you think Eisenstadt is going to make a move of any kind?'

'We rattled his cage big-time. My bet is he'll have a drop-box site where he goes to leave messages for whoever is running him. My idea is we follow him there, locate the drop-box, and wait to see who shows up.'

'That could take a week.'

'Got any other suggestions?'

'Only the obvious four-letter ones.'

'I know those already. Can you access the Internet on that cell phone? My laptop is in the back there. Hook it up to your cell, and see what you can find out about KSB and Consolidated Power Systems.'

'What will you be doing?'

'Me?'

'Yeah, you.'

'I'll be maintaining a keen vigil.'

'You will, will you? How about I maintain the keen vigil, and you do the second-string sidekick secretarial shit?'

'I've got the wheel.'

'I've got the gun.'

'Excellent point.'

Drew got out and walked around to the passenger side, while Luna slid across and took the wheel. Halfway down the block, a very large black man in a navy-blue pin-stripe suit and a crisp white shirt, his broad, flat face a little cold, and his deep-set eyes as flat gray as a shark's, sat up behind the wheel of a green Windstar van and nudged his partner.

His partner, a rangy, athletic-looking white woman in her early forties, with close-cropped black hair and wide blue eyes, straightened up and stared down the street at the black Crown Victoria. They both watched as Drew got back in the car and closed the door. They watched with a ferocious intensity, saying nothing. After a time, during which the black Crown Victoria showed no sign of moving, they gradually eased their attention and relaxed into their seats again. The woman lit up a cigarette, and blew a plume of smoke into the windscreen. Sighing, the large man rolled down his window. No one spoke. The woman turned up the radio, and they sat there listening to a sinuous tango that played softly inside the darkened van. Back in the Crown Victoria, Drew placed Luna's cell phone on the dashboard, plugged its cable link into his laptop, and hit START.

The laptop screen lit up, and a cursor blinked for a time as the connection was established. Then Drew's e-mail program clicked in, with the YOU'VE GOT MAIL indicator.

Drew hit READ MAIL, and the program began to download a string of messages. Drew recognized all of the screen names – constituent groups, family friends, people from the Hill – there were fifty-five messages, and most of them were certain to be messages of condolence, expressions of sympathy for the death of his father. There was even an e-mail from Diana in Paris. With an effort, Drew passed them all by. There was nothing he could do about his father right now, and thinking about Gerhardt Eisenstadt was a wonderful distraction from a grief that sometimes seemed unbearable.

But one e-mail stood out from all the others:
BVogel@thewashingtonpost.com
Drew hit READ and got this message:

Drew. I found an article on Constantin Desaix in Paris *Le Monde* – May 21, 1978 – I'm sending it to you as an attachment, but I can't see that it will be of any use. Kind of a puff piece. I have to file copy on this story for tomorrow's edition. I'll keep Cole out of it, but you should know most of the mainstream media are going to plaster this all over the world. The ICC is about to announce charges against the Americans they're holding, and according to our White House guy, the President has totally flipped out. Brace yourself for bad news. E-mail me soon!

Britney.

Drew hit DOWNLOAD FILE, and they watched while a PDF file transferred into Drew's hard drive. The PDF program kicked in, and in a moment they were looking at what seemed to be an archived page from a Parisian newspaper. The text was in French – a language Drew had never been able to tolerate, let alone comprehend. The article was long, over two thousand words, but the main feature was a black-and-white photograph of a striking man in a tailored black suit and a clerical collar standing in front of a desk in what looked like a lecture hall, a fiercely intent expression on his angular face, one long-fingered hand making a stabbing gesture with the stem of his pipe.

Wood-paneled, circular, the hall was packed with students whose attentive faces and fixed expressions were entirely focused on the priest leaning on the desk. He was tall, broad-shouldered, with a leonine head of long white or blond hair, deep-set eyes, and a prominent beak of a nose; not handsome, but certainly memorable, even charismatic, if you went by the transfixed expressions on the faces of the students, who seemed to have packed the large hall by the hundreds. The cutline under the photograph read:

L'autodidact Extraordinaire:
Jesuit et Renégate Père Christian Desaix
faut épater les étudiants bourgeoises.

They were still staring at the photo and trying to decipher the text – Luna's French was worse than Drew's – when the laptop beeped, and a disembodied male voice said:

'You've got mail.'

They both jumped at the sound.

Drew hit READ MAIL, and got this:

Lsloane/sscs@usgov/NSA.gov: hello

'Oh Christ,' said Luna. 'He just sent that.'

Drew hit READ, and got the following message:

Tried to call Luna on her cell and found you currently on-line, accessing your mail. Note that according to the cellular grid you – or at least Luna's phone – are somewhere in the Upper East Side of New York, which I find intriguing, since last time I looked, the Beekman was in midtown. Lots to explain here. Drew: About your father, forensic autopsy confirms cause of death pulmonary embolism – repeat, pulmonary embolism – not murder. His body will be released to you as soon as you go to Harrisburg to sign the papers. No sign yet of either Andrea Collier or Cornel Chulalongkorn, but search continues. If Luna is with you, you both need to read the attachment I have enclosed. It's a document we have just obtained, and which will be released by the Office of the Special Prosecutor for the ICC at The Hague tomorrow morning in New York. It contains some very bad news. I deeply regret what has happened. This has gone way beyond our brief, and is now out of our hands. Stay where you are. Have dispatched a unit. Sloane.

Drew reread the lines about his father's autopsy twice while a weight on his chest dissolved into a diffused feeling composed of deep sadness and quiet relief. He blinked at the screen, wondering why it was shimmering, and realized that he had tears in his eyes.

Luna passed him a crumpled Kleenex.

'Where's this been?' said Drew, smiling at her.

'It's an heirloom,' she said, smiling back. 'You better get Sloane's attachment.'

Drew hit DOWNLOAD FILE, and they waited in silence while cars slipped by them and a siren wailed from somewhere on Second. After a few seconds, the attachment popped up, a Word document.

GENERAL MEDIA RELEASE:
INTERNATIONAL CRIMINAL COURT:
SPECIAL PROSECUTOR'S OFFICE:

START: A public meeting of the ICC special prosecutor's office is to be held on Monday August 25 in New York to consider the petition of the United States government for the surrender of two American citizens, Dean Mitchell Krause and Ramiro Vasquez, as well as the remains of two other American citizens, Loman Strackbein and another male who has been tentatively identified as Jordan Kemp. Krause was picked up by a French patrol after a prolonged search. He was reportedly wounded during the attack on UN troops investigating the massacre at Cobraville. Ramiro Vasquez was captured after a firefight at Camp Casey in the hills south of Iligan City. The partial remains of Jordan Kemp were found in dense jungle a few hundred feet from Camp Casey. Soldiers on the scene report that Kemp committed suicide with a grenade as they were closing in on him. Several peacekeepers were also killed in this action. Camp Casey is the site of a former American army base. A cache of American-style weapons was also uncovered. These weapons have been linked by UN investigators to the massacre at Cobraville. At present Mr Krause and Mr Vasquez and the bodies of Loman Strackbein and Jordan Kemp remain in the Philippines, in the city of Iligan, on the southern island of Mindanao.

In this matter, the President of the United States has informed this office that Mr Krause and Mr Vasquez are citizens of the United States, with no connection to any governmental agency; that they are innocent of the charges of mass murder that are being contemplated against them by the International Criminal Court at The Hague. And he further takes the corollary position that the ICC has no jurisdiction over these private individuals, since the United States is not a signatory to the protocols of the International Criminal Court. In the face of this assertion on the part of the United States, we report that at least one of the detainees has already given an informal statement admitting to his involvement in the massacre at Cobraville, and has confirmed his willingness to testify to this crime before the ICC.

In a move intended to signal the seriousness of his position, the President of the United States has informed the UN that should the petition be denied, elements of the Seventh Fleet will be deployed to the Philippines to blockade the major ports of Mindanao, specifically the ports of Iligan, Cagayan de Oro, Butuan, Cotobato, General Santos, and Davao. As well, we are informed that elements of various fighter wings will conduct over-flights of the island, and that AWACS planes have already been committed to monitor all air and sea traffic into and out of Mindanao. Further action will be taken unilaterally, as dictated by the situation and without any consultation with the Security Council or the General Assembly.

Accordingly, the governments of France and Germany have communicated through their UN ambassadors their intention to immediately expel all American troops currently stationed in their countries, and to resist with all necessary force any intrusion by any foreign nation into an area of operations governed by the United Nations peacekeeping treaty. As a direct result of this threat of hostile action on the part of the United States President, the Special Prosecutor has agreed to a hearing to consider the American petition on Monday, August 25 at the UN HQ in New York. END

Drew's hands fell away from the keyboard, and the blood rushed from his face. He reread the text again and again, but the words remained the same:

. . . The partial remains of Jordan Kemp were found in dense jungle a few hundred feet from Camp Casey. Soldiers on the scene report that Kemp committed suicide with a grenade as they were closing in on him . . .

'Cole's dead,' he said, in a toneless voice.
'We don't know that.'
'He's dead. He was about to be captured, and he did

what the Agency expected him to do. He committed suicide rather than be caught alive. Krugman was right. They were set up for this. Lured in somehow, and set up. And it worked. The whole unit. All of them.'

Luna fell into silence. She put a hand on Drew's arm, and left it there. There was nothing to say. He was right.

Luna stared out at the street, and saw a silver Mercedes pulling out from the parking lot under Gerhardt Eisenstadt's townhouse, a fat, white, pillow-shaped man at the wheel.

'Drew.'

Drew looked up at her.

'What?'

'He's leaving.'

Drew looked up the street, and saw Eisenstadt pulling away in the direction of Second Avenue.

'Follow him.'

'Follow him? We can't. Sloane's on his way. Let Sloane –'

Drew snapped the laptop shut, disconnected it from Luna's cell phone. Then he threw her cell phone into a planter next to the car.

'Let Sloane fix it? How's that been working for us so far?'

'This is over. You have to stop.'

'Either drive, or get out of the car, Luna.'

Luna looked at his face, and saw nothing there that resembled the man she had spent the last days with. She sighed and put the car in gear, and the black Crown Victoria rolled smoothly out into the street. They caught up with Eisenstadt's silver Mercedes at the corner. He turned south onto Second. They let him get some distance, and then they blended into the stream of Friday-night traffic. Far down the avenue the towers of Lower Manhattan rose up into a blue-black night streaked with orange clouds. Nine cars back and a lane to the left the green Windstar followed them down the street, and soon all three cars – the silver Benz, the black Crown Victoria, and the plain green Windstar – disappeared into the broad red river of taillights streaming down the stone canyons of New York City.

Iligan City

The Milan Hotel
218 Truong Tan Buu Street
Friday, August 22, 11:00 a.m. local time

An orange sun was burning like a lit match in a sulfur-colored sky above the city of Iligan, and a wind off the sea carried with it the stink of rotting fish and the salty reek of the open sea. A light blue Range Rover with UN markings butted its way through the crowds on Cabili Street and made a sharp right turn onto Truong Tan Buu, its tires squealing on the superheated pavement. It accelerated down Truong Tan Buu and pulled up in front of the Milan Hotel, braking hard. Two German troopers standing on either side of the entrance snapped into present arms as a tall slender officer in the uniform of the Foreign Legion stepped out of the passenger side carrying a battered leather briefcase, his sun-dried leathery skin and sharp-edged bony features bearing the unmistakable brand of the military cop.

He snapped a blade-sharp salute at the troopers guarding the entrance to the hotel and strode, stiff-legged, favoring his right knee, into the cool, dark lobby filled with French and German troops, all of them heavily armed. They all stiffened into ramrods as he walked by and sliced the air with their salutes, which the officer acknowledged with a vague gesture, his light brown eyes

444

fixed on the duty sergeant behind what had been – until the UN peacekeepers had taken over the hotel – the receptionist's desk.

Of the well-thought-out girl named Ingrid, with crow-black hair, the off-the-shoulder sundress made out of what looked like green smoke, and the off-center smile, there was no visible trace; although a hint of her tangy scent still floated in the area like a trace memory of a long-forgotten song. The sergeant – a young blond man with blunt, Alsatian features – knocked over his stool as he got to his feet, and it clattered to the wooden floor as the boy got his salute halfway to his forehead before he realized he wasn't wearing his forage cap. He froze it there, his face reddening.

'Colonel Lazard. *Bienvenue –*'

'I need to see the American.'

'Certainly sir. Corporal!'

A legionnaire, standing by the elevator doors with his FN at parade rest wearing a tan uniform starched as stiff as if it had been cut from wood veneer, snapped into present arms and snapped his heels together, turning to press the UP button as Colonel Lazard stepped up to the elevator. Lazard's face was sharp-set and his shoulders squared, and something in his manner suggested a man who has reached the limits of his patience. The doors ground open, and the corporal stepped aside to let the colonel enter first. They rode up in a dense, charged silence broken only by the creak and groan of the ancient cage. The corporal held his breath in the – vain – hope that the colonel would not notice that he had taken cognac with his breakfast coffee. The elevator reached the fifth floor, and the colonel stepped out before the doors were fully open. Three German troopers, leaning against the stained walls with their heavy arms folded and their HKs propped against a wooden chair outside room 511, came to a much less formal approximation of attention as the legionnaire came down the hall. As far as they were concerned, the man behind the door of room 511 belonged to them. The senior noncom stepped into his path.

'*Guten Tag*, Colonel.'

'I need to see him.'

'He's asleep.'

'Wake him.'

The noncom, a heavy, slope-shouldered trooper with a shaved head, small reddened eyes, and the chest bars of a seasoned paratrooper, frowned at the colonel, resenting the official tone.

'He's medicated. What's your business?'

'He's being formally charged. An American official is coming to see him in a few minutes. I want to talk to him first.'

The trooper's face seemed to thicken, and a muscle in his cheek bunched slightly.

'An American?'

'Yes. It's the law. Once he's charged we cannot talk to him without a lawyer present. So I want a word now. *Verstehen Sie?*'

The trooper hesitated, and the colonel made a sharp cutting gesture with his left hand, lifting the battered leather case.

'I intend to make him sign a statement. This statement. I have only a few minutes. The American's plane has already landed.'

The trooper shrugged, and nodded to the guards now standing outside the door of 511. One of the troopers tapped the door three times, paused, and then three more solid raps with a scarred knuckle. Bolts drew back, and the reinforced door opened on another German soldier: tall, powerful, with a shaved head and a broad, out-thrusting jaw, in a uniform still stained with blood. He stank of sweat and cordite. He took in the scene, and grunted at Colonel Lazard, stepping away from the door.

The colonel stalked into the room, barely glancing at the grubby walls and the dirty windows. Street noise – the buzz of jeepneys and the chatter from the open market across the way – rose up from Truong Tan Buu and drifted in on a hot, wet wind stinking of old fruit and fresh sewage. An electric fan on an ancient wooden chair had been set up to play on the figure lying in the bed, but it had been shut off a long time ago, and now the heat in the room was stifling. The colonel came to the end of the bed and stared down at the man lying on it with the expression of an executioner weighing a man for a short drop.

On the bed, Dean Krause, naked under a bloody sheet, his hands cuffed to the iron bedstead, lay in a pool of his own sweat, his head turned to the left, his bruised and beaten face pulpy and covered with dried blood. His puffed eyes were closed. An IV bag on a pole by the bed, filled with something yellow, dripped into a long narrow tube plugged into the vein in the hollow of Krause's left elbow.

'He's out,' said the German, staring down at Krause with a look that had little in it that was recognizably human.

'Wake him.'

The trooper stepped around to the side of the bed and drove his index finger sharply into the middle of a bloody bandage taped to the right side of Krause's belly. Krause stiffened and hissed and his eyes flew open. He shot a murderous look at the big German.

'One day, little flower. One day.'

'Someone to see you, pig-boy.'

Krause moved his head, and took in the narrow sharp-faced man in the well-cut legionnaire uniform.

'Jesus. It's Claude Rains.'

'I am Colonel Lazard. In a few minutes you will be formally charged with war crimes by the International Criminal Court, and then you will be extradited to The Hague to face trial. Your companions will be offered what I am about to offer you. I will make this offer once, and once only. You will have a minute only to consider it, and then it will be withdrawn and presented to your companions. In my view, one or more of them will be very likely to accept it.'

'Who are they?'

'There is no reason for you to know that. Here is my offer. I offer leniency if you will testify to your crimes.'

'Yeah?' said Krause, stiffening as he tried to move in his bed. 'How about somebody tell me what my crimes are?'

'You infiltrated a UN security zone with the intention of killing a terrorist named Hamidullah Barrakha. While carrying out this mission for the United States government, you encountered resistance in the tribal areas. We accept that you may have been fired upon by some of the men in the village of Cobraville. Having said that, we contend that you and your men lost control of the situation, and in the end you killed almost everyone in the village. Just as in My Lai, during the Vietnam War. As a soldier myself, I can see that there are extenuating circumstances, that you were under great pressure, and that some members of your unit may have precipitated the attack without your approval. Nevertheless, a massacre took place, and you must accept your part in it. If you agree to a statement that reflects this generous interpretation of the incident, I can guarantee that the court will offer you clemency, and your cooperation will be taken into consideration in the sentencing portion of the proceedings.'

'Before I get into this, I want to know the names of the men you're holding, and what condition they're in.'

'Their names are irrelevant. You know who they are.'

'I'm not gonna hear what you're saying until I get an answer.'

The colonel nodded to the trooper, turned and stepped out of the room. The door closed behind him. He stood in the long, narrow hallway with the three silent Germans and lit a Gitane. A low groan, that quickly escalated into a high sharp shriek, came through the thick wooden door. It went on for a while, and then stopped suddenly.

One of the troopers chuckled and grinned at his friends, but the oldest man there snapped at him in a Silesian dialect. He hung his head and kicked at a cigarette butt. The colonel finished his Gitane, threw the butt onto the floor, and went back to the door.

Back in the room, Krause was paler now, and his lips were thinned out with pain, his face slick and his eyes filled with a dangerous light. The German trooper was smiling down at him.

'Hey,' said Krause, smiling, 'Claude Rains take two.'

'What is your answer?'

'Can you repeat the question?'

'You know the question. Now you must respond.'

'Okay. You got me. Can I read the statement?'

'Certainly.'

Lazard took the single sheet of paper out of the case and set it down on Krause's chest. Krause craned his neck trying to read it.

'I can't read this. Undo my hands.'

Lazard nodded at the trooper, who unlocked Krause's cuffs. Krause pushed himself up in the bed and picked up the paper. He read it slowly and then read it again. Lazard and the trooper watched him, while a sudden gust of sea wind billowed the dirty curtains and made the rusted blades on the old electric fan turn slowly.

'Well . . .' said Krause, looking down at it.

'Yes. *Alors?*'

Krause crumpled the sheet into a ball, and popped it into his mouth. He chewed it, slowly and carefully, with evident enjoyment, his cheek muscles bulging. After a time, he swallowed it down with an effort and then smiled sweetly up at the colonel.

'Yummy,' he said.

As Lazard rode down to the fourth floor in the elevator, the sound of Krause's pain faded away, and it was only a faint echo that filtered down through the floorboards as he walked along the hall to room 411. More troopers guarded this door, and they opened the door to the room as he came up. In this room, a twin of the one above it, three German guards sat at a card-table playing rummy. Ramiro Vasquez was lying on the thin cot with his hands cuffed to the bedstead, just as Krause had been. He looked up as Lazard stalked across the room and stood at the side of the bed.

'Your friend has refused.'

'Good for him.'

'Now you must –'

The phone by the bed rang. Lazard snapped it up and

listened to the voice on the other end, his expression altering. He set the phone down softly onto the cradle and looked at Vasquez.

'Bad news?' said Vasquez.

'The American is here. He demands to see you.'

Vasquez smiled broadly.

'Maybe you better unbuckle me. The optics are bad.'

'Go to hell,' said Lazard over his shoulder, turning away. He nodded to the guards and left the room.

'I'm already there,' said Vasquez, to no one in particular.

In a few minutes, he heard the sound of voices in the hall; a heated discussion, one voice high and lapsing into French, the other deep and smooth, and unmistakably American. Vasquez strained at the cuffs, and then watched the door. The Germans were standing now, and watching the door as well, their thick, tanned faces uncertain.

Then the door opened, and an imposing but rather elderly man with a shaved head and a lean, craggy face stepped into the room. Over six feet tall and straight as a lancer, he was wearing an immaculate and very well-cut creamy white three-button suit over a pale blue shirt, open at the neck to show his leathery skin. His eyes were pale gray, and his hands were knotted with what looked like the early stages of arthritis. He had placed his hands one on top of the other over the gold horse's head that topped a gleaming rosewood cane. It was bending alarmingly under his weight. In the silence of the moment, Vasquez saw that the man had no fingertips, just ten blunt, fleshy conclusions at the end of his fingers. Vasquez looked up at him, and the man smiled back, a bloodless smile that showed his large, yellow teeth between thin blue lips. The smile faded, and when it was gone the man's mouth looked like an old and well-healed surgical incision.

'You can go, boys,' the man said, looking at the Germans.

They looked out into the hall past the American's broad shoulders and got some kind of signal from someone in the hallway. They dropped their cards and filed out past the American, who closed the door after them and shot home the bolts. He crossed the room, pulling a set of cuff keys from his suit-coat pocket. When he bent over Vasquez to undo the cuffs, Vasquez could smell his cologne; bay rum with lime, and the sharp earthy bite of a recent cigar. The cuffs undone, the man stepped back and pulled up a wooden chair. He set it down by the side of the bed, and waited while Vasquez pulled himself upright, rubbing his wrists where the cuffs had dug into them.

'Well then ...' said the American. 'This is a hell of thing.'

'You from the embassy?'

The American nodded.

'In a way. My name is Gunther Krugman.'

The Navy Yard

The bridge deck boomed in a steady rhythm under their wheels, and off to their right the last light of the evening lay on the East River. Up ahead, they could see the strobe lights on the office towers clustered around Cadman Plaza blinking against the glow of Brooklyn that stretched out ahead of them. In the rearview mirror, Lower Manhattan looked like an ocean liner with all her lights blazing.

Nine cars up and holding steady, Gerhardt Eisenstadt's silver Benz was cruising in the inside lane, just visible beyond a FedEx truck and a couple of yellow cabs. A hundred yards behind their Crown Victoria, buried in a stream of cars and trucks, the dark green Windstar was still there, a black silhouette against the headlights all around it, and it was still keeping pace with them. Now and then Luna would look at it, floating there in her rearview mirror, and consider what, if anything, she could do about it.

Nothing at the moment, anyway, she decided.

'Still there?' said Drew.

'Yeah.'

'What do you want to do about it?'

'Nothing at the moment.'

'How long has it been there?'

'Not sure. At least since we crossed Forty-second.'

Drew looked out at the roofs and blocks of Brooklyn, and then back at the silver Benz.

'I hadn't figured on this,' he said.

'What a shock.'

They passed under the Gothic stone tower of the eastern pier, and the river slipped away behind them, to be replaced by the low, dense forest of the Fulton Ferry Park. To their right, container sheds and storage yards lined the river banks for several blocks. The bridge deck slanted downward, and soon they were rolling by Fulton Landing. Away to their right, the spire of One Pierrepoint Plaza loomed above the courthouse and Brooklyn General. The traffic was slowing as they reached the end of the bridge, and now Eisenstadt had his right-hand turn signal on.

They followed him in a slow sweeping curve through the exit ramp, less than ten cars back. The windows on the Benz were heavily tinted, but when a car making a left swept its headlights across it, they could see Eisenstadt's large round head, turning right and left and then right again as he came to a stop at the entrance to Prospect.

'Is he lost?' asked Drew, not expecting an answer.

'No idea.'

In the rearview, she watched as the green Windstar came to a stop in the lineup. She could see a dim shape behind the windshield, a man. A large black man. And beside him, a white-faced blur that somehow looked feminine.

'He's going right,' said Drew, and they watched as Eisenstadt pulled out into the traffic stream on Prospect and drove northward, crossing under the bulk of the bridge above them. They were still with him as he slowed down at the next intersection and made a left onto Pearl

Street. Now they were running along beside the rusted bulk of the eastern end of the Manhattan Bridge, and the neighborhood was changing from upscale residential and corporate into low-rent and seedy. They rolled under the Manhattan Bridge, and when they came out from under it, the lights of the Farragut Houses, a state housing project now sliding into inevitable ruin, loomed over the narrow, crowded streets lined with wood-framed houses and run-down stores. Clusters of morose teens in baggy pants and expressionless faces stared at Eisenstadt's gleaming silver Benz as it rolled westward along Bridge Street, fifteen heads turning as one to watch it go by.

When they saw the black Crown Victoria with the black-tinted windows coming down the street a few seconds later, they scattered into smaller groups and carefully avoided eye contact.

Luna, watching the Benz a block up and feeling increasingly uneasy, checked her rearview one more time and found the green van totally gone. She looked around her, to the left and right, and back again at her rearview. The entire block was empty now. No sign of it anywhere. One block ahead of them the silver Benz seemed to be headed for the Brooklyn Navy Yard. But behind her there was no one. The green van was gone. Utterly gone.

Iligan City

The way Ramiro Vasquez was holding himself changed just a little when he heard the name Krugman. Seeing this, Krugman leaned back in the chair, crossed one knee over the other, and laid his cane along it. He said nothing, but a quality of watchful and not entirely benevolent interest seemed to gather force and direction inside him.

'Gunther Krugman?'

'Yes.'

'From Washington?'

'Guilty as charged.'

'I know who you are.'

'And I you.'

'You're not official, Mr Krugman.'

'Not at all. I'm here in quite an informal way.'

'Informal?'

Krugman nodded, a glacial smile thinning his lips.

'Oh quite.'

'I was expecting to see an embassy official,' said Vasquez.

'Yet here I am.'

'And now that you're here, you can go.'

'If you really wish it.'

He reached into his breast pocket and extracted a photograph, which he laid on the bed a few inches from Ramiro's right hand. He picked it up and looked at it. He stopped breathing, and his body became very still. He didn't speak, and he didn't visibly react to the photograph, but something seemed to leave him as he looked at the picture, a color shot of a young girl lying on her side, her eyes closed, her blue-black hair tied up in a purple ribbon, her china-white hands folded around a Barbie doll. There were dark circles under the little girl's eyes, and her lips were a too-bright red, her mouth a little open. A breathing tube ran into her esophagus, and an IV drip was just visible near the little girl's left arm, a silver tube that disappeared under the soft pink sheets with the tiny white flower print.

'Pilar.'

'Yes. A lovely child.'

'How is she?'

Krugman lifted his hands, palms upward.

'How is she?' he said, finally. 'As you can see, her color is good. She breathes easily. In the half-light of her room you could convince yourself that she was merely asleep. Of course the machinery, the pumps, the monitors, they mitigate against the illusion. Still, she lives. Hope remains.'

Vasquez nodded, and a long, tense interval followed while he stared down at the picture of his daughter. Krugman watched him in silence, aware that the man was using the time to think about the implications of the situation. Krugman was quite willing to give him all the time in the world. Within operational limits, anyway.

After a while, Vasquez put the photo down.

'Is this a threat, Mr Krugman?'

'No. Not in any way.'

'You're sure?'

'You have my word on it. It is in no way a threat. Rather, I can promise you that no matter what the outcome of our conversation, your daughter will receive the best of loving care for however long she may require it. Without reservation. I place the honor of our country behind that promise, Mr Vasquez.'

'Then what . . . ?'

'We ask only that you revisit your own honor, your sense of duty as a soldier.'

'I'm not a soldier. I'm a civilian. An American citizen.'

'True. You're also a member of the CIA's Special Collections Service. Your ID number is Fox-Uniform-Hotel-zero-six-four-seven, and your pay grade is Level Nine. As a result of two very ill-considered and disastrous missions, one in Paraguay, and the other a HALO drop into Waziristan, your last performance review was negative, and Psych sector recommended a permanent transfer to Mission Analysis. Nevertheless, you were instead inserted into northern Mindanao as part of a mission to locate and repair a National Security Agency surveillance relay that had begun to malfunction. Your mission controller is a man named Levi Sloane. The other members of your unit are Dean Krause, Christopher Burdette, Pike Zeigler, Loman Strackbein, and Cole Langan. Your in-country contact man was a Filipino agent, currently missing, named Jesus Rizal.'

Vasquez stared at Krugman.

'Does it occur to you that this room may be wired?'

'I am certain that it is. I am also certain that as long as I am in this hotel these devices will not operate. I imagine that right at this moment, there are French and German officials in a nearby location who are painfully aware of that, and who are presently engaged in a desperate attempt to fix the problem. They will not be successful.'

Vasquez gave that some thought.

'I know what that takes.'

'I'm sure you do. Now. We understand that you have given the French and German military police an informal statement admitting to your role in the massacre at Cobraville. This is correct, is it not?'

'Yes.'

'We can also agree that this statement is false in detail and in its entirety. I am reluctant to believe that the officials at the UN and the ICC who are pursuing this prosecution with such unholy delight and vigor are aware that your statement is false. I am willing to accept that the latent antagonism that has always existed between the United States and current rulers of the European Union has led the UN to see what it wants to see. Or, to be precise, what Hamidullah Barrakha desires them to see. I also prefer to believe that the officials of the International Criminal Court are unaware that your statement of guilt contains not a scintilla of truth and is only being made because you are under some form of duress and have been for quite a considerable period of time. Certainly this duress predates your last two missions, to Paraguay and Waziristan and greatly influenced their outcomes. Are we in agreement on these questions?'

Vasquez looked around the room with such an expression of misery on his face that Krugman felt some pity for him.

'Don't lacerate yourself needlessly, Ramiro. I understand that you are a deeply conflicted man. I am not here to judge you. I am here to bring you the means to recover your lost honor. And perhaps also to solve your problem. As well, I admit, I hope to determine its origins.'

Vasquez said nothing for a very long time. The light changed in the room, and a shadow that lay diagonally across Krugman's left cheek moved inexorably down his face, like a living thing.

'I'm in,' said Vasquez, after this silence, 'and I can't get out.'

'Not at all,' said Krugman, kindly. 'There's always a way out.'

The Judas Gate

Eisenstadt drove the Benz slowly down a long, narrow lane alongside the tall razor-wired fence that enclosed the Brooklyn Navy Yard. A quarter of a mile back, Luna and Drew followed him down the road with their lights off. On their left, the East River rolled in the darkness, bringing the scent of rotting wood and river mud. On the far side of the river, Lower Manhattan glimmered in a haze. They could hear the boom and rush of traffic on the Manhattan Bridge, and under that, the muted roar that an entire city makes so continuously that no one in the city ever hears it. Past the thirty-foot-high fence, the stacks of the Con Ed power plant dominated the night sky. The entire compound – almost a square mile in size – was lit by sodium arc lamps that cast a green corpse-light over the roofs of the oil tanks and the clustered spires of unused derricks along the river. The Benz reached the end of the road, and turned left, passing through a set of iron gates, and disappearing into the yards. Luna brought the Crown Victoria to a crawl, and watched as the lights of the unseen Benz lit up a long, dark alley that ran between two stacks of shipping containers.

They were piled on top of one another – three high – and ran for almost six hundred yards beside a wharf that jutted out into the river. They caught glimpses of the Benz as it ran down the lane between the container lines, a brief glimmer of silver and a flash of its lights as it passed by the occasional gap in the container wall. Luna brought the car to a complete stop at the open gates.

'That,' she said, with an air of finality, 'is a killing ground.'

Drew said nothing. He looked down the lane of containers, and they both watched as the Benz came to a stop at the far end of the alleyway. The brake lights flickered on and off as Eisenstadt put the car into park. The taillights glittered in the shadowed dark at the end of the lane, perhaps two hundred feet away.

Drew sat back and rubbed his face.

'We go in there, Drew, we don't come out,' said Luna.

'We could leave the car. Go in on foot.'

'Either way, the result is the same. We don't come out. We were followed all the way here by a green van that dropped out of sight back by the Farragut Houses. My money says the people in that van are down that laneway waiting for us to roll into it.'

'Who do you think they are?'

'My guess would be more thugs from Sternhagen.'

'Sternhagen is protecting Eisenstadt.'

'Yes. Somehow he set this up after we grilled him. Now he's brought us down here to get taken out of the picture.'

'I never figured out why one of their own guys was working with Krugman.'

'Kohl Keune?'

'Yeah.'

Luna shrugged.

'Maybe he got wind of what Sternhagen was doing and

462

didn't like it. Maybe he was the one who gave Krugman the heads-up in the first place. Whatever it was, they killed him for it.'

'I thought you had Krugman tagged as the bad guy.'

'It's definitely Eisenstadt.'

'And whoever he's with.'

A plume of exhaust was tailing up from Eisenstadt's Benz, and they could hear the muted burble of its engine in the confined space between the container walls.

'I'd love to go down there and crack him open,' said Drew.

'Crack him open? The only thing you're qualified to crack open is a bottle of Beaujolais. Listen to yourself. And I thought we were going to wait and see if he had a drop-box here. Then we were going to stake it out and see who showed up. I hate to dignify this nimrod escapade with the word "plan," but that's what you said we were going to do. Remember?'

'I remember. But he's not doing anything. He's just sitting there while the seconds tick off, and I admit he's driving me bats.'

'Being driven bats is what it takes to run surveillance. How about I call you a cab and you leave the rest of this to me?'

'No. We finish this together. Maybe you're right. Maybe this is a killing ground. A trap. I don't know how he rigged it. But that's what it looks like. Which means nothing happens unless we take a chance and make them show their hand. I'm going down there.'

'Remember the green minivan? It's out there some-where. Go down there and die, then. You accomplish zip.'

'Not if you stay back and cover me. If there are people down there waiting to kill me, I draw them out and you deal with them. Then we have Eisenstadt alone, and we put him to the question.'

'No. That's lunatic. I say we pull back. Wait for a better time.'

'There's not going to be a better time. Sloane will have all the cops in the eastern seaboard looking for us by now. We have maybe a couple of hours of freedom left. The hell with this. You do what you want to. I have to finish this now.'

He opened the passenger door, and got out.

'Wait here, Luna, if you have to.'

'This is crazy. It makes no sense. It's a hundred-percent fatal.'

'So's life. See you around.'

Drew reached into his coat and pulled out a black semi-auto pistol, a Beretta.

'Where did you get that?'

'Room service.'

'You're kidding?'

'I've been staying at the Beekman for a long time. This belongs to the night manager. I got it when I went down for the paper this afternoon.'

Luna sighed and opened her door, pulling out her service pistol.

'Okay. We'll do it your way. I'll go high and try to cover you. If you manage to draw any fire, I'll do what I can about taking them out. You just get to Eisenstadt. If you start taking a lot of rounds, get down behind the wheel rims or the engine block. Nothing else will stop a bullet. Except, of course, you.'

Drew smiled at her over the roof of the car.

'Thanks, Luna.'

'Just call me Wyatt. Let's go.'

Iligan City

Vasquez looked at Krugman, trying to see into the man. Krugman returned the look with an air of calm inevitability.

'A way out? How?'

'First of all, you can ease my mind on a couple of matters.'

'And if I can?'

'Then I ease yours. As I said. I'm curious. Not about the larger picture. I have the larger picture. But the particulars? The little things that always leave you puzzled? For example, was it your intention that Cole Langan should die in the Blue Bird bombing?'

Vasquez studied the window, staring through it at a patch of blue sky. A gull wheeled across it, making a sound like a child calling.

'My intention? Half the time I had no idea who was doing what to whom. It wasn't like we all met at the secret clubhouse to share a box of Krispy Kremes and plan global domination. There were cutouts, cells. Half the time, I never knew who I was talking to.'

'You're an experienced covert operator. You've had a lot of time to put it together. You've been inside. You must have an idea of how it was laid out. I'd love to hear your views.'

'My views, hah?'

Krugman smiled a chilly smile and nodded. Vasquez studied his impassive face for a time, and Krugman waited quietly. Finally, Vasquez let out a long breath and began to speak.

'Here's my take on it. In the beginning, the idea was for Cole to die. I figure Barrakha needed to thin the crowd. Cole was the leader. The idea was, you take Cole out of the picture and the rest of the unit would be shaken up. Easier to control. He didn't need all of them. Just a couple of guys would have been enough.'

'Enough to take to trial at The Hague. Yet Cole survived?'

'Yeah. I couldn't do it. When the time came, I found an excuse to get him out. As it was, he almost ran back inside. I had to take him down in the street. The blast nearly killed us both.'

'Yes,' said Krugman. 'Of course. You have your limits.'

'Do I?' said Vasquez. 'Ask the guys who went to Waziristan with me. Ask the guys in Paraguay. You'll need a psychic.'

Krugman inclined his head and lifted his shoulders, made a wry smile, and placed his hands together in his lap.

'Just one or two other points.'

'Sure.'

'Rizal's cousin, Diego D'Aquino. How far was he involved?'

'He put Barrakha's guy into the Maria Christina plant.'

'Butuan Sabang?'

'Yeah. They called him Gideon. Odd little guy. I kind of liked him. Barrakha played that boy like a tin whistle. All

466

the guy wanted was to be part of something greater. To count. Too fucking bad.'

'Did Diego D'Aquino know that Barrakha was going to blow up the Blue Bird?'

Vasquez peeled his lips back in a sardonic, self-hating grin.

'I wasn't sure. But the whole reason for blowing the Blue Bird was to kill Diego D'Aquino. Once he had Butuan Sabang in place at the power plant, Barrakha wanted Diego D'Aquino gone. Dead men tell no tales.'

'Why not just have Diego killed?'

'That's easy. It was more fun to take out the whole club. Barrakha likes to kill.'

'Yes. Of course. Yet when Butuan Sabang – Gideon – was in place at the power station, he handled himself very badly. He blundered around on the Internet and drew us right to him. He was a security risk. Why would Barrakha tolerate such a handless clown?'

'I wondered about that. Then I figured that was the brilliance of it. That was the idea. Barrakha must have figured the NSA would be all over Gideon. They'd snap him up and play him for all they could get. But in order to play him, they'd have to leave him where he was. For Christ's sake, Barrakha had him chasing down the Jordan Kemp ID on the Internet. You might as well ring out the steeple bells.'

'Yes. The Jordan Kemp ID. Oddly transparent, wasn't it?'

Vasquez stared at Krugman, comprehension dawning.

'Damn. You did that on purpose?'

'Yes,' said Krugman. 'It was such an obvious trail. Kemp was an embedded reporter in Cole Langan's unit. When he contracted cancer, we offered him a deal. Full, free treatment at Walter Reed, and a generous pension for the rest of his life, under a new identity. In return we use his background as a legend for one of our own, a legend that can be easily broken. But once it was broken, we could follow the trail all the way back to the source of the inquiry. You must be familiar with the ruse. And it worked. It led us to Gideon.'

'Did Levi Sloane know how shaky it was?'

'No. He didn't recognize the name. We gave him the legend, and he applied it to Cole on our advice. He never asked why.'

'You never let Sloane know how shaky it was?'

'No.'

Vasquez worked that out. 'Christ. You were looking at him, weren't you?'

'I admit that Levi Sloane had drawn our attention. Failed missions in Waziristan and Parguay. Keeping you in the field after you failed a psychiatric assessment. Other factors I cannot detail.'

'So you saddled Cole with a flawed legend. A bit risky for Cole Langan, though.'

'Yes. We did what we could do to have him protected.'

'How?'

'His father is a senator. I involved him in the case to ensure that no one at the CIA would consider his son . . . expendable.'

'No. Not the senator's son. Just the rest of us.'

'He was the one wearing the target. He needed the protection.'

'Cold, Mister Krugman.'

'It's a cold game. Another question. Gideon's blundering led to the exposure of one of Barrakha's agents in Toronto. The man operating as Jorge Esquivez. He was extremely well-placed in the Canadian immigration department. He was also a cousin to Barrakha. His real name was Yusef al Ashrami. Why would Barrakha sacrifice such a valuable source?'

'That's easy. No sense playing a double game if you don't give your suckers something real. Otherwise they get bored and look elsewhere. Barrakha wanted to keep you guys focused on Gideon.'

'So what Gideon was doing was just a diversion?'

'You don't get it. The main thing was to keep Gideon in the plant. With the NSA all over him, he was too important a source for the CIA to kill. And he kept everybody's attention fixed on the power plant while Barrakha set up the Cobraville stunt. Barrakha knew we were closing in on the relay, and he knew where it was, since he was the one who had the jammer attached to it. I saw it happening. When we were in Cobraville talking to the Jesuit, a firefight broke out in the southern jungle around Marawi and Lake Lanao. I think he had his Bukidno tribesmen start that firefight with the UN troopers to draw the French and German units away from the area around Cobraville. Then he went in and cut the place to pieces. He and some of his Abu Sayaf guys. I'm sure he loved that part.'

'You disappeared right after the Germans hit your team?'

'Yeah. I knew I was supposed to testify at the trial. In order to testify, I figured I had better stay alive. The Germans were ripping up the terrain with full-auto fire. Rizal took off. I saw my chance to fade, and I took it. Later I wandered into a German patrol and handed in my tags. That was the end of my game.'

'We're told the people who massacred the village

used American weapons. Where did they come from?'

'I think they got them in the gun markets on the Sulus. You can get any weapon you want in the Sulu Sea. Anyway, as soon as the Cobraville thing went down, everybody at the CIA was looking in our direction, and Barrakha could play Gideon out one last time.'

'By getting him to raise the gates at Maria Christina?'

'Yeah. I think Gideon figured he had screwed up totally, and that Barrakha was going to kill him. I heard that Barrakha worked him over pretty good, too, and I guess Gideon thought it was for burning Jorge Esquivez. But a guy like Barrakha would't give a shit about Esquivez. I think he wanted Gideon motivated. One last act. Raise those gates, and he gets to live. And it worked like silk. We could use some guys like Barrakha on our side.'

Vasquez seemed to hear his own words and he stopped.

'Our side . . .' he said again, in a dull tone.

'Let that go. Obviously your daughter was used against you. Cooperate or she dies. You were in a very difficult position.'

'It didn't start that way. In the beginning, it was the medical expenses. My insurance wasn't going to cut it. I needed more. I went to HR, but they said there was nothing they could do. After I sold off what I had, and all of my wife's insurance money was gone, and the bills were still coming in, I ran right out of options.'

'How were you approached?'

'I was on the Internet looking for private mortgage money. I got an e-mail from this guy, says he can help. It started there.'

'Did you ever identify this person?'

'No. I had some theories. For one thing, he was American.'

'You actually spoke with him?'

'Never. Always through the Internet. Chat rooms, mainly. Subtle changes in a website. Coded programs in a JPEG download. You know how it's done. But the way he used the words? There's a thousand different ways you tip it off, and I'm a language guy. No, he was American. I'm sure of it.'

'Why didn't you report the contact to Levi Sloane?'

'I thought about it. But I didn't see how it would help Pilar, and she was my main concern. So I went along. And after the Paraguay mission, I was afraid that if I told him I had been turned, he'd be so pissed he'd just have me shot. These were *his* missions I was fucking up. His guys dying. His reputation getting shot to shit as well. You should have seen him during those days. He was literally on fire. There were times I thought he was going to have an aneurysm or something. No. I never went to Sloane.'

'So in the beginning, it was just information?'

'Yeah. But once you're in, like I said, you never get out. They upped the stakes, and asked for more and more. I'd already given them so much that I could never go back. There's no way out of this.'

'And you still have no idea who's running you?'

'Not a clue. I wish I did. I'd kill the guy myself.'

'I may be able to help you there.'

Krugman took another piece of paper out of his pocket. It was folded in three. He set it down on the bed and sat back. Vasquez picked it up and unfolded it.

It was a grainy, black-and-white photograph of a man sitting behind the wheel of a white minivan. It seemed to have been taken at a tollbooth somewhere. The light was strong and direct, but the man's upper body was lost in the dark interior of the van, his face invisible. Only his left hand and forearm showed in the sunlight. The hand was extending a ten-dollar bill, and another hand, presumably belonging to the toll taker himself, was reaching for the cash.

'What is this?'

'It's a shot taken from a tollbooth camera.'

'I can see that. So what?'

'Look at the time-marker.'

Vasquez did.

1534 HOURS 07/17/97

He looked up from the sheet, and stared at Krugman.

'That's the day Katie and Rafael died.'

'Yes. While walking on the side of the road. A hit-and-run by someone driving a white Windstar van.'

Vasquez stared at the photo.

'Where did this come from?'

'It's part of the investigation files from the Virginia state troopers. They looked at every parking-lot camera and bank camera and surveillance camera in the area, every camera that might have taken a shot of a white Windstar anywhere close to the scene of the accident. This shot was taken by a ticket-booth camera at the entrance to the Blue Ridge Parkway. The van in the shot is a Windstar. You can tell by the side mirror and the shape of the window.'

'Fifteen-thirty-four hours. Katie and Rafael and Pilar were struck down about a half an hour earlier. How far was this tollbooth from the scene of the accident?'

'About a half-hour.'

'Was the van damaged?'

'There's no way to tell from this shot.'

'Then what good is it?'

'At the time not much. It was merely one of thousands. Since the man's face was not visible, and the camera never got the vehicle's plate numbers, the shot wasn't considered important. But since then, the inquiry has narrowed somewhat, and an overlooked detail now seems much more critical. It'll come to you.'

Vasquez stared down at the picture for a long time, straining to make out the blurry details, and then he looked back up at Krugman.

'Son of a bitch.'

'Yes. My sentiments exactly.'

Sloane

Drew moved slowly down the line of containers with his Beretta at his side. Above him and to his right, Luna was walking across the top of the container stack, keeping pace with Drew with her pistol out and her arms braced. The concrete surface under Drew's feet was gritty, and it was hard to take a step without making a grating sound that seemed to reverberate across the gap. He could hear Luna's light step as she worked her way down the stack above him, perhaps twenty feet up. The silver Benz idled gently at the far end of the lane, exhaust fumes curling up in the downward glow of an overhead light. The Benz was now about a hundred feet away.

Each time Drew reached a gap in the container walls he'd edge around the side of the container and point the Beretta into the darkness. Each time there would be nothing waiting, and he'd set out to cover the next section of containers. As he moved down the lane, he watched the door of the Benz and wondered what Eisenstadt was thinking, sitting there in the cool, dim darkness of the Benz, alone with his fear. Drew was sure the man could see him coming toward him. Each time Drew passed under the downlight from one of the lamps overhead he could see his own shadow pooling under his feet.

Halfway down the next section he heard Luna's whispered warning.

'Drew. There's a truck coming along the road.'

Luna dropped into a crouch on top of the container stack, and Drew faded into a dark section between the pools of light. They both listened while a vehicle powered up the lane. They saw its light rake across the laneway and then enter it, a large black Suburban.

It rolled a few yards into the lane and stopped beside their black Crown Victoria. The driver's door opened, and a man stepped out, a heavy man in a suit. In the dim light, Luna and Drew could see he was holding a pistol. The man walked a few paces into the container line, silhouetted now in his own headlights.

'Drew. You have to get out of there.'

Drew pushed himself backward into the shadow by the container, feeling the ridges of the container wall pressing into his shoulders. The man called out again, his soft voice carrying in the damp air off the river, his tone urgent.

'You've been set up!'

Drew looked up at the container roof across the lane. Luna's voice came out of the darkness above him.

'Levi?'

Sloane stepped back out of the pool of light from the truck.

'Luna? That you? Where are you?'

'I'm up here.'

'Well, both of you get back here.'

'What about Eisenstadt?' said Drew.

'Leave him there. We'll deal with him.'

'How did you know where we were?' asked Luna.

'We got to Seventy-seventh street, and you weren't there. But we found your cell phone in the planter. We were running a sweep of the street, when this woman comes out of her townhouse. She ID's herself as Hildi Eisenstadt. She told us her husband was leading you into some sort of trap down at the Navy Yard. Now get out of there.'

'Eisenstadt's wife burned him?' said Drew, out of the dark.

'You guys shook her up badly. Apparently Eisenstadt's into something sleazy, and now she's looking for a way out.'

Luna straightened up and called down to Drew.

'Drew, he's right.'

'Damn right I am,' said Sloane. 'Come on. Let's go.'

Drew stepped out of the darkness and into the pool of light in the middle of the laneway. He heard Luna walking back along the top of the container line toward Sloane. There was no point in pushing this any further. He had come to the end of the line. He was through.

He walked slowly back to the Suburban. Sloane was leaning on the driver's door, with his thick arms folded across his chest.

'You,' he said, in a weary tone, 'are a pain in the ass.'

Drew stopped in front of him, a massive weight pulling him down, as if the force of gravity were stronger underneath him.

'Yeah.'

'Where'd you get that pistol?' Sloane said, looking at the Beretta in Drew's hand.

Drew shoved it into his waistband and shrugged.

'Hidden depths, hah? You're a caution, my friend.'

'Yes. I suppose I am.'

'I'm sorry about Cole, Drew. I really am.'

'I know. So am I.'

Luna dropped softly to the ground a few feet away, and came over to stand beside Drew. Drew saw she was still holding her pistol. So did Sloane. He gave her a hard look and came back to Drew.

'What was this all about?'

'Drew figured you for a mole,' said Luna.

Sloane looked at Drew, and in the downlight they could see that he was grinning at them.

'Yeah? I been sensing that. What gave you that bright idea?'

Luna smiled, her face half in shadow.

'He believed that only you could have put those guys in the chopper on us. That you were cleaning something up.'

Sloane sighed heavily.

'I thought we'd settled that one, Drew.'

'Yeah. Sorry.'

'And what was I supposed to be cleaning up?'

'We never got that far,' said Drew.

'All of this has something to do with Eisenstadt and the Maria Christina power plant in Mindanao,' said Luna.

'We'll follow it up. It looks like his wife is ready to make a deal. We'll sort it out. You two ought to leave this stuff to the pros.'

'I will,' said Drew.

Sloane put his piece away and opened the driver's door.

'You both look like hell. How about we all go get a drink?'

Drew looked at Luna, who smiled back at him.

'That sounds wonderful. What about him?'

They both looked down the laneway toward Eisenstadt's silver Benz. Sloane leaned into the Suburban and flicked the high beams on. The driver's door popped open and Gerhardt Eisenstadt stepped out into the pool of light from the street lamp, shading his eyes from the glare. He blinked into the dazzle and called out to them.

'It is over, yes?'

'Just about,' said Luna, raising her pistol. She fired it four times, the weapon kicking in her hand and the muzzle flash lighting up the walls of the containers. The sound of the weapon slammed around in the narrow space, stunningly loud. Down at the far end of the lane Gerhardt Eisenstadt staggered backward and fell out of the light. When Sloane and Drew looked back at Luna her heavy pistol was aimed at them.

'Tidy as you go,' said Luna.

There was a sudden puff of air between them, and Luna stepped backward, staggered slightly, and a puzzled expression came over his face. A sound carried over the container stacks, a distant muffled report. Drew and Sloane watched Luna as she reached up and touched a large black hole in her right cheek. She stared back at them with a look of mild indignation on her face, and another heavy round punched into her chest, followed by another distant report, driving her back against the container wall; but by then Sloane had put several large and arguably superfluous rounds into the middle of her chest. Footsteps sounded in the lane, and a man walked out of the dark. Sloane swiveled and put the weapon on him, but Drew reached out and touched his arm gently.

'Not in the suit,' said Vernon Geberth, stepping out into the light, his hands in from of this chest. 'This is a Zegna.'

Sloane looked at Drew.

'Who is this guy?'

'Vernon Geberth. He's with the NYPD.'

Sloane looked from Drew to Geberth and back.

'I saw a green minivan parked down the line there.'

'My guys,' said Geberth, grinning hugely.

'Christ, Drew. You took a hell of risk.'

'So did you.'

'Me? How?'

'It was either you or Luna. Detective Geberth was out of your loop. This was the only way to find out.'

Sloane considered Drew for a time.

'You're not just a pretty face, are you, Senator?'

'Isn't it pretty to think so?'

They all looked down at Luna's body.

'What about her?' said Geberth.

'The usual thing,' said Sloane.

'Ah,' said Geberth, nodding sadly.

'What's the usual thing?' asked Drew.

'Killed in the line of duty,' said Sloane.

'Military honors,' added Geberth. 'Flag on the casket.'

'A solitary piper,' said Sloane.

'Yeah,' said Geberth, looking down at Luna. 'The usual thing.'

Denver

Three separate thunderstorms, each one reaching ten thousand feet into the air and covering a hundred miles of flatland, floated like huge galleons in a bruised yellow sky over Denver, dragging a soft, shimmering veil of heavy rain across the bone-dry reaches of eastern Colorado. High up on the edge of the Front Range, the noise of the city far below was only a muted hum, and the smell of lodgepole pine and hickory smoke filled the clear air.

The ancient post-and-beam house was built out on a cantilevered platform that jutted out into the sky overlooking Denver, just down the slope from a forest of communications towers that rose up another thousand feet into the air, red lights blinking on their tips.

The house was made of square-cut pine timbers, roofed in slate, and it was sheltered from the play of the winds that always circled around the eastern edge of the Rockies by a stand of oaks and cottonwood trees over a hundred years old. A huge veranda ran across the eastern front of the old house, and a row of padded cedar chairs stood in a broad arc around the overlook. Behind the patio, under the broad, low roof of the house, two massive plates of clear glass shone with a soft amber light that poured out of the interior. The thunderclouds were reflected in that broad flat glass, lightning flickering, the last of the sun lighting up the uttermost tips of the storm, black fury below.

Alone in the middle chair, an elderly woman, whose skin was dried into a leathery hide by years and years of sitting in this very chair, was looking out over Denver, her eyes sunken into her skull but full of a hard clear light, steeping herself in the kind of comfort that only old American money can provide. In her clawlike left hand she held a heavy crystal glass filled to the brim with gin, and over which the houseboy had waved a bottle of tonic. Two lemon slices floated through the bubbles like tropical fish. In her other hand, the fingers knotted and twisted with arthritis, a Monte Cristo cigar burned, forgotten, the glowing ash less than a quarter of an inch away from her tobacco-stained knuckles. As she watched, the southernmost storm cracked open with a flare of vivid forked lightning that stabbed downward into the flatlands, striking a tiny silver tower near the far-off town of Limon. She smiled at that, her lips pulling back over a set of strong yellow teeth, listening for the muted rumble of thunder.

When it came, she smiled again, feeling like an old Valkyrie in Valhalla, and lifted the glass to her lips, pursing them primly as she drank. She let the drink burn down inside her, warming her thin blood and bringing heat into her sagging belly, her wasted thighs, her shriveled legs. She put her head back against the chair and looked up to the sky, where a pair of hawks circled, so high they were still in the sunlight, their wingtips burning, and sighed.

'Someone to see you, Mrs McDowell.'

Damn.

'Who is it, Chester?'

The houseboy made an apologetic shrug; they all knew how she hated to be disturbed at this hour of the day. These evenings on the Front Range were the only un-diluted satisfactions she had left. The rest of her life was taken up with the calculations, with bargains and betrayals, with the Goddamned family business.

'A Mr Langan. He is sorry to intrude.'

Helen McDowell twisted in her chair and glared at the boy.

'Drew Langan?'

'Yes, ma'am.'

Christ. What does that moron want?

'Okay. Send him through.'

She sat back in the chair, watching the storms glide, her mind working, trying to float up through the gin toward the light. A soft step behind her, and she put on her meeting face the way she'd have slipped in her dentures, her lips working around it, as Drew Langan walked up to her, a black silhouette in the warm glow of the house lights behind him. He was holding a flat, square box in his hands.

'Helen,' said Drew. 'Nice to see you.'

She twisted around, nodded at him with a black look in her eyes, and indicated the chair next to her with an index finger that looked like an ice-pick.

'Sit, then. I'm breaking my neck to look up.'

Drew sat down in the next chair and set the box, a wooden case, polished to a glow, with a brass plate inset on the lid, carefully down onto the wooden boards at his feet. Helen McDowell eyed it with a raptor's intensity, but made no comment. Its silent presence – the implicit promise that something inside it might be offered to her –

482

had fired up the eternal flame of her omnivorous greed, and prompted her to feign a more hospitable manner.

'Drink?'

'I'll have a scotch. Straight up.'

McDowell nodded to Chester, who padded away across the boards. She studied Drew in the fading light.

'You look like shit, son.'

'Thanks. It's been a tough week.'

She showed him her teeth.

'I've heard something about it. My condolences about your father, by the way. They ever work out who did it?'

Chester reappeared with the scotch. Drew sipped at it and put it down on the flat wooden arm of the chair.

'They worked out what happened.'

'Yeah. And what happened?'

'It seems this Cornel Chulalonkorn was something of a hustler. He had met my ex-wife at a party in Paris. My wife's friend Mitzi Gallant took him off to bed and kept him there for a week. During the week, he spent a lot of time going through drawers and cupboards, and found out all about my father's place in Camp Hill. Wrote himself a letter on Diana's personal stationery, introducing himself to my father. Stayed there long enough to win his trust and to seduce the young woman taking care of my dad. They proceeded to drain some of his personal accounts. Then my father died, suddenly –'

'They kill him?'

'No. It was an embolism. Took him in his sleep. When they realized he was dead, they knew the game was over. They cleaned up the place and scatted before anyone could find out my dad was dead.'

'Hustlers,' she snorted. 'I've had a few make a run on me. I usually send them packing. They find them yet?'

'We have a line on them. We'll see what happens.'

'You've had a time, Drew. Sorry about your boy. Line of duty and all that. Got no kids myself. But I can see how it would be hard to lose one. First your father. Then your son. That's real hard.'

Drew shook his head slowly.

She was thinking about her dinner, not wanting to be obliged to invite him to stay, but intrigued by the wooden box enough to prolong the chat until he got around to it.

'Well, Drew . . . to what do I owe . . . as they say?'

'Just a couple of things. You remember Gunther Krugman?'

'Yes. Miserable old bastard. Caused us no end of trouble. Still no sign of him? What about him?'

'You ever have any contact with him?'

She shrugged.

'Over the years, sure. Who didn't?'

'But nothing recent?'

'No. Why?'

'You called my house in Georgetown the night he disappeared. You remember?'

Her face closed up, her lips tightened into two thin lines.

'No. No recollection.'

'None?'

'I'd remember, son.'

Drew pulled a small Pearlcorder out of his coat, hit PLAY.

'Drew, this is Helen – if you get this message early enough, I'm here in Denver for another hour, and then I'm on my way up the Front Range for some hunting. I'm gonna give you my private cell number – three-zero-five-four-seven-seven-eight-six-eight-six – and where the hell are you, anyway? I know you're home, because I already woke up your daddy, and the cranky old fart told me you were still in Georgetown. I need to talk to Gunther Krugman pretty damn quick. Can't find the son of a bitch anywhere. He's a friend of yours. You get your ass in gear and tell him to give me a call!'

McDowell shrugged.

'So I called. What's your point?'

'Why were you looking for Krugman?'

She made a cutting sideways motion with her knotted right hand, sending cigar ashes flying in the still, scented air.

'I don't know. Some committee business. I forget.'

Drew smiled at her.

'Well, thanks for the talk. I have to go. There's a hearing Monday, at the United Nations in New York. We're meeting with the Special Prosecutor for the International Criminal Court.'

'This about those poor CIA bastards in Mindanao?'

'Yes. I'll be at that meeting.'

'In what capacity?'

'A party with an interest.'

'How nice for you.'

'Thanks.'

Drew leaned down and picked up the box, got to his feet. McDowell craned her neck to look up at him, her mouth half-open, her black eyes sharp.

'What's in the box, Drew?'

Drew looked down at the box in his hands, and then at her.

'It's a gift. For you.'

He held it out to her. She tried not to snatch at it, and managed a ghastly parody of a smile as she settled it into her bony lap. It had a reassuring weight and heft, and the wood was buttery under her hand. She squinted down at the brass plate:

GERHARDT EISENSTADT

She stared down at the name for a while, her breathing audible, while Drew watched her visible effort to control her emotions.

'What the fuck is a Gerhardt Eisenstadt?'

'He was the Junior Undersecretary for International Trade and Development at the United Nations. His specific duties had to do with infrastructure. Agrarian reform. Water purification. Electricity.'

'I see,' she said. Her knotted hands were shaking, and her voice was thin, strained, her throat closing around her words.

'As I said. That's what he used to do.'

'What's he doing now?'

'Cooling his heels in a federal facility, I guess. We've figured out he was involved in a conspiracy.'

'Yeah? What kind of conspiracy?'

'He had contact with an Al Qaeda terrorist named Hamidullah Barrakha. You've heard of him?'

'Of course I have. Get on with it.'

'Barrakha told him he was in a position to arrange the destruction of a hydroelectric plant in northern Mindanao. The Maria Christina plant near Lake Lanao.'

'I know all about the plant, boy.'

'That plant was built by an American company, Consolidated Power Systems. Are you familiar with Consolidated Power?'

'Never heard of them.'

'No. Well, although the Maria Christina plant was built

by Consolidated Power Systems, the cost of the construction was paid for by the American taxpayer as part of a development grant arranged for by the Foreign Aid Development Trust in D.C. You chaired that committee at the time, so it's odd that you wouldn't remember the name of the company you selected to build the plant.'

'It was ten years ago. I sit on dozens of committees.'

'Consolidated Power Systems is owned by a numbered corporation on the Isle of Man. So far, we haven't been able to figure out who the owners are. But since September Eleventh we're allowed to force the holding companies in places like the Isle of Man to divulge the details of offshore ownership. So we'll eventually get the list of corporate shareholders.'

'What's this got to do with me? You think you're gonna find my name on that list, kid? Because you won't.'

'We don't expect to.'

'Then either state your case, or bugger off.'

'Okay. Sorry to be taking so long. It's kind of complicated, but basically, the IRS has been told to look into the correlation of payments and disbursements made by this corporation and certain deposits made over several years to a registered charity called Springbuck. You're a director of that charity.'

'One of them. It's a purely honorary position. I have no influence over them, and I take no funds from them for serving as a director. If you're hoping to force me to –'

'Let's set Springbuck aside. Now, we take a look at a German company called Koenigsburg Stadtlander Bundt SA, known on the NYSE as KSB. Ever heard of them?'

McDowell closed her eyes and then opened them again. 'Maybe. Sounds familiar.'

'KSB got listed on the NYSE several years ago. They

operate coal-fired power plants all through Southeast Asia, usually under a contract issued by the government of whatever country they're operating in. The responsibility for issuing these contracts falls to the Secretariat for International Trade and Development at the United Nations. Two years ago, Gerhardt Eisenstadt took on that portfolio for Southeast Asia. Last week, when the Maria Christina plant was destroyed, KSB filed a request with the Secretariat to rebuild that plant as part of a much larger project to design and build several nuclear power stations throughout the Philippines. If the entire project came to fruition, KSB stood to make a stunning amount of profit. The funds were to come from the World Bank, but the decision to grant them the contract was going to land on Eisenstadt's desk.'

McDowell was staring out at the storm clouds crossing the Great Plains. Below the veranda, Denver twinkled in the mist. She was so still that she might have been dead. Only the sound of her breathing indicated that she was still alive.

'In the weeks before the destruction of that plant, several corporations and private individuals across America made significant purchases of KSB stock. One of the corporations that made major purchases of KSB stock was a charitable organization called Springbuck. Last week, Springbuck purchased enough stock in KSB to have thirteen-percent ownership of the company. What made Springbuck decide to invest so heavily in an obscure German power corporation whose stocks had been ticking along without much change for ten years, Helen? Any idea?'

McDowell blinked slowly, and shook her head.

'Well, what's in this box is an extract from a secret

deposition made by Gerhardt Eisenstadt's wife to the United States Attorney General's office. In the deposition, which forms part of the case we're bringing to the ICC Special Prosecutor's office in New York, Hildi Eisenstadt states that you and her husband had frequent communications through an intermediary, and that you informed him that if he were to grant the rights to rebuild the Maria Christina plant to KSB, you would look favorably on the decision.'

'What intermediary?'

'You tell me.'

'I don't play that game. Why would he need my approval?'

'Because a clause in the original contract with Consolidated Power gave them the sole right to rebuild the Maria Christina plant if anything should happen to it. That right had to be renewed by the federal government after a set period. It was due to come up for renewal as a line item in a Senate bill in October. You have already made several calls to other senators expressing your desire to have that line item defeated. Most of the senators we've spoken to said that, without your strong pressure to defeat the line item, the renewal would have passed easily. In the face of your vehement opposition, it was guaranteed to be defeated.'

McDowell looked at him.

'You've talked to the senators? Which ones?'

'They asked me not to reveal their names. Anyway, Hildi Eisenstadt's deposition is inside the box. I thought you might like to read it. If not you, then your lawyers.'

McDowell stared up at him. Drew noticed that under her tanned, leathery skin her color had drained away.

'Look – Drew – if this is what I think it is – there's a lot

489

of factors involved here. Nothing is simple in the money business. This part of what you're going to talk about at the ICC? Because if it is, and what you're really pissed off about is being kicked off the Oversight Committee —'

'I'm resigning from the Senate after this session.'

'Resigning? Why?'

'Personal reasons. Thanks for the drink.'

Drew walked away across the patio and was quickly lost to her failing sight in the blue shadows under the cottonwoods. McDowell turned around and stared out across the great plains, dreaming under a purple sky that was slowly filling up with cold, hard-edged stars.

Below her, Denver burned in the evening light like a freighter churning through a dark sea. She found it difficult to breathe, and her cigar had gone out. She lifted the lid on the box and saw several sheets of computer paper lying on top of a gold-plated Colt .45. The Colt rested on a blue velvet bed. Two gold-plated magazines glimmered in cutaways next to the gleaming gun. Both magazines were fully loaded, seven big rounds each. McDowell fumbled for her reading glasses and held the papers up to the light streaming from the house. There were eight sheets in all, and she read them twice. Then she let them fall to the ground, where they spilled out across the terrace on the soft evening wind that was rich with the scent of pine and hickory smoke. She took the gun out, pushed in a magazine, worked the slide to chamber a round, and then for a long time she sat there and watched the lights coming on out on the great plains, in all those insignificant little towns and villages where all the insignificant little fly-over people lived.

New York

Office of the Prosecutor – Special Hearing Room
International Criminal Court – United Nations Headquarters
First Avenue and 46th Street – New York City
Monday, August 25, 8:00 a.m. local time

A gray light poured into the long, high-ceilinged, wood-paneled hall from eight tall, slender windows that marched in a stern Germanic order down the eastern wall of the hearing room. The cold, recycled air was filled with the bustle and murmur of hundreds of separate voices mingling in anticipatory chatter, as the observers and the reporters filed into the hastily converted auditorium after being herded through the metal and explosives detectors. There was an air of urgency mixed with dread, a generalized feeling that the results of today's special session would be either catastrophic or triumphant. Most of the press gallery had filled up an hour before, and they lined the second balcony: a motley crowd of undistinguished men and women in jeans and sweatshirts, the men bald or bearded or shaven-headed with little goatees, and the women with short, sensible haircuts and hard uncompromising faces; serious men and women bearing the sacred burden of the free press, almost all of them far gone in self-righteous pride and the ready willingness to think badly of everyone in power anywhere.

Down on the main floor, the international observers –

with their color-coded ID cards carrying the signs of their varying degrees of importance or irrelevance – took their seats with solemn faces, heads together or leaning forward to tap others on their shoulders, faces scanning the room; and whispered commentaries, predictions.

Up on the dais, in front of a projection television screen at least five feet wide, the special prosecutor's team was already in place behind a long, intricately carved, teakwood panel with a series of blunt, heavy-handed carvings of blunt, heavy-handed figures acting out in wooden mime the various sacraments of the people's struggle for freedom and democracy around the world; all of this culminating in a joyful peasant's jig around a pillar topped by the crest of the United Nations. The prosecutor's team consisted, for the most part, in reedy young men and a few sharp-faced young women dressed in the standard-issue black suits of international courts, their crisp white linen giving the hall the air of a royal inquisition run by a staff of cranky headwaiters.

The session not yet in order and the prosecutor still blow-drying his hair in his chambers, the space in front of the uplifting carved panel – an area set aside for witnesses and lawyers, complete with a lectern and a microphone – was currently taken up with a jostling scrum of television crews and still photographers, all of them dressed even more badly than their print cousins up in the gods. Their lights blazing and their flashes strobing hypnotically, they filled the forward part of the room with the sound of a million sand crabs advancing up a beach defended by seagulls, a wall of clicking and scrabbling noises intermingled with the harsh squawking cries of the producers shrieking into cell phones and calling for close-ups.

In the fullness of time – thirty-eight minutes late –

two large doors sheathed in hammered pewter swung majestically open, and the special prosecutor emerged from the inner chambers wearing a long, flowing black robe that wafted up behind him with the speed of his advance like two black wings; portents swirled in his wake.

The vast room muttered and mumbled itself into a kind of breathing silence, and the special prosecutor, ascending to the dais and taking his position at the center of the long table, leaned into the microphone – tapped it once or twice to provide the ceremonial mike-thumping that always precedes a public address – and called the assembly to order; upon which several blue-suited civilians filed into the now-vacated area of the press scrum and took up their positions at two long mahogany tables.

This operation complete, the man went on:

'Today's meeting of the prosecutor's office, and we thank the UN for allowing us to use this facility, is to consider the petition of the United States for the surrender of the person of one Dean Mitchell Krause and Ramiro Vasquez, both citizens of the United States, as well as the remains of two other American citizens, Loman Strackbein, and an unknown male, tentatively identified as Jordan Kemp. At present, Mr Krause and Mr Vasquez, and the bodies of Mr Strackbein and Mr Kemp, remain in the Philippines, in the southern city of Iligan. We're all aware of the threatening position currently taken by the American government should this petition fail. We're also compelled to announce that rumors of an inculpatory statement that was supposed to be tendered by one of the Americans involved has turned out to be false.'

He paused here to write something with a gold pen on a sheet of blank blue paper, looking up once over the steel rims of his reading glasses to check the time, while a spate of nervous coughing made its way through the audience.

'So . . . given the grave consequences that would follow upon any unilateral action by the United States, the Special Prosecutor has convened this open hearing, at which various parties with an interest will have an opportunity to present information or to make observations that may guide this office in the disposition of this matter. Present today are representatives of various organizations, including the Organization of Public Interest Lawyers, represented by Mr Phil Shiner, and the Committee on Economic and Social Rights, represented by Mr Roger Norman. So in this regard, it is my pleasure to call upon the first speaker, Senator Drew Langan, of the United States, who has requested the right to address the assembly first, a request we have – after consultation – granted.

A murmur ran through the hall as Drew Langan – wearing a blue pin-stripe suit, a crisp white shirt, and a Harvard tie – rose from his seat beside Britney Vogel, both of them deep inside a welter of blue suits clustered around the tables. He looked at Britney Vogel, whose pale face was tight with anticipation, his expression warming, and got a brief but memorable smile in return. He stiffened, pulled in a long, slightly uneven breath, and walked slowly across to the lectern, where he did not tap the microphone to see if it worked.

'Thank you Mr Prosecutor. I'll try to keep my comments brief and to the point.'

Drew opened a laptop computer and plugged the link into the array set into the top of the lectern. The screen behind the dais flickered into blue light, and the prosecutor flipped up his own flat-screen display, as did several of his assistants lined up beside him.

'As we understand the case against Mr Krause and

Mr Vasquez, as presented by the special prosecutor . . .'
His voice, low, level, and calm, carried around the
hall with a slight echo, and the crowd – hushed now, and
attentive – grew still – 'as well as the case against the
two deceased men, rests mainly on the accounts of two
witnesses who were present at the scene of the killings.'

'And on the accounts of the German soldiers who
survived the subsequent ambush,' said the prosecutor.

'Who, as we understand it from the affidavits, were not
present at the time of the massacre.'

'That is true,' intoned the prosecutor.

'So, I have some submissions concerning these
two witnesses that go directly to the issue of their
credibility.'

'I hardly think we can question the credibility of a Jesuit
priest whose work in Mindanao is the subject of international praise, and the antecedents of Mr Rizal, who is
a direct descendant of a well-known Filipino patriot, are
equally impeccable.'

'I don't intend to challenge the professional records of
either man, Mr Prosecutor. I wish only to point out one
or two details that might help your office in their investi-
gations, so that – if my information is of interest – you can
consider what the appropriate action might be.'

'Very well,' said the prosecutor.

'Thank you,' said Drew, pressing a button on the
laptop.

A black-and-white picture appeared on the screen, of
a tall elegant man – clean-shaven – in a black suit and a
clerical collar, standing at a podium in front of a circular
lecture hall crowded with students, his hands raised,
making a gesture with a pipe, the expression on his fine-
boned face that of a man photographed in the middle of a

speech. The angle allowed the shooter to see the priest's face, as well as the faces of several rows of students in the circular hall, gazing up at the man with various expressions ranging from awe to amusement.

'This is a picture of Father Constantin Desaix, taken several years ago, when he was a visiting lecturer at the Sorbonne. It was taken by a photographer from *Le Monde,* and appeared as part of a feature article on Father Desaix, a copy of which has been provided to you. The course Father Desaix was teaching was described in the article as "Post-Colonial Divinity Studies."'

'We accept that this is a photograph of Father Desaix, Senator Langan. You said you would be brief. Please come to the point.'

'Certainly. In his affidavit, Father Desaix affirms that he was certain that the massacre at Cobraville was not carried out by any of the indigenous extremist groups such as Abu Sayaf or the Moro Liberation Front. This, in spite of the fact that he has maintained that many of the people of the village had been killed by guerrillas controlled by a man named Hamidullah Barrakha.'

'Yes. This Barrakha is known to this office. Father Desaix has been in the forefront of a social movement that is attempting to bring peace to a troubled region. Mr Barrakha's hatred of Father Desaix's mission is also well-known, but if you intend to propose that the attack on the village was carried out by Islamist freedom fighters, I must remind you that Father Desaix's testimony clearly and unequivocally refutes that contention. And a forensic investigation of the scene carried out by international experts has determined that the weapons used were American-made weapons, such as the M-16, and the M-60 machine gun. These weapons are not the type used by any of the guerrilla movements known to be operating in Mindanao and the Sulu Islands.'

'Father Desaix also asserts in his affidavit that he has never met Hamidullah Barrakha personally.'

'That is correct.'

'Then I ask you to look closely at this photograph.'

Drew used a laser pointer to single out a young bearded man in the third row, a hawk-faced young man with intense black eyes.

'The records at the Sorbonne identify this man as Hamidullah Barrakha –'

A wave of whispering erupted across the hall. The prosecutor gaveled it down, glaring at Drew over his steel-framed glasses.

'You can support this claim?'

'The copy of the list of students in attendance at the Sorbonne, and the roll of students who graduated from Father Desaix's course that year, are among the papers I have provided.'

The assistants, heads bent, ruffled through their paper-work, one young woman with a shaved head surfacing with a long sheet, which she handed to the prosecutor, whispering in his ear at the same time. The man studied the list – or affected to study it – for a time.

'Very well. Father Desaix had some slight contact with –'

'Mr Barrakha's place of residence in Paris is also indicated in the material I have provided. He stayed at Seventeen rue Sevigny, in the Left Bank region of Paris. Father Desaix's family owned the house. Father Desaix lived there while he was in Paris.'

There was a long silence from the dais that contrasted sharply with the rising chatter out in the audience. Flashes from various cameras in the press gallery began to light up the dais.

'I see,' said the prosecutor. 'It would have been a courtesy, Senator, if your government had simply brought this detail to our attention in a more private forum.'

'I apologize, sir. We have only lately come into this material. If you wish, I can present the rest of my material in your chambers.'

'You have other information of this sort?'

'I do.'

'Does any of it concern the testimony of Mr Rizal?'

'It does.'

'Is it of a similar nature?'

'I can demonstrate that Mr Rizal was in direct communication with Hamidullah Barrakha.'

'What proof of that can you offer?'

'Extracts from a classified intelligence agency that had established a form of wiretap on Mr Barrakha's communications. A voice-recognition program was used to compare copies of Mr Rizal's voice as heard during a taped conversation with a member of our intelligence services.'

'More American sources?'

'Yes, sir. In this intercepted communication, Barrakha refers to an unknown third man as "The Ferenghi." As you are aware, "Ferenghi" is a corruption of the Arabic word *franji*, which means "Frank." In the common usage of this word, "Frank" is generally meant to apply to the French knights who played major roles in the early Crusades. Father Desaix is a French citizen. We have reason to believe he was routinely referred to as "The Ferenghi" by Hamidullah Barrakha and his people.'

'Very thin. And all this from an American intelligence agency?' asked the prosecutor.

'What I have shown you seems to indicate the possibility of a conspiracy involving Father Desaix, Jesus Rizal, and Hamidullah Barrakha. This goes directly to their credibility as witnesses.'

All of his assistants were now in action, some whispering into cell phones or clacking away on their Palm Pilots and Blackberrys. The woman with the shaved head was glaring at Drew, a killing look.

'This ... conspiracy? What possible reason could Father Desaix have had to allow – to conspire in – the murder of one hundred and seventeen Samal villagers, many of whom had been literally raised under his care? It is unthinkable.'

'I do not believe – and we in no way contend – that he anticipated a massacre of his own villagers. I think Father Desaix was told that the plan was only to capture American civilians in a UN zone and then to use them to embarrass the United States, here, in your court. I will make the observation that Father Desaix's family was executed by the Viet Cong shortly after the United States pulled out of Vietnam in 1973.'

'You can prove that Barrakha was responsible for the explosion at the power plant?'

'No. I suspect it. I also suspect that the massacre at Cobraville was planned and carried out by Hamidullah Barrakha – who operates under the alias of Mr Gabriel – in order to draw the attention of UN troops away from the plant in the hours before its destruction.'

'Why would Barrakha want the plant destroyed?'

'Blowing things up seems to please him. As well, Barrakha may have been paid to carry out the destruction of the power plant.'

'Paid? By whom?'

'The distribution of electrical power in Southeast Asia is a highly profitable business. Most of the plants in Mindanao are coal-fired stations, run by Swedish and German corporations. The Maria Christina plant was a free gift of the American people, wholly owned by the Filipino people. It was seen as a Western intrusion by various Islamist factions, including Abu Sayaf and the Moro Liberation Front. The United Nations had sent peacekeepers into the area for the express purpose of keeping these factions isolated from the Christian people of Zamboanga and Iligan. Barrakha had an ideological reason for destroying the plant. But I also suspect that he had a financial motive as well. Let me show you another photograph.'

He hit a button, and a photograph flickered onto the screen, a large color shot – grainy, taken through trees – of a pillow-shaped man in a dove gray suit, talking to a young blond, whose back was turned to the camera. The masts of a sailing ship were clear in the background. A murmur of recognition went down the dais.

'This is a photograph of a man named Gerhardt Eisenstadt –'

The prosecutor's hand flew up, palm out.

'Mr Eisenstadt was a respected member of the German delegation to the United Nations. His suicide this weekend diminishes us all. He was a great man, tragically unable to cope with the abduction of his only child. You will respect his memory in the room, Senator. Gerhardt Eisenstadt served as the Junior Undersecretary for International Trade and Development and chaired several of our sub-committees. If you wish to slander a true humanitarian, whose heroic contributions to the cause of indigenous peoples all around the globe are beyond debate, you will do it in another venue.'

'With respect sir, I also have a deposition from Mr Eisenstadt's wife, Hildi, in which she admits –'

The rapid-fire hammering of the gavel rode him down, the echoes slamming from wall to wall around the suddenly silent auditorium.

'This session is closed. Senator, I'll see you in chambers.'

Mindanao

The Haribon Folk House – 213 Davao Avenue
Marawi City – Lanao del Sur – Mindanao
Tuesday, August 26, 9:00 p.m. local time

In the green northern mountains, a low, charcoal-colored cloud cover was sliding up into the twilight sky, eating up the stars, red lightning flickering inside the mass. A hot, wet wind out of the mountains was stirring the palm thatch that covered the roof of the lakeside café where Mr Gabriel was sitting, his back to the crowded restaurant, staring out across the flat, ruffled surface of Lake Lanao as a cloud of ibis lifted off the water, filling the air with a strange, shrill cry like the sound of children in pain. On the table in front of him was a plate of couscous and a copper decanter filled with hot black coffee. Next to the decanter lay a new plastic ventilator that he had just been given. On his lap sat a pale blond child with large brown eyes like a lemur. Now and then Mr Gabriel would spoon up some couscous with his fingers and feed it to the child, who gobbled it eagerly while Mr Gabriel watched him with obvious affection.

Opposite him sat Jesus Rizal; thin, haggard-looking, staring at Mr Gabriel like a man being interviewed by a cobra, his lips white and his expression that of a man who thinks of himself as prey. Rizal had brought the Therafine inhalers all the way from Iligan as a kind of burnt offering.

Mr Gabriel's hawklike face did nothing to diminish Rizal's fear; this was their first face-to-face meeting, since Jesus Rizal had found it necessary to apply to Mr Gabriel for sanctuary, now that an investigation of considerable force was underway in Iligan City. Rizal's plate of ginger chicken stew had gone untouched and was being eyed by a huge black crow sitting in the rafters, preening his feathers and dropping ticks on the patrons.

'How did he die?' asked Mr Gabriel.

'He was shot. From a great distance. His head simply exploded. I was covered with his brains. There was nothing I could do.'

'He was supposed to be on his way to The Hague.'

'He was packing. He stepped in front of a window —'

'Which hotel?'

'The Arc en Ciel, near Aguinaldo.'

'Why was he there?'

'He could not come back to Cobraville. The people would kill him. They have all come down from the hills. No one believes it was the Americans anymore. It was not safe to stay.'

'Why were you there?'

'I was going with him. He had an agreement with the French government. Since he was to be a witness at The Hague, they were sending a helicopter and some legionnaires to take him out. He said I could go with him. I had no other means of traveling. I was to assist in the hearings. As you know.'

Mr Gabriel was quiet for a time, looking out over the lake. Rain was in the air, the monsoons returning. The café was filling up with the smoke from these terrible Filipino clove cigarettes. He inhaled deeply and felt the familiar constriction in his lungs. He eyed the puffer, but decided to wait; perhaps he would not have an attack. He watched as the boy picked up a puffer and sucked on it heavily. He felt a rush of kinship with the child. They both suffered from the same terrible affliction. He patted the boy on the head and stared out at the water, thinking about Father Desaix.

'So Constantin is dead,' he said, more to himself than Rizal.

'He is,' said Rizal, his voice quavering. He had been unwilling to bring the bad news, but carrying it and the Therafine had been the only passport he could think of that would get him past Mr Gabriel's Moro and Bukidno bodyguards.

'A wonderful man,' said Mr Gabriel, his mind traveling back to Paris, to the cafés and the clubs and the girls. He would leave Mindanao for a while, and perhaps go back to Paris. There was always a welcome for his people in Paris; they hated the Americans as much as he did, although for corrupt, infidel reasons.

'So you came directly to me? After being present when Father Desaix was killed? You could have been followed.'

'Your men would have seen someone.'

'Yes. They would. So . . . what is it you hope for?'

Rizal opened his mouth to answer, jerked suddenly forward, coughed thickly, his face paling, and Mr Gabriel stared at him.

Rizal's mouth was slack, and he was patting his chest.

'What is it?' said Mr Gabriel, seeing Rizal's gray face, his staring eyes. He looked like a man having a heart attack. His hands fluttered at his shirt front, weakly, his mouth working. He looked up at Mr Gabriel and suddenly vomited a torrent of thick black blood all over Mr Gabriel's pale blue suit. Mr Gabriel leapt out of his chair, sending the blond child staggering across the floor, and stared at his suit front with a look of disgust filling his sallow face.

A pool of red blood was spreading across Rizal's dirty tan shirt, and he slid slowly under the table, staring up at Mr Gabriel, his yellow eyes glazing, a small landslide of dying flesh.

Mr Gabriel's breathing promptly shut down, and he turned to clutch at the blue plastic puffer in the little boy's hands. The boy jerked it away, cherishing it. Mr Gabriel lifted a hand to strike him, but by then his head had disintegrated with a meaty puffing crack and an explosion of wet, pink mist. The boy put the precious blue puffer to his lips as he watched Mr Gabriel's blood spreading, inhaling deeply. He took it away, two white spots showed on his pale cheeks, and began to smile. The people cowering on the floor of the café or hiding behind the low concrete wall thought they heard a peal of distant thunder from across the lake. But later they decided it was just the monsoon.

Quinalang Point

Quinalang Point – two miles north of Iligan City
Northern coast of Mindanao
Friday, August 29, 7:00 p.m. local time

The monsoons had come again, but gently, and a silken veil of rain played across the wide, palm-lined bay. The last of the sun slipped below the horizon, a thin, shimmering crescent, and then it was gone, and darkness rolled up out of the surrounding jungle. In the beachside café, the owner – a sad-eyed Bontoc whose people had left Northern Luzon after an affair of *maratabat* had gone badly for the family – shuffled along the line of tables, setting rusted kerosene lanterns down in front of the customers. The rains reached the beach, and a gentle, pattering, rustle filled the soft night air. Moths came to flutter in the yellow light of the kerosene lanterns.

Gunther Krugman watched the moths circle and dart around the light, and speculated idly on their inner lives – on the power of flame – which led his mind to consider the power of myth – the effects of belief on the susceptible mind. He was reaching for a small glass filled with what they liked to think of as brandy in Mindanao when he heard the distant mutter of a jeepney, growing louder, and the rattle of its fenders. He turned around and watched as it pulled up by the café.

Cole Langan and Dean Krause climbed out of the

jeepney, Cole extracting the keys, Krause favoring his right side. Both men looked gaunt, Krause more than Cole Langan. They stepped up onto the wooden platform of the beachside café, and sat down at Krugman's table, their drawn, unshaven faces cast in shadows by the light of the lantern. The owner materialized out of the dark and hovered, his hands together.

'Tsing Tao,' said Krause, smiling at the man.

'Me too,' said Cole.

'Another brandy for me,' said Krugman. The owner bustled off, and they stared at each other in an easy silence. He was back in a moment, smelling of cloves, carrying a tray. He set the frosted beers down in front of Krause and Cole, and bowed as Krugman received his cognac with a graceful gesture, inclining his head like a Prussian.

'Confusion to our enemies,' he said, raising his glass.

'Fuck 'em if they can't take a joke,' said Krause, draining half the beer and setting it down gently on the tabletop. Cole took a small sip and held the bottle against his cheek, turning it.

'Very damn hot country,' he said to no one in particular.

'It is,' said Krugman.

'I'd like to leave it,' said Cole, sighing heavily.

'I have a boat moored,' Krugman said, indicating the pale line of the rolling surf, just visible in the dying light.

'Big enough for two long crates?' asked Krause.

'Easily.'

'Can you bring it into shore?'

'There's a dock just down here. You can run the jeepney right down to the water, and we can have the villagers put them on board.'

'Where to then?'

'Across to Leyte. There'll be a sub in the channel.'

'Why not here?'

'Can't do that too many times. Did they give you any trouble down in Iligan?'

Krause shook his head.

'No. They just wanted me gone. Walked me out as soon as Cole showed up. Vasquez and Strackbein were already in the corridor. They're in dry ice, and sealed up pretty good. The Germans carried them out to the jeepney themselves. They want this all to go away.'

'And well they should,' said Krugman.

'Too bad about Ramiro.'

'Fuck Ramiro,' said Krause.

'How did he get the weapon?'

'Someone slipped him a cuff key.'

'Someone?' said Krause, smiling.

Krugman inclined his head with a smile and went on.

'If I understood Colonel Lazard correctly, Ramiro was being transferred to another location, and he got the cuffs off and somehow managed to reach Lazard's sidearm. By the way, he killed a German trooper while he had the weapon.'

'Yeah,' said Krause. 'I heard. My guy. The little flower who beat the shit out of me. Too bad. I was saving him.'

'Well, he put three in the guard's face before turning the weapon on himself. According to Lazard.'

'Yow,' said Cole. 'Good for him.'

'I'm glad I can tell Pike we got Strackbein out,' said Krause.

'How's my father doing?' asked Cole.

'He's in Camp Hill resting on his laurels. You should have seen him in New York. He was brilliant.'

'Somebody film it?' asked Cole.

'Everyone but Al Jezeera,' said Krugman.

'They get the Kraut?'

'Eisenstadt? Luna Olvidado killed him.'

'What about the guy at the power plant?' asked Krause.

'Gideon? Assisting the authorities in their inquiries.'

A silence settled down, and they all watched the monsoon sweeping into the shore, curtains waving in the sea wind and the eaves running, water pooling in the floorboards. The lantern guttered, failed, and then brightened.

'I'm curious,' said Krugman, seeming to speak more to himself than the others, 'I'm curious about something Vasquez said to me.'

Neither Cole nor Krause said anything; they waited.

'Vasquez mentioned that after the Germans had attacked you near the relay site, he chose that moment to run. Yet – if I recall it correctly – he was waiting for you at Camp Casey. Was that a trap? And if so, who set it?'

Cole looked at Krause, who shrugged. Cole leaned forward.

'It had to be Vasquez. Only he knew we were going to regroup at Camp Casey if it all went to hell. And he was there, waiting for us. Odd thing is, when we sent Chris Burdette into the valley to check it out, Vasquez gave him a tell and warned him off.'

'What kind of tell?'

'He had his rifle on his knees, but he was holding it so Chris could see that the magazine was missing. In our unit, that always means a trap.'

'Yet you engaged anyway?'

'Yeah,' said Cole. 'We engaged.'

'Why?' asked Krugman. 'You could have slipped away.'

'I wanted to get Vasquez out. We leave no one behind.'

'Of course, you were unaware at the time that Vasquez had betrayed you.'

'Yes,' said Cole. 'But if I'd known that, we would have engaged anyway, but with a different end in mind.'

'According to the press, you were killed in the engagement.'

'Yeah. A martyr to the cause. Blew myself to shreds with a fragmentation grenade as the Germans closed in.'

'You look remarkably together for a man of your parts.'

'There was a boar in the valley. I stumbled over the son of a bitch while I was trying to get back to Chris and Pike – he tried to gore me and I shot him. A patrol was closing in. I stripped off my tee and my boots, shoved a couple of grenades down the boar's throat, and took off. I was fifty yards away when he went off. It looked like a big red meat fountain. I was impressed all to hell.'

'So the Germans took what was left of the boar for you?'

'Yeah. Guess I'm uglier than I thought. I hooked up with Chris and Pike. We couldn't get to Vasquez, so we decided I should stay dead for a while and try to get a line on him. We wanted Pike and Chris out so they could tell our guys what really happened at Cobraville. We didn't want that one nailed to our foreheads. They caught the sub. I went deep and got myself back to Iligan City. Finally spotted Rizal in the Aguinaldo Street market and followed him to the Arc en Ciel. Got a clear shot at the Jesuit and took it. I wanted Rizal to run. He ran. I followed him. He led me straight south to Lake Lanao and Barrakha. I took them both out from across the lake.'

'Was there a child with them?' asked Krugman.

'Yeah. A little blond kid.'

'What happened to him?'

'No idea.'

'A shame,' said Krugman. 'I doubt he'll be recovered.'

'Who was he?' asked Krause.

'I imagine he was Gerhardt Eisenstadt's boy,' said Krugman. 'Perhaps the United Nations will be able to get him out of there.'

'Oh yeah,' said Krause. 'There's a hope.'

'So, Vasquez ratted out all those guys in Waziristan? And the entire insertion team in Paraguay?' asked Cole.

'Yes. I'm afraid so. Once he had given out a little, he had to give them everything. A terrible, lonely existence. A kind of tragedy. I spoke with him at length, and I felt a great sympathy for him. It was quite sad. In the end, I think Ramiro was happy to die.'

'Just as long as he's dead. He never knew that it was Luna Olvidado who had turned him?'

'At the end he did. The photograph at the ticket gate showed the burn scars on her left hand. We managed to place her close to the scene. She was in Richmond for a meeting the night before.'

'How did Vasquez know it was her? I mean, we all heard about her, Sloane's hot-shot import from the Secret Service. But none of us had ever met her. She was no-go, worked over in security.'

'When Vasquez was being evaluated by the psych team, Sloane sent her over to debrief him about possible security lapses. He remembered her. I've seen her. She truly was quite memorable.'

'Wasn't she in my father's chopper when Eisenstadt's men tried to take it out? They needed her. Why would they try to kill her?'

'I can only speculate.'

'Then speculate.'

'The situation was getting chaotic. I think whoever was running the New York end of things decided she was expendable. The stock-share deal was set. The power plant was about to go. They had to get your father off the case. If she was in the chopper, too bad. She wasn't needed anymore. A nest of vipers is no featherbed.'

'Why did she do it?' asked Krause. 'The whole thing? What was she after?'

'If you mean Vasquez, he needed a firebreak. The missions were going sour. Luna knew that eventually someone would come in to find the leak. Sloane was worried about me, and I was worried about Sloane. Neither of us was looking at Luna. She got herself inserted into the middle of it to see what was being said. If the investigation got too close to her, she could always throw us Vasquez. She had him all laid out if she needed him.'

'I don't mean just that. What was it all about for her? She was inside, a trusted agent. She was on a career track that would have taken her a long way. She had everything to lose. I can't believe she did it for something as simple as money.'

Krugman hesitated, unwilling to indulge in speculation. It had been his experience that money – the lust for it – the absence of it – was an explanation for many of the terrible things that he had seen people do in his long life. He sipped at his bitter lukewarm brandy and stared out to sea, considering what to say about her.

'You understand this is merely conjecture. I'm told that she was involved in an accident, quite early on in her career, apparently shortly after she graduated from the law enforcement academy in Georgia. She was on her way to her first assignment in Maryland. There was heavy fog on the interstate, a few miles from the Virginia border.

Shortly before she encountered the scene, a tractor trailer had slammed into a line of stopped cars, setting fire to several of them. Luna came to the aid of a family who were trapped in a burning limousine. She managed to pull three of the family members clear, but she sustained severe burns, to her torso, her left hand, and forearm. A child died in her arms.'

'What's the connection?' asked Krause.

'The burns were quite bad. She required several months of reconstructive surgery. Her rehabilitation took another year. It was all quite expensive, of course.'

'So what?' said Krause. 'The service would have covered it. She was on her way north to take a job. The trip was service business. She would have been taken care of.'

'One would have thought so. Unfortunately, a decision was made by the headquarters legal department that she had recklessly endangered herself in an incident that was not connected to her work, and they denied her any benefits. Although she made several appeals, the case was rejected, on the grounds that she was under no obligation to help those people, and that by doing so she had put herself at risk and was therefore solely responsible for her injuries.'

'She was a law enforcement agent; she had a duty –'

'The legal department took the view that, although she was en route to an assignment, she had not yet been officially sworn in. Therefore, technically, she was still a private citizen.'

'What about the people in the limousine?' asked Cole.

'The surviving members also declined to assist her financially.'

'On what grounds?'

'They were quite wealthy. It seems their lawyers made

the argument that granting Luna any payment would imply a degree of liability that could be ongoing, that might imply a basis for a lawsuit on Luna's part, for injuries sustained.'

'That sounds unbelievably cold-blooded,' said Cole.

'The accumulation of great wealth almost always requires an essential coldness. There are so many claims upon wealth – legitimate and reasonable claims – that a kind of carapace is gradually formed. It becomes easy – even reflexive – to say no. The counterargument was made that the responsibility for her treatment lay with the government, and of course the government strongly disagreed. Precedents were in danger of being set. The arguments multiplied, and in the end Luna's injuries fell into the gap between these competing forces. In the final event, she paid for her treatment herself. I assume that at some point during her totally undeserved suffering she conceived a terrible grievance against – against all of us.'

They fell into long introspective silence, ended by Krause.

'That was a tough break. But it doesn't justify what she did.'

'No,' said Krugman. 'But it does in some way explain it.'

'So what was done to her,' put in Cole, 'she then turned around and did to Ramiro? Ran down his family – I guess the kid's coma was a real stroke of luck for her – and then used it to turn him.'

'Yes,' said Krugman. 'It seems that many of our troubles here could have been greatly ameliorated – not to consider the loss of so many valuable intelligence agents – if only the legal department of our government agencies were staffed with something finer than pragmatical heartless scoundrels. *Haec nugae in seria ducent malum.*'

'How much money was Olvidado going to get out of this?'

'Since the deal is dead, Cole, it's hard to estimate what her take from the Maria Christina transaction might have been. But her regular payments from whomever was running her could run into a million.'

'Who *was* running her, anyway?' asked Cole.

'Haven't found that out yet. Since most of the players are dead, there aren't many people left to interrogate. We'll follow the money trail, of course, and I'm hopeful. We think a lot of the money paid out to her came indirectly from KSB.'

'But my father told me that she was right there when he fronted Eisenstadt. He said she ran the interrogation. Why help the enemy?'

'Again, I don't believe that Barrakha's people would have let Luna know the true extent of the conspiracy. The whole idea of a covert operation lies in cells, in cutoffs. All Luna was required to do was to supply information to an unknown buyer, accept the money, and buy whatever stock these people told her to buy. I'm sure that she had no idea it was Eisenstadt who was the source of the money she was getting, until Drew showed her the video. Even then, she was under the impression that Drew had already given the video to Sloane, so she had to appear to be pushing the investigation along. I'd say she was also painfully aware that a decision had been made to kill her in the helicopter. She'd want to know who was behind that decision, if only to prevent him from making another attempt. In a sense, she had the same motivation for taking this thing apart that your father did. What he was finding out was extremely important to her survival. When she was interrogating Eisenstadt at his townhouse, his answers were as critical to her as they were to your father. And, as I said, she figured Sloane was closing in on Eisenstadt too, so she had to maintain her credibility. But when your father told her that he had never given a MPEG video to Sloane, she realized that she was the only one who knew about it, other than your father. She saw the opening this presented, and decided to clean house.'

'How much of this did you know before you dragged my father into this?' asked Cole. His tone was far from cordial.

'Very little. A decision was made to introduce some chaos and self-doubt into the situation, and see who started to disintegrate.'

'Who did you suspect?'

'Everyone. In particular I was concerned with Levi Sloane.'

'And my father?'

'No. Not your father.'

'And apparently not Luna Olvidado, either.'

'No. I admit I had not considered her as a candidate. She was young. Dedicated. Intelligent. Her record was superior.'

'So was Levi Sloane's!'

'Point taken.'

Krause decided a change of direction might be advisable.

'And you don't think Luna knowingly sold information directly to terrorists, to Hamidullah Barrakha and his organization?'

'I doubt it very much. How could she have known? She probably never had any direct contact with anyone who knew where Barrakha was and what he was doing. All she knew was there was a market and she was getting rich.

I don't think Luna knew who the end user was. She may have suspected, but I doubt that she ever asked.'

'Maybe,' said Cole. 'And maybe she just didn't give a damn.'

'There is that element.'

'Christ,' said Krause. 'What a house of reptiles.'

'Cobraville,' said Cole.

'Yes,' said Krugman, '"Cobraville" catches it nicely.'